Annie Clark Cole

RETURN FROM
PANTHER HOLLER

A Masterful Tale of Revenge

To Jane Dear Friend,

Annie Clark Cole

Cover Design by Sanjay N. Patel
www.sanjaynpatel.com
Interior Design by Create Space
Cover Model––Rope Spinks
A Dream on Production Publication
Annieclarkcole.com
Copyright 2017 Annie Clark Cole
ISBN: 13- 9781975924577
ISBN: 10- 1975924576
Library of Congress Control Number: 2018901689
CreateSpace Independent Publishing Platform
North Charleston, South Carolina

Aclaim

Dedication

TO MY HUSBAND JIM COLE, WHETHER IT'S THE EARLY MORNING HOURS OR BURNING THE MIDNIGHT OIL, YOU ARE ALWAYS THERE TO INSPIRE ME TO BELIEVE IN MYSELF.

ANNIE CLARK COLE

Return from
Panther Holler

From the Author

*I*n my mind's eye, there exists a magical place where unexplained things happen. As children, we often played in a wooded area called, the Scout Woods.

I remember well, the old building that had deteriorated into nothing but walls and bare windows.

We children were warned that past sunset a ghost of an old woman would shine a light to scare people away. To me, there was something mystic about the place called the Scout Woods. Perhaps through this experience, I was inspired to write Panther Holler.

I hope you enjoy the climactic conclusion of Return from Panther Holler as much as I did writing it. If so, please go to Amazon and leave a review. It will be greatly appreciated.

Annie Clark Cole

There are legends recounted in the hills of Arkansas that many years ago, in a place called Panther Holler, the great ancestors of the original people left a treasure near the "Road that Roars" guarded by a Black Panther.

Return From Panther Holler

No man can understand war until he's gone to battle! And no one knew better than Vick and Cain Porter—for they lived it!

Chapter 1

IN THE BACKWOODS OF ARKANSAS, TUCKED AWAY AMONG TALL PINES and rolling streams, was a cabin, storm shelter and one lonely grave. The place was called Panther Holler. The holler was a peaceful and serene place set among a rocky hillside and hidden trails. Oftentimes, a lone hawk could be seen circling the sky as it guarded the secrets of an ancient treasure.

Vick Porter and his brother Sam stumbled upon the little cabin as children during a blinding storm as they sought to escape an abusive father.

The location was a hunter's paradise, but often—strange things happened—unexplained things.

Years after the mysticism began, a hawk summoned by the Great Spirit with a magic reserved for great deeds, led Vick and his son Cain to an ancient treasure of diamonds—hidden near Panther Holler. It was there in the clutches of death that Vick and Cain were miraculously saved by a black panther which was guarding the ancient treasure of the forgotten people. The descendants of this lost civilization later became known as the American Indians.

～

Before leaving Panther Holler, Vick and Cain took a moment to walk around the cabin and check out the storm shelter where Vick and his young brother found bodies of a murdered family. It was afterwards that a falling limb killed Sam, leaving Vick alone in the wilderness to face insurmountable odds. And finally, it was there where he was forced to become a man, framed for murders he did not commit.

Vick and Cain strolled out near the storm shelter to pay their respects to Sam, who had died years earlier. With a bowed head tears in his eyes, he looked around the place. He took everything in, from the tall grasses to the flit of a bird that had pecked Sam's grave clean.

Bending down, he laid his hand on his brother's grave and whispered.

"Rest easy little brother—until we meet again."

For the first time, Cain saw the pain and anguish of his father who still mourned the death of Sam.

The two brothers were very close, a powerful bond formed from the commonality of abuse from an alcoholic father. When Sam died, a little piece of Vick died with him.

After they rode away, there was a mood about Vick that Cain had not seen before. He must be thinking of the treasure, Cain figured.

"Pa, do you think we'll ever come back?"

Vick answered somberly, "Maybe--someday." Vick was never big on conversation, for prison had taught him that too much talk could mean trouble.

"What about the treasure?" Cain insisted.

"What treasure?" Vick grinned and rode on ahead.

I guess I know what that means, Cain thought. He knew Vick would not speak of it again until he was ready.

Now that their enemies were dead, Vick and Cain aimed to forget the past and focus on their future. Life was looking pretty good. They were anxious to get back home and start living, something Vick had little time to do since he had been released from prison.

Elizabeth will be relieved when she learns that Lonnie and Dudley are dead and no longer a threat, Vick thought. *It had been a harrowing ordeal; being kicked in the gut, and the barrel of a Colt .45 shoved in their faces, but the panther saved them. Without the Panther, we would have been dealt a different fate. Someone or something was watching over us,* Vick postulated, while gazing upward toward the Heavens.

Witnessing the unexplainable which surrounded Vick, Cain was becoming more aware of a mystery that besieged his Pa. *The little time I've known him, there's something special, almost magical about him. First: A panther comes out of nowhere to save us; and then we find a cave of diamonds. Even if I swore on a Bible no one would believe such a story.* Cain continued to marvel.

∽

Leaving the lake at first light, the treasure was still weighing heavily on Cain's mind.

"Pa, are you certain we're doing the right thing leaving the treasure behind."

"I'll know when the time's right—and it's not now," Vick stressed.

"But it doesn't make sense with what we've been through."

"Patience son—patience! We'll know when we need to know."

That's a heck of an answer, Cain thought, as he nestled into his saddle.

When they arrived at the manor in Jonesboro, Vick and Cain felt blessed to be alive. They were like two valiant warriors heading home with a reception awaiting them—one richly deserved.

Rounding the bend leading up to the stately manor, Cain saw Lucy and his son waiting together, as though they knew he was coming home.

The jagged pieces of Vick's life were all around him. But for now, Vick only wanted to get back to loving on his wife.

Seeing Cain and Vick in the distance, Lucy sighed heavily, hoping their nightmare was over as she coached Jared to look at his daddy who was flashing that big grin of his.

Dismounting, Cain took her in his arms, and then reached down for Jared, who pulled away. Lucy was overcome with emotion as she hugged and kissed Cain.

"Thank God you're safe. Need I ask about Lonnie and Dudley?"

"Let's just say they won't be bothering the Porters anymore," Cain replied.

Suddenly Lucy felt lighthearted. Perhaps it was the release of all the bottled tension of the past months.

Cain bent down and looked at his son at eye level and motioned for him to come—but Jared ignored him.

"Guess he's already forgotten me."

"Don't worry, he's being a little shy. He'll warm up!" Lucy reassured.

Her piercing blue eyes and rosy cheeks were what Cain had been waiting for. I'm a lucky man, he thought.

"I almost forgot how beautiful you are." She smiled and gently kissed him again.

Vick kept waiting for Elizabeth to come out and greet him.

"Lucy, where is Lizzie?"

"Oh, I'm sorry, — she's in town picking up a package."

Vick spurred his horse and rode off in the direction of town, hoping to catch her. After spotting her car parked in front of the mercantile, he dismounted and waited.

So, there he was, propped up against the car with his hat pulled slightly over his eyes, his boot heel on the running board, Elizabeth saw Vick as she walked from the store. She ran toward him, dropping her packages as he grabbed her and swung her around. She held him tightly as he kissed her passionately.

"Lizzie, you're sure lookin' good," he whispered softly in her ear.

"Thank God you're home and in one piece. I've been worried to death about you and Cain."

"You have nothing to worry about. Your boys home safe and sound with Lucy and the boy."

Vick's never changed from the first time I saw him as a young girl. He was just a boy loading horse feed into the back of his Pa's wagon, but as the wagon passed by, Vick momentarily glanced and flashed that mischievous smile of his. He will always be that young boy full of playful energy who melted my heart.

After the kiss, he noticed all the packages.

"Ma'am, are you gonna need some help your packages?"

Elizabeth laughed and kissed Vick again.

"It's not the same without you," she whispered. Are you sure Cain's okay?"

"Not to worry—your boy is fine. Now, you should have been home waiting for me. He picked her up and slid her onto the front seat. Vick pressed his lips to her ear.

"I'll see you at home," he whispered suggestively.

When Vick arrived at the manor, Elizabeth was waiting for him with open arms.

"What took you so long?" she laughed. They embraced and kissed once more and then everything became serious. There was something about Vick that had changed. She imagined it had something to do with the two brothers who had dealt them holy hell for what seemed a lifetime.

"Lizzie, you and Lucy don't have to worry about Lonnie and Dudley ever again. They're no longer with us."

"What do you mean? Are they dead?"

He wanted to explain, but the panther story was too much for even Elizabeth. He saw no reason to leave an image of a panther ripping the brothers to shreds. If she doesn't push, I'll keep the details between Cain and me, he thought.

Elizabeth kept waiting for answers.

"Does it really matter how they died? They're both dead and neither Cain nor I had anything to do with it. Let's just let it be for now."

Elizabeth was puzzled by his response, but she trusted him. *My husband and son are home and that's all that matters*, she reasoned.

She took Vick by the hand and led him to the kitchen which was filled with the sweet aroma of freshly baked pie.

Vick sadly remembered his old friend, Sheriff Orson Cargill, who loved pie more than anyone. *There was never a better friend*, Vick sadly reminisced.

Chapter 2

CAIN AND LUCY HAD WAITED FOR SEVERAL YEARS WHEN FINALLY, IN THE year of 1910 the courts of San Augustine, Texas reinstated Cain as sole heir to the Petty estate. The would-be heir, Jonathan Petty was declared dead, and Aggie Dawson was yet to be notified that she was an heir.

Lucy's apprehension about moving to Texas was certainly warranted, for she had never lived more than 60 miles away from her childhood home, except for the two years she spent at a finishing school in Chicago.

For them, the chance to begin a new life was exciting—yet troublesome, for their roots ran deep. They were going to miss the small town of Jonesboro, Arkansas where they had spent most of their lives.

Lucy's reluctance concerned Cain, but he managed to reassure her that the success of running the cotton business would be left up to her. She considered it a challenge that she was more than capable of handling. Cain was aware of her experience when she helped the Porter Lumber Company show a profit.

Who would expect anything less from the daughter of Orson Cargill? Cain remembered her Pa as one of the toughest and orneriest men he ever knew, and he was learning Lucy was a lot like him.

Although she was beautiful and alluringly feminine, she maintained many of her Pa's traits. She had spunk, and there was nothing she couldn't do. She was poised as a lady, yet tough as the loggers she supervised— when she had to be. There was no doubt, comparing her two tasks, that it would be no chore for her to handle the operation of the cotton business.

She had no concept of what was waiting for her, even though Cain had told her all about Pecan Plantation there was no way she could imagine living on a sprawling estate with a spaciously rambling plantation for a home.

As their Model T puttered along, Cain thought some things never change. Approaching the entrance to the plantation, the large pecan trees enveloped the white shell road leading up to the mansion—just as before. *It's like I've never left,* Cain thought. He looked at Lucy, whose concentration was on her new surroundings. She sat speechless, scanning the enormity of the place. She thought to herself, *cotton fields stretched as far as the eye could see, field hands loading flatbed wagons used to haul cotton to the gin all happening only a short distance from our plantation home.* She was amazing seeing cotton loaded and then transported to the waterways to be shipped to various destinations. *This must be the cycle, working from daylight to dark,* she thought.

Lucy saw the savagery of the hot Texas summer as it reflected in the tanned faces of the workers.

She had been unaware of the enormity of the place and she had to pinch herself to believe that the plantation was their good fortune.

Driving up to the house, she noticed large ferns hanging about everywhere.

Senor Galvez, the caretaker who had been on the job waiting for Cain's return, had planted the vivid greenery in preparation for their coming.

Brick stairs led up to the porch, with sturdy outdoor furniture donned in white tablecloths. Lucy had only seen these types of settings in books she read. The swing that hung from the porch near the front door reminded her of a privileged child's home. *Everything is perfect*, she marveled. *This is a picture of wealth and privilege—something I know little of.* For a moment, she imagined being served lemonade amongst the huge magnolia and evergreens manicured to perfection. She closed her eyes and pictured herself in a long white flowing dress made of silks and satins like the affluent women wore.

"Cain, are you sure this is ours? This place would swallow the manor." He loved seeing her so excited.

Driving up to the back entrance, Cain recalled how Jonathan, the previous owner, wrecked the house in a heated rage. I hope the Senor and Senora could put it back in one piece. I would hate for Lucy to see the house in shambles after bragging so.

Helping Jared from the car, Lucy's eyes followed the grounds to the small frame house. That must have been daddy's place, she thought. She closed her eyes, imagining Orson sitting on the porch having his morning cup of coffee. *Daddy must have loved living here with the small lake nearby.*

Senor Galvez and his wife, Carina, were there to meet them as soon as they heard the Model T puttering up to the house.

"Meester Cain, Meester Cain!" the old Mexican gentleman called out!

Carina and their young daughter stood near the door of the barn waiting to welcome the couple and help with their luggage.

"Senor Galvez, this is my wife Lucy, and our son."

"Si Mees' Lucy… good to meet you. Thees' is your boy?"

"Yes, this is Jared."

The boy hid behind her skirt, somewhat embarrassed at being in the presence of a young girl who was close to his age.

"Thees' is Senora Carina, and our daughter Maria." The Senora looked embarrassed—for she spoke only broken English. Maria was a smidge younger than Jared, and noticeably protected.

The Galvez family, not accustomed to operating such a huge estate, was genuinely happy to have Cain and Lucy home to accept the responsibility for the farm. The place was up and running, but obviously in need of attention.

"Lucy, do you think you can handle this?" Cain asked. She paused momentarily— "I had no idea of the enormity of this place."

Lucy had the skills necessary for handling responsibility. Cain had no doubt she would win over the workers on the plantation, just as she did with the loggers back in Jonesboro.

Walking up the brick stairway to the back porch, Cain swept her off her feet before entering the house, while little Jared followed close behind.

"Cain, what are you doing?" she asked playfully.

"What do you think? I want you to meet your new home."

The house was in pristine condition—without a dish out of place. *The Galvez family did a great job of cleaning up after Jonathan's mess*, Cain thought.

"Oh my gosh! I can't believe this!" Lucy said, while walking throughout the kitchen. "This home is big enough to entertain royalty." Even though her daddy had sacrificed to send her to an upscale finishing school in Chicago, she felt unprepared for her abrupt change of lifestyle.

Walking from room to room, they entered their bedroom, while Cain took her in his arms and cradled her.

"This is our special place," he whispered into her ear.

～

Lucy could hardly wait to jump into learning the cotton business. After a day of looking over the expenditures, she realized their fortune was not at all as purported. The plantation had enormous liability against it, much more than they could have imagined. Stunned by the debt against the place, she quickly realized there was a short time to satisfy what was owed, and that debt was growing daily. She ran the situation through her head and tried to come up with a solution. *There's no way we can fulfill this debt before the bank reclaims the property. If the bank can wait until our first shipment of cotton, we'll be able to pay— otherwise, how can we raise the money?* Lucy was paralyzed with fear for even, she could not correct what was facing them.

The evil Jonathan Petty, the great manipulator, did all the damage he could before he died, she thought.

It took Cain two years to reclaim Pecan Plantation, but the devastation had already taken place—thanks to Jonathan, who was not only the black sheep of the Petty family (the original owners) but also suffered from a mental illness.

No one, not even Cain's wealthy mother can save what apparently is imminent unless the bank works with us. *Jonathan managed to have the last laugh after all*, Cain thought. There's no chance Lucy and I can raise that kind of money short of a miracle—and that wasn't likely.

For the first time, he spoke with Lucy about Panther Holler and the treasure of diamonds. "Cain, do you know how crazy you sound? You can't be serious about Vick having a vision about a mountainside of diamonds? It's absurd believing he thinks he's a Cherokee...which by the way would make you one fourth."

Cain whispered, "Not Cherokee--Navajo."

"Are you sure Vick didn't snap while he was in prison? Something's wrong with the both of you," she laughed. *Wow, she's making this tough!* He thought. Cain quickly realized his mistake by including Lucy in on the secret. *Hell, I hardly believe it myself...and I was there.* Realizing the mistake, of telling her, he had to think fast.

"Ha, you almost fell for it!" he said. "I was pulling your leg," Cain laughed to cover himself.

"You need a better story than that if you want me to believe you!" Lucy said disapprovingly.

∽

The Petty fortune came with a price. Cain had been married to Eileen Petty for only one day when she and their unborn baby were murdered. Cain had no reason at the time to believe his marriage to Eileen would eventually make him the beneficiary of the infamous Petty Estate.

If it wasn't for Eileen, I wouldn't be involved in this mess, he thought. She was a rare Beauty who seduced him at a most vulnerable time. And since that day, his entire family has suffered nothing but misfortune. He hated to think ill of the deceased, but Eileen did everything she could to get me to fall for her– and it worked, he reflected.

No one was more shocked than Cain when the Petty's showed up to inform him that he was the father of Eileen's baby. Naturally, I had to do right by her because of the baby—even disappointing Lucy, whom I truly loved. Cain doubted that he would ever get over the horrible murder of his unborn child. *Had I known what I know now, I would have gladly turned everything over to Jonathan, who had been disowned by his family. There was nothing that Jonathan wouldn't do to reclaim his father's estate—even murder. Ownership of Pecan Plantation can never be worth the price it has cost my family*, Cain reflected.

The only good thing in my life is Lucy, who understands. She and Jared are all that matters now, Cain thought.

The two years it took for Cain to be reinstated as the heir to Pecan Plantation turned out to be a misfortune packaged to fool him. *I'll never find peace until I'm rid of this place*, he thought.

He and Lucy even talked of selling the mineral rights to the Dawson place in Woodville—which was the property willed to Jared from his biological mother. Although Aggie had asked Cain to take and raise their son, she intended for Jared to have his inheritance, which was her last show of her love for him.

Months passed and things did not improve, but Lucy knew they would get by regardless of what might happen. She thought about her father's counsel. *Daddy was a simple man, but he always knew how to get on with the living, and Cain and I will do the same.*

After the Porters moved to San Augustine they became the talk of the town. They were rich and down to earth, which appealed to the townsfolk. Even though Lucy was catered to, her manner never changed. When she went into a store she was offered the best; from fresh-butchered meat, to the grandest style of clothing. She was amused with the attention, for she did not see herself as one who needed special attention. She would always be the daughter of Orson Cargill, the rough and tumble sheriff from Jonesboro.

As the six-month deadline drew near, Cain decided that they should forfeit the plantation against Lucy's better judgement.

"Cain, you're a lawyer. Can't you do something?" She pleaded.

"There's nothing I can do."

"Perhaps not, but I aim to try!" she countered.

"If that's how you feel––be my guest. But being a lawyer, I say it's all a waste of time."

"Well, I'm not giving up without a fight," she fired back.

"Lucy, do you know how much you sound like Orson?"

"Well, what do you expect? You married his daughter!"

"I'm telling you, the only choice is to move into Aggie's place in Woodville," Cain said.

She hated the thought of moving into the home of her son's biological dead mother. She feared living there would be a constant reminder of the woman who gave birth to her son.

Lucy was careful not to use that as an excuse, for to Cain it might sound petty. All she wanted was for him to realize moving into another woman's home was not a good idea.

"Cain Porter, the difference between you and me is I'm not willing to roll over and let the bank reclaim this place!"

"What's it gonna take for you to understand that we don't have a leg to stand on. The bank is operating within its rights and there's not anything you nor I can do!" Cain was at his wits end trying to convince her.

"We'll see. Come tomorrow, I'm going to meet with Mr. Lee Tompkins, and after that he'll be begging us to keep this place. You just wait!"

Cain chuckled. "You're Orson in the flesh alright!" She smiled at hearing her daddy's name.

Lucy was never known to be selfish, but she had become attached to San Augustine, for it was a place where she never thought she would live. She had lived in two worlds, one of humble beginnings, and the other, of an upper-crust lifestyle she never thought possible.

As the weeks passed, she agonized over the inevitable.

True to her word, she marched into the bank to see Mr. Tompkins, who had been corresponding with them through mail. There was only one little man who blocked the door to Mr. Tompkins's office, and he was sleeping. She rapped on the desk to wake him.

"Sir, I hate to disturb your nap, but I'm here to see Mr. Tompkins."

"Oh, he ain't here today." The clerk, who was in a fog, refused to let Lucy go past the desk.

"Okay mister, but I'll be back—and next time I won't take no for an answer." Lucy stormed out the door as the beady little character looked on.

Mr. Tompkins, the owner of the bank, and Sebastian Parker were in cahoots to steal the Porters property. On that day after Lucy left, they were behind closed doors discussing a bank robbery they had masterminded in Carthage, Texas.

Holding up the newspaper, Tompkins showed Sebastian an article with the Carthage Bank robbery splashed across the front page.

"Look here! The bank was cleaned over two million dollars, and we ain't seen hide nor hair of Packer Rover nor his men," Lee said.

"I didn't know the bank had that much money!" Sebastian exclaimed.

"Why do you think I chose the Carthage bank? I been knowing ole Henry Cox had money from his mining expedition in California for a long time. The story is he lives like a pauper and ain't spent a dime of it and he's near dead."

"Lee you should have listened when I said, Rover wasn't to be trusted," Sebastian said.

Lee was visibly upset.

"That ain't all! He has our share of the robbery, and two of our accounting books." Lee pointed out.

"Don't tell me it was the Pecan Plantation accounting books!"

"Yep, the very books that could put us under the jail iffn' the Porters get their hands on 'em."

"Maybe you forgot where you put 'em!"

"No! remember that day we left and Packer pushed himself in my office? It had to be, because the next day the books were gone."

"So, what do we do?" Asked Sebastian.

"We dang sure ain't gonna standby and let Packer run off with our books and the money!" Lee said. "I'm thinking if he double-crossed us, he probably double-crossed his own men."

Sure enough, two days later the Joiner brothers came into Lee's office and confronted him and Sebastian Parker who happen to be there to witness the conversation.

"All we want is our cut," one of the Joiner brothers said. "I ain't seen hide nor hair of Packer Rover. Looks like he skipped out on all of us. If you find him—and I know you will, tell 'em we want our share of the money and the two accounting books he stole from us. If he doesn't have the money or the books—kill him."

"It'll be to your benefit," Lee instructed.

Lee was livid at realizing how easily they had been duped.

"I have an idea where he is," Saul Joiner said.

"You know where he is?" Sebastain asked.

"I overheard him talking about owning a boat down at the ship channel in Beaumont. It was quite a while ago, but it's worth checking."

"You find our money and the books and you'll be well rewarded," Lee restated.

~

Lucy did just as she promised. She waited a few days and then returned to Tompkins office. *I'll see him this time or I'm gonna break the door down!* She thought.

Lucy entered the building and there sat the same beady-eyed man. He gave her the same runaround as before, but Lucy was loaded for bear. She got in the clerk's face,

"You wouldn't be lyin' about Mr. Tompkins not being here, would you?"

Crouching like a whipped dog, he said, "No ma'am, he ain't here."

Lucy changed her voice to reflect her frustration.

"Then what's his car doin' outside? He ain't going nowhere without his car, and I batcha' ten dollars that's his coat's hangin' in the corner 'cause I've seen him wear it. Now, you git him out here right now, or I'm going right through that door!"

The clerk looked around the room as if Mr. Tompkins would magically appear and then moved toward the banker's door.

As he tapped on the door, it opened and Mr. Tompkins stepped out of his office.

"What's going on?" Mr. Tompkin's said.

"Oh, Sir…it's Mrs. Porter. She would like a word with you!"

Lee turned to Lucy. "Ma'am, what can I do for you?"

Sebastian had his ear to the door, listening as Lucy lit into Lee.

"I'm here to talk about my place, Pecan Plantation. I want you to listen carefully. My husband and I are not giving up what's rightfully ours. I don't care what you say—we are not leaving. You're going to have to wait until we collect payment from our first shipment of cotton."

Mr. Tompkins refuted, "Mrs. Porter, it must be difficult for you to accept losing your home, but I have several suitors ready to bid after the foreclosure. So, this is to inform you to get your affairs in order because you are moving—and sooner than you think."

Lucy noticed something very sinister about Mr. Tompkins. It was as though he enjoyed seeing her pain.

She gathered her shawl, but before reaching the door, she stopped and admonished him. "Sir, you may be surprised. I've learned not to count my chickens before they hatch!" And that's a lesson for you too—Sir!

The clerk was wide-eyed at seeing a woman talk to Mr. Tompkins as she did.

"Caleb, quit yer' gawkin' and get back to work!" Tompkins said.

⌒

Sadly, and reluctantly, Cain and Lucy began preparations to move. Whether they liked it or not, they would soon be headed to Woodville.

As the weeks rolled by, Lucy was concerned the bank was acting in haste and would foreclose before they were ready.

The day their life changed, Cain went for a walk to clear his head, for his concern was slightly different. He knew his wife wanted no part of moving to Woodville.

From a distance, Cain saw a car approaching the house. *Poor Lucy is all alone*, he thought.

Mr. Tompkins exited the car and walked up to the door.

Lucy reluctantly but graciously, invited him inside. "I'll get my husband. Please sit and wait until I find him." Lucy stepped out onto the front steps and saw Cain walking fast toward the house. She waved for him to hurry.

Feeling the pressure of having to move from their grand home, their only option was to relocate in the small house that Cain had purchased for Orson, which was only a stone's throw from the plantation.

Cain was hopeful that the new buyer would not like them living nearby and could possibly be prepared to present them with an offer, just to get rid of them.

He also, worried about Lucy and how she would feel moving into the small house after living in a grand home like Pecan Plantation. *I'm sure my wife will be grateful to have a place to go.*

Feeling very confident, Cain thought part of their problem had been solved since they could move into Orson's place temporarily, of course.

As Cain entered the room, Mr. Tompkins stood to greet him.

As they shook hands, Lucy noticed a calm about Cain that she had not seen before. There had been a tremendous amount of pressure on him, and seeing him regain some of his fight spirit gave her reason to believe he might pull some magic out of his hat. He's a lawyer and she believed he might save the day, but that was not to happen.

This was a sad day for them, for Mr. Tompkins' visit was definitely not a social one.

Lucy was saddened at seeing the home she loved taken from her. She remembered each time they went into the bank, how uncomfortable Mr. Tompkins made her feel. And it was the same now, as he handed over the papers for Cain to sign. There was something very cunning about him. *I would imagine he has some secrets*, she thought.

As the men spoke, Lucy's head began spinning when she heard the name of Sebastian Parker, who was prepared to make an offer on the frame house and the 5 acres of land attached to the plantation.

"I'm sorry, but we're not selling at any price," Lucy said. Cain looked at her in amazement, for he had not expected her to turn down a proposal.

"Sir, we'll talk about it and let you know." Cain replied.

"No need to talk—my mind is made up. It was my daddy's property and I'm not selling." With that, Lucy walked out of the room.

"Mr. Porter, perhaps your wife needs time. When she comes around, we'll do right by you. I'm sure neither of you will want to continue living here after Mr. Parker moves in."

"Sir, I'm afraid you don't know my wife. When Lucy makes up her mind about something—there's no change!" Cain explained.

Mr. Tompkins shrugged his shoulders, picked up his belongings and walked out.

Although Lucy knew the move was imminent, hearing the words to vacate was still alarming.

"Cain, I have to be honest—I'm not going back to Jonesboro."

He knew he had to try and find a place that would make Lucy happy.

Every day there was something new, and this day they learned Sebastian was a wealthy cotton farmer from Georgia who would be moving in within the month.

Little did they know, but Sebastian Parker was nothing but a con man involved with Lee Tompkins and Packer Rover, who were stealing everything from personal property to committing bank robbery.

~

Three more weeks passed, and just before their move, Vick and Elizabeth arrived with furniture. They had hired a truck to move the odds and ends they had from the carriage house, which at one time was used in her paint studio. Knowing Cain and Lucy's circumstance, she arranged everything.

It was a lovely thought and Lucy was grateful, but her world appeared to have turned upside down—and it showed. All she could think about was being forced into giving up the plantation.

Cain, torn with doubts and frustration, tried to pay Elizabeth and Vick for the furniture, but they would not accept it.

"Son, you and Lucy need furniture and these pieces were all extra."

"Yes, I recognize most of it," Cain laughed.

Lucy listened to their laughter.

"I wish I could laugh, but there's nothing to be joyful about," she anguished.

Although it was tight quarters with the five of them, Cain and Lucy were happy Vick and Elizabeth had decided to relocate so they could be near them. *Jared needs his grandparents*, Lucy thought.

The Porters were just getting settled into the small frame house when Vick saw a car drive up to the plantation.

"Pa, that must be the new owner!" Cain said.

The stranger drove up in his shiny new Pierce Arrow with the top down, a luxury car that only the very wealthy could afford.

Lucy strained to have a glimpse of the man whom she assumed was the owner. She had only seen picture shows with his type; lean, tall, good-looking, and reeking of wealth.

She imagined he had no problem with women. She noticed how stylish he was. His hairstyle was a bit longer and very modern. He opened the door of his car, and out of the corner of his eye he saw a beautiful woman standing outside the small house next door.

That must be the pretty little thing Lee spoke about, he thought to himself wantonly.

Sebastian grabbed the two suitcases from the back seat and placed them on the porch, then walked out to the cotton fields. Lucy watched as he explored the perimeters of the plantation which a short time ago was theirs. She thought it was unfair for the bank to sell the plantation out from under them.

Vick presumed Sebastian was just another rich fellow from a different world—not better, but certainly not one of similar interests.

There had been only one other man Vick knew who was close to Sebastian in status, and that was Johnson Petty, the original owner of Pecan Plantation—a wealthy gambler, and lady's man.

Little was known of Johnson's dealings back then with several lawyers protecting his interests. It was assumed he came by his wealth mostly by illegal means.

Cain had no feelings either way, however, he was impressed with the car.

"Pa, what do you think about the new owner's car?" Cain asked.

"Son, everything has its purpose, but my horse can do things that a fine automobile can't do."

Vick turned and walked into the house. Only Vick had the insight that set him apart from other men, Cain believed. At times, he thought Vick was living in a time warp.

Twenty years in a cell can do that to a man. His life began after he was released from prison, but to him time had stood still during those twenty years of incarceration. He was still living in the day of horseback and horse-drawn carriages.

Cain was educated and his Pa was somewhat illiterate; but no one would guess the intelligence of Vick, who had been taught the trappings of a southern gentleman. He also had a swagger about him that reflected affluence and confidence.

Although Vick's character suggested all of that, he was still of the opinion that a horse-drawn carriage could: bring a doctor to the house to birth a child, pull a hearse to the cemetery when someone dies, and be useful to the farmer who plows his fields, plus, they offer transportation around town moving within tight places that an automobile can't. Horses would always be Vick's preferred manner of transportation.

~

Sebastian Parker was a man of mystery. This aroused Lucy's interest. Each day she found herself glimpsing toward the plantation to see if the new owner might show himself.

Likewise, she had no idea Sebastian was excitedly curious about the beautiful woman whom he had quietly observed.

Some evenings, Senor Galvez would come to Cain full of information about Sebastian.

"Meester Sebastian been asking questions 'bout ya'll living so close to the plantation. I hear him talking to the foreman. He wants all the land around him. He doesn't like you and your family living here."

The Porters understood Sebastian disliked their presence, but there was nothing he could do about it unless he chose to cause trouble with Lucy.

The next day Cain and Lucy discussed the fact that living so close to Sabastian could become an annoyance.

"Cain, I have an idea. I could ask Mr. Parker for a job? That way he may not care if we live here."

"You'll do no such thing!" Cain said.

"I don't believe I heard you right! You know I resent being told what I can and can't do!"

"You may live to regret your decision. The man's not to be trusted," Cain said.

She just smiled at him.

"Don't worry, I can take care of myself."

"Do you mind telling me the real reason you want to work for Sebastian?" Cain asked.

Vick walked in on their conversation before Lucy had a chance to explain.

He could feel the tension when Lucy left the room.

After several weeks, Lucy began noticing a change in the way the townsfolk treated her. After they heard she had lost the plantation, those who once catered to her were now ignoring her. She was no longer considered special, and the tongues wagged at how the Queen of Pecan Plantation had been dethroned. Lucy went about her business ignoring the idle comments.

After leaving the store with her head held high, she knew she had to make her move.

"Tomorrow, I'll meet Sebastian Parker," she said under her breath.

Lucy no sooner left the store when she rounded the corner and ran head-on into Sebastian.

She was carrying bags, and as he grabbed her to keep her from falling, he held on a little too long.

For a moment Sebastian's world stood still, until he heard Lucy's sweet voice.

"Oh, excuse me, I didn't see you coming," she said. Her classic southern accent endeared her to him. She was a beauty and intrigue all wrapped in a perfect package. After taking a deep breath, he finally spoke, "Oh, hello…why you must be the lady I've seen living next door. I'm sorry I haven't been over to introduce myself. I'm Sebastian Parker."

"Oh, I know who you are." She hadn't intended to sound smug—it just came out that way.

She thought how nice it was to get to the point and break the ice.

"I understand it's been difficult for you and your husband to leave."

Lucy imagined he was getting a thrill as he "turned the knife".

"We moved next door, because there's a lot of sentiment tied to the place. It belonged to my father, and I'm not sure when and if we'll be relocating. In the meantime, I have plenty of free time if you need help with the bookkeeping. I'm the one who set-up your books."

"Is this the only job you've had?" Sebastian asked.

"No, I ran the office for the Porter Lumber Company and managed a crew of loggers."

"That's a big undertaking. I'm very impressed. Give me a day or two to get settled and I'll have Senor Galvez tell you when I'm ready. One other thing: It's nice to have you and your husband living next door."

It was obvious that he was not sincere. After the ice was broken they said their adieus and went on their separate ways.

For the first time, Sebastian was excited about being in San Augustine.

She's quite a woman. There's a mystery about her, he thought.

The next day, while Lucy was in town purchasing baking supplies, Caleb, the clerk of the bank walked in. He quickly turned and walked out of the store before she could say "hello." *That's strange,* she thought. She sensed he was ignoring her.

The following day, she drove into town to fetch horse feed when the same thing happened when she saw him. Only this time, he started to say something but couldn't bring himself to address her. Being curious, she pulled on his jacket before he could walk away.

"Caleb Young––that is your name, isn't it?" He looked embarrassed and nodded "yes." "What is this all about? I think you want to talk to me, so why don't we have a seat at the soda fountain and talk."

He followed her to the end of the counter where they could speak in private. "Ma'am, I ain't supposed to talk to you."

"Caleb––I have no idea what you mean by that!"

"Miss Lucy, I'm afraid to be seen talking to you, and I don't know you well enough to know if I can trust you."

"You're going to have to enlighten me. I don't quite understand."

"I spec' it's 'cause you and Mr. Cain lost the plantation––and I know why."

"Do you care to explain?" Lucy asked.

"Talking could get me in a lot of trouble." Caleb pushed himself away from the counter to leave.

"Just a minute! You can't leave without explaining." Lucy responded.

"Mr. Tompkins––how well do you know him?" Caleb asked.

"I know he owns the bank and he sold the plantation out from under us. It still puzzles me why he was in such a hurry; I'm sure our finances were in good shape, but he foreclosed on us!"

"I can't prove anything, but they're a conniving bunch of cheats. They cheated y'all and used poor ol' sick Jonathan Petty to do it! Everybody knew Jonathan was crazy and Mr. Tompkins used him to steal your plantation."

Lucy sat there in a state of shock, for she had not planned on hearing such a claim.

Caleb bent toward Lucy and whispered, "They operate out of two sets of books. The books you've seen ain't the real books."

"Caleb, are you serious? What do you know about this?"

"They swindle people all the time. They don't know, but I overheard them plottin' against you and your husband. I'm ashamed I ain't come forward sooner, but I didn't know what to do—and I need my job."

Lucy was stunned. She took a deep breath and continued to ask questions.

"Are you absolutely sure of this? Caleb this is quite an accusation unless you can prove it! Who else is in this with him?"

"If I had the books I could prove it! Maybe they been destroyed for all I know, but that Sebastian feller and Mr. Tompkins are thick as thieves."

"So, you're saying Sebastian, who bought our plantation, is in on this. If this is true, we need to find the books!" Lucy pressed.

"Ya' gonna git yourself in trouble and me too if ya' start messing with their business, tho'. They've done some bad things."

"What kind of things."

Caleb whispered again,

"People die!" Caleb was visibly upset. "I'm sorry, Mrs. Porter, I didn't mean to scare you. If they find out I told you any of this, I'm gonna be as good as dead." He looked around to make sure there was no one there he knew, obviously antsy.

"Caleb, you listen to me. They're not going to know we've talked, so stop worrying. I need you to think back and make sure you haven't forgotten any details."

"For the first time, Caleb felt absolved, and it felt good. He appeared to be very truthful as he continued to spill his guts.

"There's a lot I know, and it's far worse than being cheated."

"What could possibly be worse than what you accused them of?" Lucy asked.

Caleb spoke slowly, "Murder."

The word "murder" sent chills up and down her spine. She sat back hard in the chair. She had no idea what to do with the information Caleb had shared with her.

"Miss Lucy…maybe I shoulda' kept my mouth shut, 'cause the way you look, you ain't gonna' let this go. Please don't stir up no trouble for me."

He provided her with too much information for it not to be true. *I believe him. If this is true, Sebastian and Lee Tompkins should be hanged or imprisoned. I'll see to that!* she thought.

Having this information certainly placed a new spin on how and why they lost the plantation. *I'm going to see they pay,* she thought.

Now, she had to convince Cain to let her stay in San Augustine for awhile. It was important for her not to let Cain and Vick know until she had the proof. She knew it was possible they would jump the gun and do something rash. If that happened, *we'll never get the plantation back. Gotta take it easy and not rush,* she planned.

Caleb saw her stern face, "Miss Lucy, are you gonna be alright? I've already said too much, and if we're seen talking together, they gonna suspect something." With that, Caleb scurried away. Lucy knew she could not tell anyone—not even Elizabeth.

That night at supper, Lucy was noticeably quiet. She was planning on what to do next.

The next morning, most of their conversation centered around finding a place to live.

Vick knew something had to be done, and quickly.

"Son, before we think about moving, why don't we go to Woodville and see what's there?"

"When do you think we should go?" Cain asked.

"How about as soon as we can pack?" Vick chuckled.

"What about Ma and Lucy?" Cain hated to leave them behind with Sebastian next door.

"Oh, don't worry about us," Lucy insisted. "We have plenty to do right here," Elizabeth sensed something different about Lucy. She had known her long enough to know when something wasn't right.

Elizabeth wasn't the only one who noticed a change. Lucy had been acting very strange and moody, which bothered Cain.

"Pa, can we take a walk?" Vick followed Cain outside, lit a cigar and strolled down by the lake.

"I guess you know things ain't exactly right between me and Lucy. She thinks I should have done more to save the plantation and now it's Jared she's worried about."

"Son, you and Lucy will work it out. Right now, y'all are hung up in the curve. When you and Lucy turn the corner, you'll figure it out....Know what I mean?"

"I reckon I do, but this is the first time we've been at odds with each other. I can't believe she's asking Sebastian for a job. She's just like Orson, hard headed as they come."

Vick laughed.

"I guess as long as we have Lucy, a little piece of Orson lives on, and that's not a bad thing. Don't worry about Lucy. She can take care of herself."

"Is that supposed to make me feel better?" Cain asked.

Vick smiled, and as usual, gave Cain a quick pat on the back.

Chapter 3

THE MORNING AGGIE MADE HER DECISION TO FAKE HER DEATH, SHE HAD no one to turn to but Justin, her caretaker. She wrapped a shawl around her shoulders and walked toward the guesthouse.

Peering out the window he sensed something was wrong the minute he saw her.

"Morning, Miss Aggie. Time now to break them ears of corn and pull those peanuts. It's gonna be a mess of 'em this year," Justin said, with a bulging cheek full of chewing tobacco.

She couldn't hide the sad face she carried.

"Ma'am, ya' all right?"

"No Justin, I've learned that Mr. Seth isn't coming back home."

At first, he didn't understand, for Seth was in prison for a very long time.

"Ever?" he asked. Then it hit him that they might have parted ways.

"I'm really sorry to hear that, ma'am."

Her head dropped and her eyes filled with tears as she explained what when she had visited Seth the day before, he'd asked her to divorce him.

"Miss Aggie, I don't reckon Mr. Seth meant he didn't love ya'. He probably said that 'cause he ain't got no life to give you locked away in prison. He may have thought he was being kind to ya'."

"No, this was not being kind. It was in his eyes--I could tell. I don't know what I'm going to do now that I've lost both Jared and Seth. All I know is I can't stay here with all these memories!"

"What do you mean?" Justin asked.

"You remember me telling you about my half-brother and the big plantation I lived on? I know for sure that Jonathan wants our father's inheritance for himself and he's out to kill Jared and me. He doesn't know, but I would give him the place just to leave my son and me alone.

"That's not the only reason he wants me dead—I'm the one person who can have him hanged. He murdered my mother right before my eyes when I was a kid. Now, he has men searching for me. That's the only reason I allowed Cain to adopt my son to protect him from Jonathan. Now it's too late, and I have nothing left but bad memories surrounding this place and what I've lost. I wish I would have known what I know now, for I would still have Jared and would never have met Seth—or his father. I've thought about it and I can't stay here any longer. I have to leave, but before I go I need to ask a favor of you."

"Miss Aggie, you can ask me anything. You should know that by now."

"I do, but what I'm going to ask might seem strange."

"Yes, ma'am, you got my word."

"You're going to think I'm crazy, but I'm sending two letters… one to Cain Porter, Jared's father, and the other to Seth. They'll assume that these letters were mailed either just before or after I died. My wishes will be made known in the letters."

"Miss Aggie, you ain't got in mind to hurt yourself, do ya?" He asked in shock.

"No, but I want everyone to believe I'm dead, especially my half-brother and his hired killers, who want to harm my son and me."

"Miss Aggie, I don't know what to say. What if someone comes lookin' fer ya'? What do I tell 'em?"

"You tell them that I've died, and I asked you to stay on and keep the property intact until Jared is old enough to move here and take care of the place. One day this place will be his, and if anyone asks, tell them you have no idea where Jared is. I hope you'll plan to stay on until then. This will be a fair exchange….You keep up the property and you're welcome to stay in the guest house for as long as you want. You keep the money made from selling eggs, vegetables and livestock."

"Ma'am, that's awfully generous of you, but jest in case something happens, could I ask ya' ta put that in writing?"

Aggie assured him that before leaving she would leave a note to explain her wishes.

"Justin, I ask only one thing, and that's for you to keep my confidence. For the safety of me and my son, no one must know I'm alive or where to find Jared."

"Miss Aggie, you do what ya' have ta do. I ain't tellin' nobody nothin'. My lips are sealed," Justin said.

If only Aggie had not acted so hastily she would have learned that her brothers who had dealt her a lifetime of misery, were both dead.

Cain would never have understood Aggie's uncharacteristic behavior had he known her plan to falsify her death.

Poor timing often makes for a disappointing entrance. Aggie's timing was too early, and for that, she doomed herself to a future without her son. Had she stayed and learned that her half-brother, Jonathan, and his men were by that time dead and were no longer a threat, her life would have turned out quite differently. She had been afraid to even send an anonymous inquiry to San Augustine. There would have been no need to run, for she would have Jared safely with her, and she would never have allowed Cain nor anyone else to adopt him. Circumstances often influence decisions, either good or bad.

～

It had been about two years since Cain received a letter that Aggie had died.

Little Jared had adapted quickly to having Lucy as his mother, and he was a happy, growing child. Things could not be better.

Cain would never in his wildest dreams imagine Aggie would fake her death and be hiding out somewhere. But this was no dream, for, unbeknown to him, she was alive and well living in Beaumont and working in a boarding house.

~

Even though it had been two years since Aggie had disappeared, many times she regretted making such a drastic decision to deceive the people she cared for.

Little did she know, after all the time that had passed, her husband, serving his prison term for killing his father, was still under the impression that she was alive and possibly remarried with more children. For, unfortunately, the letter Aggie sent to him announcing her death was lost in the mail.

On their last visit, Seth had asked her to divorce him as soon as she had arrived to visit.

Married to a man who was serving most of his life in prison was no way for the woman he loved to spend her life, so he assumed Aggie had gotten the divorce and gone on with her life.

Likewise, Aggie had no idea Seth failed to receive her letter announcing her death. She was sure he knew of her ill fate. After all, she had simultaneously mailed letters to both Seth and Cain.

Because of her presumed death, Cain had an overabundance of gratitude toward her for making sure Jared was given to him and Lucy "before she succumbed to her illness." He knew of her wishes and intended to honor them at all costs. Marrying Lucy was Cain's best solution, because now Jared had both mother and father.

After Aggie went through the ordeal of falsifying her death, she would lay awake many nights reliving the day her world came crashing down around her.

Shortly after Seth entered prison, Aggie never even considered the eventuality of dissolving their marriage. She acted hastily and asked Cain to adopt Jared for his safety and, since he was the boy's biological father. To her it seemed to be the right thing to do. This was mainly how her problems began. How fast things can change. *I'm being punished*, she thought.

After Cain legally adopted Jared, the only other person she had to rely on was Seth, in prison. He was the only one left she could emotionally depend upon and found her visits helpful to go on living, but, when he rejected her by asking for a divorce—her world crashed.

She remembered the day she walked the austere marbled hallway to a room designed for prisoners and their visitors. She was looking forward to seeing Seth. Standing there waiting, she looked totally out of place in her long maroon dress, tan gloves and her red hair pulled back in a bun with ringlets framing her face. She needed his reassurance, but instead, he shocked her by asking for a divorce.

Leaving the prison with shattered dreams, she cried all the way home. *There's nothing much to live for now*, she thought. In a moment's time, she even entertained the idea of taking her own life, but killing herself was something she could never do. Her next inclination was to run away, as far as possible, to escape her pain and not have to fear her for her safety. She was now a broken woman, living each day because of the terrible choices she made. She was all alone, with no one to turn to. Her heart ached from not being able to live with her son.

Her thoughts were often of Cain and how they met. How different my life would have been if I had accepted Cain's proposal. I would never have met Seth, and he would have never had reason to kill his father.

$\sim$

Before leaving Woodville, Aggie took one last moment to gaze over her property. It's such a beautiful and serene place, she thought. She glanced at the slope above the lake with plenty of dogwood and pine trees and wished she did not have to leave. Over on the left side of the house was a pasture of tall grass that seemed to be waving goodbye. For the first time, she realized her mistake was in not allowing herself time to sort out her feelings for Cain.

She had many dreams for a happy life, but her impatience cost her dearly. She now felt she should have given Cain a chance. *How could I have been attracted to Seth when there was Cain?*

She remembered the promise she made to her Pa before he died that influenced her decision to leave Cain before she even knew she was pregnant. She agreed not to marry and saddle herself with a bunch of kids, which was his last wish for her. *Why did I make such a promise? Now, I would give anything to have Cain as my husband, and raise our child together.*

Leaving the home that had so many possibilities for her was heartwrenching, but she finally walked away never looking back. She was done.

~

Beaumont had a booming economy with oil exploration and new businesses popping up all over town. The population exploded over-night with thousands of people relocating to this small Southeast Texas town to make their fortunes. Oil had replaced lumber and the town was bursting with unprepared growth. There were several new towns including Vidor, Orange, and Port Arthur, all in close proxi-mately. Most folks lived and worked in Beaumont.

Before Aggie moved to the booming oil town, she had plenty of money, for she had sold most of her cattle and had enough to live on until she would be forced to find employment.

When she stopped her car in front of Annie Mae McGarity's boarding house, there was something about the place that reminded her of Woodville. She took an immediate liking to the light-yellow painted place. The sweetness and charm of Annie Mae was exactly what she needed, for it had been a long time since someone made over her.

"Come on in child. You must be tired from your travels. Are you hungry?" Annie Mae talked a mile a minute, and those oversized brown "cow eyes" assured you she was as genuine as they come.

Aggie hardly knew what to make of Annie Mae's friendliness.

"Thank you, but I'm in need of a place to stay."

"Well, you're just in time. I had a room come vacant this morning. This is your lucky day 'cause there ain't hardly no place in town to stay with all the influx of people. I imagine you're here because of the oil boom."

There were only a few boarding houses to accommodate the oil people who had come to Beaumont to prosper. Aggie had no idea how close to Cain's footsteps she was traveling. Before recovering from amnesia, he stayed nearby at Josey's Boarding House.

"Dear, would you like to freshen up before you have supper?" Annie Mae asked.

"Oh thank you. Yes, I would, if you don't mind. I'll tidy up a bit."

"Well then, let me show you your room. We're good around here at spoiling our tenants." She chuckled as she led the way.

When Aggie opened the door to the small room, she was impressed with how nice and clean it was. It served her needs and that was all that mattered, since she considered herself just passing through. The soft four-poster bed was covered with a pink and lavender floral quilt, and the sunlight passing through the white cotton window curtains gave a comforting warm glow to the room.

"Now Miss, I don't think I got your name...?" Annie Mae asked.

"Oh--I'm sorry. My name is Aggie Dawson." She flinched a bit, hadn't mean to use her real name, but it slipped out before she knew it. *Aggie!...hmmm*, she thought.

"Seems like I've heard your name. Sounds familiar," Annie Mae mused.

First, Aggie was concerned that her past had caught up with her already, but she wasn't sure, since Woodville was only 60 miles away. After Seth killed his father, Aggie had gotten some bad press. People gossiped, and accused her of coming between father and son.

"Well, you take your time and I'll begin my evening meal at 4 o'clock," Annie Mae, said.

"Thank you, I won't be too long."

Sitting on her bed, she prayed that she had done the right thing by sending letters to Cain and Seth announcing her death.

∽

Two years had passed quickly, and, working beside Annie Mae, they became like family. She made enough money to live on, which enabled her to continue to save the money. By anyone's standards, Aggie was a wealthy woman.

Chapter 4

HUNTSVILLE, TEXAS PRISON

SETH JACKSON HAD BEEN IN PRISON FOR OVER TWO YEARS, AND, AFTER HE had asked Aggie for a divorce, he had all but given up on life. It had been only two years since he sent her away, but it seemed much longer.

Seth had often wished he had never engaged in a conflict with his father, but there was no looking back. If Pa, hadn't loathed Aggie and tried to steal her oil rich property, he would still be alive, and I wouldn't be in prison, he anguished.

His dad, Parley, had a reputation for being a ruthless no-good, and sought Aggie killed. Now, that his plan was in place for him to take over her land, it had backfired—Seth found out what his dad was up to, and after meeting in a heated rage, Parley took it too far, which resulted in Seth shooting him.

No matter how abusive Parley was toward Aggie, without witnesses to confirm Seth's testimony, there was no way to defend his sworn statement that his father was the one who had attacked him. After a short trial, Seth was found guilty and sentenced to 20 years.

It was a tragic mistake for his father to choose to settle the argument with a gun, and with no witnesses to testify in Seth's behalf, the guilty verdict was going to be obvious.

$\sim$

Sitting in his dank cell, dreaming of the old days when life was simple, Seth heard the rattle of keys approaching him.

That was Sonny—the evilest guard in prison. There were two Sonny's—the Sonny who was having a bad day, and the Sonny who was having a worse day. It was never good for Seth or any of the prisoners when either of the two Sonny's showed up.

He was very unpredictable, but mostly he was just plain mean. He enjoyed beating up and degrading the prisoners, and if he didn't like you, well, that made things even worse.

He had a special way of using the butt end of his gun to get one's attention. It was a quick and powerful jab that one remembered long after the pain was gone.

Approaching the cell, Sonny shouted, "Seth Jackson, the Warden wants to see you, so git yourself together!"

A rush of cold chills entered his body, for being called in by the Warden was quite unusual and not a good sign.

He reluctantly followed the guard to the Warden's office, handcuffed and shackled at the ankles. Seth wondered if he'd be walking or crawling back to his cell. The Warden was also one to taunt the prisoners, and when he got angry, it could be brutal.

Warden Nelson always dressed in starched khaki pants and shirt. He was very clean cut, slightly overweight with slicked back brown hair. He was average looking, with eyeglasses and shiny black shoes. He looked like the perfect Warden, but he was considered mean and unforgiving if one ever got on his bad side.

The Warden was up to his old tricks when he withheld a personal letter from Aggie to Seth for more than two years. He couldn't take all the credit though, because somehow the letter got misplaced, in with a backlog of papers.

"Jackson, we got a letter for ya'," the Warden stated. "It must have come by Pony Express to take this long. It's kinda' old, like maybe it took us two years to read it." The Warden looked at the guard and they both chuckled.

His remark struck a nerve, but Seth let it slide. One learns to become numb to verbal abuse when locked up in one of the worst prisons in Texas.

Seth had not received mail for over two years and he wondered who would be sending a letter that took so long to arrive. It was probably from Aggie, he decided and hoped, while fearing bad news. For some reason, a chill ran over him.

Seth understood prisoners who were summoned to the Warden's office were often beaten—but not this day. It was the Warden's way of jerking him around—anything to show they were in charge.

The Warden handed him the letter. "Sonny boy, git the prisoner back to his cell!"

Seth took a moment and stuffed the letter into his shirt just as a swift jab to the back got his attention. He was knocked to the floor, but he managed to get up and hobble back to his cell as the guard continued to cajole him. Once there, he was unshackled and pushed into the small four walls that was his home for the next 18 years.

"Ain't nobody like you deserves mail, since you killed yer' own Pa. Now, who'd be sending a letter to a lifer like you when ya' probably ain't ever leavin' here alive?" Seth heard a ring of truth in Sonny's prediction. The guard was filled with curiosity as he watched Seth open the letter.

This must be the divorce papers I've been waiting two years for, Seth thought.

He remembered the last time he saw her. *Turning Aggie away may have been the biggest mistake of my life,* he reflected. He made the decision that she was a lady and did not deserve a husband who would spend most of his life in prison. His decision to divorce her was for also for her safety, due to the evil that loitered around the prison. Her beauty had a lot to do with his choice.

If it wasn't the Warden, it was the guards who stole pieces of his life. Seth convinced himself that he had nothing left to give Aggie, even if he lived long enough to be a free man.

Opening the letter, Seth's hands shook. Only those locked away with no hope and shut off from the rest of the world would understand the excitement felt from receiving something as simple as a letter—a symbol of the intimate human need for others. Sonny continued to harass him. He had an attitude much like Seth's Pa—sarcastic and demeaning. But there was nothing Seth could do but go along with what Sonny and the Warden had to dish out.

"You heard the Warden! The letters git lost in here—maybe even read by everybody else before it gits to ya'," Sonny provoked. He laughed out loud at believing he got under Seth's skin.

Examining the envelope, Seth thought it looked as though it had travelled around the world before it got to him. But he didn't care. It was a letter from Aggie, and that's all that mattered.

His eyes watered as he read her words.

Seth Darling,

Should you be reading this letter you will know I have died. Our life changed when you went to prison, and since then I have had to make decisions without you. I wanted to speak of this the last time I saw you, but you sent me away.

I had received news from my doctor that I am near death with a mysterious illness, and will no longer be able to take care of Jared. Had you been here I would have worked something out with Jared's father so you could continue your relationship with our son. Cain Porter is a good man so you need not worry. You were good with Jared and I know he loves you like a real father. I hope you understand what I had to do. I have no other choice but to leave Cain in charge of the home place with Jared. I know he will do what's best for our son and be fair with you. Seth, you have the Jackson place in Woodville for your return, but I have left my home and the mineral rights to Jared. I'm sure he will share any residuals from the oil exploration. Should something happen to Jared, I know Cain will do right by you, for I have not forgotten our love and what we had.

This letter specifies my wishes since you are unable to share our place with Jared.

I will always love you. Seth, I tried to go through with the divorce, but I couldn't. I am enclosing a picture that was taken on our wedding day.
All My Love, Aggie

Seth felt sick to his stomach, and his face was flushed with anger that Aggie had to die alone, possibly from a broken heart. He again remembered the last visit they had and how crushed she was when he told her to divorce him.

Out of disdain for himself, he wadded up the letter and the picture and threw it between the bars. Sonny continued to taunt Seth, who was enraged enough to take it out on a guard.

Death would be easier, Seth thought. At least I would be with Aggie, he imagined. Sonny had never seen Seth so angry and sensed a fight on his hands if he intervened.

Sonny bent down and picked up the letter. Walking back and forth in front of the bars, Sonny taunted Seth unmercifully.

"Now let's see what has you so riled up….I'll jest keep this letter close to my heart."

He looked at Aggie's picture. "Whew-wee…she's a pretty little thing." He laughed at seeing Seth with such contempt.

Regretting that he had thrown Aggie's letter away, he reached through the bars for it, but Sonny was too far away.

Waving the letter in the air, Sonny laughed and sauntered away.

Momentarily, Seth thought how easy it would be to kill Sonny and not look back. No one should have to endure this insanity–no one, he thought.

∾

Sonny Bilbo was a rodeo cowboy—the kind who was considered ruggedly handsome but lacking in refinement. The years were beginning to catch up with him as he got careless with his appearance.

He was a muscular man with dark features, brown eyes and a wicked little smile that appeared devilish. For years he travelled the rodeo circuit as a bull rider until he was gored and had to call it quits. After a year of convalescing, the Huntsville State Prison hired him as a guard. People had heard of Sonny, and a few knew of his dark side.

He had quite a past that was certainly not pearly white. Some said he was the ultimate irony as a prison guard, since he was the one who should have been behind bars. His friends pulled away from him when his disposition got worse as he got older.

In the back of Sonny's mind, he had always imagined finding a pot of gold—or stealing it. Either way was all right with him. He was a dreamer with an entitlement mentality, having no morals or decency about him. One thing for certain: if he ever got rich, it wasn't the result of hard work. Women on the other hand could never figure him out, until the real Sonny showed up. It only took a couple of weeks before his nasty behavior took over. His life was a mess, making one bad mistake and decision after the other. When the results turned sour and his plans blew up in his face, he wondered what happened, and why?

He loved the danger involved in bull riding. But the wrong bull cost him his rodeo career and left him with a bum leg. He ran with outcasts most of his life, Gill Morrison being one. In fact, Gill was serving time in the same prison, although Sonny did his best to avoid him. *Don't need guards or inmates knowing Sonny had paled around with one of the inmates.*

Sonny lived on the south side of Huntsville in a small rustic, dilapidated shack, spending most of his free time in a small cantina not far from the place he called home. This is where he did most of his hustling with cards—and women.

His money was spent on whiskey until his bottle ran dry, and then he would turn his attention to a woman—any woman. It didn't matter what she looked like, for when morning came, he was left alone with his own thoughts.

After Seth had his meltdown, Sonny was anxious to get to the cantina and read Aggie's letter. It had been raining and was "country dark"— so dark you couldn't see your hand in front of your face. After having a couple of drinks, he took out the crumpled letter to read. The woman he had been sharing eye contact with saw the letter and became curious. While straightening the letter, he felt someone standing over him. It was the woman from the bar. She began teasing him about what she thought was a love letter.

"Whatcha got, cowboy?...Did ya' jest learn your lady run off with another man?" She had a big smile with bright red lips, and her hair was slightly windblown from the storm. She purposely had left too many buttons on her blouse unfastened so her cleavage would show.

As usual, the saloon was dimly lit. Sonny was squinting his eyes to read the print when suddenly the woman reached over and turned up the kerosene lamp.

"I reckon I'm gonna have to wait until I can see. I can't see a thing," Sonny mumbled and turned to the other side a little, hoping to end her inquiry. Before he had a chance to put the picture and letter back into his pocket, she snatched them from him.

"Well then, I'm gonna read it for ya," she demanded. She straddled a chair, ready to read.

"My eyes can see this just fine," she said mockingly.

"See here now, ya' just can't start reading another person's mail… this is personal," Sonny said.

"Well, it ain't no more," she laughed.

She read the part where Aggie told Seth she was dead. "Why this letter is to a man named Seth. The bartender told me your name was Sonny." She stared at him like he was part of a joke.

"Well Miss know-it-all, Sonny happens to be a nickname. My real name is Seth." He grimaced, hoping she fell for it.

"So yer real name is Seth?" She scrutinized him carefully.

"Seth don't fit ya', but I guess if yer wife calls ya' Seth, then that's yer name."

At the time, he had no idea of what might be revealed in the letter. Reading out loud she suddenly stopped. "Seth, I'm so sorry about yer wife dying, but it ain't like yer gonna be hurtin' fer nothin'."

He almost choked on his whiskey. "What do you mean by that?" Sonny reached and grabbed the letter from her hand. "You ain't got no right to this letter. Now, git out of here and let me be."

The woman was alarmed to see such agitation from a man she was trying to seduce. I've had my share of hotheads, she thought as she hurried away.

Sonny stuffed the letter in his coat, and then got up and stormed out of the cantina into the blinding rain. Before he got home he was soaked to the bone but kept the letter and photo dry. *The woman forced me to pretend to be Seth. I've got to hurry and read that letter.*

All the way home his heart was pounding, wondering what the woman at the bar was talking about. Once inside, he sat on the edge of his bed and lit the lantern. He read the letter carefully, but couldn't believe its contents. After reading it a second time, he realized his excitement was warranted.

"I'll be wallerin' in riches if I can pull this one off," he said aloud to himself. "Poor ole' Seth ain't gonna see what's coming!"

Sonny celebrated by drinking a bottle of whiskey. He became convinced that he was onto something big. *This could end up being a windfall... all the money I could hope for,* he schemed.

"This is the best thing that ever happened to me," he exclaimed aloud. He didn't care that Seth had lost his wife. All he cared about was cashing in on Seth's dead wife's oil-rich land.

The weeks that followed were all about what to do next. At night, he lay dreaming of his boundless wealth and what money can do for him. He carefully studied the picture of Aggie and Seth together. *With a little trim here and there, and grow a beard, I might be able to make this work,* he thought. There was a great deal of uncertainty because of Aggie's son, but he was desperate to do anything rather than the mundane routine work that he had grown to hate.

After a few days of building his courage, he began hanging around the Warden's office, just in case there was a chance he could slip in without being seen. Usually the office was locked, so he had to find a way to unlock the door. One late afternoon offered the perfect opportunity, but the door was locked tighter than a drum.

This ain't gonna work, he thought. *I should think of something else.*

Since it was Friday night and Sonny had just gotten paid, instead of going to the cantina, he went shopping for some similar clothing from the photo he seized from Seth. Afterwards, he stopped by the barbershop for a haircut.

The barber looked at the picture, "I think we can do this."

Sonny was pleased with the new look that closely resembled the picture. Even the Warden commented on how different he looked.

The only thing left to do was to take care of Seth and figure out how to do it, Sonny thought.

That same day he got lucky when he saw the Warden leave his office door unlocked. He knew there was a small window of time, and he had to move fast or it could land him on the other side of the bars. *Nothin's gonna git in the way of my plan—not even the Warden,* he thought.

As soon as the coast was clear, Sonny popped into the office and began sifting through papers. He had to find copies of discharge papers to tempt his partner in crime. He was midway through the files when he heard footsteps coming down the hall. He was sure it was the Warden, for he recognized his cough and someone stopped the Warden and asked a question. *Good!*

Papers were scattered about and there was little time to put the office back together. Luckily, Sonny opened a cabinet door, and found what he was looking for. He moved fast to take care of his mess, then popped inside a small closet to keep from being caught.

Sonny took small breaths to prevent the Warden from hearing him. He watched through a crack as the door opened and the Warden entered, apparently searching for his keys. Scratching his head, he remembered they were in his coat across the room.

Cold sweat popped out on Sonny's forehead as he thought of the consequence. Sonny saw the perplexed look on the Warden's face as if he sensed something wasn't right.

How quickly things can change from bad to worse, he thought, when suddenly the Warden left his office again, locking the door behind him. Now he had the time he needed to work on forging documents for a prisoner's release.

Sonny was successful in carrying out the first phase of his plan. Now it was time to visit the cell of an old friend and try to convince him to kill Seth.

～

Sonny was having a day off when Seth received a letter from Cain Porter. Confused with the timing, he wondered why Cain would be contacting him. After reading the letter, he learned that Cain was about to take over Aggie's place, and wanted to know if Seth would sell the old Jackson Place to the Porters.

Seth hadn't thought of selling the property and needed time to decide, since it was the place where he was born and raised.

After a few days, he had an epiphany that selling would be the right thing to do. A lot of bad memories relate to that place, he thought. *After I'm released from prison, I'll begin anew womewhere else without reminders of what happened between me and Pa. Selling might be the answer,* he considered.

~

The days were flying by, and soon it would be time for Cain and Lucy's big move to Woodville.

Looking toward the future, Cain asked his Ma and Pa to move with them for the sake of their son. Little Jared was growing up fast and it was important to Cain that Jared share a bond with his grandparents. Feeling cheated by not growing up with a father, Cain wanted only the best for Jared.

Eager to find a place for his Pa and Ma to live, Cain waited for Seth's reply.

~

When Sonny returned from his day off, the new guard told him that Seth had received a letter.

"Do you know who the letter is from?" Sonny asked.

"Somebody by the name of Porter," the guard stated.

Sonny could feel a cold sweat forming on his brow, knowing his plan may be in jeopardy. Things were moving a little too fast, which worried him. Sonny asked the guard if Seth had answered the letter.

"No, ain't no letter gone out. Why'd you ask?" the guard quizzed.

"Oh, no reason, other than we need to know when a prisoner receives mail and sends mail….Guess you didn't know that."

"Ain't nobody told me that rule," the guard said.

"Well, I don't know if it's a rule, but it's for safety. Jailbait like him don't need no special privilege—know what I mean?"

"I reckon I do," the guard agreed.

"We have to keep watch on prisoners. Caged men do desperate things."

The guard shook his head "yes" and walked away. Hearing that Seth had a letter, Sonny visited Seth's cell.

"Jackson, I heard you got a letter while I was gone."

Seth wondered why Sonny was so interested. He didn't respond, just looked at him.

The next day Seth was escorted to the prison rec-yard for a walk, while Sonny searched his cell for the letter in question. After discovering it beneath the mattress and reading it, he dropped onto Seth's cot. *Times a-wastin'. I gotta get going before I lose out.*

He knew he had to take care of things before the outside world found out what he was up to. Desperate, he knew it was time to see his old buddy from whom he had tried to distance himself.

Gill Morrison, who was two years away from being released from the Huntsville Prison, was a lot like Sonny—weird looking, and considered to be mean as a rattlesnake. Gill grew up with a bunch of misfits and had to fight for everything he ever got. The knife scars on his face and arms were evidence of too many fights in sleazy saloons. The burly feller with sharp features never backed down from nobody. *If there was anyone who'd go along with murder it would be Gill. Especially after he sees these release papers I have. This will entice him to do it,* of that Sonny was sure.

That same day, Sonny stopped by Gill's cell and passed him a cigar, lighting it through the bars.

"How about this! It's like old times," Sonny said. Gill took a long puff and shook his head 'yes.' "Where ya' been? I thought I'd be crow bait 'fore I seen ya', so don't say it's like old times."

"Oh, I've been around. I've stayed away 'cause there ain't a dang thing I could do about it until now. Good ta see ya'."

"Yeah, minus the bars," Gill chuckled. "Now, what do ya' know that I don't know?"

"Things are about to change!"

"What do you mean by 'thangs could change'?"

"How much longer you got?" asked Sonny.

"Too long to talk about," Gill replied.

Sonny shook his head and looked him square in the eyes. "Gill, I been thinking about that time you saved my life—and I owe ya'!"

"Then why ya' waited till now?" Gill gave him a snarly grin, and Sonny chuckled.

"Least ya can do is git me some chew. Think ya' can do that? Besides ya' owe me for that time I saved yer ass."

"Son, that was a long time ago, and I don't reckon I hardly remember, but I need your help."

"Ain't nothing I can do all caged up here like an animal!"

"I been thinking, and I got a plan if you're interested. I can get you outta here, but I gotta know I can trust you," Sonny said.

"I'm listening...."

"I need you to take care of someone for me."

"You mean kill 'em? Forget that, Sonny! I ain't lookin' to rack up more time."

Sonny turned to walk away—slowly.

"Maybe this ain't such a good idea," Sonny said as he continued to walk away.

"Wait, hold on....Why don't ya' stay and tell me what you got planned? I got time to listen."

"Not until I know I can trust you?" Sonny restated.

"What about that time I saved your skin?" Gill reminded Sonny.

"A few minutes ago, you didn't remember," Sonny said jokingly.

"Well, I do now...so shoot."

"But you ain't never killed nobody," Sonny pointed out.

"Let's just say—as far as you know, and leave it at that. You say you can get me outta here?"

"That's right. I have a plan that will escort you right out the front gate."

"Ya' ain't just tellin' me that, are ya'?" Gill asked.

Sonny pulled out the forged prisoner release papers and showed them to Gill.

"Got yer name right here."

Gill's hands began to shake as he read his name on the paper and at the thought of getting out of his hell hole.

"You do this for me, and you're a free man," Sonny promised.

"Just tell me who, when and where," Gill whispered, now eager to do the job.

"When I get it worked out, Seth Jackson will be outside in the yard and I want you to kill him," said Sonny with a nervous chuckle.

"What with–my fork?" he asked.

"No–with this." Sonny gave him a knife that he had smuggled into the prison.

"You hide this where it can't be found, ya' hear?"

Gill took the knife, turned, and hid it under the lining of his cot.

This ain't gonna work. They'll find it when they search me."

"They ain't gonna search you, 'cause I'm the one that's gonna be taking you outside."

That makes sense, Gill thought. "What time is this gonna happen?" Gill asked.

"I can't give you a time—so be ready. I gotta make sure there ain't nobody around."

A few days later, Seth gave Sonny a letter to mail. It was addressed to Cain Porter, accepting his offer for him to purchase the Jackson place. He stuck it in his pocket with a plan to read it later.

Time was closing in on Sonny, and he began imagining that one of the Porters might show up at the prison to see Seth.

I can't let that happen. I gotta do this–now!

Seth was lying on his cot when Sonny approached his cell.

"Jackson, you're going to the yard, so get dressed. I ain't got all day."

Seth wondered why so early, when everyone else went later, but there's no arguing.

It was a beautiful day when Sonny led Seth to his death.

It was too late to turn back. He felt a twinge of guilt, but not enough to stop what was about to happen.

Just as planned, Gill was waiting for Sonny to take him to the yard. Seth thought it was unusual that a guard would take two prisoners out of the cellblock together.

Sonny unlocked Gill's cell saying, "Come on, Gill, you're going outside for some sunshine," Sonny said for Seth's ears, but, before they could get to the rec-yard door, Gill jumped Seth on the spot—knifing him in the heart.

"Not here—you crazy or something?" Gill looked at Sonny as he pulled the knife out of Seth's chest.

Sonny cringed, for he had not planned on seeing the murderous act played out before him. The awful part was experiencing a madman with gleefully no respect for human life watch his victim struggle to stay alive. Seth's eyes had a cold stare as he focused on Sonny and then his head dropped to the side.

Gill looked accusingly at Sonny, knowing it was him who was responsible for Seth's death. "Dang it Gill, you should have waited."

"No use ta' wait. The job's done, now let's go."

Sonny had tipped off the guard that something was going down, and before Gill reached the door, the new guard came in and saw Gill with the knife.

Sonny knew guards didn't care if inmates murdered one another. Murder only added to an otherwise boring day. Gill dropped the knife as both guards grabbed him. He was taken into custody, wrestling and he Gill screaming that Sonny had set him up. He shouted at the top of his lungs, and kept trying to remind Sonny of the time he saved him, but the other guard didn't thought that was a lie, too.

"You're the same dirty scumbag you always were! I shoulda' let 'em kill ya' that day!"

One week later, Gill stood before the judge for the murder of Seth. He was still insisting Sonny had set him up, but no one believed him. With no witnesses to back Gill's story, the trial was expedient, and the sentence was swift.

Early on a January morning, Gill was escorted back to his cell to await execution. Leaving the courtroom, he shouted to Sonny, "I'll see you in hell!" This was the day Sonny became—Seth Jackson.

Chapter 5

Immediately after Seth was murdered, the Warden prepared a letter to Seth's next of kin, which was addressed to Aggie. The letter explained that a fellow prisoner had murdered her husband and there would be an ongoing investigation. Since Aggie was "dead" and there was no response from the family, the Warden decided to dispose of Seth's body in the usual manner—the incinerator.

∽

Two weeks later, Cain received a letter from the "new" Seth stating that he had been released from prison and would be moving back to Woodville in Aggie's home that he had legal rights to. He also informed them that he expected to have time to spend with Jared and he wasn't interested in selling the Jackson Place. *When they hear I'm interested in the kid, they might do anything to keep me away from 'em.*

After receiving the letter from Sonny, Vick and Cain decided they needed to have a face-to-face with Seth and see what he had in mind, for there was no way Cain was going to go along with letting a man who killed his father have partial custody of his boy.

∽

Sonny soon quit his job at the prison and headed east to his future and his fortune.

Everything's gonna be all right," Sonny kept saying to himself as he hitched a ride to Woodville. The East Texas road was heavily wooded, which made each mile seem like ten. Dread twisted in his gut with the uncertainty of how he would be received as Seth Jackson.

"It's got to work," he kept repeating to himself.

It was a brisk winter morning when Sonny arrived in Woodville as Seth Jackson. He reluctantly walked into the mercantile to talk to the storekeeper about Aggie's place. His face felt cold as he pondered how it would feel hearing his own voice introduce himself as Seth Jackson.

Relieved that only one clerk was working, he looked through the merchandise as if he was going to make a purchase. Finally, the clerk walked up to him to help.

"You new around these parts?" the clerk asked.

He took a big gulp before he spoke. "Not really, but it's been awhile…I've been away a long time." Sonny gave a nervous chuckle. "I reckon I'm gonna need some directions home."

"What place you talking about? I bet I can help–been living here practically all my life."

"I'm Seth Jackson, I reckon ya' know me—it's been awhile." He cringed, anticipating the storekeeper's response.

"Don't tell me you're Seth Jackson. Why, I would recognize you anywhere." The clerk did remember Seth, but thought he had changed a bit. "I see ya' got that same beard." The storekeeper didn't question Sonny's claim, for he did not want to appear rude. "How you been?"

Sonny sighed with relief. "I guess you remember what happened to me."

"Yeah, we knew that Pa of yours. Weren't no love lost. Nobody in this town thought you meant to kill 'em. You were always a good kid. By golly, it's good ta see ya' back. You've changed some, but I guess prison will do that to a man."

"You're right about that! Them constant beatings by the prison guards have even affected my mind, especially my memory—then

I've got this bum leg. It's embarrassing having to ask how to get to my own place, but the town looks a bit different after the years I've been…uh, away."

The clerk looked Sonny up and down as he sympathized with him. *There's a resemblance, but that sure don't look like the Seth Jackson I remember. Prison sure can take a toll on a man, but he looks taller somehow,* the clerk thought. After talking to Seth, awhile longer, he finally convinced himself that the mistreatment in prison could have caused the change and he must be mistaken about Seth's height.

"I'm sorry to hear about your suffering, but if you go about four miles north of town you'll come to a fork in the road. Go to the right and you'll pass by Aggie Dawson's place—your wife's place. The Jackson place ain't more than a mile farther down the road. Too bad about yer wife dying. I liked her a whole lot."

"Yeah, I been missing her really bad."

"I guess I better git going. You can see I'm on foot," Sonny said. "All I got is the shirt on my back."

"Well you ain't gonna be on foot fer long, 'cause I got my son working in the stock room and he's gonna drive ya'. You take it easy, ya' hear…Seth?"

That was a whole lot easier than I expected, Sonny thought.

~

With hundreds of thoughts racing through his mind, Sonny was practically unaware of the constant chatter of the storekeeper's son. He didn't even notice the rough ride down a cleared trail that now generously was called a road. Soon, they arrived at the Dawson place. He couldn't believe his good fortune. Everything was manicured as if someone was taking care of the place.

"Are ya' sure ya' want to stop here before ya' go to your home place?" asked the young man.

"Yep, this is my home, too, and it'll do for now," he said, then added for effect, "and this is where Aggie lived, rest her sole."

He grabbed his suitcase, thanked the driver, and then walked up to the front door to peek through the window. It was finer than he imagined. He laid his suitcase near the front door as he walked around to the back of the house.

This is a fancy place, he thought happily.

His main excitement was the potential for an oil strike. He smiled inwardly, thinking how rich he would be when all the drilling took place. Mixed in with the smell of honeysuckle that was growing along the back-picket fence, Sonny was sure he caught a whiff of the "black gold."

He walked up the back steps to the porch and was peering through the window when he heard movement behind him. It scared the heck out of him.

"Mister…can I help you?"

Sonny turned slowly to find himself facing Justin Miller, the caretaker of Aggie's property. He was her sole confidant when she lived there, and who knew Aggie was very much alive somewhere around Beaumont—but he was still sworn to secrecy.

Justin immediately discerned that something wasn't right. Even though the stranger introduced himself as Seth, there was a little part of him that did not believe the stranger. It was an uneasy feeling he couldn't shake. His gut instinct told him to be cautious. The resemblance was similar, but there were certain characteristics of this man that he didn't remember or just didn't pay attention to before Seth went to prison.

If he ain't who he says he is, it'll come out sooner or later. Maybe I'm wrong and it is Seth, Justin tried to convince himself.

Sonny didn't know if he had done a good job passing himself off as Seth, but one thing for sure, the place wasn't big enough for Justin and him, too.

"I reckon you want the key to the house since you're home. You remember the hiding place don't ya'?" Justin thought it was a clever ploy to find out if Seth was who he said he was. He would surely remember where the key is hidden.

But Sonny was no dummy—*not gonna fall for this one*, he thought.

"Yeah, I remember, but I'm mighty tired. Why don't you git the key while I fetch my suitcase and look around the place. It's been a long time and sure is good to be back home."

Justin sensed the cunningness of this character, and thought it best not to cast any doubt for fear of being thrown off the place. This man hadn't even mentioned Aggie or her death, either. *Doesn't seem right*, Justin thought.

"Mr. Jackson, I been taking care of the place ever since you been gone."

Sonny thought this is the perfect time to bring up his release papers, just in case there were questions. "Yeah, no one was as shocked as me when they pardoned me, but I got my papers, jest in case I have to show 'em."

"Well, it's good ta' have you home. I was real sad when Miss Aggie died." Justin stayed true to his word.

Sonny decided the caretaker was a liability he couldn't afford. *He'd ask too many questions, he's talking too much, could trip me up*, Sonny thought.

"Mr. Jackson, you enjoy your stay. I usually work around the place a couple days a week for my keep. Miss Aggie told me I was welcome to stay in the guest quarters as long as I keep up the place."

This was Sonny's perfect opportunity to get rid of Justin.

"I'm sure Miss Aggie had no idea I would be released from prison. Now that I'm home, I suspect I'll be taking care of the place myself. You need to clear out the guest quarters as soon as you can."

Justin couldn't believe he was being thrown off the property. *Somethin' sure ain't right*, he thought. Justin remembered Miss Aggie saying that Seth wasn't returning to the place. He remembered how heartbroken she was the day Seth asked her for a divorce.

"Mr. Jackson, I ain't thought about leaving 'cause Miss Aggie said I always had a place here until Jared growed up to live here."

Now, more than ever, Sonny thought, *it's imperative I get rid of Justin.* Encountering the caretaker living on the property did not fit into his plans, and was something he never even considered. *I don't even know the man's name,* Sonny thought. Finally, he decided to ask Justin to leave.

"I'm really sorry to disappoint you, but prison life can change a man, and now that I'm home, I need to have my own privacy."

Justin was plenty smart and had good intuition. He convinced himself that "Seth" or whoever he was, was up to no good. Justin packed his things and left without another word to this man who was supposed to be Seth.

Sonny rested up a day, checked things out around the place, fed the livestock, rummaged through papers in Aggie's desk, and then went into town. He knew he had to make an appearance sooner or later, but he hadn't expected to see Justin. Sonny gave him a dirty look, then Justin practically ran out of the café. Thank God nobody paid attention. *I gotta get rid of that weasel before he blows my cover.*

Sonny rode his horse into the alley near the café and waited for Justin to appear. He had always had someone else to do his dirty work, but now it was up to him if he wanted to save his own skin.

Justin underestimated the evil in the new Seth. Justin left the café on horseback, headed toward Aggie's place. Sonny followed. *He must be up to something. I gotta stop him and put an end to his snooping once and for all.*

Sonny trailed Justin until he reached a wooded area where no one would see. *This must be the best place,* Sonny decided.

Suddenly, Justin heard a rider approaching from the rear at full gallop.

He spurred his mount, but it was already too late. Due to the years of training, Sonny had as a rodeo calf-roper and bull-rider, Justin was no match. Sonny caught up to him in a flash, leaped from his saddle, grabbing Justin by the neck and twisting as if it were a falling steer. Justin's neck was broken before the two hit the ground. Dusting himself off and kicking dirt in Justin's face, Sonny hogtied his body, then dragged it into a nearby field to be left for the buzzards.

"Ain't nobody gonna even miss you!" Standing over the body, Sonny lit his cigar and waved away the little cloud of smoke that hovered above his head. There was no sadness, no regret for killing Justin—only satisfaction. Exactly what one should expect from a sociopath.

There's only one last thing for me to do, and that is to notify Cain Porter that Seth Jackson is alive and well and free. They need to know, I'm here to stay.

Chapter 6

AFTER TRAVELING FROM A LITTLE TOWN UP NORTH, A TALL, SLIM, WIDE-shouldered man in his early thirties checked into Annie Mae's boarding house. Aggie was on hand to greet the prospective patron. He had a genial smile and was well mannered. Removing his hat, he apologized for "bustin' in," but he "needed a place to stay for a couple of weeks."

His manners were better than his appearance. He was poorly dressed, right down to his heavily scuffed shoes. He was an interesting fellow who introduced himself as Kyle Rover, the nephew of Packer Rover/ He had come all the way to Texas to work for his uncle on a boat. Kyle was not the type Aggie would be interested in, but he had quite the endearing personality, and he made her laugh. His eyes were too close together, which added to his already comedic nature. To put it plain and simple—Kyle brightened her life. Soon they became close friends and began confiding in one another. He told her more about what brought him to Texas and his missteps getting there. She loved his northern accent, and listened carefully as he told his story.

"My uncle worked on a boat and was after me to come work for him. When I arrived, I ran into a bit of bad luck."

"Oh, I'm sorry. I hope it wasn't serious," Aggie said with empathy.

"As it turned out, it was more than serious—my uncle died, and now I have to pick up his belongings at the shipyard! I hope he remembered me fondly, and left me enough to get by on. I've heard about Spindletop, and people coming here to make their fortunes.

Maybe a little of it will rub off on me," Kyle followed with a nervous laugh.

"I'm sorry about your uncle. If there is something I can do, please let me." She felt sorry for him.

"I do need help, but I wouldn't want to impose," Kyle said.

"I think I can relate to how you feel."

"I really need a way to the ship channel to pick up my uncle's things."

"Of course, if you can wait until after 2 o'clock, I can take you." She needed to help Annie Mae with the dinner crowd. Aggie had no idea her life was about to change.

That afternoon she drove Kyle to the ship channel. Her first senses were that of fresh air over water and people busy everywhere. There was something exciting about hearing ship whistles that made her take notice. She was hooked immediately. *I could go for this*, she thought. She marveled at the large steamboats coming and going, imagining what it would be like sailing away from her pain.

As they waited for the clerk, she studied Kyle's appearance—disheveled, but actually not dirty. *He could use some help*, she thought. He was the rugged type, with hair slightly longer than most. Not a bad looker, but certainly not her type. His energy level and personality endeared him to her, but that would not be enough for her to take romantic interest. When he walked, it was more of a glide, but it was the twinkle in his eyes that projected honesty that made her trust him.

The wait was only a few minutes before the clerk addressed Kyle with a letter.

"I was told my uncle had personal belongings to pick up."

The extremely thin clerk peered up over his low-riding reading specs and said, "And you must be Packer Rover's nephew?"

"Yes sir, I am."

"Nice to meet ya'. I just read a letter that you'd be calling, and here you are! It's a shame your uncle died 'fore ya' got here. This letter I got for ya' explains that Packer committed suicide....I'm sorry to say. Ya' say yer here to pick up his personal belongings?"

"Yes, I am," replied Kyle nervously.

The clerk hesitated, "Well, it ain't nothing you can pick up, if you know what I mean." Kyle looked disappointed and the clerk continued. "Yer in luck, for yer uncle just sold the old Stump Dumper and bought him a steamboat...a big one. Too bad he never got to try it out." Kyle heard the words, but it wasn't registering with him.

"What's the Stump Dumper?" Kyle asked with crinkled brow.

"Well, it's a big barge used to pull stumps and debris out of the waterway of the Neches River. Jest before your uncle died, he bought the High Stepper, that big steamboat ya'll musta' seen as you came in. Guess you got somebody to help ya', ain't ya?"

"Sir, I have no idea what you're talking about. I'm here to pick up my uncle's belongings and any money he might have left me."

"I imagine if ya' uncle had money he spent it buyin' that steamer outside, 'cause there ain't none here!"

Money was all Kyle was interested in.

"The High Stepper can make ya' a good living if ya' know what yer doin'."

Kyle stood there frozen with his mouth agape as the clerk handed him the title to his boat, along with papers that appeared to be a contract. He turned to Aggie, who was just as surprised as Kyle. He hurriedly scanned over the fine print, which indicated a large shipment of cotton.

"If all goes well, the High Stepper will be transporting freight to Galveston within the month. The clerk took a deep draw off the butt of his cigarette.

Rice was a staple in the Beaumont area and was also shipped to different ports, such as Houston and Galveston.

Somehow it didn't register to Kyle that he was now a businessman and the owner of a steamboat.

Aggie's mind was racing, trying to figure out how Kyle was going to make it in this business with neither experience nor money to back him. She seemed to now comprehend much more than Kyle, who was trying to catch up.

"We got a load of cotton on its way, all inventoried and ready ta' go," the clerk said enthusiastically. You ain't gonna have no problem with the shipment are ya?"

"Sir, I need a job—not a steamboat! And I don't know a dang thing about navigatin' or drivin' that monster boat."

"It's piloting…. It's called 'piloting'," the clerk corrected him. "I take it you ain't been listenin'. You better learn how to pilot fast, 'cause you have a contract with Stoker Farms. Ya' sure don't want to tangle with them people. You fail with this contract and you'll be black-balled from ever working in Beaumont agin, young man!"

Kyle shrugged his shoulders and looked at Aggie in disbelief.

"I don't understand!" Kyle said. "I just don't understand."

"Mr. Packer, what's there to understand? You are now the proud owner of the High Stepper, and it's waiting for you…right out that door," the clerk said laughingly, getting a huge kick out of the situation.

Aggie could see the despair on Kyle's face. He was so nervous, his hands began to shake.

"By the way, you'll not only be transporting freight, but also people," the clerk stressed.

Kyle stood there scratching his head.

The clerk tried to explain a bit to Kyle about steamboats, but Aggie was sure it was going right over his head.

The clerk got close to Kyle's face and said,

"Son, listen here—that steamer of yours is a packet boat, 'cause it hauls both people and cargo. Now, if you were transporting only people, your steamer would be a dispatch boat—so, don't forget that. Now your uncle made sure there were workers onboard who knew how to load, unload, and to 'pilot' the boat. Now, at least act like ya' know something about a steamboat.

"Don't worry, 'cause I checked the boat out after yer uncle died, and it's plenty nice. One thing I don't understand is why 'yer uncle hung himself when he just bought the High Stepper. It don't make no sense. Guess we'll never know." Kyle and Aggie were also puzzled.

"You saying that my uncle killed himself?"

"That's right, just like the papers say, he hung himself." Everybody around is talkin' 'bout yer uncle. His death was even written up in the newspaper. I didn't know 'em well, but he seemed like a nice enough feller. In case yer wonderin,' he's buried right outside Beaumont in a little town called Vidor. They say that's where yer uncle was stayin' before he died. I spec' yer gonna be goin' there to pay yer respects, ain't ya?"

"How far away is Vidor?"

"Ain't no distance at all, I'd say about eight miles or so—jest 'cross the Neches River Bridge. I think ya need to know that the steamer's been around for quite some time, but don't let it bother ya' for it's still a mighty good steamboat and people know about it."

The clerk was still talking a mile a minute, but all Kyle heard was his uncle had hung himself.

Kyle kept wondering how Packer got the money to buy the boat. *Something ain't right! Ain't no way he'd hang himself after making that kind of investment.*

~

The High Stepper was majestic compared to the barge anchored nearby. Of the two boats, Kyle related more with the Stump Dumper than the stately steamboat, about which he knew nothing.

"Aggie, I'm at a loss. I came to Texas to work, and not become an heir to a steamboat without a dime to my name."

She responded, "I would be scared, too."

"Girl, you ain't helping!" Aggie was amused with Kyle; they both finally chuckled.

It was difficult for him to imagine hauling people and cargo up and down open waters when he knew nothing about the mechanics or finances of a steamboat.

Thinking about the way Packer died, left suspicions that he might have been murdered.

"What if my uncle didn't hang himself?" Kyle suggested.

"You really think there was foul play?" Aggie responded.

"From what I remember of my uncle, Packer Rover ain't one to die by hanging himself. What I'm wondering is where the money came from to buy this monster boat."

"Kyle, did you know your uncle as well as you thought? Perhaps he realized he made a mistake and decided this was the only way out." She was comparing his uncle to what she went through early on when she faked her own death.

"You mean he hung himself because he was sorry he bought the steamboat?"

"It's possible," Aggie said, not really believing in her suggestion.

"I'm gonna have to think about that another time, 'cause right now, I have to figure out what I'm gonna do with this monster of a boat—I mean, steamboat—and a boat load of crap to Galveston."

"See, you're already getting the hang of it," Aggie laughed and patted his back good naturedly.

~

When they stepped aboard the High Stepper to examine the great steamer, a man of American Indian decent, stepped from the shadows to introduce himself.

"Excuse me, my name is Bidzill Franklin and you are on private property."

Aggie was immediately attracted to him. She presumed he was only half Indian, for he was lightly tanned, tall and thin with blue eyes and the most incredible face she had ever seen. His coal black hair framed his face, since he had not pulled it back. Their eyes locked for a moment as if they each had an untold story. There was something about him that was different from the Indians she had seen before.

Embarrassed for showing his interest, the handsome stranger quickly looked away. Aggie noticed a Beautiful and most unusual necklace around his neck. The pendant was shaped like a diamond.

"What brings you aboard the High Stepper?" Bidzill asked.

Quickly assessing Kyle and Aggie, he was sure they had no business aboard the steamer.

"Excuse me sir, but I inherited this steamboat from my uncle Packer Rover, and this is my friend Aggie." Kyle declared.

"I see, but I'm going to need your papers." The Indian scratched his head and stared intently, obviously suspicious of Kyle who did not look the part of a steamboat owner considering how he was dressed.

"Since you are the new owner, I need to explain." I'm Bidzill Franklin. I have been working on this steamer a long time, and I reckon I was going to be speaking with the new owner about a job. If you're new to the business I can be of help to you."

Kyle was still confused as Bidzill continued to talk. Then the conversation shifted to his uncle and how he died.

"I suppose you want to know about your uncle. It was early morning when I found him. Don't mind telling you—something doesn't seem right about how he died. The place was a mess, stuff thrown everywhere, like someone was searching for something." Aggie noticed that Bidzill had impeccable English, unlike half-breeds she had met before.

"The little time I knew Packer I don't think he would hang himself—that was my feeling. He was excited to own the Stepper and eager to take her out. Right now, I suppose you're going to have your hands full figuring out how to operate this thing," Bidzill said as he continued to read the paperwork Kyle had handed him.

"You know anything about navigating?" Kyle asked.

Bidzill smiled, "I reckon I know as much about piloting as anyone, but I don't have papers."

"I don't care whether you have papers or not—if you know how!"

"Well then,—I'm the one. Let's start on the bottom deck and I'll show you the ropes." Bidzill took his time going over all the fine details of the cargo business on the Neches River, and they both paid close attention during the tour. Aggie wondered how Kyle would be able to run the business without operating capital.

As they walked throughout the lower and upper deck, Aggie learned Bidzill was excellent at giving orders.

This is no ordinary man, she thought.

"Mr. Rover, what I am about to explain is very important, so listen carefully. We have seasonal months between December and May—a period when upstream water levels are right for shipping cotton. The bales are piled high at the landings, all inventoried and waiting to be transported." Aggie listened, but everything was a blur to Kyle, for his mind was busy trying to figure a way out of the steamboat business.

"Our off season begins in June, and our steamer is usually tied up in the Neches, or someplace else in the tidewater region. That's when we do some excursion trips transporting people and freight to their destinations."

"Are we only hauling cotton?" Kyle asked.

Bidzill could see Kyle was preoccupied, for he had already told him what the steamer transported. "Remember, we were talking about cotton and rice. That's mostly what we haul, unless we have a contract with someone else. We do a lot of work for Stokers Farms."

The more Bidzill explained the ins and outs of the business, the more Kyle felt he could not do this.

Aggie, on the other hand, saw great potential for the steamer. She was excited about the possibilities of the upper deck. She could visualize cruising down the river into open waters. Kyle saw her excitement while she was listening to every detail Bidzill was telling them. They were both impressed with the questions she asked.

Walking up the steps to the upper deck, Aggie stepped ahead observing as she went. While passing through the kitchen, she saw all the pots and pans, along with fine china and silver with the name of the ship engraved on the silverware. She remembered seeing similar antiques when as a young girl, she lived at Pecan Plantation.

She strolled through the Grand Saloon which was furnished with large chandeliers, sofas, tables and chairs for gamblers. Her mind raced as she imagined being on an exciting journey to places far away from people who might recognize her. She began seeing ways she could improve the looks of the upper deck should Kyle ask for her assistance. The main improvement would be ripping out and replacing the carpet. This would make a world of difference, she thought.

The cabins were in good shape, but could stand some new curtains, otherwise it was a grand ol' steamer. She worried that Kyle needed help attracting the more sophisticated class for he was not a stylish man. He lacked polish for the kind of people who would be boarding the boat would be expecting someone with more class. She worried that he might fail if there was no one to help him. He looked more like a deckhand than the owner of the High Stepper. *If only I could help Kyle develop more taste*, she thought. Aggie, had a desire to tell him he could begin by sprucing himself up and looking more like the owner of the High Stepper instead of owner of the Stump Dumper.

As they continued to explore the top deck, it was more than Aggie imagined. It contained a full bar, dance floor and lots of tables for gamblers. There was even a piano strapped on a platform for entertainers to perform.

She was as overwhelmed as Kyle, but in a different way. But both were trying to figure out how the steamboat could operate without money.

I'm just one person, and there's no way I can operate this on my own, Kyle thought.

Without hesitation, he offered to sell the steamer to Aggie—something she had not expected

"Aggie, I been thinking. What if I sell you this steamboat?"

Aggie could not believe what she was hearing.

"Kyle, that's impossible. I don't have that kind of money."

Bidzill looked up as he heard Kyle's offer.

What a mistake if he takes on a woman, Bidzill thought.

"Aggie, if I sell the steamboat to you—I can work for you. I think together we can make this work."

"But I don't know any more than you do."

"Aggie, I need someone like you to work for and I can tell you know how to handle people."

"Kyle, you're not listening. I appreciate the offer, but you would want much more than I could give you. All I have is twenty-five hundred dollars, and that wouldn't make a dent."

"Would you be interested in buying the upper deck and let me keep the lower deck for the transport business?"

Without hesitation she replied, "Yes!"

"You got a deal!" he said and held out his hand to seal the deal.

"Aggie, I've been thinking. You can save rent by staying in one of your cabins. I'll have mine on the lower deck. We'll both save, and I'll work as your deckhand."

Hearing that Aggie accepted Kyle's offer—Bidzill quickly walked away.

It was obvious to her that Bidzill did not like dealing with a woman.

"Kyle, I don't know. How would that look with both of us living on the boat?"

He laughed. "What's the difference? We're both staying under one roof at Annie Mae's. It's like a boarding house that floats!" They both laughed.

Aggie had misgivings of her own after accepting the offer. After all, she was embarking on something completely out of her comfort zone. Although she was excited, she had great apprehension about the possibility of failure at her new venture, and that would mean the loss of half of her entire fortune. Aggie had made some foolish mistakes in the past, and she hoped this was not going to be another one.

The next morning, she talked to Annie Mae about accepting Kyle's offer, and was completely surprised when Annie Mae encouraged her to go for it.

"Aggie, you have to do this for yourself. If you fail, I'll always have a place for you here." She loved mothering young Aggie, and Aggie loved her for it.

Aggie had butterflies thinking of what might go wrong, if she were to lose what money she had left. She also thought about Bidzill Franklin, and imagined how he would feel, since she would be part owner and he would be working for her also.

"Annie Mae, I worry about leaving you like this."

"Child, you don't worry about me. I have a little money if things go awry."

Before Aggie realized what she was saying, she asked Annie Mae to come work for her. *After all, Annie Mae was used to handling a man-crowd*, Aggie thought. Perhaps she may want a change for herself. She was certain Annie Mae would laugh at her idea, but she had to try.

"I'll sleep on it. A change might be what I need. Maybe I've been working at this business too long."

With both Aggie and Annie Mae working together, the High Stepper could be a profitable income for both.

Once agreements were made, everything began moving quickly. Annie Mae contacted the owner of Miss Josey's Boarding House and sold her property on the spot.

Aggie was smart. The first thing she did was to take part of the Great Saloon and make it into two separate living quarters for Annie Mae and herself. This still left plenty of room for guests to be entertained and have the privacy of their cabins.

She thought the best thing to do concerning Bidzill was to ignore him and keep to herself. She was sure his negative feelings towards her were strictly caused by the fact she was a woman.

~

After operating only cargo shipments for nearly three months, the High Stepper was ready for excursions, and both operations began regular trips. Both Kyle and Aggie were pleasantly surprised with the profits which allowed Aggie to improve the steamer.

Once again, she thought back to another time when she was poor as a church mouse, and living in a little shanty outside of Henderson, Texas. Thank God, I had the baking business. Aggie became amused as she remembered Miss Jones, the proprietor of a local store that she did business with. Miss Jones always reminded her that she was not a proper lady and would never be able to afford the couture fashions that were advertised in her store.

She remembered how her luck had changed. After Aggie's stepfather died, she had discovered 5,000 dollars hidden in his mattress that he had saved for her inheritance. *My father will never know how that huge amount of money changed my life.*

The first thing she did was purchase two of the most expensive couture dresses Miss Jones had. Aggie felt vindicated by having the last laugh. *If only she could see me now.* Aggie, thought. Although that had been a few years back, it seemed like a lifetime. Now, there was no doubt in anyone's mind that she was a proper lady who was half owner of a well-known steamboat.

Chapter 7

AT FIRST LIGHT, LUCY AND ELIZABETH SENT THEIR MEN OFF WITH two-days' supply of food they had prepared for their travels.

With heavy hearts, they watched as Cain and Vick rode away. Concerned about Jared and the outcome of the visit with Seth, Lucy was unsure how she would handle giving partial custody of Jared to a man she knew only as a convicted killer. She tried to temper those thoughts by remembering that Vick had been convicted of murders he hadn't committed. She hoped Seth's case was similar.

Traveling to Woodville, Cain and Vick had plenty of time to talk about the 'what-if's'.

"I'm gonna do whatever it takes to protect my son," Cain said.

"Son, I should warn you—don't push too hard," Vick offered.

"What do you mean?" Cain asked.

"Don't come across as desperate. You're the one who makes the calls…not Seth."

"This reminds me—how did you handle the threats when you were in prison? I can't imagine spending twenty years in the hell hole I saw—yet you're alive. How did you do it?"

"It took a while before I figured things out, but when I did, I began weighing out all the dangers before I made my moves and kept my eyes open. You'd be surprised how much you learn around a poker table. When you listen, you learn a lot. So, remember…when you deal with Seth, let him do the talking and you'll be surprised the information you collect. And there's one other thing—try learning a little patience. Don't rush! That's when you make mistakes. I had plenty of time to learn patience when I was in prison."

"Pa, why do you always compare life to playing cards?"

"I guess being in prison for so long, there's little else I have to measure life with. I take one day at a time and keep on dealing until I win."

"Pa, I've been dealing all my life and I haven't won yet!" Vick smiled when he knew better. *Cain's got a lot to learn*, he thought.

~

The Porters rode into Woodville about the time the sun's flaming rays left no doubt that it was summer. Woodville was a well-established Texas town, bustling with visitors from the surrounding area. One could hear the creaking wheels of wagons as they traveled through town. There were buckboards, horses, and a few cars that crowded the narrow dirt streets, with cowboys coming and going. Despite the hot summer, there were farmers and ranchers loading their wagons with 50 pound bags from the feed store.

It was a homey little town, but nothing like San Augustine where they left behind the women they loved.

~

Sonny was anticipating his first meeting with Cain. *It's only a matter of time before he comes calling. Can't anything foil my plan. Not now*, he thought. *I'll use the boy as a bargaining chip if I must. Whatever it takes.* Sonny wasn't going to allow anyone to reposition what he had already killed for.

Being a father was of no interest to a man like Sonny, but if he expected to have the rights to the oil and land, he would have to show interest in Jared.

Watching from the window, Sonny saw two men dismounting near the gate. He mistakenly had assumed Cain would come alone. Seeing the two together made him uneasy. They commenced with the usual greetings, but Cain could feel a chill in the air. *I must be careful when I explain the damage it will do to Jared should he want to share custody.*

Gathering his composure, Cain explained, "My boy has already lost his mother, and my wife and I are concerned that Jared will have a setback. He's been through a lot since he lost his mother." Underneath Cain's façade was a quiet desperation he hoped Seth would not sense.

He'll do anything to keep that boy of his, Sonny surmised.

Sonny is hard to read. I'll just play along and see what happens, Cain thought.

"Mind if I ask you why you want to have a boy underfoot?" Cain asked.

With a pathetic tone, Sonny said, "I miss the little feller."

They sensed that the man they thought was Seth, was not suitable to be a part-time father.

Cain took a quick glance at Vick. Both being perceptive and wise, they had come to the same conclusion as to the kind of man Seth was.

Cain continued to try and reason with him.

"Seth, if you will, I'd like for you to look at this from my perspective. It's been a long time and my boy is not likely to remember you."

"Sure, the little feller remembers me," Seth retorted.

He's looking to rake in on Aggie's fortune, Vick was now sure.

Cain recalled his Pa's propensity for comparing life to a game of poker.

"Seth, I don't know if you are aware, but my family and parents were in the process of moving here when we heard you were released from prison. We lost our place there, and we have no other option but to continue with our plan and move here. I'm sure you understand."

"You plan to what?" Seth was noticeably concerned.

"Let me explain my plan so you'll understand. I have custody of Jared since I legally adopted my son."

"And what might that plan be?" Seth grimaced.

"Move in here with you and share the property. I'm sure you know that the property was willed to Jared. After the boy reaches 18, we can all sit down and talk about what's fair. But it's going to be a while before we have that conversation. In the meantime, we'll all be one big happy family until my boy comes of age."

"No, that ain't right. Aggie didn't know I would be pardoned. She would never agree to such a plan."

"Perhaps so, I can see you're not happy but you're only one, and there's five of us counting my Pa and mother. We have no problem sharing this place, if you want to live here and see Jared grow. If this doesn't please you, there's your ranch. That's a mighty fine spread you got, and you'll be close by to help with the boy."

This ain't working out, Sonny thought. He suddenly remembered the offer Cain made in the letter to Seth about buying the Jackson place. Without giving much thought, he mentioned Cain's offer to buy it.

"Are you still interested in buying my place?" Seth asked. I reckon if I sell, we can be neighbors and I can stay put until the boy comes of age.

This is better than I thought, Cain mused.

"Cain, I don't rightly remember your offer?" Seth asked, acting as if he had been privy to the discussions.

"Ten thousand!" Cain said. The ranch was worth much more, but to a crook like Sonny, Cain thought he would probably jump at the offer.

Without hesitating, Sonny agreed. "Done!" Sonny had never seen ten thousand dollars–only dreamed about it.

With a handshake they consummated the deal, which was all in Cain's favor. There was yet one other problem for Sonny—the deed! *Cain and Jared might end up with both places,* Vick calculated.

The following morning, Sonny rode over to the old Jackson place in a panic to find the deed. This was the first time he had seen Seth's property and immediately resented taking Cain's offer. *So this is how ol' Seth was raised. Don't look like he hurt for much*, Sonny thought.

Looking over the place, he could have kicked himself for selling. *This was a big mistake!* He thought.

Sonny had a deadline to meet and the deed in question took hours to find.

That afternoon at the County Clerk's office, Sonny sat twiddling his fingers before signing the papers. Concerned that there might be questions, he wanted to hurry and sign over the place. He had practiced Seth's signature over and over and had mastered it. Just when things were about to get better for Sonny, they got worse.

The clerk had a sharp memory and remembered Cain from the time he adopted Jared. And then to Sonny's dismay, the clerk let it drop that Cain was a lawyer.

Sonny began boiling inside after hearing this.

Life is full of little surprises, he thought. *I should have been more thorough and asked more questions. I didn't even know who I was dealing with. This is gonna be plenty sticky living this close to a law man.*

Arriving back at Aggie's, Sonny was frustrated more than ever. He grew increasingly annoyed that Cain may have gotten the better deal. *Hell, that Jackson place could have more oil than what I might find here.* The more Sonny thought about it, the more he fumed. *I ain't got nothing but a big ol' house with a lot of land to take care of, while I wait 14 years for a kid to grow. That sonofabitch got the best of me.*

Then he remembered another part of his original plan. A lot of things can happen to a boy in 14 years.

Chapter 8

While Cain and Vick were in Woodville surveying their new property, Lucy smoothed her beautiful blonde hair, buttoned the top of her dress, and walked toward the barn to take a ride into town. She glanced toward the plantation and saw Sebastian smoking a cigar and staring at her. His eyes were very concentrated, which made her uneasy, since she knew what he was capable of. Handling a man like Sebastian was going to be difficult, she thought. He's a charmer and unpredictable, which makes him dangerous.

Once in town, Lucy went to see Caleb. She found out that he had no family, and as a loner, was prone to never settling into one place for very long. She didn't dare go see him during banking hours.

"You got a few minutes? I might need your help."

"No ma'am—I'm leavin' town. I gotta be careful 'cause they been watching me like a hawk. I think they know I might talk. I can feel it. Right now, they don't know I'm on to 'em and I'm leavin' before they put two and two together. If they see me with you, it ain't gonna take them long to get suspicious. Yesterday, I found out something else"

"What did you find out?" Lucy asked.

"A man came in the office asking to see Mr. Tompkins. I hadn't seen the man before, and when Mr. Tompkins saw him he looked at me like I shouldn't know what was happening. He was a bit shaken if you ask me. When they went in his office I listened and got an earful.

The man wanted to know if Mr. Tompkins and Mr. Parker had seen some man by the name of Ace—can't remember his last name. The man wanted his money and was there to collect. Mr. Tompkins started shouting and said this man Packer Rover had double-crossed them both. Then I heard something about him being a dead man and he was going to the Beaumont ship channel to try and find him. The man told Mr. Tompkins that he thought Packer worked on some boat. Can't remember the name of the boat."

Lucy had no idea if that would help her clandestine inquiry.

"Caleb, I know you have to go, but I need to ask you one more time if you are sure that Mr. Tompkins and Sebastian have killed people for personal gain."

"Yes ma'am. The men they kill ain't even cold in their graves when they swoop in and take over their property. A wife can't stand up against two rattlesnakes like Lee Tompkins and Sebastian Parker. The ladies just let it go 'cause there ain't nobody to stick up for 'em. It's terrible. Now, they plannin' on killing this man Packer who's in Beaumont."

"You say they're going down to the ship channel in Beaumont?"

"Yes ma'am. That's what they said. You ain't planning on going after 'em, are you?"

Lucy reached over and patted him on the shoulder. "Don't you worry about a thing, Caleb. There's something you should know. My Pa was the Sheriff of Jonesboro, Arkansas, for as long as I can remember. He had a mind of his own and a nose like a hound dog. If he smelled blood, he hunted 'em down until he caught ever last one of 'em and I'm a lot like my Pa."

"Miss Lucy, if they find out, they're gonna be onto us."

"Caleb, they're not onto us—we're onto them—and they'll never know unless you tell 'em. I need you to keep what you've told me just between us. I'll do the worrying for you and me both."

"It ain't me I'm worried about—it's you!"

"Caleb, when you leave have you thought about where you're going?" She asked.

"I don't rightly know. I meant to talk to Mr. Cain before I left, bein' he's a lawyer and such."

I should have told you before but we're moving to Woodville.

"Where 'bouts in Woodville?

"Right near the old Jackson Place."

"Well, I be,—that's Seth Jackson's place. I ain't seen 'em in a hundred years. Used to ride horses with 'em when we were kids. At one time I worked for his Pa. Have y'all met Seth Jackson?"

"No, we haven't! Guess you don't know, but he's been in prison for murdering his Pa. We heard he was pardoned."

"Naw, that ain't right! I think Seth was defending himself if he did what you say. One thing for sure, ain't no love lost between the town folk and Parley Jackson. Just so you know, Seth is good as gold and would give ya' the shirt off his back."

Hearing Seth was a good man gave comfort to Lucy.

~

After Cain arrived back in San Augustine, he had a truck ready to make the move. Lucy was pleased to hear that they would not be moving into Aggie's place. Living in a dead woman's house who just happened to be her son's biological mother, gnawed at her. And she still refused to accept that she was a bit jealous.

Now, to break the news to Cain that I'm staying in San Augustine a while longer. Perhaps Elizabeth can help me, she thought.

When evening approached, Lucy asked Elizabeth to take a walk with her. It was a beautiful night as they strolled around the lake.

"This is the one place I'm going to miss when I have to leave," Lucy said.

Elizabeth was sympathetic, for Lucy was still mourning the death of her father.

"I understand how you feel about Orson. He loved it here!"

As they remembered Orson, Lucy thought of the perfect solution to keep Cain from worrying. *Why didn't I think of this before?*

It was though she could feel Orson's spirit admonishing her from above. *"Be careful Lucy, you're about to get in over your head."* She ignored the feeling and explained to Elizabeth that she would not be leaving until she went back to Jonesboro to visit her daddy's grave.

"I think you'll agree that it's easier leaving from San Augustine than leaving from Woodville."

Although Lucy seemed sincere, Elizabeth felt there was another reason for her staying behind. *If it has something to do with Cain, they'll have to work it out themselves,* she thought.

"Lucy, I worry about you, but if you stay, Vick and I will help Cain sort out the house. Will you have a problem with that?"

"Goodness no, I would be grateful for your help. You know your taste is better than mine."

Cain was also suspicious that there was more on Lucy's agenda than just going to visit her father's grave. *How can she stay behind when I'm leaving with our son? She's not confiding in me,* he thought.

The next morning, Cain and Lucy had an awkward moment as they held each other to say goodbye. "Lucy, it's not too late to change your mind."

She could hardly stand to look at Cain without bursting into tears, but she knew it was important that she stay and get to the bottom of Lee Tompkins and Sebastian Parker's chicanery. *Cain can't know that I'll be following Lee and Sebastian to Beaumont to spy on them.*

$\sim$

With a truckload of furniture and household goods, the Porters drove through Woodville. The town was near dark, with only a flicker of light from the windows of small homes as they made their way toward the Jackson place. Cain pointed out where Aggie used to live. He was sure he saw Seth smoking on his front porch.

"That's a real nice home," Elizabeth replied.

She could sense her son was worried about Lucy.

"Cain, I'm worried about leaving Lucy here alone."

"I reckon she's not ready to say goodbye to a place that reminds her of her daddy. That's the only thing I can figure. She'll join us when she's ready. I've learned not to push."

"She has had a hard time since her daddy died. Don't you think she's a lot like Orson?" Elizabeth asked.

"You think? It's just like living with him," Cain chuckled.

As Elizabeth thought about what all Lucy had gone through in her short life, she wondered about Lucy's judgment. *It's hard to know what might be going on with her. Since Orson's death, Lucy's only sanctuary has been with Cain and Jared*, she thought.

Cain was excited to see his mother's face when they arrived at their new home.

"Ma, if you think Aggie's place is nice—wait till you see the Jackson place. If Seth's Pa knew how much his son sold me the place for, he'd turn over in his grave."

"Perhaps it's too painful remembering what happened there," Elizabeth reasoned.

As they rounded the bend, there was just enough light for Elizabeth to see a beautiful rambling ranch house set among huge trees. "Cain, I love the magnolias, but what are the other trees called?"

"You've never seen dogwoods?"

"No, I've never seen them before," Elizabeth replied.

"Just wait till spring when they're all in bloom; they're every-where."

Elizabeth pointed to the guesthouse, which reminded her of the carriage house that sat near her beloved Manor in Jonesboro.

"Cain, I love it. It's like home! The yard can use some work, but we'll have it trimmed and weeded before you know it!"

"Ma, you wait. Lucy's gonna love this place, just like you," Cain's voice faded, for he was unsure about Lucy and what was going on with her.

Vick noticed Elizabeth's excitement but it wasn't Jonesboro. He still felt guilty urging her to leave the home she loved. *I'll be taking her back someday when she least expects it, he thought.*

In a matter of weeks, Elizabeth had changed the ranch house décor into a warmly enticing place. They did not stop until they completely renovated the guesthouse where Vick and Elizabeth would be living.

After she completed the job, Vick came from behind and whispered into her ear, "How did I get so lucky?" He grabbed her and twirled her around, then held her close. "It doesn't matter where we live as long as I have you," she said. Feeling his closeness, she lifted her head and kissed him.

"Lizzie, don't you know, you can get in trouble kissing a man like that?" She loved his tenderness. *No matter how serious life had become, he always makes me feel loved*, she thought.

During the following week, Cain and Vick took a ride over to Village Mills, a small, but thriving lumber town halfway between Beaumont and Woodville. They spotted Seth going into the feed store. The more Cain observed him, the more he wondered why Aggie settled for an older man with a bum leg when she could have had him. *She certainly complicated her life*, he thought.

"Pa, did you see Seth when we passed the blacksmith shop?"

"Yeah, I saw him."

"Did you notice he had a bad leg?"

"That can happen if Seth got on the wrong side of a prison guard. I think we should give him a break, unless we find out different."

"You're right, but there's something about the man that rubs me the wrong way."

~

As the weeks passed, Cain decided to track down Hop Babcock. He heard he was living in Lufkin, which was not too far away. Cain remembered how close Hop and his Pa were. *They're made from the same cloth*, Cain thought.

But fate was way ahead of Cain, even before he had a chance to plan the trip, he saw a horseman from a distance. There was a familiarity about the rider, but he wasn't sure. As soon as Hop's horse jumped the cattle gap, Vick recognized the rider and smiled. I'd know that feller anywhere with his tweed suit and laced up boots. It had been a couple of years since he had seen Hop.

"Well, I'll be danged! If you ain't a sight for sore eyes," Vick flashed that big smile of his. "It's about time you came home."

Hop dismounted, and the men had a warm welcome.

"You know me, I go where there's good cooking. Elizabeth spoiled me. You don't think I came back because of you, do you?"

They both laughed and walked toward the house.

Elizabeth was overjoyed to see Hop. *Things didn't seem the same after Orson died and Hop left. Now he's back where he belongs*, she thought.

After supper, the men sat on the front porch sharing stories. It was a beautiful evening with the sweet smell of jasmine mixed with a hint of honeysuckle and cigar smoke. Elizabeth had thought of everything. For the first time Vick and Hop enjoyed the new brick terrace with a huge wall of shrubbery planted for privacy.

After laughing and remembering some of the old times, Elizabeth joked, "There'll be no more secrets now that we planted the shrubbery. You'll never know if there might be someone on the other side listening. So be careful."

"Oh, so that's why you planted this big wall. Eavesdropping on us, huh?" Vick countered.

"I want to make sure there's no family secrets among us," Elizabeth mused.

Cain looked at his Pa and smiled, since they had never shared their secret of the diamonds they left in Panther Holler.

Chapter 9

By THE YEAR 1910, STEAMBOATS HAD IMPROVED VASTLY. THE BOILERS, which were once considered dangerous, had now been improved and brought up to a new standard. Experienced pilots knew what to look out for, such as sandbars, river snags and such. Even though steamers had changed, one tradition remained—and that was racing. Oftentimes, a race between steamboats would ensue to the next port; the winner being the boat that was first docked to unload its cargo of cotton or rice.

Kyle Rover was a risk taker, and he loved pushing the Stepper to its limits. Gamblers alike involved themselves with the folly of the next race, drawn into the sport betting on which boat would arrive first. Kyle loved this, and now, since he and Aggie had been in commerce for more than two years, they were ready to take on a new business: hauling freight and gamblers from Galveston to points up the Mississippi River.

One afternoon, after the boat was loaded, Bidzill approached Aggie about a storm brewing.

"Miss, we're not likely to make it to Galveston if you and Mr. Kyle plan to leave as scheduled. There's a stillness—can't you feel it?" Aggie had noticed a slight weather change, but had not paid much attention to it. "I've felt this same stillness before, and it's always before a storm," he said.

Kyle had very little respect for half-breeds and, therefore, little confidence in Bidzill's knowledge and skills.

Aggie was alarmed that Kyle refused to listen, allowing his prejudices to overrule common sense.

She rushed through the great hall and down the steps into the engine room where Kyle was checking out the boilers.

"We need to delay the trip until morning," she advised.

"You want to disappoint our passengers? We have over 50 gamblers that'll be bellyaching, and I ain't up for that. I think you listen to your half-breed Indian friend when you should be listening to me. Remember who's the Captain. When I say she moves—she moves."

"Captain Kyle, you need to watch it. And don't ever refer to Bidzill as a half-breed. Not in my presence."

"Well that's what he is—a distrustful half-breed. We have nothing to worry about!"

Aggie turned and stared at Kyle with disdain.

"Whatever you say—Captain!" she snapped! "You're responsible if anything happens."

She had experienced many thrills with Kyle's racing, but this time it would be racing against Mother Nature, which could be devastating.

Knowing a storm might overtake them, Bidzill was subdued as he prepared the boat. He was more concerned that someone might get hurt. His alternative was to retire from working with Kyle and Aggie, which he was contemplating very seriously.

After the return trip, I don't intend to be part of this, Bidzill decided.

He felt used and disrespected. For he had trained Kyle to pilot the steamer, only to be demoted to standby in case of an emergency. Kyle also refused to allow him to make any decisions which interfered with Kyle's recklessness. Bidzill's number one job was to act as the strong-arm in case a gunfight ensued among gamblers over a woman's affection, or a dispute over a card game got out of hand.

Although it had been only two years, Aggie had begun reevaluating her partnership with Kyle because of his ego, and because of the way he treated Bidzill. She worried about the safety of the passengers and the strain he placed on the steamer. It was an old boat in relatively good condition and would stay that way with proper care.

As the sky darkened, there was a strange quietness that crept aboard the steamer. It made the rattling and creaking noise of the boat uncharacteristically and eerily frightening. In her gut, Aggie knew they should have listened to Bidzill, but Kyle had a mind of his own, and refused to allow an Indian to tell him what to do.

During times when Aggie sought solace, she would always turn to Bidzill, whom she had developed a likeminded relationship. This was her only contentment, and the feeling was mutual. Bidzill, who otherwise would be interested in more, knew that it was ill-advised to have more than a friendship with a white woman. The two years they worked together, they masked their feelings because of the social barriers of the times. Yet, there was always that look or touch that kept them drawn to one another.

Most white people still considered Indians savages because of their strange customs and behavior, but Bidzill was different. For this reason, Aggie kept her feelings to herself, and Bidzill did likewise. He acted more white than Indian. His black hair and blue eyes were uncharacteristic Indian physical traits. To her, his eyes were like flaming rays of sun that penetrated her soul. However, his Indian features were distinct, although he had mostly white man's similarities. He carried himself with dignity and spoke English as well as most white people did. He was proud of his heritage and confident as a man.

There was also secrecy and mystery surrounding him that he had not revealed to her. Socially, it was taboo for a white woman to be seen "cavorting" with an Indian, and Aggie was quite aware of what the consequences would be. Early on, she cautioned herself about associating with him because she did not want to draw public attention to herself. After all, she wasn't even supposed to be alive.

$$\sim$$

Before leaving the Port of Beaumont, Bidzill thought he would have a serious talk with Aggie—possibly sharing his feelings. Although drawn together like a magnet, unmistakably, a cultural wedge stood between them.

When he walked through the grand hall, weaving his way through all the tables of gamblers, he saw Aggie standing near the railing overlooking the Neches River. There she was, beautiful as ever, with her shawl wrapped around her shoulders. She was the loveliest woman he had ever seen. *I can never have her, he thought. My skin is just a little too olive for her. She knows nothing about my background.*

Bidzill thought he would speak to Aggie one more time before they left port, and possibly share a bit of his past with her.

He hardly remembered the early years of his life, for he was a very young boy when the Navajo people were forced to take the deadly march to Bosque Redondo (named for a grove of cottonwoods by the Pecos River). The great Navajo Chief Atsa was Bidzill's grandfather, who died on the trail to Bosque Redondo.

A Cavalry soldier who was leading them raped Bidzill's mother, and afterwards, he was born from that union. His name means "strong" among the Navajo.

When it became known that a white man fathered Bidzill, he and his mother suffered persecution from their own people.

Along the way, a group of Navajo managed to escape, including Bidzill and his mother. While wandering, they lived in deplorable camps, caves or simply beside trees. After they crossed into Texas, the harsh winds of West Texas spurred fatal sandstorms, taking their toll. Everyone traveling with them died except Bidzill and his mother. A doctor who had been trapped in the storm had successfully sheltered, and afterward he found Bidzill and his mother among the bodies and debris. Bidzill's mother was near death, and he was cuddled in her arms. The doctor lifted the two onto the back of his wagon and traveled to a safe location to give them food. Having taken the oath of saving lives, the doctor was sympathetic towards these Indians. He found a small lake, providing much needed water for all, including his horses. He tried his best to nurse Bidzill's mother back to health, but she died a day later in his arms.

Dr. Franklin had no reluctance when it came time to adopt Bidzill and raise him as his own. Ignoring his wife's wishes, he signed papers giving Bidzill his last name and making him an heir. Early on, the doctor learned from Bidzill that he was the grandson of the great Chief Atsa, which impressed the doctor but he had already discerned a greatness in him.

The boy was a natural born leader and Dr. Franklin decided to teach him medicine. It was always after a patient was asleep that Bidzill would assist his father in surgery. Several years after Dr. Franklin died, Mrs. Franklin chose not to read her husband's will concerning Bidzill's inheritance. Consequently, when she sent Bidzill away, she sent him with his father's medical kit, which unknowingly contained his father's will hidden within.

He loved practicing medicine, but it was impossible to be accepted into a white man's profession. With little other choices, he put the medical kit away and used it only in cases of emergency.

After Bidzill left home, he found a position on the High Stepper and was taught to pilot the steamboat. He worked there for 10 years until the owner's death. Fate then brought him back aboard the High Stepper, but this time with new owners. During this time his adopted mother died, and his inheritance was stated in the will that was tucked away inside his medical kit.

~

Kyle disregarded Bidzill's warning and pulled the steamboat out of port just before the water became choppy. There were worries after a couple hours into the trip that the oncoming storm may be worse than what Kyle anticipated.

Aggie, with the help of Annie Mae, ran through the boat strapping down the piano, and closing all windows and doors in case the steamer shifted. Now that they were out of range of the port, there was no turning back. "Kyle should have listened to Bidzill!" She shouted. They watched as whirling rain and wind dumped a bounty of water onto the deck of the boat.

It was icy cold water, pelting down from the clouds, even though it was spring. *The boat could roll over,* she fretted. *I should have defied Kyle and made him stay in port. Please God… don't let us die,* Aggie prayed.

"Kyle takes too many chances," Annie Mae remarked.

"If we make it to port, some things are going to change. If not, I'm selling him my half of the boat. I'm not going to be responsible for what might happen because of his stubbornness." *Never again,* Aggie thought.

Kyle insisted that Bidzill be in the navigation cabin in case there was an emergency, but it didn't keep Bidzill from blasting Kyle for his negligence.

"You should have listened—and now it's too late. I knew if we left Beaumont we'd be in the wake of a storm. We have to think about Aggie and Annie Mae–and the passengers."

Kyle objected, for he knew Bidzill was pandering for Aggie's attention. Unknown to Aggie, Kyle also had feelings for her. *Bidzill's gotta go and the sooner the better.* The more he thought about an Indian being with Aggie, the angrier he got.

"Boy, you need to keep your head in your job. I know what's going on with you. She ain't gonna fall for no half-breed." Bidzill turned and walked away, for he had too much pride to stay and take the ridicule.

I'll handle Kyle when we get to Galveston—if we make it!

Rushing to the boiler room, Bidzill saw ropes dangling in the water. We can't lose those ropes, he thought. Although they were connected, he knew the ropes were needed to tie down the steamer when they arrived in port.

Bending over the railing he tried to reach the ropes when a huge wave thrust him overboard. *This is it,* he thought. *I'm going to die.* Lucky for him though, the rope in question entangled him, saving his life. Bidzill hung on tightly as he shouted for help. Aggie heard his cry and ran to Kyle for help.

"You have to lower your speed and try to save Bidzill," she shouted.

In the meantime, Bidzill was enduring the roughest ride of his life as he continued to hold onto the rope. "Help, anyone?" he tried to shout over the noise of the storm.

"Aggie, what do you expect me to do? You go and find someone to help you. I must stay and pilot this steamer. Go now!"

Aggie ran frantically asking for help, but no one was willing to risk their lives to help a stranger. In desperation, she forged her way through the blinding rain, leaned over the railing of the boat to find Bidzill. For a few seconds, she thought he had drowned, for she did not see him. Straining to get a closer view, she leaned further over the railing. The chaotic power of the wind-driven waves lifted the boat, then slammed it down again, hurling Aggie into the water. Bidzill was watching in horror, "No Aggie!" Aggie began fighting for her life, thrashing around—trying to keep her head above the water. She would go down and then come up, choking as she tried to call for help. The water was freezing cold. *My body must be frozen,* she thought. I must try to relax and keep afloat. Bidzill tried to swim toward her, but his first attempt failed, as he was too entangled in the rope to reach her.

"Aggie, I'm coming for you!" he screamed.

She relaxed a bit and tried to maintain a calm but the water was so rough.

"Bidzill, please hurry!" She gulped more water as she was thrown about. She was losing the battle and there was nothing she could do. The freezing cold water was shutting down her body, and she felt as though she were paralyzed. The surging waves and turbulent wake of the boat again were throwing her up and down. I'm dying, Oh God, don't let me die, I want to live! she prayed.

For a moment, she thought of giving up to the angry sea, but she continued to fight to survive.

Bidzill managed to loosen the entangled rope and swim toward her amidst great odds. The minutes seemed like hours before he reached her.

"Here, help me put this around you!" he yelled.

Aggie looked at him with despair, for she was frightened that neither of them would make it.

"Aggie, you must hold on tight!" Bidzill commanded.

She put her arms around his neck, still convinced they might die together. She loved his strong arms around her, even though it was hardly the time for such thoughts.

"Hold on, I don't want to lose you!" he yelled as their eyes met.

The way he said, "I don't want to lose you" touched her. *There was such passion in his voice*, she thought.

Several passengers braved the wind and rain, throwing life preservers to them. It was a struggle, but they were finally pulled to safety.

Bidzill looked deep into her eyes for one brief-moment. *It is all there,* she thought. There was no doubt he loved her. Lost for a moment in fantasy, she suddenly came to her senses. *This is crazy!* She was soaking wet and just short of hypothermia, and she was thinking of Bidzill and if he loved her.

As soon as she reached the door, she turned and watched him untie himself from the rope. The strong waves had torn off his shirt, bearing his chest and broad shoulders. Every part of his body shook as his muscles flinched from the cold. Seeing him excited her and she quickly turned away, but it was too late, for Bidzill caught her staring at him. Embarrassed to think she might be encouraging him, she dashed to her cabin. Leaning on the inside of the door, a warmth came over her which she had never experienced. She peeled off her soaked clothes and dried off; then wrapped herself in a warm blanket.

Even though Bidzill caught her looking at him, he remained puzzled. *She probably felt gratitude toward me*, he thought. "I wonder how she would feel if she knew I was the grandson of a great Navajo Chief," he wondered aloud.

It had been awhile since Bidzill had thought about his grandfather or his mother, but he felt their presence when he thought he was drowning.

Chapter 10

The raging storm pushed the Steamer farther inland.

As Kyle struggled with the controls, he put aside his sense of self and asked for help.

"Bidzill, you're going to have to help pilot this thing. I don't know what in the hell more I can do."

Just as Bidzill was about to take over the helm, they heard a loud thud on the starboard side of the boat. They did not know what they had struck, but it sounded like it was serious. Shortly thereafter, a shudder went through the complete vessel. Kyle knew he was no match for Bidzill's experience.

"What did we hit?" he asked.

"How would I know?" Bidzill replied. "You need to check, since you have a free hand."

Running to the port side of the boat, Kyle saw everyone standing near the railings, ready to jump if the steamer began to sink. People were panicked, and imagined the worst.

One man, who was a bit calmer, rushed to Kyle's aid and asked if he could help.

"I think we hit a log," the man said. Can I help calm the passengers?"

"Thanks, tell them we're doing everything possible and try not to worry."

No sooner had the man spoke, the steamer slowed and began to rock. Passengers became sick; many vomiting uncontrollably. This went on for quite some time, as the boat swayed and creaked. Bidzill was not sure what had happened. He feared that the steamer might drift onto a sand bar and be beached. But nothing could be done until the storm passed.

The storm went on for hours until it eventually turned into a lite rain. Kyle did not have the experience to know what to do next.

"One of us is going to have to get wet, and find out if there's damage before we start to drift." Bidzill offered to go, but Kyle wanted to be the hero in Aggie's eyes.

Stripping down to his undergarments, he dove into the churning water to see if the steamer was damaged. Everyone became concerned, for they did not see Kyle resurface. "Where did he go? Did you see him?" one gambler asked.

People scrambled, for they were afraid they might be asked to volunteer to help in some way.

Frantically, Aggie ran to Bidzill.

"We have to do something—Kyle's in trouble."

"What do you mean 'in trouble'?"

"I think he's drowned. Passengers say he never resurfaced."

There was no moon visible, only a dim glow from behind the clouds as Kyle became disoriented underneath the water. Due to the circumstances, visibility was zero. A strong feeling of loneliness and despair came over him, as he had no idea if the boat was in front or back of him. Blindly groping his way, he touched a rope he thought was attached to the boat. Making matters worse, the rope itself was now meshed with seaweed. He felt himself losing consciousness, as he had been in the frigid water too long. And he was running out of air. Now in a panic, his fighting and disorientation caused him to become entangled in the rope, and seaweed. He could not free himself in time, and ultimately succumbed to the sea. His last thoughts were of Aggie.

$\sim$

"Aggie, do you think you can hold the control steady until I find out what's happened to Kyle?" She was reluctant, but agreed.

"I'm not sure, but I'll try. If you see the Chief Mate, have him hurry and take over for me." Aggie said.

"Where in the hell is he? I haven't seen him all day." Bidzill complained.

"Forget him, and just go. Kyle needs help."

Bidzill turned and ran toward the railing, undressing as he went. He hated going back into the water, but there was no one else to help rescue Kyle.

Finally, a cowboy saw Aggie struggling with the controls and came to her rescue.

"Thank God, I was about to lose it," she said.

"Missy, I have some experience with steamers. You go and see what you can do with passengers. Practically all 'em are sick."

"Are you sure you're okay by yourself?" she asked.

"Don't worry—I'll be fine," the cowboy said.

By the time Aggie got to the railing, most of the passengers had gone back to their cabins. She stood by the railing and prayed, trying desperately to see any sign of Kyle or Bidzill. This can't be happening, she thought.

Instinctively, she threw two life preservers into the sea, then screamed for help. Where is everyone, she thought. Screaming at the top of her lungs, no one answered her call.

As soon as Bidzill slipped into the water he realized what Kyle might have been up against. He dove deep, feeling all around as he surfaced. Taking deep breaths, he continued to feel under the dark water. Shortly, he felt Kyle tangled in one of the ropes. He resurfaced for air several times more before Aggie finally saw him. She prayed that neither of them were hurt. Bidzill shook his head, trying to indicate that Kyle was dead. He dove down one more time and pulled the lifeless body of Kyle up to the surface with the help of a life preserver.

Seeing that Bidzill was safe, Aggie got the attention of a cowboy who lowered himself close enough to the water that he could pull Bidzill to safety.

She wept at seeing Kyle's body being lifted onto the deck, wrapped in seaweed. Bidzill, in his own fight for life, received a very serious cut on his arm. One that required stitches.

He ignored his injury as he and one of the cowboys took Kyle below where they could cover him and await his burial. Seeing the blood gush out of Bidzill, Aggie rushed to his aid. "We have to take care of that cut. Let me help you." she demanded.

"Oh, poor Kyle, I can't believe he's gone," she said.

"I'm sorry, I tried to save him, but he was already dead."

"If only he had listened and stayed in port until after the storm," Aggie lamented. "I can't worry about that now, your wound needs taken care of."

He suggested they go to his cabin. After all, he had extensive training from his father who taught him how to perform many routine operations.

Aggie followed him to his cabin and watched as he pulled out a medical kit. It was more of a medium size suitcase filled with all kinds of surgical tools.

She was confused. What is he doing with all the medical instruments? she thought.

"Aggie, I'm going to explain this to you later, but right now I need your help."

"Of course. What can I do?" She continued to be puzzled.

"First we need to stop the bleeding."

Bidzill took off his shirt and raised the bloody arm over his head to help stop the bleeding. "Here, take this solution and cleanse the wound. Then you're going to suture me up!"

"Sew you up? You mean you want me to sew you up?" she kept saying.

"I don't think you understand, but I don't know a thing about sewing a body up. I can't do this. Let me see if I can find someone who can help you."

"No Aggie, you're the one who is going to help me. Now, listen to me and you won't have any trouble. First thing—take this bottle and pour over the suture. All I have is alcohol to clean the wound and use for sterilization."

She had no other alternative but do what he asked. She cleaned the wound as per Bidzill's instruction, and then slowly but surely sewed him up. "There–you've done it," he said.

She could not believe he led her through the entire procedure without having difficulty. As soon as the bandages were ready, she doused the wound with more alcohol and bandaged him up.

"Aggie, you did a great job for a beginner."

She was impressed with the education level he apparently had. It wasn't until after the surgery that she realized he was no ordinary person. He doesn't sound or act like an Indian, she thought.

In her mind, he was as white as she was, even though her culture would never consider him white. She admitted she was baffled, because he had the medical kit and knew how to administer first-aid.

"What are you not telling me that I should know?" she asked.

"It's a long story. Are you sure you want me to tell you now?"

"I'll make time for this," she said.

"My father was a white man. He was part of the Cavalry that were marching my people to Bosque Redondo, I'm sure you've heard of that march. Hundreds of my people were murdered except for my mother and me.

After a Cavalry soldier raped her, and I was born, our people turned against us. When the time was right, my mother and I escaped. The only one who knew we were leaving was my grandfather, who encouraged it. We had no food and hardly any clothing to keep us warm. My mother died in the arms of Dr. Franklin who adopted me. He was a renowned doctor who taught me all about medicine and loved me as his son. I operated with my father, but it was only after a patient was sleeping or too drunk to care. The kit you saw belonged to my father."

"Do you know where your people are now?"

"One day I hope to find them."

"Bidzill, why aren't you a doctor? People need you."

"I think it's obvious! I'm an Indian."

"But you are more like a white man. If your hair was cut no one would know the difference."

This was the first time he had shared anything about himself.

"Bidzill, you've been through so much. I think you need to rest. Perhaps we'll finish this conversation another time," Aggie said.

"I want to thank you for doing such a fine job suturing," Bidzill complimented.

She looked into his eyes and knew she had deep feelings for him.

"You had me worried–with all the blood you lost."

She walked over to his bed and pulled back the covers for him.

I can't allow him to know how I feel, she thought.

After Aggie left, Bidzill was about to put his medical tools away when he noticed a letter. Upon opening it, he saw that it was a legal document that belonged to his father. This is the Will of my deceased father. Reading it over, he thought how many years he had gone without a job or a place to live. And all the while he had his father's place, and a sum of money left to him in the Tyler Bank.

～

While mourning the loss of Kyle, it suddenly hit Aggie that she was now the sole owner of the High Stepper. It's up to me to forge ahead and make the steamer a success, she thought. Running the business alone created insecurity and made her ashamed that she had not given Kyle enough credit.

All I have is Bidzill, she thought.

The next day they pulled into Galveston a little behind schedule, but the cargo made it without any loss. Once there, they felt relieved and fortunate that they had made it through the storm and that Kyle would finally be laid to rest.

While in port, Aggie hired an experienced crew to inspect the steamer for damage. After inspection, they reported only minor damage was done to the hull from what appeared to have been hit by submerged logs. One log was still with them; a stub of a branch caught in one of the ropes they had allowed to hang over the side. Finally–an answer to the mystery of what perpetrated the unusual rocking of the High Stepper. Luckily for all aboard, the hull had not been breached.

That same day, Kyle was laid to rest. After the short service for him, Aggie called Bidzill and Annie Mae into the Captain's quarters to sort out their schedule.

Annie Mae began weeping, for she was still grieving for Kyle, who must have suffered a horrible death.

"I'm sorry Aggie, I can't do this today. We've just come from Kyle's funeral. I hope you understand."

"I feel the same as you, but there's a shipment waiting for us in Beaumont." Annie Mae hugged Aggie's neck.

"Honey, you do what you have to do—I'll be okay."

After Annie Mae left, Aggie became distraught.

"I'm sorry, this is going to have to wait," she said.

Tears welled up in her eyes, for she could not hold back any longer. She threw her arms around Bidzill's neck, which was a shock to him at first. They held each other and then he lifted her face and kissed her. It was a tender passionate kiss; one they had waited for from the first time they met. As soon as they embraced, all the fears and heartache went away, for she was in the arms of the man she loved. They kissed several more times until the passion ran deep.

"Aggie, I had no idea you felt the same," he whispered. His eyes seemed to penetrate right into her heart.

Embarrassed for her aggression, she broke away and ran toward her cabin.

I can't believe I threw myself at him, she thought.

"Aggie! We'll make it to Beaumont in time." His voice trailed off into a whisper.

Throughout the trip, Aggie was embarrassed for her aggression.

After arriving, Bidzill handled the arrangements for the transport of cotton to Galveston for a Mr. Sebastian Parker, whom he had yet to meet.

It became apparent to Aggie that owning the High Stepper might become a burden, since ownership might expose her identity. For that reason, it was necessary for her to depend on Bidzill to do what Kyle had done to protect her. She preferred to keep the ownership of the High Stepper a secret to protect her from anyone finding out she was alive.

After leaving the shipping office, Bidzill ran head on into Sebastian, with whom he spoke briefly. Bidzill tried to recall where he had seen him but he couldn't remember. I've seen him somewhere, he thought.

It did not ring clear at the time that Sebastian Parker may have known Packer Rover and was looking for him. Perhaps he wasn't aware that Packer had killed himself.

Boarding the steamer and reviewing the ship's manifest, Bidzill noticed something very strange. He had become aware of Lee and Sebastian making round trips to Galveston without disembarking. *Why would Sebastian travel round trip to Galveston without taking time to rest up and enjoy the sights?* Bidzill thought.

~

Aggie grew to love the creaking sound of the steamer, which reminded her of escape. As she stood on the upper deck and watched people board with trunks and suitcases, she noticed they were mostly cowboys, professional gamblers, and women—all headed to Galveston for fun.

It was the last sail of the season, and Aggie had planned a masquerade ball, which was advertised as a special event. This was her way of showing appreciation to passengers who had traveled with her.

Invitations were in staterooms, along with masks for passengers who wanted to participate in the event. The ballroom was decorated Galveston style with ivory faces and red lips scattered about. The ragtime sound of the piano was heard throughout the ballroom, creating just the right ambiance. Anxious cowboys were dressed in their usual attire, while businessmen were dressed more formal with masks of their choice provided by the High Stepper. Card tables were set up all around the dance floor, for gamblers who were waiting their turn for a game of poker. Sebastian stood out among the guests with his erect posture and sandy hair. He's very handsome, Aggie thought. For a moment, she tried to forget about Bidzill, but it was no use.

Even with her mask, she had reservations about entering the ballroom. Her large rhinestone earrings flashed like the morning sun as she tossed her hair about. Dressed in an elegant evening gown with a feathered mask, it was determined early on that she was the hit of the evening.

She felt exciting and quite daring as she walked through the crowd of men, who, by their stares, were in awe of her. With such Beauty and grace in what they could see, they were left to allow their imaginations to discern as to what splendor was hidden behind the mask. She longed to find someone who could take her mind off Bidzill. Accomplishing that, while maintaining a low profile would be no easy task. No one must ever know I am the owner of the High Stepper.

As soon as she entered the ballroom, Aggie caught the eye of Sebastian Parker. He was talking to a man she remembered as a young girl when she lived on Pecan Plantation. She looked more closely to make sure it was Lee Tompkins, who lived in the hometown she was raised in as a child. She was not aware he was traveling aboard the Stepper. She remembered hearing that Lee Tompkins was a man not to be trusted.

Seeing him reminded her of her childhood, a dreadful time when she lived with her siblings who did not accept her. She also thought of her mother's involvement with the owner, Hamp Petty, a land baron and wealthy cotton farmer.

Before Aggie was born, her mother, Betsy Dawson, became the mistress of Hamp Petty. After her mother's murder, Aggie fled the plantation with the man she thought to be her father, and it wasn't until he was dying that the truth came out that Aggie was the forgotten daughter of the wealthy Hamp Petty.

Before her father's last breath, he warned her that her half-brothers would kill her to keep from sharing their inheritance, which Aggie was entitled to.

Eventually, being an heir to the Petty fortune became an encumbrance.

She had been running from her half-brothers for years, but there was no way she would know that they were all deceased, including her half-sister Eileen. All the while, she and Cain were sole owners of the Petty estate, but she had no way of knowing. So many of her mistakes were the direct result of her trying to protect Jared—and of course, herself.

Aggies recollection of the plantation brought only sadness. She would always remember the devastating day when her half-brother, Jonathan, murdered her mother before her eyes. Seeing Lee Tompkins reminded her of a time she sought to forget. She was sure Mr. Tompkins would never recognize her as a grown woman in a different environment, but the fear of being found out made her uneasy. Now that Kyle was dead and she was the sole owner of the High Stepper, she needed someone to become her confidant and help keep her secret.

Living a lie is difficult if there is no one to share your past.

On the eve of the dance, Aggie entered the ballroom and was noticed right away by Sebastian Parker. She appeared to be very mysterious as she wore her feathered mask.

This is one I'll have to tame, he imagined. *She must be mine by evenings end*, he thought.

The Chief Mate had taken over the piloting of the boat during the ball and this left Bidzill available to keep an eye on the passengers.

As the evening wore on, his senses were treated mostly to vast darkness, piano music and a woman singing in the background. Occasionally there would be a moon glow cast across the water as the steamer sailed onward. He thought about how many times he had made the journey from Beaumont to Galveston. Thank God, it's a packet boat that carried both cargo and passenger or he would not be able to stand the loneliness and boredom. He wondered how Aggie was handling the cowboys. He wanted to keep an eye on her, but without her knowledge.

Fearing for her safety, he had an idea to disguise himself. There was extra clothing aboard the ship for emergencies, but it was only cowboys attire.

After braiding his hair, he placed his mask over his eyes and then stuffed his braids underneath his hat. It's doubtful anyone will recognize me, when half the steamer is dressed just like me.

Sebastian had maneuvered his way closer to Aggie and was about to ask her to dance when a tall cowboy slid in between them and asked

Aggie first. Using a different accent, Bidzill managed to fool Aggie, while Sebastian felt cheated and annoyed that a low life cowboy cut in before him.

Aggie noticed a familiarity, but seeing Bidzill outside his normal appearance fooled her. He was just another cowboy.

From that moment on, Aggie and Bidzill danced the night away. It was the most fun evening she could remember, and she hated for the night to end.

It wasn't until Sebastian and Lee left the dance hall, that Bidzill decided to follow them, leaving Aggie alone.

It was so abrupt that she decided to follow him.

Bidzill walked about the deck checking boilers and making sure the motor hands were at work.

Aggie was perplexed at watching the cowboy show such interest in the mechanics of the steamer. She wanted to confront him, for he had no business being in places that were off limits to the public. He sensed he was being followed, and stepped into a very private area of the steamer. Hoping to catch him red-handed nosing in places he shouldn't be, Bidzill grabbed her and pinned her up against the wall. He was surprised when he realized it was Aggie.

She knew she should have walked away, but she couldn't for this cowboy wouldn't let her go. She hated to admit it, but she rather liked him holding her.

She felt she was acting out of character, but it didn't matter. Bidzill, lost in the moment, got carried away and kissed her. It was with such passion that finally he had to pull himself away to keep from taking advantage.

Finally, Bidzill said, "Miss, may I escort you to your cabin?"

She was completely out of breath, but she took his arm and walked in the direction of her room.

Before she walked inside, Bidzill tried to kiss her again, but she pushed him away.

"I can't do this," she said.

"Why?" he asked.

"Because my heart belongs to another. I don't know what came over me. Please, you have to excuse me." Bidzill released her, and she walked into her cabin.

He was afraid to tell her who he was, for fear she would never forgive him.

Later that evening, Bidzill noticed two men talking together. They were the same two men he had seen the day Kyle's uncle, Packer, hanged himself.

He was sure they were onboard up to no good, for he remembered the shambles of the Captain's quarters.

They must have thought something was in the cabin. As he approached the corner to the Captains quarters, he saw a figure run away furtively. It was dark and very difficult to make out, but he was sure it was a man interested in what was inside the cabin.

Bidzill decided to follow in the same direction, hiding in a dark corner to observe Sebastian and Lee Tompkins talking together. Seeing them together he was sure that they were aboard when Packer was found dead.

Puzzled by the low tone of voice and hand motion pointing in the direction of the Captain's quarters only substantiated what he felt. They had to be involved someway with Packer Rover's death. What are they looking for? Bidzill wondered.

Confiding his suspicions to Aggie would appear paranoid, when what he saw could be a mere coincidence.

I'm going to keep my eyes on these two and see what they're up to, he thought.

Bidzill continued to observe the two men until Sebastian shook hands with Lee and then went inside. It was only a few minutes later that Aggie came outside with Sebastain.

Why would Aggie leave her cabin? Bidzill thought.

Seeing her engage with the passengers made Bidzill uncomfortable.

He also felt a tinge of jealousy, for he had no idea what the man's interest in Aggie was, other than she was breathtakingly beautiful.

Sliding closer, he overheard Aggie introduce herself as Carmen Davis.

"Very nice to meet you, Miss Davis."

"Likewise," she said.

It didn't make sense that she would introduce herself as, Carmen Davis.

"Are you all staying in Galveston?" Aggie asked.

Sebastian lied in the affirmative, for he knew it would be strange if he told her he was doing a turnaround with Lee on the Stepper.

"We may be there a couple of days," he continued his ruse.

"How about you, Miss Davis?"

Aggie lied as well by saying she was staying to visit an Aunt.

Too many questions made her feel suspicious.

"Will you men excuse me? I need to find my sister."

"May I walk you to your room?" Sebastian asked.

"How nice of you to offer, but I see my sister ahead. Will you excuse me?"

Aggie rushed toward a very plainly dressed woman.

"Do you mind if I walk with you?" The woman smiled and nodded "yes".

Sebastian and Lee assumed that she was Aggie's sister.

"Did you get a good look at the sister?"

"Yeah, I guess Carmen got all the looks in the family," Sebastian chuckled.

Bidzill was totally confused, but was glad that Aggie excused herself. Still there was something very troublesome to him about Sebastian and Lee—and now Aggie. He wondered what was going on with her.

Bidzill rushed to his cabin to change clothes before Aggie found him out.

She was about to enter her living quarters when Bidzill appeared out of nowhere.

"Oh, Bidzill…you frightened me."

"Do you have time? I need to talk to you. Those two men you were talking to—do you know them?"

"I don't believe I do," she lied. She did not want him to know she knew Lee Tompkins.

"I saw the passenger list and I know that we are transporting cotton for Sebastian Parker, but I don't believe I know the other gentleman."

"Aggie, these two men are the very ones I saw snooping around the Stepper the day Packer Rover hanged himself. Tonight, one of them was snooping again. Remember when you and Kyle saw the mess in the Captain's quarters after Kyle's uncle hanged himself?"

"I'm afraid I don't see the connection," Aggie replied.

"I think they're up to no good!"

"What do you think is going on?" she asked.

"I don't know yet! I saw one of them checking out the door where I sleep. Then I saw the two of them talking. If they had anything to do with Packer's death, they might be looking for something right here under our noses."

Aggie thought of the reputation of Lee Tompkins and his shady past.

She started to tell Bidzill about her life, but decided she should be careful until she knew one hundred percent she could trust him.

After the Ball was over, Aggie retired to her room, but before she did, she knew she had to tell Bidzill about her past. On the way to his room, she saw him carrying cowboy clothing, boots and a hat back to the closet where they kept extra clothing.

She stepped back so he could not see her.

The man who kissed me was Bidzill! She placed her hand over her mouth to keep from saying something. I can't believe he tricked me, she thought.

Chapter 11

Lucy worked fervently performing outdoor chores since there were several animals left behind that needed care. She had just finished up milking when she saw, in her peripheral vision, a shadow of a figure standing near the barn door. It frightened her upon recognizing it was Sebastian. She wore old boots, and her hair was knotted with one piece of hair hanging over an eye. She had not planned on him seeing her poorly dressed and in such disarray before she went to work for him. Sebastian has now seen me grim and bedraggled. It's a shame it wasn't yesterday, when I was dressed to the hilt, she reflected.

"Oh, I didn't see you," she said.

"I've been watching you milk. Very interesting, I don't know much about milking cows."

Typical city boy, she thought. She picked up the pail of milk, glancing in his direction. He doesn't look like a criminal. Could anyone like Sebastian squander our property and be part of a plan to murder someone? She wondered.

Walking in the direction of her house, he offered to help her carry the milk.

"Here, I'll carry that for you. A beautiful woman shouldn't be carrying anything this heavy. Before he took the milk, he brushed the hair away from her face. "Now you can see," he said.

She gave him a half smile and handed him the milk. He was very impressive. I can see why he would attract women, she imagined.

"You should have your husband milk the cows," Sebastian said.

Lucy thought he was just nosing around, since he was not aware that Cain had moved away. She wondered how long it would take, for him to find out that Cain, and the family had moved to Woodville.

By the time they got to the house, Sebastian asked if she was still interested in bookkeeping for him.

"It's only right that I ask you first, since you're the one who set up the books. You don't have to answer now for, I am sure you want to talk it over with your husband."

Lucy jumped at the chance for fear, he might change his mind.

"When would you want me to start?"

"Wow, that's quick! I thought you might want to talk it over with your husband."

Again, she thought he was fishing for information.

"I make my own decisions," she said.

This is an independent woman, he thought.

It was late afternoon when Lucy saw Sebastian drive away. She imagined he was going into town to visit with Lee.

This is a good time for me to do a little investigation of my own, she thought. Having a key to the plantation home place, she planned to pry and see if Sebastian was careless enough to leave the accounting books out in the open before she went to work for him.

This is a great time to do some snooping, she reasoned.

Lucy, tried the key and to her amazement he had not changed the locks. A chill of excitement ran from head to toe as she tiptoed through the house toward the office. "Oh, my God, I can't believe, I'm doing this," she said.

The very first thing she saw, was an article on Sebastian's desk concerning the death of Packer Rover having killed himself.

She sat down in an office chair with a thud. *I can't believe he's already dead! If only, I had acted sooner with the information Caleb gave me, I might have been able to save him.*

Lucy, being so much like her father was not going to let this rest. Orson was one who had a mind of his own and Lucy was just like him.

When Sebastian and Lee go to Beaumont, I'm following them, she planned.

She continued to look through different rooms in the house, but the accounting books in question were not there. With all the digging and pilfering, she managed to place things back the way they were.

She hadn't planned on searching so extensively, but curiosity got the best of her.

As she walked up the stairway, she looked down on a beautiful grand piano that she had not seen before. He must be a pianist, for there were sheets of music all around the piano that apparently were some of his favorites. She sat on the stairwell and thought of all the things Sebastian had taken from her. This would have been a grand place for a Ball, she imagined. She hated that she was deprived of having the opportunity to show off her new home. *Lee and Sebastian took everything*, she anguished.

Time must have slipped away for the next thing she knew a key was opening the door.

"Oh no, Sebastian is back."

Lucy jumped to her feet and ran to the front door but it was locked.

I'm trapped, and there is only one way out. How am I going to get to the back door without being seen? She thought.

Lucky for her, Sebastian walked directly into another room making way for her to leave without being noticed.

She practically ran out the back door, terrified that she might have been seen.

Lucy was half way home when, Sebastian looked out the window and saw her running. *Why is she running?* He thought. It appeared strange that she was leaving from the direction of the Plantation. It made no sense.

Perhaps she saw one of the foreman, and had been talking to him. She knew Senor Galvez for he had worked for the Porters before he moved in. *That must be it,* he thought.

The next day, Lucy made a run into town for supplies when she noticed Lee and Sebastian talking. When they saw her, Sebastian shook hands with Lee and then walked over to Lucy who was getting in the car.

"Are you ready to go to work? Sebastian asked.

She placed her packages in the car, and then smiled at him like nothing had happened.

"When you're ready, I'll be ready," she said.

"You won't have a problem, since you know the routine. All the invoices are in place, and if you can begin tomorrow, you can work for me, while I'm out of town."

"Oh, you're leaving?"

"Yes, I'm driving to Beaumont on business. If you have time on Saturday, I will go over the books, and you can see the extra columns I've added, say 4 o'clock in the afternoon? Is that a good time for you?"

"Yes, I'll be there, but for now, I need to get home and feed the livestock."

Sebastian took her hand again, which made her uncomfortable.

Lucy planned to follow them to Beaumont, and gather as much information as possible, but she didn't know how she would pull it off.

Saturday afternoon, she was on time and ready for the meeting with Sebastian.

She was dressed beautifully, not overdone, for she did not want him to lure him with her good looks.

After going over the books she asked Sebastian if she could begin work the following week, which he agreed. This would give her time to follow them when they were in Beaumont.

Lucy had to make a choice, for this would be the perfect time to have stayed behind and searched for the books in question, with Sebastian and Lee out of town. Although the books could prove that she and Cain had been cheated out of the plantation it was more important to find something incriminating about them that could help build a case. She had no idea what she might find out, but something was gnawing at her about following them. That was the Orson in her. Bring 'em to justice!

Monday morning, Lucy was packed and ready to leave for Beaumont. Her plan was following Lee and Sebastian. Being anxious, time seemed to creep by. When are they going to leave? she wondered. She finally realized that they were already gone, having left much earlier than she had anticipated.

As Lucy drove the lonely road she thought of Cain. She knew that neither he nor her deceased father would approve of the risk she was taking—exposing herself to the danger of Lee Tompkins and Sebastian.

Before nightfall, she found a nice boarding house on the outskirts of Woodville, where she stayed the night.

The next morning, she was on the road again and arrived in Beaumont before mid-day, staying in a local boarding house called Aunt Josie's.

Later that evening, sitting across the table for supper was a young man who asked if she would like to read the local newspaper. She was astonished to see more headlines that Packer Rover was found dead aboard a steamboat called the High Stepper. She looked at the date and it had been several weeks earlier.

This was a more extensive article than the one she had seen in Sebastian's office. Her blood turned cold, for she knew it was not a suicide. It was murder! she almost blurted out. And I know who did it!

Frantic, and disappointed that she failed in her mission to warn Packer, she decided to head down to the ship channel and ask questions. It was very busy, with passengers everywhere carrying trunks and suitcases. There were several tugboats being loaded with cargo. Seeing all the activity excited her. But she managed to stay focused, for she had come too far to ignore her plan. *Maybe there'll be someone who can give me answers.*

Lucy scanned the ship channel until she saw Sebastian's car. This concerned her, for she had not planned on seeing them there. Now, she had to wait until they left before beginning her inquiry. It was near sundown before she walked into the shipping office. Lucy was very uncomfortable, but she was a Cargill, and she needed answers. *Daddy would have done the same thing*, she thought.

As she entered the office, the clerk was behind his desk making out schedules for the steamboat. "Ma'am, can I help you?" he asked.

"I hope so, I'm looking for information about Mr. Packer Rover."

"You and everybody else. What is it with this Packer feller? I just got the third degree from two men who were looking for information about Packer. I'll tell you what I told 'em.

I don't know why they're just now investigating, when the man's been dead over two weeks!"

"Sir, can you tell me if those men left their names or what they were looking for?"

"Well, they were both businessmen. One ain't no Texas feller, with that accent of his. If you want more information, ya' might wanna talk to that Indian feller that's aboard the High Stepper.

"Indian?" Lucy asked.

"Well, he's a half breed—don't rightly look like he's full blood Indian. He came in with the High Stepper. Then Packer Rover bought the steamer. Poor feller, never even took it out of port 'fore he hung himself."

Lucy thought Lee and Sebastian might have found a way to make claim of Packer's steamboat; since they are known for killing people before they steal their property.

"The two men you saw asking questions…are they the new owners of the High Stepper?" Lucy asked.

"No, the new owner is Packer's nephew who came in from out of town. He thought his uncle had left him a few of his belongings. Instead, he found his uncle dead and had fell heir to the High Stepper."

Lucy was impressed with the information she received by asking only one question.

"Do you remember where the two men went who were asking about Packer Rover?"

"I 'spect they left town."

Lucy thanked the clerk and then walked outside toward the steamboat. Once aboard, she ran into Bidzill Franklin, the Indian whom she spoke with.

Bidzill failed to mention Kyle Rover as the new owner for he did not feel it prudent to divulge the new owners' names. Instead, Bidzill took Lucy's name and information on how to reach her. She gave the Jackson place in Woodville as her address for she thought she might be home with the family before she received any worthwhile information.

Bidzill wondered why a woman who was unrelated to Packer would be so interested in Packer's death.

To Bidzill, Lucy was much too classy and beautiful to be tied to Packer Rover, who was not of her class. There must be another reason, he thought.

Walking back to the captain's quarters, Bidzill placed Lucy's information in a file on his desk.

∽

Soon after the Porters moved into the Jackson Place, it wasn't long before Sonny planned his first visits with Jared. He dreaded taking time with the boy, but that's what he had to do if he wanted his plan to work.

I must be careful and not make them suspicious of me, since Cain is a lawyer I could land in jail or better yet—hung, he thought.

A few days later, with a sickly dazed look, Sonny got the courage to pay the Porters a visit. This could be a mistake, but he was ready to take the plunge. I've got to get this thing movin' before it blows up in my face, he acquiesced.

Cain, on the other hand, had time to think of the predicament and was still unsettled on whether to trust Seth. I'll be able to tell if he's playing me, he thought with certainty.

When Sonny rode up, Vick and Cain were breaking in a new mare. Neither of them were having luck with the high-spirited horse.

"Cain, I'm getting too old for this," Vick said. This was the first time Cain had seen signs of age creeping up on his Pa. It appears it happened overnight, for now Vick was showing a little grey hair around his temples although he had the looks of a thirty-five-year-old man.

Cain had bought the mare at a nearby auction for a good price and thought between he and his Pa they could break her. She was a beautiful Mustang Cain got for Lucy. But now things were different since she had disillusioned him.

Seeing Sonny approaching them, Vick and Cain climbed over the corral fence to greet him.

"Pa, take it easy with Seth! I don't want Jared all messed up with Seth and me fighting over him."

"Don't worry about what I think. But if I see something I don't like, I'm going to be the first to let you know," Vick countered.

Cain smiled and patted Vick on the back. "I'd expect you to do no less."

"Jared comes first, no matter what!" Cain agreed.

Sonny was apprehensive as he rode closer. To show his friendly side, he stopped near the corral and looked at the mare.

"You trying to break her?" Sonny asked.

"Trying is right...she's not cooperating," Cain smirked.

Sonny thought it was a perfect time to gain their trust.

"Mind if I try? he asked. There's nothing like breaking a Mustang."

"Be my guest! Don't let her fool you— she's tough."

Sonny smiled and nodded that he understood.

Vick and Cain hadn't expected Seth to know anything about breaking horses.

Sonny walked into the corral with a lariat in his hand. They were amazed with the confidence he showed as he slipped the lariat over her neck. She pulled away, but Sonny tightened the rein, showing her he was in charge. She's a strong one, he thought. He held on tight as the horse pulled him around the corral, digging his boots into the ground. It was now a contest between Sonny and the Mustang.

"What do you think?" Cain asked Vick.

"He's a professional, no doubt. I ran into a few of 'em when I was in prison."

After Sonny gave several efforts to calm her down, the mare tangled one leg in the lasso and Sonny brought her down.

"Now there, settle down," he whispered. The mare was panting, moving her head about. Her eyes were glaring at Sonny who was now the victor. It was beautiful, almost artistic how Sonny worked the horse. She continued to snicker and move her head back and forth using the last bit of strength to try and get up. Taking one step at a time, he walked up close to the mare whispering.

"I'm not going to hurt you." He was careful as though they were communicating.

"There now," Sonny said as he began to pet her, talking quietly to comfort her. After kneeling there for some time, he untied the horse's foot and gently pulled her up on her feet. He then walked around to the side and stepped into the stirrups. The mare began to buck again, but not as much as before. Sonny rode her near the corral gate, opening it giving her full rein. As soon as the horse felt the command, she galloped as they rode hard. When they returned, the horse was wet, but Sonny hadn't broken a sweat.

"Good job," Vick said. "We can tell you've done that before."

Sonny, who had been thrown in the past one too many times, forgot momentarily that he, was impersonating Seth Jackson.

"Well, I've done my share of rodeos. That's how I got my bum leg." Sonny instantly changed the subject, for he realized what he said may come back to haunt him. Perhaps they didn't notice, he hoped.

"Where's our boy?" Sonny asked. "I've been missing him."

Cain cringed when he heard him address Jared as their boy. He had doubts about Seth, but the patience he saw while breaking the horse made him more comfortable in allowing a stranger to take Jared. Perhaps he'll be as good to Jared as he was with his horse.

"Seth, what do you have in mind?"

Sonny sensed breaking the mare created trust between him and the Porters.

"We'll take it slow and easy. My idea was to take the boy on a ride today. Has he ridden before?"

Vick wondered why Seth kept referring to Jared as "the boy". It was almost like he hadn't known him before.

"Yeah, he likes to ride, but I'm careful with him," Cain replied.

"I'll make sure I ride slow, so not to scare the boy."

After Vick fetched Jared to go with Sonny, he could see how tense Seth was. He appeared to be very uncomfortable relating with a child.

Sonny dismounted his horse when he saw Jared.

"Well, you're just growing like a weed." Sonny couldn't believe he was buttering up a kid he would never be fond of.

"Get 'em home within the hour and you can have supper with us," Cain said.

Sonny hated the idea of being under the microscope, but he felt having dinner with them would also gain some trust. "Well, that's mighty nice of you to invite me. I'll make sure I have the boy back in time."

They watched as Sonny rode away.

Vick was not so trusting.

"Cain, something ain't right. Did you believe the story about him riding in the rodeo?"

"No, and Aggie never mentioned anything about his bum knee.

"I hate to say it, but maybe she just needed a daddy for Jared."

"Looks like she would have told you more about Seth when she asked you to adopt the boy. I remember hearing she loved him."

"What are you trying to say?"

"I don't know, but there's something about him. He has a past and I'd like to know what it is. Now that I think of it, he reminded me of a prisoner I knew when I was in the Huntsville Prison. Just saying, we need to be asking more questions and find out what makes him tick. Frankly, I don't believe he cares about Jared. Did you notice that he never once mentioned Jared by name?" Cain thought Vick might be exaggerating, since he and Jared had become close.

That night, while gathered around the table, Vick questioned Seth about his rodeo days, as Elizabeth served supper.

"You handled that Mustang like a professional. Very impressive."

"Why don't you tell us something about your rodeo days?" Elizabeth asked.

This was a subject Sonny was not prepared to go into to.

"Ma'am, some of us unemployed cowboys did what we could back in the day, I pretty much had a steady job traveling mostly performing in rodeo's— bull riding. I was in Cheyenne when I rode my last horse, and that's when I hurt my leg. They thought for a time that I might lose it. After that, I made my way back to Texas working for my Pa. That's when I met Aggie and you know the rest—it's too bad what happened between me and my Pa."

After Sonny left that night he became paranoid about how he answered some of their questions. *Why did they drill me like they did? That ain't gonna happen again.*

The next visit with Sonny didn't fare too well. When Jared realized he was going to be left alone with Sonny again, he pulled away and ran to his Pa, grabbing tightly onto his leg. That was a red flag to Vick.

"Maybe Jared should stay home today," Vick suggested.

"You don't worry about the boy, 'cause him and me get along just fine," Sonny said.

"Where ya' plannin' on riding today," Vick asked.

"Maybe town! I was thinking the boy might like a candy bar."

Cain and Vick reluctantly let him go. However, as soon as Sonny was out of sight, Vick jumped on his horse.

"Pa, where you going?"

"I'm following him. Couldn't you tell Jared didn't want to go with Seth?"

"Yeah, but I figured he'd settle down. I ain't lookin' for friction between me and Seth," Cain pointed out.

"Tell Lizzie I'll be back before dark."

Vick followed Sonny, but it was in the direction of the lake and not town.

Due to Sonny's lack of character, he learned early on in life that he needed to always be looking over his shoulder. Because of that, he developed an extra sense that helped keep him out of trouble. That sense had kicked in again, as he felt he was being followed. So, he stopped shy of the water. Instead of walking his horse in the water as he planned, he took Jared out of the saddle and they walked beside the lake.

"Boy, you ever seen any arrowheads?" Sonny spoke loudly of arrowheads for Vick's benefit. He didn't fool Vick for a minute! He walked his horse right up to where Sonny was standing.

"You taking the long way into town! In case you didn't know, town is in the opposite direction!"

Sonny looked Vick square in the eyes.

"You following me?"

"My grandson acted up with you, and I thought you might need some help with him."

"Y'all got the boy spoiled, and it's gonna take time. This is why I decided to ride out to the lake and look for arrowheads."

"You take care of my grandson, you hear?"

Sonny watched as Vick rode away.

He was livid after Vick, rode out of sight.

"Come on boy and git ready to hang on!"

Sonny hopped in the saddle and snapped Jared up by the arm. The boy whimpered when he saw Sonny's eyes.

"Shut your mouth kid or I'll throw you in the lake!" Jared was terrified.

As Sonny left, he intentionally rode hard, jumping logs, and taking unnecessary risks, just to frighten the boy.

Chapter 12

Lucy left the ship channel very confused, not knowing what her next step should be. She was now unsure of who murdered Packer Rover. On her drive, back to the little yellow boarding house, all she could think about was getting back to San Augustine safely without Sebastian finding out she had been in Beaumont. She continued to dwell on Bidzill Franklin and wondered what else he failed to tell her. Time was of the essence, and making it back to San Augustine before Sebastian was foremost on her mind. I'll get an early start in the morning, she planned

The next morning, as she entered the dining room, guest were seated around the breakfast table. She froze in her tracks when she saw Lee and Sebastian sitting at the table talking. They glanced her way, but Lucy turned around just in time, certain that she had not been seen. Frightened because of a near miss, she ran back to her room and began throwing her clothes into her suitcase. I've got to leave before they find I'm here, she thought.

Both Lee and Sebastian were certain they caught a glimpse of what appeared to be a beautiful woman.

"Lee, did you see the lady near the stairs?"

"All I saw was her dress."

"If I didn't know better, I would think Lucy Porter had a look-a-like, Sebastian remarked. I failed to mention, but yesterday, I interviewed Lucy to keep books for me. She knows I'm in Beaumont. Surely she would have told me if she planned to be in Beaumont."

"I can't believe you asked her to work for you." Lee mentioned critically.

"Surprisingly, she said yes, without talking to her husband—can you believe that?" Sebastian asked.

"You know that Cain Porter is a lawyer, don't you? Knowing our history, I'm shocked you asked the man's wife to work for you. I presume you remember how she threatened me in my office." Lee related.

"I wouldn't hold that against her. I think she reacted because of losing the plantation. She's not the same girl you remember," Sebastian explained.

Lee was very curt. "Sounds like you've forgotten she's married."

Sebastian hadn't understood how much Lee wanted Lucy and her family out of town—and his life.

"I don't know if she's married or not. I haven't seen her husband around lately," Sebastian said.

"Are you sure?" Lee asked.

"It's been several weeks since I've seen him, and the other morning Lucy was milking her cows. Why would he allow his beautiful wife to tend to the animals if he was there? He's nuts if you ask me," Sebastian replied.

~

When Lucy returned to San Augustine she was an emotional wreck. *What am I going to do with this information?* she thought, and what if they saw me?

The next morning, she noticed that Sebastian's car was parked near the back of his house. Now, I must face him.

She always thought of her daddy, when she got herself in trouble, and it was as though Orson was speaking to her.

Lucy girl, you have to act as though nothing happened. If they ask you if you were in Beaumont, deny it and keep denying it. "That would have been my daddy's counsel if he was here," she said out loud.

As much as she hated to face Sebastian, she knew she had no other choice.

Lucy dressed very modestly, picked up her umbrella and walked over to the plantation. She knocked on the door exactly at the time they agreed for her to begin work. Before Sebastian came to the door, she took a few deep breaths to muster up courage.

"Are you ready to begin work?" he asked. She reconciled in her mind that everything was okay, for he acted his usual self until he asked her if she had a body double.

"You may not believe this, but I saw a woman in Beaumont who looked just like you," he said.

There was a moment of panic, as she was caught off guard by his comment.

"I suppose everyone has a double," she laughed.

"Well, she wasn't as pretty as you."

"Thank you for the compliment, but it's best we get to work."

She was relieved to know that Lee did not see her, for she believed he would have known it was her.

"Do you want me to show you what needs to be done?" Sebastian asked.

"Have you changed the books from the time you've taken the place over?" she asked.

"No, mostly what I have are invoices ready to be entered and those two columns I spoke to you about. I do have an itinerary, I want to go over with you. Most of my travel will be aboard the High Stepper, out of Beaumont. We'll be shipping cotton and rice to Galveston. I have everything laid out for you, and I'm sure you'll be fine. Lucy, I'm sorry to leave you on your first day, but I have a new Arabian that needs to be ridden. By the way, do you like riding?"

"I used to ride all the time. Riding has been part of my life since I was a kid," she replied.

"Good, then one day we might ride together. I have several champion horses you may want to ride."

Lucy had no desire to ride with Sebastian, but she loved the idea of riding an Arabian.

"Are they all Arabians?" she asked.

"Yes-—before I came here I owned an Arabian farm."

Sebastian failed to tell the whole truth, yet, he did live on an Arabian Farm, but it was never his. He left out a few minor details of how he charmed a wealthy widow out of her fortune. When her children found out, they ran him off.

"Arabians are beautiful horses," Lucy said.

"Would you like to join me for a ride one day?"

"Sebastian, thank you, but it's better that we keep our working arrangement strictly business. You need someone to keep your books, and this is what I was hired to do. I hope you will respect my wishes."

"Oh, I'm sorry, I didn't mean to embarrass you." He quickly changed the subject.

As soon as Sebastian left, she wasted no time looking for the books. *I must make good use of my time if I'm to prove Lee and Sebastian stole our property.* She rummaged as carefully as possible, making sure everything went back in its original order.

She rambled throughout the house again, looking in every crook and cranny. *The books must be here, they should be,* she thought. *Caleb would never make up such a story about Lee and Sebastian stealing our property if it wasn't so! Perhaps they're destroyed or somewhere else. Maybe the barn, she thought.* She remembered hearing Sebastian say he spent a lot of time in the barn. Lucy was relentless, and after she finished, she was certain the books had been removed. *It would be only natural for him to remove them in case I became a bit meddlesome. I must find a way to get into the barn. Perhaps when he asks me to take a ride.*

A few days later, Lucy asked to ride one of Sebastian's Arabians. He was puzzled by her timing, but agreed. "Of course, but hadn't you rather I go with you?"

"I think I should ride alone. I don't think Cain would approve. I hope you understand."

Sebastian knew that Lucy was living alone and wondered why she lied.

"Lucy, why would you mislead me about your husband? I know Cain is not living with you."

"So, you know! I hope you will respect my wishes and not speak of my business. It's not what you think!"

"I'm sorry, you don't have to explain. I only want you to be truthful with me and if I can help, let me know.?" Sebastian stated.

"My intention is to keep my personal life private. It's really not open for discussion."

Sebastian knew if he kept pushing he might lose her as a bookkeeper.

"I'm sorry, Lucy. I didn't mean to interfere. I'm here if you need me."

~

The days were everything but normal, and the more she was away from Cain, the more she missed him.

One afternoon, Elizabeth and Cain were alone when the subject of Lucy came up.

"Ma, what do you think is going on with Lucy? Do you think she loves me?

Elizabeth just stood there and listened.

"Something has got to change for I'm not living like this much longer. Jared misses his mama, and I miss her too. I've refused to admit it but I think she's hiding something from me. Ma, have you noticed anything?"

"Son— what I think doesn't matter, but you and Lucy need to spend time together. After all, I'm a woman, and I know these things. You have to be sweet and let her know how much you love her."

"Perhaps you're right! I'll plan on driving to San Augustine in the morning."

~

Meanwhile, Lucy continued her charade, as she went about trying to find more information. *I need to find the books, Cain and I may never save the plantation if I can't find the truth!*

Although Lucy missed her family, she couldn't give up her quest. *They need to pay for what they've done.* Lucy had tried being firm, but buttering him up might prove to be more beneficial. She was confident that she would prevail.

Sebastian had noticed a slight change in Lucy. She had become more personable and with this sudden change, he decided to ask again if, she would go horse riding with him.

She hadn't thought of what might happen if they rode together. Her only desire was to gather as much information as possible, if there was an opportunity.

Sebastian was excited that she had finally given him hope that there might be a chance. *This woman doesn't belong with a man like Cain*, he thought.

When Lucy walked out to the horse stables she looked more beautiful than ever in her riding outfit. She had to be careful when, she began observing, her surroundings. Searching for anything that seemed unusual or out of place, her eyes became fixed on a locked door. *What can be behind this door?* She wondered.

Jokingly, she asked Sebastian if he was afraid that someone would come in and steal his feed.

"Why would you ask that?" he replied.

"Because you have a lock on your storage door. That is where you store your horse feed isn't it, or is it your valuable saddles you're protecting?" She said, laughingly.

No sooner had she mentioned the saddles, he walked over to the door and unlocked it, which surprised her. The room was not at all as she expected, for there was nothing out of the ordinary, just feed and a few saddles.

"You're not trying to appease me, are you?" she asked.

"No, but you have a curiosity about the room, so I want you to see that it's nothing more than a storage room. Suddenly, she noticed a slightly sinister look on his face—one that she had not seen before.

After Sebastian helped Lucy into the saddle, he slapped the horse on the hindquarters, and the Arabian went flying out the stables and through the open fields. It was unlike any horse ride she had ever taken. She always enjoyed pushing her horse, but with the Arabian it was like floating on air with the cool damp air hitting her in the face. It was exhilarating.

She could hardly hear Sebastian as he said,

"Be careful." He was stirred at seeing Lucy's beautiful blonde hair flying through the cool breeze. She hadn't noticed, but there were dark clouds gathering—suggesting they may get wet. She didn't care about that, for riding the Arabian was the best ride she had ever had, plus she needed a diversion. Lucy had always respected and loved horses and it was apparent to Sebastian she knew a thing or two about riding. They continued to race, jumping boulders and splashing through streams as they road into the deepest part of the woods. There was a single trail, which wound its way in and out of one wooded area after another. And then came a fine mist, brushing against her face. Suddenly, it began to sink in that they were a distance away from home, which concerned her. Suddenly her horse burst from the woods into a breathtaking pasture. She stopped to look around at the land she was seeing for the first time. Pecan Plantation is more gorgeous than I ever imagined. Then Lucy, spurred the horse and galloped at top speed again.

Sebastian was purposely lagging so he could study the gorgeous woman who was in well control of her horse.

So, she wants to race, Sebastian thought.

As they rode, the mist turned into a sprinkle. As she slowed down, Sebastian rode up beside her and grabbed the horse's bridle forcing the Arabian to stop. He led the horse into a small pond used for a watering hole. Lucy thought the mist of rain on a beautiful Arabian was sensual and triggered her desire for Cain. If only he was here with me, she imagined.

However, Sebastian had other thoughts of sensuality, which included Lucy.

She's one rare beauty, he obsessed. The mist began turning into a drizzling rain and he noticed how stunningly gorgeous she was with the rain dripping off the end of her nose.

"Lucy, we're going to get soaked if we don't find shelter! Follow me--I know a place where we can wait-out the rain."

She was reluctant to follow, but she did not want him to know she distrusted him, even though it appeared he was saving them from the approaching storm. Sebastian had plans for Lucy, for he was feeling very much aroused.

She was several miles from her home, and overcome with apprehension as they approached a small cabin. It had been built as a shelter for ranch hands that got caught in the same type of storm.

Riding up to the cabin, the clouds turned to black as night. Being trapped with Sebastian by a severe storm was the last thing she expected to happen.

~

It was late evening when Cain drove up to Lucy's house. He could hardly wait to see her. The rain had stopped momentarily, and all he wanted to do was hold his wife and make love to her. I should never have left you here alone, he thought.

He opened the door to Orson's old home and called out her name, "Lucy, are you here?" After checking the house, he was concerned, *where could she be? Her car is here*, but no sign of Lucy. After waiting awhile, he decided to drive into town and see if she was at the local café having supper. Perhaps a friend took her out for the evening, he imagined, and then he thought, what friend, for Lucy had no close friends.

◡

Lucy and Sebastian, dismounted the Arabian and ran into the cabin. She was soaked to the bone and so was Sebastian with his hair dripping wet.

We must be miles from home, she reminded herself. Sebastian was very close to Lucy when they entered the cabin and took liberty grabbing her and forcing himself on her. She did not want to be in his arms but it happened so fast there was nothing she could do but kiss him back when he caught her off guard. It was not a simple kiss, but a forced long passionate wet kiss, which terrified her for she had never been kissed that way before.

"Sebastian, stop it! You have no right to do that!" She twisted and pulled herself away.

"Lucy, please, I know you feel like I do." He grabbed her wrist and tried to drag her onto a pile of hay that covered part of the floor. For a moment, she saw evil and desire in his eyes. She feared he might rape her. *My God please help me*, she thought. Her mind went back to the Jackson Whites, a nomadic cult who kidnapped and raped her years earlier. She was determined that it would never happen again.

She fought to stop Sebastian, until, she thought she heard the voice of her daddy. *"Lucy, remember what I taught you— kick him."*

Feeling Orson's presences around her, she kicked him in the groin. She watched as he rolled up into a ball.

"That'll teach you!" she shouted. "Don't ever touch me again!"

He was still spewing profanities as she opened the door and ran to her horse. She climbed in her saddle and rode hard, but Sebastian managed to limp to his horse and follow her. She was whipping and spurring the Arabian as she rode, running through streams and jumping anything in sight. She had to make it home before Sebastian caught her.

"What did I get myself into?" she said out loud.

Arriving back at the house after his trip into town, Cain drove just out of view in time to see Lucy ride into the stables with Sebastian right behind her. He couldn't believe his eyes. Now he understood why Lucy refused to leave with the family. *What a fool I've been, thinking she was going back to Jonesboro to visit Orson's grave.* He quietly backed away from the house to prevent being seen, and headed back to Woodville. Lucy was unaware that Cain had seen her with Sebastian.

She dismounted and had to push Sebastian away when he tried to touch her. He realized he had alienated her. *Lucy's special and I'm afraid I've come on too strong. Now, I've lost her,* he thought. *Somehow, I must convince her that I am no threat to her,* Sebastian pondered.

"Lucy, I'm sorry. It's just that you're so beautiful and I couldn't help myself. I promise I will never allow this to happen again."

Her only thought was how she messed things up and may never have another chance to find the accounting books. She knew that Sebastian was drawn to her, but agreeing to ride with him might be dangerous. She was angry at herself. *What should I expect? I'm married and Sebastian has no idea why, I have chosen to stay in my daddy's place, without my husband. I've caused this and now all my efforts have been in vain. Daddy would not approve.*

That night, as she retired to bed, she thought about the events of the day, and then it hit her. The books could be at the cabin where Sebastian tried to seduce me. The cabin, must be it, she thought.

~

By the time, Cain arrived home; Woodville was pitch dark, with not a flicker of light from anywhere, not even in the cantina that usually stayed open late at night. Cain drove through town, down the country road leading to the Jackson place all heartbroken after learning that Lucy had betrayed him. His thoughts were of her and why she had fallen for a man like Sebastian. It must be because Sebastian has Pecan Plantation and can give her things that I cannot, he thought.

When he arrived home, he refused to go inside to face Elizabeth and Vick. He sat in the car until sunrise sorting out what he must do next. He watched the daybreak as the ranch hands began their early rounds, herding cows to be milked and fed. It was the first hint of fall; a long-awaited chill in the air. The tractors were already in motion, ready to plant new crops. All Cain could think about was how to break the news to his Ma and Pa about Lucy's deception.

Chapter 13

THE STEAMER PULLED INTO THE SHIP CHANNEL ON A COOL BRISK evening as folks were waiting to board the Stepper. There was only one young woman and her son who stood out. The boy had light brown hair with a few freckles—just the age of Jared who kept pulling away from his mother. Such a sweet, mischievous boy, Aggie thought, as she watched from the upper deck of the steamer. He reminds me of Jared. Seeing the young boy, brought up her painful past. Tiny tears welled in her eyes, rolling down her blushed cheeks. She walked to the Captain's quarters to look over contracts that needed approval. She was having a bad day, hating the life she had chosen without her son. She wondered what he would look like now that he had passed through the toddler stage. Cain must be happily married by now, she thought. Shuffling through the mess of papers, trying to redirect her thoughts, Aggie saw a name she recognized written on a sheet of paper. How can this be? The name was "Lucy Porter". It also told where she lived and how she could be contacted. Aggie thought the worse. They must know I'm alive, she thought. She began to panic as she paced back and forth across the floor of the cabin. What is this information and how did it get here? She still had tears in her eyes as the door opened. Bidzill saw her holding the paper and thought she must have received bad news of some sort. Of course, Bidzill knew absolutely nothing of her past. He had respected her privacy, for fear of overstepping his boundary.

Aggie held the paper out in front of him. She was more than upset and angry as she pointed to a name.

"What is this?" she asked sharply.

He looked at the paper and then at Aggie. "I have no idea." He had not remembered the woman who came aboard the steamer asking questions about Lee Tompkins and Sebastian Parker.

Aggie immediately thought Bidzill had betrayed her and was not to be trusted.

"How did it get in among your contracts? Have you been spying on me?" she asked.

"Honestly, I have no idea what you're talking about. Why are you so upset about a name?"

Bidzill's mind was racing back in time when suddenly he remembered a beautiful young woman who was interested in the events surrounding the man who killed himself on the High Stepper.

Aggie, calm down, I think I remember this woman! She came aboard asking questions about Packer Rover's death."

"You mean Kyle's uncle who owned the steamer?"

"Yes, she seemed to think Packer might have been murdered. When I mentioned Sebastian Parker and Lee Tompkins she became frightened as if she knew them. She wrote down her name and how to locate her in case there was information about how Kyle's uncle died. After that, she left as suddenly as she came. Now, would you like to tell me what this is all about?" Bidzill walked over and placed his arms around her to console her.

"Aggie, I hate to see you this upset. Do you mind telling me what happened? You can trust me. Let me help you."

"I don't know what good it would do to burden you with my problems." He looked into her eyes, searching for any clue that might suggest she wanted him to kiss her. Feeling the intensity of the moment, slowly they surrendered and desperately clung to each other. "Aggie, you must know how I feel about you! I've thought of you constantly. I think I'm falling in love with you. I know, I am," he whispered. She pulled away again and walked outside the cabin near the railing. Now was not the time for distractions when there was such concern that she might be found out. She wondered if she should allow him to know of her past. She watched as the deck hands piled bales of rice on board the packet boat, and then took Bidzill by the hand. "Come with me," she said. Once in her living quarters, she made a pot of tea and waited for the right moment to tell Bidzill of her past. She had no idea how to begin, or how many of her secrets to reveal. He was sweet, and understanding, which made it easy for her to tell him everything. She shared her life from the time she was a young girl to when she became sole owner of the steamboat. She explained how she found and nursed Cain back to health years earlier, and later how drawn they were to each other which resulted in having a child. She told him about her stepbrothers' plan to kill her and why she had to give Jared to Cain to protect their son. "I had to save Jared, and I welcomed his father to adopt him." The one thing she did not tell Bidzill was that she was an heir to Pecan Plantation, which would make her one of the richest women in the state of Texas. She was afraid that he would be frightened off.

For the first time, she did not care of Bidzill's ethnicity. He was half white, as well as Indian and had beautiful olive skin with clear blue eyes just the same as hers. I've never seen such a handsome man, and I love him, she thought. He's everything I want in a husband and being half Indian doesn't matter anyway, she reflected.

"Aggie, thank you for trusting in me, I know you miss your son."

"Yes, and it was difficult to lose him. I couldn't allow Jared to grow up under the shame of my husband being sent to jail for murdering his father. My biggest fear was the danger of my two-stepbrother's finding me and killing Jared. After I allowed Cain to take our son, my life was over, for I had no one. At the time, it was easy to fake my own death, but now, I realize what a mistake it was to do what I did."

Bidzill took her hand and kissed it.

"Aggie, I don't know what I would have done if I were in your position, but you mustn't continue to punish yourself. Everything is going to work out. Do you know where your boy is now?"

"He's in Woodville. My home place is only a short distance from where they are living. What puzzles me is how the Porters acquired the Jackson home. This must mean that Seth sold his childhood home to the Porters, which disturbs me. My last wishes were to have Jared inherit my home and property."

He looked at her tenderly.

"Aggie, I want to help you find out what's going on for your peace of mind. I think you know you can trust me.

"How can you help?" she asked.

Bidzill took her in his arms and held her. "I'm going to Woodville and find out for myself."

Chapter 14

Lucy did not know that Cain had seen her and Sebastian together after they returned from their horse ride. What appeared to be two lovers riding together, was really Lucy trying to find the books that would prove Lee Tompkins and Sebastian swindled them out of Pecan Plantation. In addition to that, she had just escaped from possibly being raped. Had Cain confronted Lucy at that time, he might have understood why she refused to move with the family to Woodville, instead he allowed his jealousy of seeing them together get the best of him.

After Sebastian apologized for his bad behavior, Lucy reluctantly continued to work for him. In her mind, the only way to make things right was to find the accounting books. Several times a week, Sebastian and Lee would join each other for a horseback ride. But before leaving, she would notice they would engage in conversation near the barn. Lucy was suspect of those meetings. During the time they were gone, she would look for the books, being very careful in the event a trap might be set for her. Finding proof that they had stolen Pecan Plantation was her top priority, and time was running out. Never mind that she was a woman placing herself in danger, for she was smart like her daddy, and could handle a gun like a man, she was convinced of that.

One afternoon, Lucy saw Lee and Sebastian prepare for another ride and she planned to follow them. She was beginning to feel the pressure of being away from Cain and Jared too long— and it was haunting her. She couldn't continue misleading Cain, for it might put a strain on her marriage if she insisted on staying longer—she had to act fast and find those books. Her heart ached for Jared and the guilt was killing her inside.

After Lee and Sebastian rode away, Lucy slipped into her riding gear and hurried to the barn to saddle up and follow them. It was important to stay far enough behind to keep out of sight. Knowing they killed before left little doubt that they would do the same to her. She had to be careful, for she couldn't chance them finding out she was spying on them.

Lucy felt her stomach tighten as they neared the same stream they had stopped before. She knew it wasn't far to the cabin. She edged her horse closer so she could hear the conversation since their voices carried well over the water. What she heard were only bits and pieces of a conversation, which did not make sense. Sebastian asked Lee if he thought the men would be there with the money. They must be expecting someone. *What are they talking about?* She thought. As they continued their journey, Lucy's horse began to nay. She pulled on the reins immediately. *What if they heard me? I think I'm far enough behind, but I'm not sure. I must be careful.* With her riding farther behind, Lee and Sebastian rode past the cabin heading toward a forest which had only one small trail. She hesitated when she noticed she would be entering a narrow trail that would be difficult to escape should they see her. She hadn't gone far when she smelled meat cooking. There in the distance she could see a campfire and tent with two men. *These must be the men Sebastian and Lee were talking about who had their money.*

She walked her horse as close as possible without being seen. It appeared the two men knew Lee and Sebastian. She could hear more clearly and they spoke of the High Stepper. *That's the name of the steamboat,* she remembered. Lucy strained to hear more when one of the men mentioned they wanted their cut of the money for killing Packer Rover.

"What about the books—did you find 'em," Lee asked. The conversation began turning ugly as they argued, but Lucy heard the name "Packer" and "the books".

"You were supposed to give us our cut! Now you're trying to double-cross us!"

One of the men shouted, "we didn't find no books." Lucy heard "books" again. *That must be where the books are—someplace on the High Stepper. So that's why they go to Beaumont so much. They're looking for the books on the steamboat!*

"We told 'em if he didn't tell us where them books were that we'd kill 'em, but he didn't think we would. I guess we showed 'em."

"You two are just alike. Why didn't ya' wait till he told you where they were before you killed him? What you did doesn't make sense. Now we'll never know where they are. "

"Well, we looked and there wasn't nothing around."

"Just maybe you didn't look good enough. They're someplace on that steamboat and now we're gonna have to find 'em. You're two sorry scumbags," he said. Lucy watched in horror as Lee pulled a gun from his jacket and shot both men dead. This time, she witnessed first-hand what kind of men Sebastian and Lee were. *My life is more important than the plantation and those books*, she thought.

She remained still until she gradually came to her senses. For the first time, she realized she was way over her head. *I'm a woman with a husband and son. This is something the sheriff should be handling.*

"Search the horses and the tent. I know they have the money," Lee shouted. Now motivated by fear, Lucy carefully turned her horse and walked with it a safe distance away and then mounted and beat the hell out of there. Sebastian motioned for Lee to be quiet.

"Do you think someone followed us?" Sebastian whispered. "Hell, I don't know! Could be they had somebody watching."

Lee turned and rode over to the men's two horses and found two huge sacks hidden in the brush. "It's here, I got it!" He assumed the

Joiner brothers had planned to double-cross them for the money they were promised for killing Packer. As it turned out it was kill or be killed, which made Sebastian feel better after watching Lee kill in cold blood.

"We need to hide the money before we ride out of here. Let's hide it in the cabin and then come back later."

"Why not take it with us?" Sebastian asked.

"It's not safe. Supposin' somebody is waiting to for us?" Better to hide it before we leave for home."

Lee continued giving orders. "When you leave go through the woods so you won't be seen and be sure there ain't nobody following you. Meet you at the cabin." Sebastian jumped on his horse and rode off.

Lucy managed to move quickly through the trail until she found a good hiding place with heavy brush. She decided to wait until she saw the two men go by before proceeding. She guided her horse off the trail and waited. *Oh my God, I hope they didn't see me!* Too frightened to move, she waited for what seemed forever until both men passed her. In truth, only minutes had passed. She was pretty sure the bags contained the money they were talking about. Now she knew for certain that the accounting books she had been looking for were on the steamboat.

Lucy made sure she took a different route to the cabin.

The men met up short of the cabin, tied their horses, and walked cautiously up to the cabin with the bags. They had been in the cabin nearly half an hour when they came out empty handed.

Lucy continued to stand in the shadows of the trees until long after they had ridden off. When she was sure the coast was clear, she walked her horse up to the cabin. After entering, she noticed there was only one table and a few chairs scattered about, with two mounds of hay on the floor. There was also a fireplace with a pot hanging over scorched kindling. As she thought of possible places to hide the money, there was only one option and it was the hay. Had she not known about the money, she would have no reason to suspect there was anything of value hidden inside the cabin. It seemed strange to her that the hay was not altogether. She raked the small pile of hay aside and examined the floor. There appeared to be a board in the floor that was slightly raised—not noticeable unless one was looking. She bent down and looked more closely, and through a tiny little crack between planks she saw what appeared to be a sack. She couldn't believe she found their hide-out so soon. There was only one problem—she had no tool with which to get the board up. *They must have used something to pry the board with*, she thought. She looked around the cabin but could not find anything that would work. I'll have to come back, she thought. Riding away, she saw a pitchfork with a broken handle. She tied her horse and ran back to the cabin, thinking the pitchfork might work. Her concern was Sebastian and Lee changing their minds and coming back for whatever was in the sacks, which panicked her the entire time she was trying to get to the bags. Lucy scarred up the floor bad before she could lift the plank, but finally managed to remove it. Bending down on her knees, she grabbed the two bags and ran from the cabin as if someone was chasing her. Throwing the bags over the neck of the horse, she mounted up and maneuvered her way home without incident.

Upon Sebastian's arrival home, he noticed Lucy's lights were out. He had taken delight having a beautiful woman living alone next door. He wondered where she was, for her car was there but no sign of life in the little frame house. Only a few months earlier, the house was nothing but a sore thumb to him, but now that Lucy was living there, all was well. He walked over and knocked on her door. "Lucy, are you home?" he called out. *She's either sleeping or she's gone somewhere*, he thought after getting no response. Her house was pitch dark. He walked to her barn and saw that she had taken her horse out of the stall. Perhaps she took a ride somewhere. The thought never entered his mind that she was the one following them. He was sure Lucy had a good explanation, which was of no business to him. When she finally arrived home, she came through the back of the barn, put her horse away and walked around the lake, so not to be seen. Before she walked onto her porch, she threw the two big bags under her steps out of sight. *They'll be safe here until I'm ready to leave,* she planned. Her heart was racing as she bolted her door.

The next day, Lucy put on the performance of a lifetime acting as if everything was alright. She gave no indication that she was the one who stole their money.

I must make an excuse to leave before they find the money gone. She thought of her Pa and what he would do.

Reporting for work the next day, she was uneasy when she saw Sebastian. He smiled at her, hardly remembering that she had left work early the day before. "It's good to see you this morning," he said.

"Sebastian, you weren't here yesterday, and I had to leave early. I'm still a little under the weather."

"I'm sorry to hear that. You're okay now, aren't you?"

"Somewhat, but yesterday— not so good." Sebastian suspected Lucy was not sharing something with him, which was of no business to him. He imagined the breakup between her and Cain was disturbing her.

The entire day she tried to act normal, but it was difficult knowing she had seen Sebastian and Lee kill two men in cold blood. All she could think about was the money and the two strangers they murdered. *I'm in way over my head,* she thought. *I need to go to Woodville before they figure out I'm the one who stole the money. I only hope Cain will forgive me. What a fool I've been.*

That night, after work, Lucy packed a bag and hid the money under the things she packed inside her car. She then placed a note on Sebastian's door explaining she had an emergency and had to leave.

Driving to Woodville she had no idea how she was going to approach the subject of Lee and Sebastian with the Porters. There was a lot at stake, for she feared if either Cain or Vick learned they were swindled, they might take matters into their own hands and possibly both be killed. This weighed heavily on her, for Sebastian and Lee were evil men. *Perhaps I'll hide the money and wait for things to settle down. Now is not the time.*

It was late afternoon when Lucy drove up to the ranch. It was more stunning than she ever imagined. Elizabeth was in the yard with Jared, while Caleb was planting flowers for Elizabeth. Lucy was glad to see that Caleb made it to Woodville. *Now, I have a confidant*, she thought. All she hoped for was that he had not spilled the beans about why she stayed in San Augustine. *This could blow everything if Caleb told Cain, what he knew about Lee Tompkins and Sebastian cheating them out of the Plantation. I'll talk to him when I get him by himself*, she thought.

Elizabeth heard Lucy's car when she drove up. She was also embarrassed, for it had been a long time since she had seen her— at least two months. Cain had shared the news about Lucy and Sebastian with Vick and Elizabeth, and neither of them were ready to forgive her. They had seen Cain at his lowest ebb after he returned home from seeing Sebastian and Lucy together. They felt Lucy had abandoned her son and Cain.

Lucy walked up the path to her new home in awe of what she had missed by not being there to help Elizabeth. She had no idea how stunning the old Jackson place was having never seen it. Her original thought of Woodville was it would be a big step down from Pecan Plantation. What a surprise it was, for she liked it even though she had not seen what Elizabeth had done to the inside. The carriage house next door was the place Vick and Elizabeth had taken as their residence, and it too was very nice. Lucy spoke to Caleb and Elizabeth, but they seemed very quiet.

Seeing Jared again reminded her of all she had missed. She acknowledged Elizabeth, and then bent down to talk to Jared.

"Mama, missed you, son."

Jared had grown since she had seen him.

Caleb excused himself ostensibly to give the women privacy.

Lucy did not want to overwhelm her son, so she readdressed her attention. "Elizabeth, it's good to see you," she said, almost forcing Elizabeth to speak.

"Yes, it's been a while," she responded. For the first time, it was obvious that the family was not happy to see her. Lucy thought, if there is a misunderstanding she was sorry but for now all she wanted was to be at home with her husband and son.

"The men are at a cattle auction and won't be home until late," Elizabeth informed.

"I had no idea the house was so beautiful. Did you do all this?" Lucy asked.

"I had some help, but thank you. Would you like to see the inside?"

The rest of the evening was rather cool between Elizabeth and Lucy but they managed to be civil. Just before they set the table for supper, Cain and Vick walked in. Lucy ran into Cain's arms and held him. He didn't know what to do with her display of affection, for he wasn't feeling the same for her. He reluctantly held her looking at Vick who gave him a half-cocked look. "I'm so glad to be home. I missed you," Lucy said.

Cain was still very much in love with her, but he kept seeing the image of Sebastian and her together when he went to San Augustine to surprise her.

He was very abrupt! "Why are you here?" he asked.

She had not expected the unwelcoming way Cain responded to her.

"What do you mean? I'm finally home."

Elizabeth broke in and suggested they have supper before it became cold. This was not what I expected, Lucy thought.

After supper, the two women cleaned the kitchen without a word between them until Lucy broke the silence. "Elizabeth, do you mind telling me what's wrong with Cain?" Elizabeth thought it was a strange question after being away from her husband so long. "Lucy, you need to ask Cain. It's not my place to involve myself with yours and his business."

"Very well, I'll find out soon enough, I suppose." Not another word was spoken between them. For the first time, Lucy grew concerned that all was not right with the Porter family. As bad as she wanted to tell Cain and Vick about Sebastian and the money, she decided the risk was too great. She tried to convince herself that all she needed was a little more time to figure things out.

Later, Jared began warming up to her.

"Mama, why you been gone so long?" he asked. Cain listened intently to the conversation, for he was interested in what Lucy might say for herself.

"Mama, couldn't come home right away. There were things I had to do. But I'm home now." Jared hugged his mother's neck. "I'm glad your home Mama, I missed you."

Elizabeth and Vick felt very uncomfortable and gave each other the eye that it was time to leave. "We're going to call it a night. I expect we'll see y'all in the morning?" Vick said.

"Yeah, I'll be here," Cain answered.

"Wait Pa, before y'all go, do you mind taking Jared with you?"

Lucy had totally underestimated Cain's intentions. She walked over to Jared and kissed him goodnight.

"See you in the morning son."

As soon as Vick and Elizabeth closed the door, Cain jumped right into it with Lucy.

"Why are you here?" he asked. She was very troubled with the way he spoke to her.

"What do you mean, this is my home— isn't it?"

"It was before you started living on your own. You made it clear that your home was in San Augustine. That's where you've been for the last 2 months and you lied to me about going to Jonesboro to see Orson's grave. Lucy, no one makes a fool of me, not even you!"

"Cain, I can't explain things now but I ask that you trust me, that's all I ask." He was livid with her response.

"Trust you, why would I trust you when you've lied to me. I know you didn't go back to Jonesboro to see Orson's grave. All this time you've been in San Augustine and I need you to tell me why?" Cain had too much pride to admit to her he had seen Sebastian and her together. He wanted the truth without forcing it out of her.

"Cain please, I can't tell you!"

"Okay, if that's the way you want it—I'll be upstairs. You can have the downstairs bedroom to yourself. I don't want you anywhere close to me."

She was sure he was over-reacting. *She wondered what she had done to warrant such defiance? Perhaps I didn't know Cain as well as I thought!*

Chapter 15

SEBASTIAN WAS NOT HAPPY WHEN LUCY LEFT SAN AUGUSTINE, BUT there was nothing he could do. *She didn't even tell me goodbye.* Several days Later, Lee and Sebastian decided they should go back to the site where the Joiner brothers were murdered, and bury them. Sebastian was concerned about someone discovering the bodies.

Riding up to the site, the tent was still there, and the horses were tied to a tree as before. Sebastian walked over and unsaddled the horses and then slapped them on the rear-end. "Go find another home!" he shouted. The horses took off like scared rabbits, surely in search of water.

"I suppose the horses would've died if we hadn't come back," he said sarcastically.

"They're just horses," Lee mumbled. "Give me a hand and we'll pile the bodies in the tent and burn everything— even the saddles. Ain't nothin' these outlaws had worth keeping."

They placed handkerchiefs over their noses to help combat the stench. Afterwards, they rolled up the bodies in the tent, resting the saddles on top. Lee took out a match and lit the makeshift pyre watching the orange and blue flames encircle the area they prepared to torch.

"May you burn in peace," Lee said. "Now let's get outta' here," he shouted.

After returning to the cabin where they hid the money, Lee took his bowie knife and walked into the cabin ready to pry open the floor. He looked around as though he could sense someone had been there. Lee was breathing hard as he pried open the plank that covered the money. He reached down to retrieve the two bags, when cold sweat popped out on his forehead.

"What the hell!" he shouted. "Someone has stolen the damn money!" He looked at Sebastian.

"Do you know anything about this?"

"Don't look at me, I didn't steal the money!"

"Ain't nobody but me and you knew about the money. You better start talking!"

"Maybe you took the money and you're trying to blame it on me, or just maybe someone followed us that day and found out where we hid it. Remember we thought we heard someone after we killed the two brothers?"

They were livid, cursing and shouting obscenities-—both in a tirade.

"I knew I was right! Someone was watching us. Now they have the money," Lee continued to anguish.

"What are we going to do now?" Sebastian asked, not expecting an answer.

After they left the cabin they rode at full speed until they got to the ranch. Once there, Sebastian put on a pot of coffee.

"We gotta figure this out."

"Where is your helper?" Lee asked. Sebastian thought that was a strange question amid what just happened.

"She left. I thought I told you she had an emergency and had to go home."

"So, she left, huh?" Lee asked. "When did she leave?"

"You don't think she had something to do with this money, do you?" Sebastian quizzed.

"Well, she's a mighty pretty little thing that I imagine likes money. I imagine you liked her working for you, didn't you?"

"Lee, I'm telling you—don't go there with me."

"If I were you I'd think it's rather strange, she left about the same time the money went missing! Here someone stole our money and Miss Goodie-two-shoes, who just happens to live next door and works for you, ups and leaves town. When did she leave?"

Sebastian took a moment and then quietly answered.

"She left the day after we came back from hiding the money."

"This means if it's her, she's on to us," Lee said.

"Sebastian, think back. Was there anything unusual that happened during that time?" Sebastian became nervous after he remembered Lucy's lights were out the same night they returned from hiding the money at the cabin. He thought it strange that she would not hear him knock on her door.

"Lee, maybe she did steal the money!"

"Second thought, it ain't possible. No woman could ride like that unless she's an expert. I don't think that pretty little thing has it in her to ride a horse like that," Lee said.

"I don't think you know Lucy Porter like I do. I've rode with her. She can handle a horse better than most men. She's tough," he said.

Lee saw a look in Sebastian's eyes and knew he was telling the truth. I had to know for sure, he thought. Lee thought back to the time Lucy came into his office. She was livid, for the bank was about to foreclose on the plantation.

"Well, if it's her, we have problems—she's a sly one. Where did she go?" Lee asked.

"They're living in Woodville. I think they bought a home there." Sebastian answered.

"In Woodville, huh! I got me a little piece of land there myself.

"Thinking back, I was surprised when she left a note that she had a family emergency. She gave the impression that there were problems with her husband, but I guess not. Now I wonder why she stayed behind and didn't leave with her husband. Doesn't make sense." Sebastian was deeply stressed now that he thought Lucy had ulterior motives working for him.

Lee was sure Lucy had something to do with the disappearance of the money.

"Sebastian, we need to find her. She may have seen you shoot those two men. I mean us, shoot the men. He saw the look on Lee's face and decided to correct what he had said.

I hope it's not a waste of time but if it's her, we need to find out, and quick. We'll leave early in the morning." Lee ordered.

~

Lucy's first night home was very stressful to the point of being traumatic. Her secret was causing great harm to her relationships with the people she loved, and who loved her. *I cannot place my family in danger, she kept reminding herself. So far, the only good to come out of my return was seeing Jared. But I'm to blame for all of this*, she thought.

The next morning, she walked over to Elizabeth's to fetch her son, when she saw Caleb. He knew if he stayed in San Augustine and they found out he was the one who started Lucy on this journey, that he would be killed.

Lucy waved at him as he left the smokehouse. "Caleb," she shouted! He didn't let on the day before, but he was relieved to see Lucy was safe, since he had warned her about Lee and Sebastian.

"Miss Lucy, I was worried about you," he said.

"Caleb, how long have you been here?"

"I been here a couple of days. I rode to Carthage first where they had that big bank robbery. I was gonna ask for a job, but after the robbery they didn't need any new hires."

"Caleb, I have to talk to you about Lee Tompkins and Sebastian. You were right about them. I hope you haven't spoken to Cain about what we talked about."

"No, I ain't said a thing, I thought I would leave that up to you."

"There's been a lot happen since I last saw you. When we get a chance, I want to tell you what happened after you left San Augustine."

"Miss Lucy, I hated seeing you stay behind when your family moved on without you, but you understand why I had to leave when I did?"

"You needn't feel guilty," Lucy explained.

"Well, I do, 'cause all this time you've been in San Augustine risking your life, and I'm the only one knowing why."

Lucy started to walk away and then stopped. "Caleb, do you mind going over to see Seth Jackson and ask if he can meet with me? I need to see what kind of man will be helping raise my son."

"Yes ma'am. You want me to give him a time?"

"Tell 'em 4:00 o'clock this afternoon or same time tomorrow if he's too busy."

Caleb still hadn't seen Seth, so he had no way of knowing the Seth he knew was a fraud. After hearing his old friend had met with some misfortune, he was looking forward to catching up since he heard Seth had been released from prison. *They got it wrong sending Seth to jail for killing his Pa.* Caleb remembered Seth's father as a sorry individual. He knew if Seth shot his Pa he was provoked into doing so. *The man I know wouldn't do something like that*, he thought.

Caleb was only a short distance from Seth's place when he saw three men talking together in front of the house Seth supposedly lived in. He quickly turned his horse around and rode as fast as he could back to the Porters. Caleb jumped from his horse and ran to the back door of the house to see Lucy. He waved his hat and she came out to see what had him in such a stir.

"Miss Lucy, they've come after me!"

"Who you talking about? Slow down and catch your breath, now start all over. Now, who did you see?"

"Mr. Tompkins and Mr. Sebastian. I saw them at Seth's place talking to another man, but he didn't look like Seth. Miss Lucy, did you let on that I told you about them?"

Her heart fell, for she hadn't expected Lee and Sebastian to show up so soon. They know, she thought. She was frightened, but she tried not to let on.

"Caleb, they know nothing about you. Get down off your horse and walk with me to the barn. Caleb knew she had something important to tell him about why Tompkins and Sebastian were there.

After they reached the barn she explained what happened. "I saw them shoot two men in cold blood and before the men were shot Lee called them the Joiners. I think they saw me. Caleb, I was frightened, but I followed them anyway, and then that's when I saw the two big bags. They were filled with lots of money, maybe even hundreds of thousands of dollars."

"Miss Lucy, how ya' know it was money in them sacks?"

"Because I stole it from them."

"You what?" Caleb couldn't believe what she was saying.

"Yes, I followed them and saw where they hid the sacks and then waited until they left. After that, I found the money.

Caleb reluctantly asked. "And where is the money now?"

"I have it hidden until I can figure this thing out. Caleb, can I count on you to look out for me? You mustn't tell Mr. Cain anything about what I have shared with you. I don't want to get him, or Vick killed. Do you understand?"

"I'll do what you ask, but I think you're placing yourself in a lot of danger. You need someone to help you. Now, they know you saw them kill those men."

"Caleb before the men died, I heard them talking about a steamboat down in Beaumont. This is when I heard one of 'em say they wanted their money for killing Packer Rover and their share of the robbery. I suppose the money I have is the Joiner's share of the robbery."

"Miss Lucy, you've got yourself in a mess of trouble and there ain't nothing I can do about it. I reckon they killed those men 'cause they didn't find out where them accounting books where hidden."

"And without those books there's nothing I can do to protect myself or my family. Caleb, I'm sure Lee and Sebastian have figured out that I'm the one who stole their money. They're probably on their way here, right now!"

"Miss Lucy, I should have never told ya' about Mr. Tompkins. Just look at what's happened 'cause I opened my big mouth. Now you're over your head and there's nothin' I can do if you won't let me tell Mr. Cain what's going on."

"I don't want you worrying about me. Do you have any idea why they're talking to Seth Jackson?"

"Miss Lucy, that man I saw ain't the Seth Jackson I know."

"Well, people change and I'm sure being in prison didn't help." Lucy thought Caleb was wrong about Seth.

Lucy was one who could never be underestimated and now it was time to say goodbye. She had to leave before Lee and Sebastian saw her. *I must try and talk to Elizabeth—perhaps she will understand.*

Elizabeth was completely confused when Lucy ran to tell her to take care of Jared. "I know you don't understand, but I have to go." Lucy tried to explain as much as she could. "Elizabeth, you have always trusted me. Whatever you think, I have always put my family first and this is what I am doing now. I wish you could find it in your heart to believe in me."

"But how are you going to live? You need money and I do not have it to give."

"Elizabeth, please don't worry about me taking care of myself, just take care of my son."

Lucy ran inside and grabbed her suitcase, which still had her clothing in it.

Before she left she mentioned Orson and how Elizabeth always trusted him. All I ask is to please trust me as you did my daddy. I know you don't understand, but I'm doing this to protect my family.

Despite the anger, Elizabeth grabbed Lucy and held her. For the first time, she thought there was a thread of truth in what Lucy was telling her. Before Lucy left she bent down to talk with Jared,

"Always remember how much your mama loves you." Lucy clung to her son and then locked eyes with Elizabeth. "I'm sorry—I have to go." She fought back tears as she gave Elizabeth one last hug. Elizabeth watched from a distance as Lucy loaded her car and left.

How am I going to break the news to Cain that Lucy left.

I have no idea what's going on with her but there was something different about her when she mentioned protecting the family, Elizabeth fretted.

Cain was visibly upset when Elizabeth told him that Lucy left.

"I don't know what's got into her. She never showed this side before we married. Something is going on and it has to do with Sebastian Parker."

"Cain all she said, was how much she loved you and to trust her. I'm not ready to pass judgement on Lucy and I don't think you should either."

Lucy was well on her way to Beaumont when Sebastian Parker and Lee Tompkins drove up to talk with Cain. Lee was careful not to accuse Lucy of anything since Cain was a lawyer. They pretended to be there out of concern since the Porters had hard feelings when they lost Pecan Plantation. They also mentioned purchasing Orson's house and the 5 acres of land that is connected to their property, the one Lucy had been living in.

Vick was glad he did not have to answer questions.

It was hard not to show contempt for Sebastian since Cain was under the impression that Lucy and Sebastian were romantically involved.

"What can I do for you men?" Cain asked.

"If you don't mind, we'd like to speak to your wife?" Lee asked.

Elizabeth broke in before Cain could speak.

"What makes you men think Lucy is here? The last we heard she was in San Augustine." Cain looked at his mother rather sharply but knew to go along with what Elizabeth said.

"My wife's not here, but perhaps you, Sebastian, would know since my wife has been living within eyes view of your plantation?"

Sebastian saw fire in Cain's eyes. *Perhaps Lucy skipped out on all of them*, Sebastian thought.

Cain did not believe for a minute they were there for the reason they fabricated, but he went along with their charade. He was convinced the reason they were there was because Sebastian loved Lucy and wanted her to leave with him. In Cain's opinion, nothing they said held any merit. Plus, he respected that his mother had reason to say what she did.

"We knew how upset Mrs. Porter was when ya'll lost the plantation," Lee said. "Please give her our regards when you see her."

After Lee and Sebastian drove away, they were uncertain if Cain was telling them the truth. "There's something funny going on," Lee said. After they rode past Seth's place, he thought about the property he acquired in Woodville after foreclosing on a poor widow.

"Sebastian, we need to stay in Woodville and keep an eye on the Porters. I'd be willing to bet that woman has our money."

"What about my plantation?"

"I don't give a damn about your plantation," Lee retorted.

"We got men who can take care of business while we're out of town. Right now, I've got to find this Porter woman who has outsmarted us."

Sebastian was having a difficult time believing a sweet, pretty lady like Lucy had it in her to steal.

"Lee, I've been thinking. I don't think Lucy stole the money. What if we have it all wrong and it's someone else?"

"She's got our money alright! Couldn't you tell Cain Porter was lying? He knows where she is. She has a son and there's no way she's gonna stay away from that boy of hers. I figure we'll still be here when she comes home."

Chapter 16

Aggie feared that Cain was a step closer to finding out she was alive. She was troubled until Bidzill took her in his arms and kissed her. At that moment, she knew her feelings were undeniable. He was soft and caring toward her, more so than anyone she remembered. She even loved him more when he offered to go in search of her son.

There was something very intriguing about Bidzill. She found him to be more spirit than substance. She was certain this trait reflected his Indian heritage, which made him even more appealing to her. He seemed genuine, but at the same time she sensed he was part of a mystery she had yet to discover.

Her love continued to grow, and soon she found a connection far greater than friendship. She loved everything about him; from his coiffured long black hair pulled smoothly back into a knot, to his tan skin and blue eyes. Being half Indian, Bidzill stood stately and proud, but favored the white man since he did not have the dominantly chiseled features that most Indians have.

Late May was considered out of season for the Stepper because of upstream water levels in the Neches River. During this time, hauling cotton was considered out of season. Like many times before when the steamboat was in port, Aggie would stand on the balcony watching boats come and go. There were only a few scheduled excursions to Galveston, and during the major part of the summer the Stepper remained in port. Aggie stayed aboard as much as possible so as not to be seen in Beaumont. She feared she would never have a life beyond the Steamer for being seen by Cain, or someone who might know him would be devastating.

One such evening, as she watched the moon glow dance across the Neches River, Bidzill found Aggie standing at the railing. He imagined her thoughts were a million miles away. Since they had kissed before, but denied their passion for each other, Bidzill decided it was time to make his move. Seeing her standing there, he wondered what she might be thinking. *Perhaps she's thinking of me.* He hadn't planned on marriage at the time, but something inside urged him to go into the Captain's quarters, where he fetched a box that he had held dear to him since he was a young boy. He knelt to the floor and pulled out a black slender box from underneath his bed. It was aged with time and resembled a small suitcase.

Aggie was curious when she saw Bidzill walking toward her carrying a box, however, the glow in his eyes seemed to penetrate through her heart and into her soul. He set the box down and then pulled her close to him. She did not resist as he kissed her more passionately than before.

"I had to do that," he whispered. "Aggie, I think you know how I feel about you!" They clung together as their embrace lingered on. Their feelings were very intense, but Bidzill refused to take advantage of the woman he loved before marriage. Knowing how important she was to him, he opened the box and pulled out two magnificent leather robes that had been given to him by his adopted father. Bidzill's mother had given the robes to Dr. Franklin before she died, and requested that he give the robes to her son before he married.

As a young man, Bidzill became more and more aware of his Indian culture, and along with that knowledge came the significance of the robes. Bidzill cherished them for what they meant. They were a special gift from his mother, who intended for her son to marry with the same moral standards and guidelines she had. Both robes were rolled up and bound with a thin white rope.

"What have we here? Aggie asked.

"Wait right here and I'll explain." Bidzill went to the his cabin and came back with a wash pan of water.

Aggie, before I explain this tradition to you, I want to ask if you'll marry me.

She was taken completely off guard.

"Bidzill, are you sure?"

"I am as sure as I am standing here; I want you to be my wife. Please do me the honor and say yes."

It did not take her long to reply, and when she said yes, they kissed and clung to each other like two lovers who had been reunited.

Afterwards, Bidzill untied the white rope and opened the box with Aggie looking on.

"These are ceremonial robes that represent my people's heritage, and this pan of water represents purity. Bidzill took a deep breath and took the robes from the box. "Aggie Dawson, I am asking you to take this robe and wear it as my wife." There was something very special and endearing as he slipped her arms into the robe. In turn, he slipped into his robe and then took her hands and washed them. The minute her hands touched the water there was a warm feeling that she had never felt before. It was though she and Bidzill were whisked away to another time and place. There was a spiritual awaking of their souls and she immediately felt a presence. It was a spiritual encounter that was so convincing, she wept. Bidzill wiped her eyes. "Don't cry, I don't want to see you cry," he said. He smiled and wiped her tears again. She looked at him as if she was under his spell. The ceremony was magical and Bidzill could feel his great grandfather's spirit, Chief Atsa's, the exalted Navajo chief who died on the trail to Bosque Redondo (the trail of tears). A shudder went up and down Aggie's spine as she became aware of who Bidzill really was. She heard the singing of his ancestors who suffered unmerciful death on the trail of tears to Bosque Redondo—yet there were no people to be seen. She felt that she had crossed the threshold into the spiritual realm that only the chosen could enter. Before the ceremony was over Bidzill, spoke a few words in his native tongue, reciting poems he had learned as a child, and afterwards slipped into the white man's culture by pulling a ring from his pocket. "Aggie, this ring I give to you as your husband." She held her hand out as he slipped it onto her finger.

She was spellbound by the sparkling diamond.

"Bidzill, this is beautiful. When did you get this?"

"My white father gave it to me before he died. I am from two cultures and this ring represents the white man that's in me."

She held her hand out and looked at the ring. "I'm without words, she whispered. It's more than I ever imagined."

"Now that I have slipped this ring onto your finger, I have fulfilled the tradition of both my people."

"Does this mean we are married?" Aggie asked.

"Yes, we are married."

Before she knew it, she was swept from her feet and carried to her cabin. Once inside, she walked to her cedar chest and chose a nightgown that she imagined would be special enough for her wedding night. As she changed he watched with great anticipation.

As he gazed at this breathtaking Beauty, she slithered into her gown and then walked toward him.

There was no surprise, displeasure, or self-consciousness, nothing to keep them from each other. When he reached for her, she was like a bird sailing into his arms. Without a word, he lifted her to his sensual kiss. "Aggie, you are everything to me." Her heart was beating so fast that it was hard to breathe.

Their feelings were heightened as they journeyed into the soft moments of their affection. It was a glorious experience beyond her imagination as their bodies became one. As they lay beside each other

Aggie felt unimaginable tranquility, and for the first time their hearts overflowed with love. *What more can I hope for, except one day I am re-united with my son*, Aggie thought.

The next morning, she awoke and immediately felt for Bidzill, but he was not there. For a moment, she thought she had dreamt the events of last evening until, she saw him gazing out the window of her bed-room. She watched him for a moment. *I can't believe we married*, she thought.

"Bidzill, is something wrong?"

"No, I was thinking about your boy. If I'm to find your son, I must go now before the summer is over. I will have Winston do the piloting in my place. I think it's time you found out about your boy."

Aggie could not hold back her sobs, he really does care, she thought.

Bidzill took her in his arms. "You mustn't cry. Everything will be alright."

Before he left, they spoke about the trip and where he should go. She suggested he go first to her place in Woodville, and then on to San Augustine.

"Bidzill whispered in her ear. "I'll be back soon, I promise."

Within the hour, he was packed and ready to leave.

Chapter 17

It was late evening when Lucy arrived in Beaumont exhausted from worry. Her foremost plan was to find a clean boarding house, and stay put until she sensed everything back in Woodville had settled down. She hated to part with Jared, and leave Cain without an explanation, but her hope was he'd believe that she left him and Jared for the safety of her family. In the meantime, she assumed there was well over two hundred thousand of stolen money in the two heavy bags. Frightened and alone, she stopped in front of a yellow boarding house just before she entered Beaumont. It was like history repeating itself, for the house was where Cain stayed many years ago when he had amnesia, however she had no clue.

Miss Josey met Lucy at the door, as she did all her guest.

The minute the landlord opened her mouth and said, "Welcome child," Lucy felt right at home.

Afraid that someone might come searching, she introduced herself as Ginny Smith.

The next morning when she went to breakfast, Miss Josey had a special meal waiting for her. All the guests had left and it was just the two of them enjoying the morning together.

"Ginny, what brings you to Beaumont?"

"I'm looking for a place to stay—a permanent place," Lucy replied.

"A permanent place, hmmm… If you give me a couple of days I might think of someone."

"Thank you, I would appreciate anything you can do for me."

The rest of the day was spent thinking of what trouble she was in and if anything would ever be normal again.

The next day, Miss Josey had a place in mind.

"Ginny dear, I know of a widow woman who lost her husband several years ago who has offered you a place to stay. I rang her up, and she said she would like to meet you. Would it be possible to meet with her today?" Lucy thought the name Martha Cormack was familiar, but had momentarily forgotten Martha was the same lady that had taken Cain in when he had amnesia. There was no way the two could connect since neither of them knew each other.

"Yes ma'am, I'll plan on going today if you think she's ready for me." Lucy felt great relief knowing she found a place to stay.

"I 'spect she'll be waiting with bells on. Now you go get ready 'cause I don't want you driving after dark."

Lucy hoped to find Miss Cormack the same as Miss Josey--sweet and understanding.

"Miss Josey, how far is it from Beaumont?"

"Not too far. It's on the way to a little town called Nederland. Ain't much there, mostly farming. Have you heard of Nederland?"

"No ma'am, I'm from Jonesboro, Arkansas."

"Hmm, seems I've heard of Jonesboro. I guess it'll come to me later," Miss Josey said.

"Ginny, before you leave I'll have a little map for ya."

Lucy was very nervous, when she drove up to the ranch and saw Martha outside waiting– she relaxed. Suddenly it came to her who Martha was and recalled Cain talking about her.

The closer she got to the sprawling ranch house the more excited she became, knowing she would soon be meeting the woman who became like a mother to Cain when he had amnesia. So, this is the place Cain stayed the two years he was lost to us.

The Cormack ranch was nothing but barren ranch land with several huge rose bushes and a herd of Herefords grazing in the distance, just as Miss Josey said. There was also an old barn, bunkhouse with farm tools laying around and a big stone water well in front of the house.

She parked her car and then walked up the steps to meet Martha.

"Hello, I'm Ginny Smith---you must be Mrs. Cormack." Lucy felt a sense of connection with Martha from hearing Cain talk about the Cormack's. She hugged Martha like she'd known her forever.

"I can tell we're going to get along just fine," Martha said. Why don't you step inside and let's get acquainted?" Lucy had seen all she needed to see to make her decision. She knew she had come to the right place.

"Martha, I don't know if Miss Josey told you, but I won't be staying very long."

"Well, as long as you're here I want you to feel like you're at home. You can stay as long as you like."

Martha had sized Lucy up and knew she would be pleasant to be around. She had missed Glen immensely after he died, and having someone like Lucy, would be very comforting to be around."

"We'll just take it a day at a time, but you're welcome to stay as long as you need. I have your room all ready for you. Why don't I get one of my men to help you bring your things in.

"Ooh, don't worry. I don't have much." Lucy was very protective of her two bags of money, and knew she would have to wait until after dark to bring them in.

"Well then, why don't I show you to your room?"

Lucy grabbed her suitcase, then followed her to another part of the house that had its own sitting area with a nice large bedroom across the hall. It had been Glen's room before he died. At one time, Martha used the bedroom, but after Glen's death she never had the desire to stay there again.

After breakfast, Lucy went back to her room and reorganized the closet, so she could hide the money bags. They should be safe here, she thought.

The next few days were spent helping Martha around the house and exploring the ranch. She loved to ride, and there were plenty of horses of which to choose if she decided to do so. In late afternoon, there were always batches of cookies, cakes, coffee, and long talks with Martha. To be away from Cain was miserable, but living with Martha and having Butch around made it much easier.

Butch Clark, Martha's right-hand man, was a lot like Orson, and Lucy related to him right away. After Martha's husband died Butch missed the old place and returned to help her run the ranch

Chapter 18

CALEB CONTINUED TO WORRY ABOUT THE MAN WHO CLAIMED TO BE Seth. *That man, ain't Seth and something fishy is going on*, he thought. The man had no resemblance to his childhood friend, and this worried him. *Miss Elizabeth needs to know that man ain't Seth*. One afternoon. Caleb spoke with Elizabeth about his suspicions.

"I can't tell much from a distance, but there ain't nothing about that man that reminds me of Seth. He don't walk like 'em, he's shorter, and Seth didn't have no limp."

"Caleb, you seem to forget that it's been years since you last saw him. People change, and you can't go accusing when you have no proof."

Caleb was very convincing, yet she was still careful not to cast doubt.

"I think it's time I do a little snooping for you," he said.

"Don't do it for me—you're the one who has the problem. If Seth finds out it could mean trouble for Cain, and I don't want that!"

"Miss Elizabeth, don't you think you need to know who the man really is? If he ain't Seth, then why is he pretending to care about little Jared?" Caleb asked.

"Of course, but the way you're going about it sounds risky, and if Seth finds that someone has broken into his house or suspects him, then Lord knows what could happen!"

"Ma'am, don't you worry—I ain't breaking in his house. If that man's Seth, he'll know me."

Elizabeth hadn't known Caleb long, but she knew he was sincere.

After Caleb left, Sonny came by unannounced to take Jared for a ride. Elizabeth was concerned, yet polite as she greeted him. She wondered if there could be any truth to Caleb's claim. If so, she would expect Vick and Cain to find out.

"Ma'am, I hope I ain't calling at a bad time," Sonny said.

"Sorry, you've missed Cain…he's not here," she offered.

"I just thought I'd pop in on ya' 'cause it's a pretty day and I thought I'd take the boy on a little ride."

If only Caleb was here to question Seth's identity, she thought.

Elizabeth tried to think what to do, but she was taken off guard.

"Alright, I'll just check and see if Jared is awake." She excused herself and then walked into the house while Sonny stayed on his horse. "Yes, ma'am!" he answered.

Jared did not appear to be happy when Elizabeth told him Mr. Seth was there to take him for a ride. *Most boys would want to go*, she thought.

Reluctantly, Jared walked outside to go with Sonny. He did not want to tell his grandma that Seth frightened him.

"Well, well, ain't ya' growin' like a weed. You ready for a ride on this pretty day?"

Jared glared at him, for he remembered the last ride Sonny took him on.

"You take good care of our boy," Elizabeth instructed.

Jared looked at Elizabeth with an expression she had not seen before. *The boy looks frightened*, she thought.

Sonny spit his tobacco, then said, "Yes ma'am!"

Elizabeth wished Caleb had arrived before Jared rode away, but Cain had made it clear that Seth had his rights with the boy.

~

Caleb had no idea his former boss, Lee Tompkins, was in Woodville and was about to be seen. He wasn't two steps out of the bank when Sebastian spotted him.

"Well, I be dang if it ain't 'ole Caleb," Sebastian said. "Look at him…he don't know we're anywhere around." Lee was still upset with the way Caleb up and quit his job without telling him.

"Why do you think Caleb is in Woodville?"

"I don't know, but I have an idea. Let's follow him and see if I'm right."

They mounted their horses and followed Caleb until he rode near Seth's place. Without warning the two men rode up beside him and grabbed the horses bit, stopping Caleb on the spot.

"Ain't you a sight for sore eyes," Lee said.

Caleb winced with fright. He had that look of guilt written all over his face.

"What brings you to Woodville…or need I ask?" Lee questioned.

Caleb had to think fast, and being in front of Seth's place, he made up a story about being there to see his friend.

"I came here to see Seth Jackson. I saw him from a distance, but I'm thinking it ain't the Seth I know," Caleb stuttered.

"Why you suppose it's not him? Lee asked.

"Oh, I don't know, maybe 'cause it don't look like him." Caleb quickly realized he was speaking jibberish and tried again.

"Because Seth was sent to prison for murdering his Pa. You remember people talking about Seth Jackson about five years ago, don't ya? It was in all the papers." Caleb kept blabbing a mile a minute, hardly making any sense.

"I think you quit your job to come to work for the Porters. Why don't you admit it or maybe you have some reason you don't want me to know?" Lee countered.

"No sir! You got this all wrong 'cause I hardly know the Porters. I'm here to see Seth. When I see him I'll know if it's him." Caleb felt his face turn a fiery red.

"Why would the man be claiming to be somebody he's not?" Sebastian asked.

"Cause there's a lake of oil as big as the Spindletop underneath this ground. That's a good enough reason—don't ya' think? I'm thinking this is someone trying to cash in on Seth's bad luck, being in prison and all."

Caleb thought Lucy would not be happy with him breaking her confidence but he was frightened enough that he spilled his guts.

"Sounds like you know a lot of what's happening around here!" Sebastian mocked.

Caleb continued to make up stories about the oil rich land.

"I heard town folk talking about it, and that's why I got suspicious of Seth. Ain't no man gets released from the Huntsville Prison for killing a man unless they're taken out in a pine box," Caleb kinda liked the way he was telling his story and embellished as he went.

Lee's deceptive mind began plotting. As he listened to Caleb's gab, he thought he smelled oil. *Just maybe there's a hint of truth in what Caleb's saying.*

Lee was a master at stealing land, and since he owned a couple thousand acres in Woodville, one more piece wouldn't hurt, especially if it's oil rich land. *One man's loss is another man's gain*, he smiled inwardly.

"Well Caleb, whatcha' gonna do? We'd like to see if the man is who he says he is." Lee egged him on to see if he was telling the truth.

"I don't want to spring nothing on him, so if y'all don't mind, I'll be calling on him tomorrow," Caleb tried to resist.

"Now, you got me wondering! I say let's all meet Seth Jackson."

Caleb had no other choice but walk up to Seth's door and knock. All the while he was thinking of Lucy. *She would be in trouble if she suddenly arrived on the scene,* he thought. Caleb was also concerned about himself and what might happen if he stayed around. He knew Lee and Sebastian were up to no good and he didn't want to be caught in the crossfire.

He was relieved when there was no one to answer the door. He sighed and then walked back to his horse.

"Guess I'll be calling on Seth tomorrow!"

"Before you leave, where you staying?"

"Right now, I ain't staying nowhere. I just checked out of my place today—but I'll be around. Caleb was breathless by the time he walked back to his horse.

"Well, you may as well check yourself back in. I'm curious to find out if the man you're talkin' 'bout is Seth. I got a little business proposition to make with 'em," Lee shouted.

"See you tomorrow at the same time— here!" Lee called out as he rode away.

Reluctantly, Caleb replied, "Yeah, tomorrow…right here!"

Riding away, all Caleb could think about was finding Lucy. "I gotta get the hell outta' here before I get myself killed. Frightened of what might happen, he went in a direction he knew nothing about. He didn't even take time to pack for fear of being caught.

~

Traveling the backwoods was the safest, and as he journeyed farther into the woods he saw something that deeply disturbed him. A man and boy on horseback were riding together at a high rate of speed. Caleb recognized the boy's voice as he shouted, "stop, please stop," the boy cried over and over. *Jared's in danger*, Caleb realized.

"Shut your mouth!" he heard the man yell.

"Wait, that's Seth he's with!" Caleb said under his breath.

Riding at a moderate pace, he could see the boy acting up. Then the unimaginable happened. The boy was sent sailing through the air after being struck by Seth. Caleb cringed, for he knew a blow like that could kill the boy. "That's not the real Seth! That man ain't Seth at all!" he muttered out loud to himself. Reining his horse off the trail, he hid so he could spy on the stranger. *I must get to the boy before he finishes him off*, Caleb planned. The only thing, Caleb was afraid that the man would kill him and the boy too.

Bidzill had been following a hawk as it seemed to beckon him to follow. This is very strange, he thought. Coincidentally, or perhaps better explained as mysterious, Bidzill, Sonny, and Caleb converged simultaneously near the same lake. He watched as the hawk flew across the lake in a purposeful direction. Feeling a sense of urgency, he rode hurriedly around the edge of the lake just in time to see the hawk viciously attack a man standing over a boy lying on the ground.

It was something out of a dream as the hawk attacked the man posing as Seth. "I can't believe it," said Caleb. It's as though the hawk was there to save Jared. In a distance Caleb could see another man, who was in the nearby woods, racing toward the hawk and the man to save the boy. As the rider got closer Caleb noticed the man's long black hair. He must be part Indian, he thought. The instant the Indian reached the boy, the hawk flew away and Sonny managed to flee, leaving Jared behind with the Indian. Caleb was stunned by the strange experience, and somehow, he knew that the hawk and the Indian were there for only one reason, —to help Jared. He watched as the Indian knelt and cried out to the Great Spirit to help the boy. After a ceremony of incantations, he went to his saddlebag and pulled out a bottle that contained a liquid which he rubbed on the boy's forehead. There was a special aura about the Indian, Caleb sensed. In an instant, he knew there was no one better than the half-breed to take care of Jared. Having this consolation, Caleb just watched and waited until Bidzill rode away with the boy.

Caleb now felt a new surge of fortitude and was no longer concerned about himself, for he knew he had to find Lucy and tell her what happened. At least the Indian will protect Jared from the man posing as Seth. Caleb convinced himself that he was in too deep and had an obligation to Lucy but he allowed his fear to control him. *What good would it do if I'm dead*, he thought.

After administering to the boy, Bidzill instinctively turned his horse around and headed back to Beaumont. Wrapped in a saddle blanket, Jared was rushed aboard the Stepper, being carried by Bidzill. There was no need to try and find a doctor, for he had been well trained and knew more about medicine than those permitted to be doctors. Aggie saw Bidzill from a distance and sensed something was wrong. She ran toward him from the cabin. "My God, what happened?" she asked.

"Not now, I'll tell you later! Quick, get water."

Aggie hurried to her cabin and ran a pan full of water to assist Bidzill as he worked with the boy, trying to awaken him. "Aggie, stay here and wash the boy's face while I get my doctor's bag," he said.

"While he was gone, Aggie took the cloth and began wiping the blood from the young boy's face. It took only a few minutes before she slowly noticed a familiarity. When Bidzill walked through the door of her cabin she shouted,

"Bidzill, what have you done!?" He had no idea what she was talking about. "What do you mean?"

She turned to him, "This is my son...what did you do to him?"

"Aggie, what are you talking about? I'm trying to save this boy."

"Bidzill, this is Jared—not any boy, my boy!"

Shocked with reality, he pushed her aside. "I don't have time to explain, I have to save your son."

Bidzill examined every part of Jared's body while Aggie stood over him wringing her hands.

"Is Jared going to be okay?"

"I don't know, He may be seriously hurt, but I can't be sure. I can't find anything obvious on his body. He is breathing okay and his heartrate is good, but he's still unconscious. Only time will tell for now. I saw a man do this to your boy."

"You mean someone caused this? Oh my God, who could have done this?" She asked more sternly. "Please tell me what happened."

He knew better than tell her about the hawk, but he wanted to be honest.

"Aggie, I was riding through the woods on my way to Woodville and I saw a hawk. I don't expect you to believe what happened, but the hawk behaved like it was trying to get my attention. It circled above me and dove right above my head several times to get my attention. So, I followed it out of curiosity. This is when I saw a man standing over your son. There was a lake between us and there was no way I could get to them in time. He had picked up a large rock and was about to hit your boy when the hawk viciously attacked the man. Aggie, I couldn't believe what I was seeing, but if it wasn't for the hawk, Jared would not be with us."

Aggie gasped. "I've never heard of such."

"By the time I got to Jared, the man was gone—and the hawk flew away."

"Oh my God, I can think of only one man who would do this?" Aggie thought of her half-brother Jonathan whom she thought was still alive. She thought of the threat she was as one of the beneficiaries of the Petty estate.

"Bidzill, I think my step-brother did this."

Again, she explained that she was the living one who could send Jonathan to prison for killing her mother.

Bidzill could feel her pain as she bent down and kissed Jared on the forehead. Please God, don't punish my son because me." Bidzill could feel her agony and took her in his arms to comfort her.

"God is punishing me for giving my son away."

"Aggie, you did not give your son away. You allowed his father to take the boy and protect him. What do you plan to do?"

"I'm going to protect Jared— I have to."

"What about Cain, he'll be worried." Bidzill addressed.

"And what about the woman who has been caring for him like a mother?" Aggie retaliated.

She was angry that Cain and Lucy had failed her son.

"They haven't cared for him if they allowed something like this to happen. It was Cain's responsibility, not his wife's, to make sure our son was safe. I'm keeping Jared here with me. They had their chance and now it's up to me."

"Aggie, Cain has no idea you're alive and he's going to think the worst. You are not thinking clearly, and rightfully so. You may change your mind about things in the morning. Remember, we don't know how this happened."

"Bidzill, you don't really think I will change my mind, do you? All my efforts to protect Jared have been for nothing. Now, I'm going to protect my son. I'm his mother, and I won't sleep tonight until I know my child is going to live."

Bidzill could see the love Aggie had for her son, and she was not going to listen to him or anyone else.

"We'll sleep in shifts. Wake me if you notice any changes in him," Bidzill offered.

Chapter 19

Elizabeth began to worry when Seth failed to return with Jared. *I should have listened to Caleb after he warned me about Seth. What if he's right!*

As Elizabeth sat in the garden waiting for Jared, she noticed the wall of shrub, which offered no privacy, for anyone could be on the other side of the hedge without being detected, and there's no way to know when someone is driving up.

By coincidence in making her point, she was surprised when Seth suddenly appeared without Jared.

"Seth, where is my grandson?" She had little time to think of what might have happened to him.

Waiting for an answer, she watched as he tied his horse and walked slowly toward her with his hat in hand. She noticed his blood torn shirt in several places. Something is wrong, she imagined.

Sonny hoped his lying face would not give him away.

She walked slowly toward him with her hand over her mouth, waiting for him to explain. Deep down, she knew something dreadful had happened.

"Seth, please--where is Jared?"

"Miss Elizabeth, I don't know how to tell you this, but something bad happened to Jared."

"What do you mean—what happened to Jared?" Tears welled up in her eyes fearing that she might hear the unbelievable.

"Please?" she pleaded.

Sonny stood there fumbling with his hat and then began his story.

"An Indian came out of nowhere and ambushed us. I tried to fight 'em off but he was too much for me. He had friends hiding out in the trees ready to kill me and there was nothing I could do."

What Sonny said made no sense to Elizabeth. "I'm afraid I don't understand."

"Well, we were riding along when a half-breed stepped out in front of us. I tried to fight 'em off but in the end, he took the boy. See my shirt?" He turned around so she could see his torn and blood-stained clothing. Her mind was whirling, as she imagined what Cain might do when he heard someone took his son.

As fate would have it, Vick and Cain rode up at that very moment. It was almost as though their arrival was predetermined, for they showed up just when she needed them.

When Cain heard the news, he was not only furious but over-whelmed with grief and fear. Vick, more levelheaded at the time, spoke up.

"So, which way did the Indian go?"

"He left with the boy and rode into the woods. He was a half-breed up to no good with some of his friends. Plenty scary if ya' ask me."

By this time, Cain was pacing back and forth—a sure sign he was about to lose control.

"Pa, what are we going to do? I can't lose my boy."

Vick felt he had to pump information out of Sonny. Something ain't right here, he thought.

After Sonny repeated the story, he did a bit of embellishment to throw off suspicion. "That Indian had long hair pulled back in a knot on the back of his head. That's the best I can tell ya'. I think they were headed for Beaumont. I'm not saying for sure, but if I was the one hiding out, that's where I'd go."

Vick turned to Elizabeth who was visibly upset. He whispered in her ear. "Try to stay calm, we'll find the boy. Lizzie, do you think you can get us a few days rations ready? I'm leaving the car with you in case you drive into town. We'll be taking the horses, so we can check out the countryside and clear our heads."

"Where y'all going," she asked.

"We're going to Beaumont."

~

Aggie had been sitting by Jared's bed day and night when the boy slowly began showing signs of consciousness. She ran to Bidzill and asked that he come and look at her son.

"He's going to be alright—isn't he?"

"We won't know until he is fully conscious, but this is a good sign."

Aggie was overcome with joy at seeing Jared's arousal.

Bidzill prayed for the sake of his wife that her son would not be traumatized by what happened to him. Waking up to virtual strangers was sure to upset the boy. He wondered if Aggie was prepared for what could be heartbreak. He assumed that she imagined her son would wake up and recognize her.

On the fourth day, Jared's eyes began to flutter as if he was trying to wake up, but he remained in a coma. She would not leave his bedside. Her only priority now was to be there when he woke up. Finally, on the 5th day, Jared opened his eyes, but it was not what Aggie expected. She had not thought that far ahead. The boy lay there and looked around the room as though he was looking for someone. He kept looking at Aggie and then looking away time after time until he spoke.

"Where's my daddy?"

For the first time, she was in a dilemma for she did not know how to answer. She did not want to upset her son by shocking him.

"I want my daddy," Jared pleaded.

Aggie suddenly knew it was a mistake to keep Jared. I can't do this to him. It's not fair, she thought.

～

The next morning Cain and Vick arrived in Beaumont. Though exhausted from the trip, they went directly to the Sheriff's office to solicit help to find Jared. "Pa, the Sheriff has a poster file we can look through in case that Indian is a wanted man. Who knows, he may know of Indians kidnapping children."

After speaking with the Sheriff, they found that there were not wanted persons matching the description of the Indian in question.

"Sorry, I ain't been no help to ya', but if I hear of anything I'll be sure to let ya' know. Before you men go I'll need an address to git' back with ya'."

Cain filled out the form and then asked if there were any half-breeds in Beaumont that he knew of.

"Not to my recollection, son. If I hear or see any half-breeds I'll be sure and let you know. Now, good luck to ya'. I hope ya' find your son," the Sheriff said. I'll make sure all my men get this information.

The men shook hands and exchanged pleasantries before they left.

"Nice meeting you, Sheriff! We appreciate you keeping an eye open in case you or someone else might hear of an Indian kidnapping children."

The men left and went about interviewing people in every business they could find. One of the places they inquired was Miss

Josey's boarding house, where Cain stayed when he had amnesia. Although she was awfully glad to see him she knew nothing that could help.

~

To Aggie's dismay, Jared would regain consciousness for a few minutes and immediately slip back into his coma. She smiled at him when he asked for his daddy. Once he asked if she was his mother. She thought he was confused and therefore said, "Yes, Jared, I am your mama." He would smile and go back to sleep. This may be the only time I might have to admit to my son that I am his mother.

Annie Mae was puzzled when she heard that Bidzill was treating a boy for injuries. When she popped in to see the boy, it did not take long for her to piece together that the boy was Aggie's son Jared, a fact she had confided in her.

Aggie shook her head "yes" to Annie Mae, indicating that it was her boy.

"You best be resting up so you can get well," Annie Mae would say to Jared.

She looked at Aggie with the most pathetic look and then patted the boy before walking out of the room. What on earth is she going to do? The boy has no idea that Aggie is his mother. What a pity, Annie Mae thought.

Aggie fought back tears for she knew her confession to Jared could break his heart. The boy must go back to his family. I just need a few more days before I let him go. She was sure that her change of heart was what was best. He must go home, she surrendered.

~

After checking into Miss Josey's boarding house, Cain and Vick were greeted with a warm welcome, since Miss Josey often wondered what happened to Cain after he left Beaumont.

"Sakes alive, I was thinking about you just the other day, and now yer' here. This must be yer' Pa 'cause y'all look jest' alike. Nice ta' meet you. This boy of yours is a real fine man."

"Thank you, Miss Josey. I've heard a lot about you."

"What brings you back to Beaumont?" she asked.

"It's not good–my boys' been kidnapped."

"Oh no, I'm sorry to hear that! I didn't even know you had a son. You never told me that."

"Miss Josey, if it hadn't been for you, I would never had a place to stay while I was recovering. Martha and Glen treated me like a son and I'll never be able to repay you for what all you did for me. I reckon we'll be going by Martha's house when we leave here and I'll ask if she's heard of any Indians on the prowl. We've been told an Indian took my boy!"

"Cain, I wish I could help but all the Indians I know are peaceful and wouldn't hurt a flea. Now, before y'all go, I have a good meal waiting in the kitchen. Cain, why don't you show yer' Pa where he can wash up…you remember where it is, don't ya?"

Cain looked at his Pa and smiled. "Yes ma'am, I reckon I do."

~

Lucy and Martha became the best of friends and it wasn't long before she was helping around the ranch, taking on chores that Martha couldn't do herself.

Each time she completed a task, Martha would tell her how she loved having a good girl around.

She thinks that now, but what would she think if she knew I was hiding thousands of dollars that belonged to the Carthage Bank? How would I ever explain that? she thought.

Every now and then, Lucy would ride into Beaumont and visit the ship channel, in hopes of seeing Lee and Sebastian doing something illicit that might incriminate them. She found that the steamer was making excursions to and from Galveston two and three times a week. She planned to be aboard on one of those trips. She would use time aboard the Stepper to search for any possible clue as to where the books might be hidden. *I'll wait until the weekend when many people travel, so as not to draw attention to myself.*

The next day, Cain and Vick decided to ride out to the Cormack ranch to see Martha. It happened to be the same day Lucy drove to Beaumont.

It was in the early morning hours when she left, but just before she reached the outskirts of town she saw two men who looked a lot like Cain and Vick. It can't be them, she thought. Unsure of who the men were, she shopped in her favorite store instead of boarding the Stepper. After a full day, she drove back to Martha's.

~

Martha was outside doing chores when she saw two horsemen riding up to the house.

She walked toward the horses, wiping her hands on her apron, when she recognized one of the riders. Why that's Cain!

Happy to see her, he slipped out of the saddle and grabbed Martha, swinging her around.

"Now, what do we have here?" She asked.

"It's been too long," Cain replied.

"Ain't you a sight for sore eyes. What are you doing in town?" she asked.

"Martha, it's not what you think. My boy's been kidnapped and we're trying to find the man who has him. I thought it'd be a shame to come this way and not stop and see you. I also want to ask if you know of any half-crazed Indians up to no good?

She didn't hear anything he said after, Jared had been kidnapped. "Oh no! That sweet child! I can't believe someone would do such a thing! Cain, do you have any idea who might have taken him?"

"We're looking for a half-breed. We have an eyewitness who said he fought with the Indian until he was overpowered and that's when Jared was taken."

"I declare, I can't believe an Indian would do such a thing. The Indians we know keep to themselves and they're peaceful. This is the first time I've heard of an Indian kidnapping. Have you been to the Sheriff's Office?"

"Yeah, but he didn't have much to offer.

Martha, I hate we can't stay longer but we have to make time while it's still daylight."

"I'm so sorry—I hope you find 'em. Please let me know."

"By the way, this is Vick—my Pa."

"I see a strong resemblance between you two."

"Miss Martha, Cain's told me a lot about you and your husband," Vick said.

"I wish you had time to come in and sit a spell but I know y'all are in a hurry. Just a minute, I have something for you."

She ran into the house and brought out a sack of cookies.

"Now, you take these and be careful. You don't know what you're gonna be up against."

"Cain took the sack and smelled it. "I bet I know what this is," he said, jokingly.

"They're yer' favorite. I must have had a premonition that you were coming."

"Well, thank you, I'll be seeing you after all this is over."

"By the way, I'd like to meet that wife of yours."

"That's a story for another time. I hope you understand."

Martha could see the pain in his face.

"You've got a lot on your plate—don'tcha?"

"I'm afraid I do. Good to see you again."

Martha walked over to Vick and shook his hand.

"It's so good to meet you. That son of yours is a good boy. You should be very proud."

"I am—his mother did a good job raising him," Vick answered. Cain looked at his Pa and smiled. No mistake, he loved hearing those words from Vick.

As they rode away, Martha felt a great sadness. *I pray Jared is still alive.*

Later that afternoon, Lucy came in from shopping and Martha was crying. "Is something wrong?" she asked.

"Yes, honey. I've just received some bad news. A young man who used to live here stopped by and told me his boy was kidnapped. I wish you had been here, so you could have met him. He's such a good man and I hate what's happened. He's had such a hard life and he doesn't deserve what's happened."

Lucy had no idea what Martha was talking about.

"I can't think of anything more horrible than having a son kidnapped. I hope he finds who did it," Lucy replied.

"He said a half-breed kidnapped the boy, but I don't know of any half-breeds around here."

Lucy remembered meeting Bidzill, whom she knew was a half-breed but much too kind to do something like that.

"Martha, I met a man who was half Indian on the High Stepper—you know the steamboat that runs back and forth from Beaumont to Galveston? But it can't be him—he's not the type.

"Honey, you never know in this day and time. I wish I would have known that before they left."

Lucy was certain Bidzill could not have done anything that despicable.

The next morning, Lucy found Martha crying again.

"Martha, what can I do? You're taking this much too hard. I'm concerned."

"If you only knew. Jared was such a sweet boy, and on top of that I think Cain's wife left him. I love him as much as my own son and that boy was a joy the entire time he stayed with me."

She sat down with a thump. "Martha, did I hear you right? Did you say Jared?"

Lucy was dying inside. "Oh no, not my son," she thought.

Martha noticed a change in Lucy.

"Dear, have I upset you? With all my crying, I didn't mean to trouble you."

"I had no idea you were talking about Jared Porter and his father!" She began crying as she explained that Jared is her son, and that she had tried to protect Cain from knowing the plantation had been stolen from them. She told Martha the entire story, so she would understand.

Martha's head was spinning with all the information that Lucy kept secret. Hearing how she plotted to expose Sebastian and Lee as frauds, and the danger she had placed herself in by taking the stolen money from the men who robbed the Carthage Bank was almost too much to grasp.

"Martha, I have to leave and go home. Cain needs me now more than ever."

"Lucy, you need to stay here. If you go home, you won't be helping Cain one bit--not now while he's looking for Jared. Please let me help you. We'll figure this out."

That night as she tried to sleep, she dreamt about Jared and what might have happened to him. She blamed herself. Cain hates me, she thought.

During the night, she came up with another possibility, which hadn't occurred to her. *What if Sebastian and Lee have figured out it was me who stole the money, and they had an Indian kidnap Jared. Yes, that must be it. They know that if they kidnapped Jared that was a sure way of bringing me out of hiding—and then they would force me to give them the money. I must go home and explain everything to Cain. Somehow, he must understand that what I did was to help our family.*

When Lucy came to breakfast the next morning, she had her bags packed and ready to go.

"Martha, last night it finally came to me that Sebastian and Lee might be holding Jared until I come forward with the money. I hope you understand that I must leave."

"Lucy, are you sure that's the right thing to do? You'll be risking your life and possibly your entire family."

"I can't think about that now. What I did was inexcusable, and I should have moved with Cain when he moved to Woodville. Once I tell him the truth I hope he can forgive me."

"You don't worry, I know Cain very well and he's a fair man. After you tell him what happened he'll understand and love you more for it."

"Let's hope. My husband was vulnerable when he lived with you, but a lot has happened since then and he's changed quite a bit."

She hugged Lucy's neck and then walked with her to the car.

Like always, food was prepared for Lucy's travel.

"Dear, you take this with you in case you get hungry."

"Now I know why Cain loves you so much. You've been a mother to me just like you were to him," Lucy explained.

Martha wiped her eyes on her apron.

"You both are just like family to me," she cried. Lucy, I'm not going to rest until I know y'all have found Jared."

"Martha, please be strong and pray!"

She started her car and then rolled down the window.

"Martha, I hope you know I never meant to hurt Cain. After we get our lives back together we'll be back."

She cranked her car and drove away.

"Be careful!" Martha called out.

Chapter 20

Lee and Sebastian expected to meet Caleb in front of Seth's place, but after waiting several hours they figured that he had run out on them.

"I shoulda' known that he wouldn't show. I could see it in his eyes," Lee complained.

"Wonder where he is." Sebastian asked!

"No telling! I bet that Lucy gal and him are in cahoots with each other–that lying devil, I ain't placing a bit of stock in what he told us about oil being on that land. What did he say the man's name was?"

"I think it was Seth or something like that. His name should be on the mailbox."

They nudged their horses and trotted to the mailbox. Lee opened the box and pulled out a letter from the Huntsville Prison. They examined the envelope that was addressed to Aggie Jackson.

"You reckon it's his wife?"

Lee held the envelope up to his nose and gave a cursory sniff. "I'm about to strike oil," he said.

"Hold on--let's make sure Seth ain't home. I would hate for him to see us messing with his mail," Sebastian warned.

"Well, then why don't ya' go knock on the door?"

Sebastian walked his horse up to the house, dismounted and then knocked, but there was no answer.

"Ain't nobody home," he said.

Lee smiled and held up the letter. "I've already opened the envelope and Caleb may have been right. This letter says Seth was murdered and the prison did away with his body."

"Well, ain't that something! The man is an imposter," Sebastian exclaimed.

"I don't know who he is, but I aim to find out," Lee replied.

Later that evening, Sebastian and Lee rode out to Seth's place again.

"He ought to be home by now, don't you think?" Lee asked.

When they arrived, they noticed the lights were on. It took a few minutes to figure out how to approach the man they had never met.

As they walked up to the house a dark shadow moved toward the back of the house. "That must be him." Sebastian whispered. "He must know we're on to him. Why don't you walk around to the back of the house and see if he shows himself? I'll stay here in case he comes around front. I think he might know something ain't right," Lee said. "Don't let 'em git the upper hand on ya!"

Sebastian retrieved his gun from his saddlebag and walked around to the back of the house. As he approached the backside the barrel of a shotgun brushed the side of his head.

"Drop your gun! What you doin' messin' 'round my house?" Sonny asked.

Sebastian was startled, feeling the gun barrel at his temple.

"Hold on fella, don't shoot. Sebastian quickly thought, *this ain't the right time to tell this man I know he is an imposter.*

"Take it easy man—I mean no harm. Just put that gun down." Sebastian was quick to come up with an excuse. "Me and my partner stopped by to find out if you know a Caleb Young."

"I don't know any Caleb Young," Sonny replied, "and I don't know you!"

"Me and my partner had some unfinished business with Caleb and we heard we could find him here." Sebastian explained.

"Best ya' git going. Next time ya' might git your head shot off. It's dangerous snooping around a man's house after dark."

"Next time, I'll know. Nice to meet ya' Mr. Jackson."

"Jest one minute! How'd you know my name?"

"It's on your mailbox."

"Oh! Sonny replied."

As they walked to the front of the house, Sebastian tried to be cordial since he saw Sonny's gun. "You got a mighty nice place here! My partner and I buy property."

"Well, my place ain't for sale!"

Sonny scratched his head as he lowered his gun.

Lee knew the kind of man Sonny was and he wanted to get out of there as fast as he could.

"Well, thanks for your time. My partner and I will be moseying along," Lee said.

"Wait, hold on, I want to introduce you to Seth Jackson," Sebastian, said.

"Nice to meet you, Seth. We're sorry to barge in on you this late but we were admiring your place. We plan to be in the area indefinitely so we may see you again."

"I ain't likely to be around--I stay pretty busy," Sonny said.

"Well, it's been nice meeting you. You did say your name was Seth Jackson, didn't you?"

The way Lee repeated Sonny's name made him agitated. They're on to something, he thought.

"You men better be careful in the dark. We got some wild animals on the prowl around here."

Lee didn't care to know what Seth was talking about.

"You have a good evening, you hear?" Lee tipped his hat.

Riding away, Lee was curious about what happened when Sebastian went into the back of the house.

"He pulled a damn gun on me! He would've been shot me if I hadn't weaseled my way out. I wasn't about to tell him that we thought he was an imposter," Sebastian explained.

"So you lied and said we were looking for Caleb. Do you think he fell for it?"

"I think so."

"The next time he'll know why," Lee said.

⁓

After leaving Martha's, Lucy drove to Woodville in a fog of despair. Sobbing, she continued to blame herself for being away from her family while knowing her first responsibility was with Jared and Cain. Feeling the pain of losing Pecan Plantation seemed distant in her mind as she reflected on why she thought she was doing the right thing. *How could I have been so foolish?* She kept asking herself. Normally, she would have given more thought and explained to Cain, but now all she could think about was her son and what might have happened to him.

Driving home, she had a sixth sense about the account given of an Indian taking Jared. She questioned its validity. By the time she arrived in Woodville she was in a state of despair, wondering who could have taken the boy if it happened to be someone other than an Indian. While exiting her car, she inadvertently left the door open, exposing the bank money and luggage. The only thing on her mind was hearing some news about Jared. She had an idea Cain and Vick were still away somewhere trying to find their son.

Elizabeth was sitting in her private garden waiting for Cain and Vick when she saw Lucy drive up. The timing of her arrival and the kidnapping of Jared seemed strange and puzzled her. How could Lucy know about Jared? she thought.

Seeing Lucy so upset, Elizabeth thought it best not to show her bitterness. Now is not the time, she thought.

She welcomed her home with open arms. They both took a seat on the garden's bench.

"Elizabeth, have you any word about Jared?"

"You know about Jared? Have you seen Vick and Cain?"

"It's a long story, but first, I need to know what happened. I heard it was an Indian. How do they know it was an Indian? Lucy was asking a million questions.

"It appears you know as much about the kidnapping as I do. How did you know?" Elizabeth questioned.

"Martha Cormack, the woman who looked after Cain when he had amnesia. You remember him talking about Martha, don't you?

"How would you know Martha?" Elizabeth asked.

"That's who I was staying with, the same Martha. As a matter of fact, I just found out last night that she had taken care of Cain when he had amnesia. After explaining, she told me about Jared.

Cain had come by Martha's asking if she knew of any Indian trouble-makers. I was in Beaumont at the time and found out only after I got home. Elizabeth, I want to explain to you why I left Woodville when I did."

"Before you say anymore, I think you should explain yourself to Cain.

"I plan to do just that, but you are equally important to me and I want you to have a clear picture of what I have been through and what caused me to leave."

"Well, if it's important to you," Elizabeth stated.

Lucy explained everything from the first time she learned that Pecan Plantation had been stolen to the time she came home.

"Lucy, you can't possibly be sure of this!"

"Oh, yes I can! There's two accounting books that can prove the plantation was stolen. It will explain how they swindled us out of the ranch, but I need to find the books so I can prove it. We need the books for evidence. But that's the least of my worries right now. Jared is missing, and we have to find him." Lucy began crying. "Elizabeth, I never meant for any of this to happen—and poor Cain. I knew I should have told him, yet I couldn't. I was afraid of them being involved in another conflict and being murdered. I wanted to spare them from another war! I hope you understand that!

Trying to find the books was why I stayed behind and refused to move with the family to Woodville. And that's not all—I also found that it was Sebastian and Lee who robbed the bank in Carthage. Remember that robbery everyone was talking about?"

"I remember. They got away with a lot of money," Elizabeth replied.

"I was foolish following them to their hideout. That's where I found the money they stole. I think they know I have it," she explained.

Lucy had a sheepish look on her face as she continued telling her story.

"Are you telling me you stole the money from them?" Elizabeth asked.

"Yes–I have it. I took the money to prove they stole it. I also saw them murder two men in cold blood."

"Oh my, you saw them kill someone? I'm surprised you thought you could handle this alone. Where is the money now?"

"It's in the car. Oh no, I meant to bring the money inside."

They both ran around to the front of the house where Lucy had parked the car only to find that she had been robbed of everything but her suitcase. The two large sacks of money were gone. After seeing that she failed to close the car door her blood ran cold. She turned to Elizabeth in disbelief.

"Oh no, someone has taken the money."

"Are you sure you had the money?" Elizabeth responded.

"Yes, you don't doubt my story, do you?"

"No, but Cain may since he hasn't seen you in over a month. He may think you made up a story, so he would forgive you."

"Elizabeth, I don't want you to doubt me. Anyone could have rode up and stolen the money. Lucy became so upset that she cried. "Cain will never believe me now!" she sobbed.

Elizabeth felt sorry for her.

"I want you to listen to me. What's important is finding Jared and if Cain loves you he will try to understand. Now please, dry your eyes and let's try to figure out who might have taken the money.

It had to be someone on a horse because if it was a car we would have heard it. What about Caleb?" Asked Elizabeth.

"Have you seen him?" Asked Lucy.

"I haven't seen him in several days. I think he's gone. The last time I saw him he had suspicions about Seth. He said he thought Seth was an imposter. Now he's nowhere to be found." You may never see that money again," Elizabeth noted.

"I don't think it was Caleb. Perhaps it was Seth or whoever that man is!"

"Lucy, I don't think Seth had anything to do with stealing the money. The day he came to tell me about the kidnapping I could tell he had been in a fight—his shirt was torn all over. I think we can believe he was telling the truth," Elizabeth remarked.

"But Elizabeth, Caleb was raised here, and he knew Seth growing up. What if he's right and Seth is not who he says he is?" Lucy countered.

"Now, not only do I have Lee and Sebastian to worry about, but I have Seth. The logical people who took the money would be Sebastian and Lee. They could have followed you and saw you leave the car door open," Elizabeth added. "They're probably counting the money as we speak!"

The night was cold and still as a corpse when Vick and Cain arrived back in Woodville. It had been a long tedious journey on horseback and they were exhausted. Passing by Seth's place they got their first scent of hickory burning.

"Pa, it ain't long and we'll be around a warm fire."

"I know and I worry about Jared. I hope he's warm," Vick mentioned.

Jumping the cattle gap, the horses began a fast trot. They too seemed anxious to get to the barn. Vick visualized Elizabeth sitting around the fireplace waiting their arrival. "It's good to be back home," he quipped.

"Pa, are you going to be the one to tell mother it was a wild goose chase?"

"Don't worry—she'll know by the look on our face."

As they rode closer to the house they saw Lucy's car, which puzzled them.

"Pa, I don't believe it! Lucy's home— I wonder why she came back?"

"I reckon we're about to find out. Son—one word of advice—hear her out."

"I don't even want to see her, much less hear her lies," Cain replied.

"Just listen to her– and then you can make your decision."

"How did you learn so much about women being in prison?"

"You learn a lot just sitting around thinking. My feeling is if you really love someone you're gonna try and understand. We all have our faults."

"Yeah, but I didn't take up with another woman. How am I supposed to forget about Lucy and Sebastian?"

Elizabeth heard the doorknob turn and knew immediately it was Vick and Cain. She ran to the door.

"Cain, you didn't find him?" Elizabeth quizzed.

"Sorry, but it was a dry run. We tried everything and came up with nothing. Not a soul knew anything about Indians kidnapping children. For all I know Seth could have lied to us. Has he been around since we've been gone?"

"Only one time, and that was to find out if we found out anything."

"I don't know—it's a mystery to me." Cain replied.

Lucy was in her bedroom and did not hear them come in.

"What about your visitor?" Cain asked. "How long is she planning to be here this time?"

"You need to talk to her! She knows about Jared and that's one reason she came back."

"How did she know about Jared?"

"She was staying with Martha in Beaumont."

"Martha? Are you sure, or is this another one of her lies?"

"I can't speak for Lucy—she'll explain."

When Cain knocked on the door she thought it was Elizabeth.

"Elizabeth, you don't have to knock," Lucy spoke.

"It's not Elizabeth," Cain whispered. He opened the door and there she was lying on her bed all red-faced from crying. Her Beauty took his breath away. I must keep it together and not allow her to know how much I care, he thought.

Lucy stood up in her plain white gown looking ravishing but very sad. Cain had to clear his throat before he spoke.

"Why did you come back?" he queried.

"Did you find Jared?" Lucy asked.

"No, we didn't and why would you care. You abandoned me and our son."

Lucy turned and began sobbing. He wanted to take her in his arms but he was much too angry.

"Cain, it's time you know what I've been through."

"You came here to plead your case when our son is missing. Is that all you can think about?"

"No, of course not! I came back because I found out our son was kidnapped by Indians. Martha Cormack told me. She said, ya'll came by so she could meet Vick. That's how I found out—from Martha."

"So, you've been staying with Martha? Ain't that funny—and she didn't even mention it."

"Martha didn't know I was your wife."

"Then young lady you better start talking. And, while you're do-ing it you might explain your relationship with Sebastian, because I know about you and him. Several months ago, I saw you two together. Perhaps you want a divorce, so you and your lover can be together— is that it?

Cain was skipping from one subject to the other leaving little time for her to explain.

He did exactly what Vick cautioned him not to do but after losing his temper, he finally settled down.

"Cain, your perception of what you think you know could not be furthest from the truth. Months ago, I found out that Lee Tompkins and Sebastian stole Pecan Plantation from us. I learned this while we were still living there. They took advantage of Jonathan Petty and his mental illness, forging numbers to reflect losses so we would lose our plantation. After Jonathan died, the accounting books were already in place and that's how we lost Pecan Plantation."

"How do you know about this?" Cain was very skeptical.

"From Caleb, he worked for Lee at the bank."

"You mean our Caleb?"

"That's right! Caleb told me everything and I've been trying to gain evidence, so we can reclaim Pecan Plantation."

"And Caleb knew of this and did not tell me?"

"Please don't blame poor Caleb, I begged him to keep my confi-dence. I did it to keep you and Vick from going to war with Lee and Sebastian until I obtained the truth. Suddenly, I was over my head and it killed me that you thought the worst of me."

"But Lucy, you told one lie after the other."

"Not because I wanted to. I was trying to protect my family and I had no choice once I got involved with my deception. These are evil men, and I didn't want you and Vick to find out and be killed. And they would have found a way to kill you, Elizabeth or God forbid our son!"

Cain was overcome with shock and had to sit down. He could not believe what he was hearing.

"Cain, please try and understand. I'm sorry I didn't come to you before, but I was afraid." She was very tender as she told what all happened to her. Her genuine sweetness was evident to the man who knew her best.

Cain sat quietly as she told him the entire story, from the beginning to the end, explaining how she discovered that Lee and Sebastian were bank robbers and murderers.

"Lucy, why didn't you tell me?"

"I wanted to spare you, I've seen their handiwork and they would have murdered you and Vick."

Hearing what all she had done to protect them, he became very concerned about Lucy and the money she had taken from them.

"I can't believe that you thought this was something you could handle alone. What about the day I saw you and Sebastian together at the plantation. I saw you at the stables after you had come in from your ride. Y'all looked mighty friendly to me."

"Cain, I know how it must have looked but nothing happened, I was trying to get away from him. When we got back to the stable I tried my best not to foil my plan, so I had to make him believe that everything was okay—but it wasn't. By that time, I was in too deep. Knowing what I know now, I should never have agreed to go riding with him, but I thought the place he was taking me might possibly be where our accounting books were hidden. My only desire was to get my hands on the books, so we would have proof to reclaim the plantation— don't you see?" Lucy left out the part were Sebastian tried to rape her. She knew it would invoke rage within Cain.

"I still say you should have told me what was going on. You could have been killed," he admonished.

"Cain, my one mission that day was to find the accounting books. I knew about their hideout and I figured if they were going to hide the books somewhere that it might be there. That's the only reason I accepted his invitation to go for a ride with him."

"I would imagine he planned to take you to his hideout and seduce you."

"I wasn't thinking like a man, all I could think about was finding where the books were hidden," Lucy retorted.

"Well, did you find them?"

"No, but I think I know where they are. When they murdered the two men I told you about, I was close enough to hear them talk about a steamboat in Beaumont called the High Stepper. When I was in Beaumont, I went aboard the steamer and met the captain."

"Lucy, do you know how your snooping has placed our family in danger? I can't believe you would do that. The captain you met could be in cahoots with Lee and Sebastian."

"I don't think so–he was nice. He looked like he was half Indian."

"Did you hear what you just said? This could be the Indian that took Jared. Can you tell me anything about him?" he asked.

"He looked and dressed like a white man, but I could tell he was a half breed. He was not your ordinary Indian. I don't know where he came from, but he was educated and looked very kind and certainly not the type."

Cain's expression changed. "Lucy, every one of the men could be connected, waiting to exchange Jared for the money you took from them."

"But Cain, the money is gone—I don't have it."

"What do you mean you don't have the money?"

"When I drove up to the house, I was frightened about Jared, so when I got out of the car I left the door open. When I realized what I had done, I found the money gone—someone stole it!"

"Oh my God, how can things get any worse?" he stated.

"Cain, I was anxious to hear about Jared and I didn't think. Please don't be upset with me?"

"I'm upset, because this might have been our only chance to get Jared back. If Lee and Sebastian were following you, they may have seen your car door open and taken the money."

She shook her head in disgust for being so careless. "What can I do to ever make this up to you and Jared?"

"I know you're as sick as I am, but I have to go to Beaumont and see if I can find the Indian you are talking about."

After their talk Cain felt sorry for Lucy and what she had gone through.

For a minute, he wanted to forget all his pain and just hold her. He had missed her so much and her standing there waiting for him to touch her was more than he could take. He walked over to her and tilted her head back for a kiss, but it turned out to be more than just a kiss—it was much, much more, as the heat of passion swept throughout their bodies. Lucy was consumed with the love she thought she had lost—it had been so long and they clung to each other. She felt a warmth fill her heart as he caressed her. The room began to sway as Cain picked her up and laid her in bed. This was their haven away from the world.

"Lucy, I've missed you," he whispered tenderly. "Thank God you've come back to me."

"Please Cain, just love me. I've waited so long."

His love was sweet and tender as they became lost in their ecstasy. As they held each other, she began to cry quietly, tears running down her face from the corners of her eyes. They were happy tears. For a moment, there was no heartache or pain for everything felt right again, except for the emptiness she felt for not having her son.

During the night, they reached for each other to make sure they were not dreaming and again the heat of passion overcame them. It wasn't until the next morning that the reality of a new day crept in. We must find Jared, Cain thought.

Chapter 21

SONNY REVELED IN HIS NEWFOUND WEALTH. HE HAD STOLEN THOU-sands of dollars and the burden of being unable to drill for oil was soon to be forgotten now that he had money to begin construction.

His mind worked a mile a minute as he strategized on how to hide the money and prevent being caught.

Combing through the bags of money, he was amazed that it was more than he could count. The money was bound together in ten, twenty, and fifty dollar allotments along with hundreds of Silver Certificates. In his wildest dreams, he never thought it possible to have the kind of money to do with what he pleased. *Now I must hide it and make sure no one knows I'm the one who stole it.* He trembled and pondered over how he would act if questioned. He figured the Porters might come around sooner or later asking questions. Cold sweat beaded up on his forehead as he wiped his face with his sleeve. *I can't believe the Porter's had this*, he thought. I gotta keep it together and not let on. Them Porters are plenty smart and they bound to try and find evidence of who stole the money.

Them Porters ain't so high and mighty after stealing this money from the Carthage Bank. They're nothin' but a bunch of thieves. They ain't no damn better than me. Why should I feel guilty when it was them who stole the money! Sonny rationalized away his guilt.

The next morning the temptation to use the money was much too strong, so he put together a generous portion of the money and rode into town to buy a new car. Once there, he spotted several cars, but only one shiny tan car caught his eye. He checked it out carefully, running his hands over the smooth contours of the finish. He began to imagine himself cruising down Main Street with everyone gawking at the rich man in the expensive new car. Then he took a seat behind the wheel, and it felt good. He had never even imagined being able to afford such a fine automobile. He looked at himself in the rearview mirror and thought, *I look damn good and it's about time I join in with the rich folks. I wonder what they'll think now?*

Sonny felt powerful paying cash for his car, something he had never experienced before. He took a few spins in his automobile and then dropped by the local mercantile company for clothing. I gotta look like I feel, he convinced himself.

The power of money was overwhelming him and continued to burn a hole in his pocket.

Sauntering into the mercantile, he tried on several shirts and pants until he found what he was looking for. *These look nice*, he thought. After purchasing five of everything he walked next door to a shoe store and bought new boots and shoes. Before he left town, he stopped in for a shave and haircut. He was tired of hiding behind his bearded disguise. *If anyone questions, I'll cross that bridge when I get to it.*

~

Elizabeth and Vick were stunned as Lucy repeated to them the events concerning what all happened during the months she was gone. They wish that she had not suffered alone as she set about her investigation of Lee and Sebastian. Upon learning the truth of her ordeal, they felt ashamed that they had thought the worst of her. Knowing the truth made all the difference to them, and now the family was together again and closer than ever.

When morning came, Vick and Cain drove Elizabeth's car to Beaumont to board the High Stepper for Galveston. Cain was hopeful that he would either find Jared or gather information of where he might be.

"Pa, I hope we're not running on another wild goose chase."

"Remember what I told you—we're taking one day at a time and the way things look, this could be the day." Somehow Vick's energy and optimism always made Cain feel secure. *What if Pa's right and I do find my boy?*

They arrived a day early and had to stay overnight since it was off-season for the Stepper. Instead of every other day of travel the boat only sailed twice a week.

Strangely enough, when they boarded the steamer Lee and Sebastian were only a few people in line ahead of them. Cain and Vick didn't know what to do, but it made sense that the Indian would be part of Lee and Sebastian's scheme, whatever it was.

How much clearer can it be? Vick thought. *What business would they have boarding the Stepper if it wasn't to make connections with the Indian who was nowhere in sight.*

Fortunately, Vick and Cain could hurry along to find their stateroom before being seen by Sebastian and Lee.

Night and day, Aggie sat by Jared's side loving every moment she had with him. Even when he was asleep, she could not help but kiss him on the forehead and whisper how much she loved him.

That evening she grew uneasy as she tended to Jared. It was as though she sensed something was about to happen. Annie Mae was in and out of her cabin and had seen many of the passengers aboard the steamer. Vick and Cain were two of the passengers whom she had never met before and naturally had no connection. She did recognize Lee and

Sebastian spying around the aft of the boat again. Something is going on with these two, she observed. Concerned, she went to Aggie and told her that the two strangers had repeatedly been seen snooping about the boat.

"I've seen them a number of times and it's beginning to worry me," Annie Mae said. Aggie was pleased that she was keeping tabs on the passengers.

"Would you mind staying here while I go find Bidzill?" Aggie asked.

She placed her shawl over part of her face and went in search of her husband. At the very same time she walked from her cabin, she saw two other men spying. It was the last two people she ever expected to see onboard the High Stepper. By the time it registered with her that one man was Cain and the other possibly his father, she turned to run. But it was too late—they had seen her. Instead of running, which would have drawn attention to her, she turned and walked slowly in the opposite direction. She felt confident they did not recognize her since her shawl covered part of her face. Aggie's heart was pounding a mile a minute.

"Oh my God!" she mumbled to herself. "*What am I going to do if they find me?*" She hurried to the captain's quarters to find Bidzill. The minute she walked in the door he knew something was wrong. She threw her arms around him. "Bidzill, Cain and his father are onboard with us. What are we going to do?"

"How do you know? Did you see them?" he quizzed.

"Yes, they are searching for Jared or me, I don't know, I'm confused."

"Aggie, this is the best thing that could happen. We can take Jared to another cabin and send them a note telling them where they can find Jared. We don't have to be a part of facing them. That way, we won't be involved. Can't you see this is the best way to protect you and me."

"I suppose," Aggie whispered. She was very distressed and could hardly speak.

"Bidzill kissed her before he left. "You stay here and try not to worry."

Leaving Aggie was the hardest thing to do, for he knew her heart. He made his way through the saloon but it was too late for he was seen by Cain and Vick.

"Pa, that's the man Lucy told me about. It has to be him."

They ran as fast as they could toward Bidzill who just stood there. Cain called out. "Captain, we need to talk to you!"

Bidzill who had nothing to hide waited for Cain and Vick to approach him.

"I'm Cain Porter and this is my father Vick. We're here about my missing son. We have an eye witness that an Indian meeting your description kidnapped my boy. I need you to tell me if you know anything about a kidnapping?"

Bidzill had no idea he would be accused of a kidnapping. He was much too reputable to allow anyone to think he was capable of such an act. He was also concerned about Aggie and protecting her identity. He knew that Cain was a lawyer and he would grow suspicious if he had the slightest hint of her living and being his wife.

"I'll be happy to answer your questions, but not here," Bidzill said. "Come this way so we can talk. They followed as they were led to an empty stateroom. Bidzill was concerned that he had incriminated himself by saving Jared.

Entering the stateroom, the men sat on the end of the bed waiting to hear Bidzill's story.

"Well, we're waiting," Cain said.

"I take it you two gentlemen are looking for a young boy that I rescued several weeks ago. I'm glad you came for him. I had no idea who the boy belonged to."

"Cain was livid and unable to control his temper."

"So, you kidnapped my boy!"

By this time, Cain had Bidzill by the throat, until Vick pulled him off.

"Cain, please, calm down and listen to the man!" The last thing Cain wanted to do was let go of the man's throat. His last action was slamming his fist in Bidzill's face knocking him backward onto the floor.

"Cain, get a hold of yourself! You don't know that this man is lying." Infuriated with Cain, Vick pushed him aside and gave Bidzill a hand and pulled him from the floor.

As soon as Vick pulled the man up he felt a shock wave through his hand. It was so intense he had to pull his hand away. Bidzill appeared not to feel the shock.

Cain was confused seeing his Pa show concern for a renegade Indian.

"Now, let's hear what you were telling us before my son interfered." Bidzill rubbed his mouth, and wiped away a trickle of blood.

"Thank you," Bidzill said. He looked at Cain, unsure if he would strike again.

"Now, as I was about to explain—I was on a trip riding through the woods when a hawk distracted me. I know it sounds crazy but it's true. Once beginning the account of what happened, he had no control over his voice as he spoke of what transpired that day. He was sure Vick and Cain would think he was loco.

While listening to Bidzill's story it was surprising to them that a hawk had a significant role in the Indian's account. *How can this be?* Vick thought.

Bidzill studied the men as they sat there immersed in what he was telling them. *They don't believe me*, he thought. He continued to explain that he thought the man he saw was about to murder Jared.

Cain shivered as he heard the word murdered.

Speaking slowly Bidzill said, "the hawk and I saved your son. As crazy as it seems, I speak the truth. The man who was standing over your son was about to kill him."

Vick and Cain looked at each other. It must have been Seth, but that doesn't make sense why he would want to harm Jared? Vick thought.

Cain only wanted his son and nothing else mattered.

"Right now, I don't care about you and this hawk you said helped save my boy. What I want is to know is my son alive? Do you have Jared here with you now?" Cain asked.

"Yes, he is resting. Your boy drifts in and out of consciousness but I have been caring for him. I have the skill of a doctor. You see, my white father was a physician, and he taught me."

Cain and Vick sized Bidzill up as being no ordinary Indian. They thought of him to be honest and Cain felt embarrassed that he had jumped to conclusions. Listening to Bidzill carefully explain Jared's condition, they were thankful that he came along when he did and saved the boy.

"Your son will be okay but you must give him more time to recover. I brought him here to treat him until such time that he could travel. He needed my care and it was not good to move him. You do believe me, don't you?"

"Yes, but I need to see my boy!" Cain demanded.

"Of course, but keep in mind he's in and out of consciousness."

"I understand," Cain answered softly.

They followed Bidzill as he led them into Aggie's stateroom. Annie Mae was there tending to Jared, while Aggie remained in the captain's quarters. She was not aware of what was happening and when Bidzill nodded to Annie Mae, she left.

Seeing Jared laying there asleep, Cain could not hold back the tears.

"Pa, I can't believe we found him." He wiped his eyes with his sleeve seeing his son with a blanket tucked around him. He placed his hand over his mouth unable to speak and finally asked, "Is my boy going to be okay?"

"Yes—you have my word," Bidzill answered.

"When can we move him? I want to take him home."

Bidzill smiled, "You're going to have to wait until we get back to Beaumont."

"Do you think he'll be awake by the time we get back?" Cain asked.

"If you want, you can talk to Jared and see if he responds to you. I can't explain why, but sometimes an unconscious patient can know you're there and yet, not give any indication that he knows."

He walked over to the boy and bent down to kiss him. "Jared, this is your Pa. Son—I'm here to take you home," he whispered. Cain continued to talk to him and finally there was a bit of eye flutter.

"Pa, Jared knows I'm here. Did you see his eyelids move?"

Vick smiled for he had a feeling that his grandson was going to be okay. His other concern was of Bidzill and his interaction with the hawk. It had been a long time since Vick thought about his phantom friend Hawk who promised many years ago that he would always be his protector. Could this be Hawk protecting my grandson? How similar we are, he thought. There is something special about Bidzill. I have a connection to him, but why?

Vick recognized a familiarity with Bidzill. Perhaps it's because of the similar experience with the hawk, Vick thought.

Overwhelmed with a feeling he did not understand, Vick excused himself.

"I'll be outside getting some fresh air while you talk to Jared." Cain nodded that it was okay for him to leave.

Vick walked over to the boat railing and stood there for a few minutes, allowing the cool Gulf breeze to dampen his face. He could hear the piano and violin music playing as cowboys were laughing and having a goodtime. Vick felt weak and had to sit on a bench that was braced against the wall of the boat. The sound of the music began to muffle and Vick's mind flashed back to another time when Cain and he were led by the hawk to a cave of diamonds near Panther Holler. He tried not to think of the diamonds and the responsibility given him, but he knew one day it would be time to deliver the diamonds to the "Original People". He felt a sense of enlightenment as the memory from his past resurfaced. Once again, he was swept away in a vision clothed in a stunning multi-colored tribal robe as a reoccurrence of his last vision repeated itself. He watched many spirits rise from their graves and ascend into the heavens. He knew it was his people who lived many years before him. As he watched, the apparition began to twirl in speeding flashes of gray, white and black lights mixed together as he was thrust into a scene that was as vivid as noonday. He could not believe the horror that was shown to him. This must be hell, he thought, but it wasn't. It was a man-made hell here on earth called the "trail of tears" that Vick had heard about as a boy. Thousands of Indians, in the worst possible conditions, began a march with nothing but the clothes on their backs forced to walk for hundreds of miles, suffering inhumane treatment through unbelievable harsh terrain that no living man should ever have to endure. Vick cried as he held out his arms as if to cradle them. Of course, it was impossible, but the instinct to comfort them was his desire. As he followed them with his eyes, there among them were Bidzill as a child and his mother. The huge panorama of events stopped and suddenly before him stood Bidzill, robed exactly like Vick. Bidzill was crying as he spoke.

"These are our people." Vick was overcome with sadness as the scene slowly returned to reality. As quickly as the manifestation appeared—like a flash it was gone. This was the first apparition he experienced since he and Cain found the diamonds. He hoped he would never have to endure another vision of how bitterly his people were treated. Vick sensed that the time was approaching when he would journey again to the cave to fulfill his destiny. Afterwards, he thought of Bidzill and how they must be related. He kept hearing his voice as he said, "these are our people."

∼

Aggie had been held up in the Captain's quarters for hours waiting to hear from Bidzill until Annie Mae came in to warn her that he was talking to two men.

"Oh no! It must be Cain and his father."

"What can I do for you?" Annie Mae asked.

"There's nothing you or anyone can do—they're here to take Jared." She wanted to face Cain and plead with him to leave her son with her but she could not risk what might happen if she allowed them to know she was alive and aboard the High Stepper.

Vick, who was weak from the manifestation, walked back into the room to see how Jared was doing. He walked over to Bidzill and touched his arm.

"Can I ask you to join me outside?" Once again, Vick had the same sensation as he did before when he shook Bidzill's hand. The two men walked on the deck about the time that Lee and Sebastian were walking to their stateroom.

Vick quickly turned away, for he did not want Lee and Sebastian to see him. Bidzill noticed Vick's reluctance to be seen.

After Lee and Sebastian passed them, Bidzill asked,

"Do you know those two men?"

"Why do you ask? Vick said. He was completely sidetracked seeing Sebastian and Lee.

"I'm sorry, it appeared that you might know them. There's something going on with those two men," Bidzill said. "They travel back and forth to Galveston without leaving the boat, which is strange since everyone goes ashore. I think they're looking for something. It's been a puzzle to me. Perhaps you know what they are looking for."

"Unfortunately, I do know of them through my son and his wife. And I have an idea what they are looking for."

"Since you know, can you enlighten me? Bidzill asked.

"If I had to guess I would say they're looking for money they stole from the Carthage Bank and two accounting books which can incriminate them if they're found. You see, they stole my son's home place— Pecan Plantation."

"I'm afraid I don't understand."

"You're not prepared to hear this, but those two men either killed Packer Rover or they're responsible for his death. I'm sure you know the previous owner of this steamboat." Vick explained.

"Hmmm, I think you must be mistaken. I was on the boat at the time he died, and I didn't see any obvious connections with him or anyone else," Bidzill said. "Why would you say they murdered Packer?"

"It's a long story and we need proof but we're sure they had a hand in killing Packer. They also robbed a bank in Carthage, Texas, and it's a matter of time before it comes out that they were all in cahoots with one another."

Bidzill was perplexed when he heard that money from a bank robbery paid for Aggie's steamboat. Momentarily he was concerned, for the boat was their source of income and hearing that a bank in Carthage, Texas could confiscate the steamer was alarming. His main fear was for Aggie and how she might respond if she heard that the High Stepper might be taken from her. Their only other option would be to relocate to Tyler and live on the property he inherited from his father, which Aggie knew nothing about.

"Mr. Porter, this is my wife's steamboat and there is no way she'll give it up without a fight. Her business partner who owned the boat, sold the upper deck of the boat to her. They were equal partners, and when he died, she inherited the entire boat."

Vick could see the disbelief in his eyes.

"Mr. Porter, good luck with finding your books. If I find them, I'll see you get them back. Now, if you don't mind, let's join your son and see how Jared is doing."

Vick let it go since he did not want more of a confrontation.

Sooner or later he's going to have to face the truth about the boat, Vick thought.

Bidzill excused himself and rushed to Aggie's stateroom where she was hiding. It was evident she had been on pins and needles waiting to hear what had transpired. She threw her arms around his neck as soon as he walked through the door.

"Bidzill, is everything alright?"

He did not want to alarm her for now about the boat and what he had learned.

"I'm sorry you've had to wait so long. They're both with Jared. Tomorrow when we dock they'll be taking Jared with them." She began to cry.

"I thought I was prepared to give him up, but I'm not," she said. "I can't even tell him goodbye."

Although Bidzill had good intentions, he could not tell her that the Carthage Bank is the legal owner of the High Stepper. *Now is not the time for another disappointment.*

That night, when all was quiet, Aggie thought of Jared. *I must see him before he is taken from me,* she thought. In the early morning hours Aggie, while fully clothed, walked quietly into the stateroom where Jared and everyone else lay sleeping. She was very careful as she unlocked the cabin door so not to be heard. Vick was catnapping as he often did in prison when he heard a sound. He thought for a time it was Lee and Sebastian until he saw a woman's image. He was curious as he watched and listened.

Aggie bent down by Jared and placed a necklace with a ring on it around her son's neck. "Jared, this ring I gave to you as a child and it's the last thing of yours I had left to give you. Wear it in remembrance of your mother who should never have let you go. You be a good boy and always remember your mama loves you." She kissed him on his forehead and quietly left the room. Her voice was muffled as she whispered, but Vick was sure he had heard enough to know that the mysterious woman was Aggie who was very much alive.

Even if she is alive I can't put my son through another disappointment— not now! Vick thought.

He felt guilty keeping such a secret but he knew that Cain must never learn from his lips that Aggie is still alive.

The rest of the trip was non-eventful and anchoring in Beaumont was a momentous occasion. Jared had awakened and was beginning to form sentences. When he realized he was with Cain he asked where he was. "Son, we're on a steamboat. Jared kept looking around as if he was searching for someone, finally he said, "Where is Mama? Isn't she coming with us?"

Vick held his breath knowing the boy was speaking of Aggie. He later tried to justify the woman he saw possibly had some weird fixation on Jared.

Cain noticed the necklace with the small ring around Jared's neck and asked Vick where it came from?

"I don't know, why don't you ask Jared if he wants to wear it?"

Cain didn't know if the ring had something to do with a ritual of some sort since Bidzill was an Indian.

"My Mama gave me this ring and I want to keep it," Jared argued.

"Pa, Jared wants to wear it!"

"Frankly, I see no harm in the boy wearing a necklace."

Vick decided then and there that he would not tell him what he had seen and heard from the woman who visited their room the night before.

Cain could not wait to start home with his son.

"Jared, are you ready to go home and see mama?"

"No, we can't leave Mama, she's here!" Jared insisted.

Cain dismissed it as a form of delusion since Jared had been injured.

"Son, Mama will be home when we get there. You wait and see."

"No, Mama's here with me. Every night she talks to me," Jared said.

Cain did not try to explain further. *If he saw his mother while he was in a coma, perhaps that's a part of the healing process.*

～

Lucy had no idea what she was going to do since she did not have the stolen money she confiscated from Lee and Sebastian. Between the loss of Jared and the money, she was so despondent that she retired to her bedroom unable to carry on a simple conversation. Elizabeth would bring food but she refused to eat.

"Lucy, you have got to eat to preserve your strength," Elizabeth encouraged.

"I'm sorry, but I can't eat until I know my son is safe. All I want is Jared safely home with me and his family."

After two days, Elizabeth heard boots coming up the front steps of the house.

"Lucy, come quick—it's Cain and Vick!"

Dreading of what might be, she pulled herself out of bed and walked to the porch. She stood there wringing her hands, waiting in hopes of seeing Jared.

Unable to speak, she stood in one place and sobbed. Vick got out of the back seat and lifted the boy so that Elizabeth and Lucy could see they had him and he was okay.

"Grandma," Jared whispered. Lucy had not expected him to overlook her until she thought how long it had been since she had seen him. Two months in a young boy's life is a long time and will take a few days before he is used to her being home again.

Lucy walked over to Jared and kissed him on the cheek.

"Mama's home," she said.

"You're not my mama!"

Jared remembered Aggie reassuring him that she was his mother. Lucy looked at Cain confused.

"Jared, you misunderstood! The lady that took care of you on the boat was not your Mama. I'm your Mama."

"The pretty lady who cried, told me she was my Mama."

Lucy walked over to Jared and tried to hold him but he turned away.

"I want my Pa." Again, Cain saw Lucy's sadness.

Although Jared ignored her, nothing was more important than her son being safely home.

～

Sonny's newfound wealth continued to burn a hole in his pocket and he began splurging on equipment he thought he needed to run his farm. Now that he had his new car, he was running all over the place buying mostly farm equipment and tools. From the beginning, spending the money seemed like an addiction he could not control.

Time and again, Vick and Cain would drive by Seth's place and see something new. The fine new car was the first thing they noticed, and then a steam tractor.

"Pa, do you reckon it was Seth who stole the money from Lucy? Look at all the farm equipment? He's getting money from somewhere."

"I've noticed. I'm wondering the same thing. How can a man released from prison come up with that kind of wealth? I think he's the one who stole the money," Vick said.

"I think you're right—who else would have access to buy what he's bought? He probably followed Lucy home and then seeing the sacks of money in the back seat of her car, he simply helped himself," Cain added.

"Yep, he was possibly curious about Jared since we know he wanted to hurt the boy. It makes sense but without proof there's nothing we can do," Vick said.

"Pa, we're gonna have to find a way to take the target off Lucy's back. Lee and Sebastian think she stole the money and they're not giving up until they get it back. Now that we have Jared home we must concentrate on Lucy and how we can help her.

"Son, we can't let Sonny know that we suspect him of any crimes. If we give him reason to think we're on to him, things could get ugly—and quick!"

～

After a few weeks Sonny grew careless with the money. He took bundles of his stash and spent it carelessly on frivolous things, even things he did not need. Being careless, he became forgetful, leaving currency straps thrown about the house. He also took the money from his hiding place, and for convenience hid it under his bed.

Along with his stupidity he continued to drink and spend money on women who were regulars in the saloon. He was becoming his regular goof-for-nothing self.

One evening Vick and Cain saw Sonny staggering drunkenly to his car. They parked temporarily in a secluded area so not to be seen and decided to follow him in hopes of him leading them to the money. Due to a half moon, they followed him all the way home without the use of headlights, and without being seen by the drunken Sonny.

Somehow, we're going to find clues to the money, Vick thought.

Chapter 22

AGGIE WAS HEARTBROKEN WHEN BIDZILL ALLOWED CAIN TO TAKE JARED. She couldn't eat or sleep after giving up her son for the second time. *Nothing is worth this kind of misery.*

Day after day Bidzill watched his wife suffer. *There must be something I can do about her pain*, he anguished.

⁓

Months passed and Aggie and Bidzill finally were getting back to normal, although the emptiness she felt for Jared lingered on.

Lee and Sebastian were still booking trips back and forth from Beaumont to Galveston having little hope that they would find what they were looking for. Bidzill watched them like a hawk as they continued snooping. *There must be some truth to what Vick told me about these two men. Perhaps I should begin a search of my own and find out what they're looking for.* Bidzill knew the boat well and began looking in places that no one knew existed.

One late night before locking up he misplaced his keys. He combed through everything until he came to a drawer that had not been opened for years. Out of curiosity he opened it and saw a large roll of blueprints that he had not remembered. *Why didn't I think of this?* He thought. He unrolled the blueprints. Examining them, he saw the outline of a secret panel in the captain's quarters, which he did not know existed. *This must be where the Captain kept his big bankroll.*

Bidzill followed the blueprints and pressed on a section of the wall where the undisclosed compartment was shown to be located. A large section of the wall began to move, exposing quite a stash. Sure enough, there were papers, books and several huge bags of money.

The bags were enormous, and holding thousands of dollars. There was also gold bullion, silver certificates and silver, much more than Sebastian and Lee could have imagined Packer Rover had in his possession.

Bidzill's first thought was keeping the windfall, and if ever questioned about the ownership of the Stepper, he would simply pay it off. There was no doubt the money came from the Carthage Bank with the bank straps around the money. And now, he knew for sure that Sebastian and Lee were the masterminds of the robbery just as Vick suggested. Packer must have found the blueprints and hid the accounting books and money there for safe-keeping. As much as Bidzill wanted to justify keeping the money, he could not bring himself to do so. He was an honorable man and he hoped that Aggie would understand. He figured when the time came for him to tell her about the stolen money and what it was used for, there would be no amount of rationalizing that would condone them keeping the steamboat.

For safe keeping, Bidzill placed the accounting books and money back behind the wall. I must tell her tonight, he convinced himself.

Aggie had not felt well since Cain took their son and all the symptoms pointed to her being with child. She and Bidzill had not been married that long but remembering how susceptible she was to pregnancy there was no doubt. At first, she was uncertain of her feelings about being pregnant, but the more she thought of a baby, the more she felt a child may heal her broken heart. *Children represent the most important thing about a family*, she thought. *But raising a child aboard a steamboat would not be a normal life for a child of any age*, she imagined.

Bidzill had arranged for a special table for supper that evening to tell Aggie the news about the ownership of the Stepper. Of course, she had her own message to deliver and she too was not sure how her husband would react, since they had only been married a short time.

She was especially lovely with her long flowing hair and shawl wrapped around her shoulders. She was a picture of Beauty and he hated that he was going to break her heart when he delivered the message that the Carthage Bank owned the High Stepper.

Approaching the dining room, he could see she was already waiting for him.

"Aggie, you're early! I wanted to escort you to dinner."

She smiled as he bent down and kissed the back of her neck.

As the meal progressed, he continued to think whether he should tell her the real reason for the evening. There might not be another evening like this, he imagined.

After the meal, they both spoke at the same time.

"Aggie—you go first," he suggested.

"No, this can wait—you tell me what you were about to say?" she insisted.

"Well, I'm afraid it's not good news. I've been holding back telling you for I knew you were not feeling well."

She didn't know what to say, so she just sat there and waited for him to continue.

It took everything he had to recreate what Vick told him.

"Aggie, what I'm about to tell you involves Kyle's Uncle Packer and how he purchased the High Stepper. It also involves Sebastian Parker and Lee Tompkins, the two men who have been searching about the steamer trying to find money and important books that can incriminate them for stealing property they swindled."

Although her head was spinning, she sat very quiet and listened intently to what Bidzill had to say.

"It saddens me to tell you this, but Kyle's Uncle Packer robbed a bank in Carthage, Texas and used part of the money to purchase the High Stepper."

"No, that can't be. I paid Kyle for half the steamer and when he died I became the sole owner. I have papers to prove it."

"I know, but his uncle used money he stole from the Carthage Bank to buy the steamer and Kyle sold you part of the boat when it wasn't his to sell. Aggie, I found the rest of the stolen money that was left over and hid it until we have time to figure out what to do."

Aggie sat there listening with a blank stare on her face.

"I know you'd rather not believe this, but I met Packer and there's no way he could have purchased a big steamboat like this on his own. I learned of this from the Porters when they were here for Jared. I wish I didn't have to tell you, but to claim ownership of the Stepper would be wrong since we know the truth. It's better we face it now than later, don't you agree?"

"I don't know, this is our livelihood," Aggie rebuffed.

"But if we wait, we would be breaking the law, and we can't chance that."

Aggie sat there in a state of shock until she could speak.

"Bidzill, what about Sebastian and Lee, what do they have to do with this?"

"They're the ones who masterminded the bank robbery and Packer double-crossed them. That's why they've been aboard the steamer looking to find the money and accounting books that involve the Porters."

"I'm afraid, I don't understand."

"I don't know all the details, but the books belong to a plantation and I understand they can prove Sebastian and Lee are criminals."

"Do you remember the name of the plantation?" she asked.

"Yes, it's Pecan Plantation."

Aggie felt as though her world was coming down around her. She felt lost.

It all makes sense now, she thought. *They're at war with Jonathan.*

Aggie had yet to find out that Jonathan and all her kin were dead, which would leave her and Cain the sole heirs to the Petty Plantation.

Her mind was racing a mile a minute afraid for Jared and herself. All her insecurities flooded back for she knew if Cain got his hands on the books and learned they were found aboard the High Stepper it would only be a matter of time before her step-brother Jonathan would find her. Not only would he kill her like he did her mother, but Cain who thought she was dead would learn that she was alive. The more she thought of her options, the worse it played out in her mind. Cain can never know I have the accounting books, she thought.

"Bidzill, I don't know what to say. If we give the money to them I will be giving up my rights to the steamboat. I also could be recognized and then possibly go to prison for lying about being dead. But that's not the only problem I have, we're going to have a baby."

Caught off guard, Bidzill was slow to speak. "Are you sure?"

"I think so, it's a feeling I'm not likely to forget." She gave him a faint smile.

"Stunned with the news, Bidzill sat there for a moment and then responded."

"I hadn't thought of a baby. How far along are you?"

"I think a little over two months."

"Well then, we've got some planning to do," he said. He tried to show excitement at the most inopportune time. He rose from his chair and picked her up, swinging her around, which surprised her.

"Who cares about the steamboat, we're having a baby," he whispered.

He looked down and saw tears in her eye. She was radiantly happy and relieved but also sad.

"Aggie, I don't want you to worry because I have a place in Tyler. It's far enough from town that your secret will remain safe. It's a perfect place to raise our child and no one will bother us.

"She wanted to be excited, but her thought was protecting her newborn and herself from an unsafe world. She knew if Jonathan Petty found out she was alive he would want to kill her and her family.

"Bidzill please, do you mind slowing down a bit?"

"What's wrong?"

"I just need to gather my thoughts," she said.

Bidzill could see disappointment in her face and thought it was because of him.

"Aggie, you have to trust me. I will do my very best to always protect you from your siblings. If they ever find you, they'll know your life is with me no matter how wealthy the Petty's are. Aggie, all I want is your happiness."

"Bidzill, I've cried a million tears through the years, and all I care about is being with you and having a place for our baby to grow up."

His only desire was to reassure her that she would have a nice place to go to.

"I think you'll like our place, although it needs some work. The house is in good shape and we have over a thousand acres to do with what we want. I'm sure you'll be safe there."

He hadn't expected Aggie to be agreeable.

"Bidzill, I think this is meant to be. It makes perfect sense!"

Even though she was relieved that they had a place to go, her mind kept plotting how she could get her hands on the Petty books to prevent Bidzill from taking them to the Porters. *I can't allow them to know I'm alive*, she thought.

"What about Annie Mae?" he asked. "Will she want to join us?"

"I don't know—everything is happening so fast. I hate that she will be disappointed when I tell her that we must move. She'll want to know why, Aggie stated.

"Should I be honest and tell her?" Bidzill asked.

"I think it's best that I tell her we're having a baby and she's welcome to come with us. Annie Mae is like a mother to me."

"I think she'll like Tyler after we get moved," he remarked.

"Bidzill, you surprised me when you told me you owned a thousand acres and a home in Tyler, and now I'm going to surprise you. I should have told you before. I bring it up only because I've done the same thing but it's time to be completely honest—I want you to know I did not set out to deceive you but I have a past that few people know."

Bidzill paused as he thought what he might say. He wanted to be understanding.

"Aggie, whatever it is I hope you know that I'm here for you. Why don't you just tell me what it is that I don't know?"

"Will you understand when I tell you my real name is Aggie Petty Jackson?"

"Petty? Where have I heard that name before?"

"I'm an heir to the fortune of Hamp Petty—the owner of Pecan Plantation. Do you remember now? My father was one of the richest men in Texas. The only problem, I can never claim my part for I have three siblings who are out to have me killed. So, I think since I am the next heir, no one needs to have the accounting books other than me. You see, I'm a bastard child. My mother, Betsy Dawson was a governess, but she acted as a caretaker of my father's wife who was ill at the time. I had no idea that Hamp Petty was my father until much later in my life"

"So you are a Petty. I'm happy you're telling me this for it helps me to understand you when I see that faraway look in your eyes."

"The accounting books that Cain would like to have can never be his. I hope you will understand how important it is for me to keep them.

Bidzill, should you turn over the books to the Porters, I'll be found out, and if they find out I'm alive, I could be killed by my siblings or go to prison for lying about being dead. I don't want this kind of burden for you or our child. No one must know about these books or that I'm alive. Can you support me?" She asked.

Bidzill stood up and pulled her into his arms. He whispered into her ears.

"Aggie The books are yours to do with as you please. What would you like to do with the money from the bank robbery?"

"Of course, we should return it as soon as possible," she stated.

∿

The next morning, Aggie handed a note to Bidzill to give to the Banker stating that part of the money from the Bank robbery was used to purchase the High Stepper and that she was turning over the steamboat to the bank to do with as they please.

∿

Lee and Sebastian were disappointed that their search aboard the High Stepper failed and they had given up on it. However, there was another fortune waiting for them. They decided to go after Seth Jackson's land. Now that they had proof that Seth had been murdered in the Huntsville jail, they imagined it would be easier for them to manipulate the man claiming to be Seth.

On their way to Woodville, Lee and Sebastian planned how they would approach Seth.

"We're not going to spring it on him, are we?" Sebastian asked.

"I don't know, it's hard to figure until I look 'em in the eyes."

Deep down Sebastian disliked the recklessness in Lee, but for the first time, he talked with a little common sense.

The next day, Sebastian and Lee drove out to speak with Sonny, but when they got there they were surprised to see several pieces of expensive farm equipment.

"Wow, he musta' struck it rich to buy those kinds of tools," Lee said.

"There's some money somewhere," Sebastian replied.

Parking their car outside the gate, they walked up to the house and knocked.

"Don't look like nobody's at home, you wanna' take a look around?" Lee asked.

The men walked carefully to the back of the house and then made their way out to the barn near where Sonny burned trash. They noticed something strange about the garbage pile. Sebastian took a stick and began stirring around in the black rubble until he saw something that got his attention. There in the burn pile were bank straps with the name of the Carthage Bank clearly printed on them.

"Well, well, well, what have we here?" Sebastian asked pompously. "Looks like there's hundreds of these."

"Don't you think it's strange how these Carthage Bank straps are surprisingly close to Lucy Porter's house?" Suddenly things became very clear that the man thought to be Seth might also have something to do with the loss of their money.

"I bet it ain't no coincidence that he lives right next door to the Porters. I reckon this man and Lucy have been in cahoots with each other all along," Lee stated.

"Something ain't right! Why would any normal man have this many bank straps? There's a ton of 'em here and the ones he's burned don't even count." Sebastian continued to talk and rake the rubble at the same time.

"It seems Mr. Seth Jackson used the money to buy all that farm equipment setting in front of his house. I hope he ain't spent it all!"

"What are we going to do?" asked Sebastian.

"We're striking while the iron's hot. Ain't no reason to wait around and watch him spend our money." They walked around to the front of the house to sit and wait for Seth.

It wasn't long before Sonny came driving up in his new car. Lee punched Sebastian.

"I spec' that's were some of our money went. We might be riding back to San Augustine in a brand-new car." Lee continued to ramble.

By the time Sonny got within sight of his place he saw he had company. As he got closer he could see it was the two Banker's.

"Oh no, not them again," Sonny said under his breath.

As he walked past Lee and Sebastian, he showed his displeasure.

"I told you men I ain't interested in selling my house so why y'all still here?"

"We ain't here about no damn house. We're here about our money," Lee shouted.

"What are y'all talking about—yer money?"

"Don't play dumb! The money you been spending buying all that farm equipment and that new car of yours. The Huntsville Prison don't give that kind of severance pay.

Sonny was stunned to hear they knew about him working in the Huntsville prison.

"I don't know what yer talkin' about," Sonny lied.

"I spec' you'll talk when we tell you we know you ain't Seth Jackson."

A shock wave went through him as beads of sweat began popping out on his forehead. He kept thinking, I gotta keep it together. He could hardly speak. His vocal cords felt like they were tied in knots.

"I don't know what y'all are accusing me of."

"Well, why don't ya' think real hard and tell us how the real Seth Jackson died. And don't bother to lie 'cause we got the proof," Lee chastised.

Sonny kept thinking how he was going to get himself out of this one.

"Well, show me your proof. Y'all can't, 'cause there ain't none! Y'all need to git off my property, and now!"

"We got a letter here we reckon ya' gonna want to see before we go see the Porters," Sebastian chided.

"What letter?" Sonny asked

"The letter that came from the Huntsville Prison. You know the letter that informed us that Seth Jackson was murdered. So, you better start talkin' or you'll be talkin' to the Sheriff. He's gonna be mighty interested with all those half-burned money straps you've got laying around in plain sight!"

"Who are you and what the hell do you want?" Sonny asked. He swallowed hard for he knew he would most likely be arrested and thrown in jail if the Sheriff's involved. *I gotta git myself outta this*, he thought. He listened to them, but all he could hear were muffled sounds as he continued to think of his plight and the predicament he was in.

"I'm Lee Tompkins and this is my partner, Sebastian Parker. Now, tell us who you are."

Sonny, having worked in the penal system knew how inmates would likely treat him. *No I can't chance it*, he thought.

"Why don't you all come in so we can talk?" he suggested.

Lee thought this was easier than he imagined. They followed Sonny inside and sat around the table.

"Would you all like coffee or something stronger?" Sonny asked. His attitude seemed to change.

"We don't want coffee, just our money and we'll be on our way." Lee said.

Sonny tried to explain. "Look we can work this out! We can be partners!"

Lee laughed seeing Sonny scramble for a way out.

"Why would we want to partner with a squatter? That's what you are 'cause this place ain't even yours."

"You're not hearing me," said Sonny. "If it's money you're interested in, I'm gonna have more money than I know what to do with. All I have to do is get enough money to drill."

"We ain't interested in being partners with anybody who steals from us," Lee informed.

Finally, Sonny decided to come clean and let it fall where it falls.

"If that's what you want, the money's still here. But I didn't rob no bank and I didn't steal money from you. I stole it from Lucy Porter's car. She lives down the road a piece. I stole it to have money to drill my wells. Up until that boy of theirs went missing I didn't have a chance of drilling 'cause them Porters said their son had to be of age before we could divide our property," he explained.

"You just said their boy was kidnapped and now you've changed your story."

"No, No! —I heard the boy was kidnapped, so I rode over to ask if there was something I could do. That's when I saw the bags of money in the back of Lucy's car. Between me and you, that boy of theirs ain't nothing to me. If he's living he's standing in the way of my fortune and yours too— if you join up with me."

"You are doing some tall talking," Lee said.

"Lucy Porter is the one y'all need to talk to—not me." Sonny insisted.

He wasn't about to give up to Lee and Sebastian until he won them over.

"When you men were here before you said you wanted to buy my place. I'd be interested in hearing your offer."

"It would be rather difficult to make a deal with a dead man since we've just learned that Seth Jackson ain't around no more." Sebastian chuckled.

"What if I make you a deal that you can't refuse?"

"And what would that be?" Sebastian asked.

"I got a lake of oil underneath the ground. It might be bigger than Spindletop for all I know."

Lee listened intently.

"How you know there's oil on the property?" Lee asked.

"I can smell it and you can too if you want to follow me out back."

The men looked interested and followed Sonny to the backside of the house.

226

"I need one thing from ya'. Y'all can't blow my cover 'cause if you do people will know I ain't Seth Jackson and there's no hope for us drilling," Sonny explained.

Sonny directed them to the area of the yard that showed signs of oil.

Sebastian stooped down and ran his fingers over the ground and then smelled it.

"It's oil alright," Sebastian said.

"This all sounds good but we want our money!" Lee shouted.

"You'll get it, but first I need to know if I can trust you?"

"You can trust us after we see our money!" Lee fired back.

Sonny led them to his bedroom, with them following behind. He bent down and pulled out several large sacks filled with thousands of dollars. There were hundreds of bundles that Lee thumbed through.

"You're kinda careless leaving our money hidden under your bed. Ya' ain't too bright! But I ain't complaining!" Lee wiped the perspiration off his forehead with his shirt-sleeve and then turned to Sonny.

"Now, tell us who in the hell you are and why you're claiming to be Seth Jackson."

Sonny kept thinking. *This ain't the way it's supposed to happen.* But he was caught, and his only hope was that Lee and Sebastian lived on the wrong side of the law just like him and would go along with his plan. *It's a chance I haveta' take*, he thought.

"I can see y'all ain't going to give up, so I might as well come clean with ya. It's more than just the oil, it's about a promise I made to Seth before he died." *Lying was his best way out*, he thought.

This is when Sonny began spinning another tale that only he could spin.

"Ya'll realize we ain't no different—don'tcha? Think about it! "Y'all robbed a bank and I stole this place, so what's the difference except y'all have money in hand and I gotta dig a well to have mine.

We both got something on each other so why not work together. I need a couple of partners, and I take it y'all like money!"

Lee and Sebastian looked at each other and wondered where this was all going.

"There's something about me and Seth y'all need to know. He was a poor feller that was framed for a murder his wife committed. She tricked him into marrying her 'cause she was having a baby—one she later told Seth was his. She claimed he was the daddy of her bastard son, of course, Seth later figured it out. He was head over heels in love with her and agreed to take her bastard son as his own—that's how good he was."

Wiping his eyes with his sleeve, Sonny continued his charade.

When Seth's "old man" found out that the bastard kid wasn't his real grandson he disowned Seth. That's when that wife of his took a gun and shot Seth's Pa. She shot 'em dead as a doornail and blamed it on Seth. After hearing Seth's story, I swore that I would keep that bastard son of his from taking over his land. Just before Seth was murdered he told me there was oil on his land—lots of it. Maybe the biggest vein in the state of Texas. That's when I promised him I would do my best to see that the Porters didn't take what was his. That bastard kid, I was talking about turned out to be Cain Porter's boy and he ain't got no right to this land.

Plain and simple, I'm here because of my promise to Seth and I need y'all as my partners. Seems like there ain't no love lost between y'all and them Porter, so we need to work together."

Sebastian and Lee just stood there with their mouth agape. Lee thought, either he's one of the biggest liars ever or he has a big heart caring for ole Seth Jackson the way he did.

"So, is that it?" Lee asked.

"Just so ya' know that we ain't no different. Y'all robbed a bank and I stole this place. There ain't but one thing standing in my way of more money than what ya' got in those sacks of yours, and that's that bastard son who belonged to Seth Jackson's ex-wife. Seth was a good man and I'm taking up his battle 'cause he ain't here to fight for himself." Somehow, Sonny's lie-filled tale convinced them that he was telling the truth. Neither could think of a reason not to believe the story he told.

"So that's how you came to know Seth–in prison?" Sebastian repeated.

"That's right. I met him behind the walls of the Huntsville Prison. That's when he told me about his wife marrying for his money and making him believe he was the baby's daddy. Just before y'all rode up I found out the kid was kidnapped and most likely dead. Ain't nothin' standing in my way now since the son's out of the picture. Y'all came along just in time 'cause I been lookin' for me some partners. I'm gonna have a fortune we can share.

Sebastian and Lee turned around and walked out the door.

"We'll be back in just a minute. We need to talk!"

"Yeah, sure thing, I ain't going nowhere." Sonny stood there nervously sliding his boot back and forth on the floor, which was a habit he had developed over the years. His knees were even beginning to shake, so he sat down. After a few more minutes passed, he got up and peered out the window just as the two were heading back inside. He quickly walked over to the coffee pot to give the impression he wasn't particularly anxious about their decision. "Ain't no way they gonna git their hands on anything I've got. I'll just make 'em believe I trust 'em."

Lee spoke for the two of them, "Well, we talked it over and decided to take you up on that deal. We think we can be partners and all get rich!"

"I guarantee that you damn sure made the right decision. Partners it is!" Sonny agreed.

Clinching the deal, Sonny had one more thought in mind and that was sharing a nice bottle of whiskey—tainted whiskey "Why don't you men have a chair in the front room and I'll fix a drink to toast our partnership. What better way to begin a new partnership than have a couple of drinks?" Sonny was pleased with his charade and just so happened to have a nice bottle of whiskey for such an occasion, along with a handy bottle of strychnine close-by that he had for rodents. With a wicked little sneer on his face, he carefully mixed the whiskey with the poison.

Sonny came into the room and sat the tray of whiskey and glasses on a table near the men.

"You men ready for a drink?" Sonny asked.

"Reckon we are a little thirsty," Lee answered.

"Well y'all enjoy these drinks made from a little home brew recipe of mine."

Sebastian looked at Lee and raised one eyebrow as if to say, "I'm not used to drinking home-brewed whiskey."

Sonny handed each one a drink and then raised his own drink to toast. The men took two big gulps and with a strange look on Sebastian face, he said,

"This is a mighty powerful drink, but I would prefer my favorite Kentucky bourbon."

"We never got your real name…what is it," asked Lee.

Suddenly, the men began squirming in their chairs, then turned to look at one another.

"What kind of gall-dern stuff did ya' give us? I ain't feelin' so good," Lee said.

Sebastian was in a panic, because he had a good idea what Sonny had done. The effects of that much strychnine were lethal.

"Lee, we been poisoned!" Sebastian was holding his throat as he tried to stand, but instead, his knee's buckled and he fell to the floor. Lee was already slumped to one side breathing heavily. Sonny was standing over them smiling as he watched every move they made. In his cruel mind he was justified, *I didn't make 'em drink the stuff.* Lee put his hands to his throat as he slid out of the chair. Sebastian lay there suffering as the poison slowly flowed through their veins to their brain. He was dying slowly and kicking every now and then.

Sonny who was enjoying the effects of the poison finally answered their question loudly and sarcastically, "Gentlemen, I never told y'all my full name. I'm Sonny Bilbo and I never liked partnerships. And now if ya don't mind I'm reclaiming my money."

Sebastian and Lee could only move their mouths, but nothing would come out except for yellowish white foam drooling down their chins. Sonny felt powerful as he continued to stand over them until each took their final breath. Sonny reached down and with two fingers closed their dead eyes, and then sat down and finished his drink. After he realized what he had done, he began repeating aloud.

"Ain't nobody gonna push Sonny Bilbo around-— ain't nobody!"

The next morning, before daylight, Sonny placed the bodies of Sebastian and Lee in their car and drove them to a nearby lake that happen to be on the Porter's land. After carefully checking the depth of the lake, he drove near the water's edge and with the engine running, placed a heavy rock on the accelerator, then shoved the car into drive. When the car hit the surface, it was travelling at a fast-enough speed that it hit just right for the interior to begin absorbing the water. After he backed away, he was a bit disappointed that it didn't make it to the deepest section of the lake. *Let's hope we don't have a drought,* he thought. He continued to watch as it slowly took on more water and sank.

Good riddance! That'll teach 'em to mess with Sonny Bilbo, he thought.

Chapter 23

Bidzill assured Aggie that moving before they returned the stolen money to the Bank of Carthage would be in their best interest.

Before driving away, Aggie took a walk over to the loading dock and did a bit of reminiscing. She thought back to the time, she learned she would be owner of the High Stepper. She had grown to love the old steamboat, but there was something she loved more; and that was Bidzill; and of course, the child they were about to bring into the world. She walked down closer to the water and took in a long deep breath as if to capture the damp clammy air she had learned to love for the last time. As she stood there, several sea gulls flew past as if to say goodbye. Walking away, she thought of Kyle, who had provided so much for her. She bent down and picked up a small amount of sand and scattered it in the wind. "Rest in peace dear Kyle."

This time it will not be a lonely life, for I have Bidzill. It's time to begin a new life, she thought. After giving her past considerable thought, the three of them headed north to start a new chapter in their lives.

$\sim$

Driving down the brick streets of Tyler, Aggie and Annie Mae were impressed with all the new buildings.

"Tyler is nicer than I expected." Aggie said.

"They've done a lot of building," Bidzill offered. "We even have a new courthouse."

Annie Mae sat there taking it all in, thankful to be with the people who were now her family.

"Did your father like practicing medicine?" Annie Mae asked.

"Yes, he was a good doctor. When he learned medicine, there was no formal training but later, he did get 16 weeks of training and learned a lot by treating his patients. When he was a boy, he got plenty of practice by caring for and treating livestock for sickness and injury, and that's how he got most of his early experience."

Aggie smiled.

"You must have been very proud of your father?"

"It would be hard not to be, since he saved my life. Without him I wouldn't be here. He was a man who had great respect for people—all people."

Bidzill turned down a narrow dirt road two miles out of Tyler. It was well traveled but there were few houses.

"My land starts at the turn," he pointed out.

"Are we just about there?" Aggie asked.

She was beginning to think the road would never end, until she saw two large fence posts with a sign that was dangling sideways. The chain had rusted through and the sign dropped to one side. The pathway up to the house had been taken over by weeds, but it was apparent that at one time it was a driveway that was heavily travelled.

"We don't need a sign anyway," Bidzill said.

They continued down the long driveway, then turned onto a short brick road that led up to the house. There was a soft wind and the white-budded trees were waving in sync.

"What kind of trees are these?" she asked.

"They're flowering plum trees. We have a yard full of 'em. They're beautiful this time of the year, and the woods are covered in dogwoods. I forgot to tell you, but north of the house we have a place for a garden. I hope you and Annie Mae like gardening."

"I've missed gardening," Aggie said.

Annie Mae noticed a small house in the back of the stately two-story house and thought it was for her.

"Bidzill, the house is lovely, it's a two-story and just the right size." What she liked most was the huge wrap-around porch with all the white gardenia bushes.

"The house might need a little work," he said.

"Not to worry, we have plenty experience after refurbishing the steamer."

"Annie Mae, I hope you like your house. You'll have it all to yourself," Bidzill said.

"It looks very nice. I didn't know what to expect."

Entering their new home, the girls were pleasantly surprised when they saw all the furniture. Bidzill hurriedly snatched the sheets from the furniture they used for protection. He stood back so they could see the condition the furniture, which was surprisingly good.

Aggie walked around the room, sliding her fingers over the wood and peaking in various rooms as she toured the premises. "It's really quite lovely," she said. "Your father and mother enjoyed fine things."

With a baby on the way, for the first time in a long time, she felt like a normal person.

One week later, the house was taking shape. They worked hard, and before long the old place was back to life.

After all was completed, and everyone was all settled in, it was time for Bidzill to head to Carthage to return the money. His main concern was protecting his cargo, for he feared someone might rob him. He didn't relax until he drove up to the bank in Carthage.

Walking into the bank, a young woman jumped to her feet seeing a very handsome Indian with two large bags thrown over his shoulder. Bidzill was not the typical Indian she had seen before. She was certain with his blue eyes that he was half white. He stopped momentarily and smiled at her, then headed to the back of the bank where the banker's office was located.

"Mister, you can't go back there," she said.

"I need to see the banker," Bidzill replied.

"Sir, you take a seat and I'll have someone help you."

Bidzill sat down with the heavy bags by his chair and waited until the banker came out to meet him.

He quickly noticed the bags.

"What have we here?" the banker asked.

"This is the money that was stolen from your bank," Bidzill replied.

"Well I'll be damn—wonders never cease. But mister, how in the world did you come to acquire it? Do you know that this is only part of it—where is the rest?" the banker asked.

"This is all I have. I found these two bags hidden aboard the High Stepper, a steamboat in the ship channel, and I'm returning what I found."

"I'm afraid I don't understand how the money got on a steamboat," the banker stated.

"I can only tell you what I know. A man by the name of Packer Rover robbed your bank and took part of the money and bought a steamboat called the High Stepper. You can find it docked in the Port of Beaumont. It's a long story if you have time to listen."

"Take all the time you need." He directed Bidzill to a table nearby were they had privacy. The banker continued to stare at the sacks of money and then Bidzill.

"I have no way of proving what I know, but Packer Rover, the man who owned the High Stepper, robbed your bank then shortly thereafter-- was murdered. His nephew, Kyle Rover then fell heir to the steamer. I became Kyle's Captain and when he died, my wife and I became sole owners of the steamer. It was much later that I found the money. After the discovery, I knew I had to deliver it to you and set things straight…but to be clear, I had nothing to do with the robbery. I have no doubt that the steamboat was bought with stolen money from your bank. As of now, your bank owns the steamboat. I have the deed right here." Bidzill handed over the deed to the stunned banker.

"What in the hell are we going to do with a steamboat?" the banker asked, not expecting to get an answer.

After their discussion, the Sheriff was called to come in and take pictures with Bidzill, and of course, the banker along with the large bags of money. The photo was for the fanfare that ensued later, which was not at all what Bidzill wanted, for there was always a chance that the identity of his wife might be found out. The people of the town were also very grateful to Bidzill when they found out that much of their money had been returned.

In this instance, being a "half-breed" didn't matter to the townsfolk, as they were overwhelmed by Bidzill's honesty. Afterwards, he kindly dismissed himself for the return trip home. He was concerned that the pictures might make the rounds to the East Texas towns, which greatly troubled him. *This could threaten Aggie. I promised her she would be safe, and I may have let her down*, he worried.

~

Although Bidzill's name was not mentioned as the one who returned the stolen money, his picture was plastered all over the front page of newspapers throughout Texas, along with the tale of his valiant courage and honesty. Little good did it do to ask that they keep his identity a secret.

It was evident, with his hair pulled back in traditional style, that he was Indian. This made Bidzill a celebrity of sorts since he did what most of, white people thought an Indian was incapable of doing.

It was a weight lifted from Aggie's shoulders when Bidzill returned home from Carthage. It took several days before he told her that his picture was in the paper along with an article explaining that the money had been found aboard the High Stepper.

"Bidzill, what's going to happen now that the town knows we're here? You'll be recognized and then people will come nosing around asking questions." Tears welled up in her eyes as she thought about the ramifications of returning the money.

"Aggie, I've been thinking. What if I cut my hair? I'm just as much white as I am Indian, and now with all that's happened, I need to draw attention to the white man inside of me. What do you think?"

"I don't know—I like you the way you are," Aggie said.

"Do you think people would know the difference?" he asked.

His hair was of little consequence to her.

"Are you sure you want to do this?" she asked

"What I want is to keep our lives private. I've noticed that with my long hair people see an Indian. With short hair, perhaps they'll see me as a white man."

The next day she cut his hair without considering how it would change his appearance. After she finished, he excused himself to bathe and change clothes. Afterward emerged a man she was certain she had never seen before. His olive skin, cropped hair, and deep blue eyes took her breath away. He was the most handsome man she had ever seen.

"What do you think? he asked.

"I'm surprised that a haircut would make such a difference. You make the most handsome white man I have ever seen."

She walked over and put her arms around him, "I love you anyway you are, so don't forget it." That day, she fell in love with him all over again. She could not believe the change and from her perspective, no one would believe that he was Indian.

From that day on, Bidzill became a white man.

◡

For the Porters, everything returned to normal. Lucy and Jared were home and that was all that mattered. It took a few weeks for

Jared to warm up to her but he soon became more attached than ever.

Cain was shocked to read that Lee Tompkins and Sebastian Parker went missing. Soon after, the word circulated that they had met with foul play, but there was no evidence to prove otherwise.

It was the time of year when all the flatbed trailers were lined up in the fields to haul sweet potatoes to the barns. This year there was an overabundance of crops and Vick was concerned with the spoilage.

"There's a fortune of surplus sweet potatoes and they're going to ruin," Cain said.

They had often thought about shipping, but they had no way to transport their crop from point A to B and there wasn't time. This was their chance to do well since they had a couple of bad years after moving from Pecan Plantation.

This had been the main topic of conversation for months until they read a very interesting article about the High Stepper being auctioned off in Beaumont.

"Pa, it says here that the High Stepper is going to be auctioned off in Beaumont!" They say it's gonna to be a quick-sale."

"What do you mean—quick sale."

"It means they'll take whatever they can get! Apparently, that Indian gave up on the steamboat. Cain explained.

"Well then, are you in for another trip to Beaumont?"

"Why do you ask?"

"We need to have one last look and see if we can find the accounting books. They have to be somewhere on the boat unless that Indian found 'em!"

"I don't really care about the plantation now that we've put it behind us, but I'm all for making Lee and Sebastian pay for stealing from us if they are ever found."

Vick was quick with a response. "Son, I think this is something we have to do."

"If that's what you want!" Cain said agreeably.

Two weeks later Cain and Vick boarded the steamer and checked out places they had overlooked before. After they finished and once again came up empty-handed, it seemed only right to stay for the auction since Vick had never been to one.

"Pa, I think you need to see the auction."

"We may as well, since we're here."

The men registered as though they were going to make a bid, and found seats in the back of the room where it was difficult to see or hear the auctioneer.

They first began the auction bidding on furniture. Vick was fascinated, watching people as they bid. Because of where they were seated, he decided they needed better seats. He walked to the front of the building and motioned for Cain to move to the front. There was only one problem. He raised his hand just in time to hear the auctioneer holler, "Sold to number 12". The auctioneer was pointing right at Vick (#12) when he brought down the gavel. At that point, the people began to scatter.

And there was Vick, standing facing the auctioneer from across the room with his hand in mid-air. It finally registered that he was part of the final bid. Cain saw his Pa's reaction, which was one of dread and confusion. Cain wanted to laugh but he knew the harm had been done.

The bank was not happy with the way sales went until they sealed Vick's bid. Understanding what happened, Vick's heart skipped a couple of beats and then he broke out in a cold sweat. *How am I going to get out of this?* He wondered. People were already moving out and there wasn't time to make the "wrong" a "right". He shuffled his way through the crowd toward Cain.

"Pa, do you know what you've done?" Cain asked. He couldn't help but laugh.

"Son, how am I gonna git my ass out of this? I was motioning you to come closer but instead they think I bid on that damn steamboat!"

"I thought you knew not to raise your hand at an auction unless you're bidding."

"I was only trying to get your attention. Hell, how would I know?"

"I hate to say this, but it's too late. They're gonna hold you to the bid."

"I've got to straighten this out. You wait here," Vick said.

Vick walked in the direction of the auctioneer but he was approaching Vick faster than Vick could approach him.

"Sir, I want to thank you for your bid. We needed to sell. I know the man you bid against was disappointed, but that's how auctions go." (Just the words Vick did not want to hear that he had beat an interested party out of a bid.) "Glad you worked your way up front so you could be seen," the auctioneer said.

Vick fumbled around trying to explain but little good did it do.

"So, you're telling me that you didn't bid when I saw you plain as day?"

Vick started to use the excuse that he had been away in prison for twenty years, but he knew that wouldn't fly. He could see the auctioneer was about to lose it.

Seeing Vick's frustration, Cain interceded.

"Sir, excuse me but I need to speak to Vick in private."

"So, the two of you are in this together?"

"Yes, we won't be but a minute."

The Auctioneer watched them like a hawk in case they tried to make a run for it.

"Pa, I've been thinking. We can either take a bullet in the back when we make a run for it or we can put our money together with a little help from Ma. We haven't had time to talk, but this could be our answer—plus, a very good investment. What do you think? We could give him a promissory note and ask for time to get our money together."

Vick looked dazed as he listened to Cain's strategy.

"Son, I see what you mean but my problem is your Ma finding out what an idiot I am. I ain't never gonna live this down!"

"She doesn't need to know. We'll say that we've been talking about the transporting business and what better way than to invest in transportation."

"I don't know, I've always tried to talk to her first before I make a decision."

"Well then, let's tell her I bought it. I like the idea of an investment like this."

Two days later Cain and Vick were the proud owners of the High Stepper.

After struggling with the thought of running the business, they hired an outside firm to run it for them.

It took another month for the Stepper to begin full operation with a new crew and Captain, but business went on as usual without missing a step. As it turned out, the next two years the potato and rice business grew in proportion to more than pay for the steamer. It proved to be one of the best investments the Porters ever made.

Chapter 24

AGGIE THOUGHT SHE WOULD NEVER OUTGROW THE PAIN AND OBSESSION she had for Jared, but when Rafe was born he became the center of her world; and once again she found happiness. God has given me another chance and now I must make a future for my son, she reconciled.

Aggie and Bidzill had been married almost 2 years when he informed her that he was going away to medical school. The medical profession was changing rapidly, and many schools had gone out of business and were reorganizing. Bidzill's timing could not have been more perfect. For the new school needed his help more than he needed the school. He was often amused that the administrators treated him with the respect of a white man, never seemingly recognizing him as half Indian. They would never have accepted him had they known that he was half Navajo. Laughingly, he thought of what they would think if they knew his grandfather was the great Chief Atsa, who led his people on the deadly march to enslave his people.

Now that he was thought of as a white man and with the experience of a seasoned doctor, they listened to him and within months he had his license to practice medicine.

Years Later

Bidzill was driving home from Tyler when he and Rafe saw a young woman standing by her mailbox waving them down. As Bidzill got close he could see that she was in distress.

"Why are we stopping, Pa", Rafe asked.

"I think there's something wrong with that woman," he said.

He stopped the car and she ran toward him. "You've gotta help me!" Sir, please?"

"What can I do for you Miss?"

"My name's Margie Conway and we ain't lived here long. I got a step-daughter inside the house that just lost her Pa."

"Ma'am, you're not making any sense. You're going to have to calm down and tell me what's happened! Bidzill said.

"My husband, Bert, got caught in a fire at the Lawson's place about five miles down the road. They say he was burned up. I need my neighbors to look after my stepdaughter till I can git back. Can y'all do that for me? I spec' they gonna need me to make funeral arrangements."

A very attractive young girl in her early teens walked out of the house, apparently very upset that her father had been killed.

"Sir, this is my step-daughter Jessie—I hope y'all don't mind looking after her until I can get back this evening," she promised.

Feeling neighborly and wanting to help, Bidzill agreed to have Jessie stay with them until the arrangements were made. He gave her directions to his house so that later in the day the woman could pick Jessie up.

"We're glad to help ma'am, anything we can do."

Rafe, who was only ten years old, felt embarrassed when Jessie slid in the car beside him. "Son, I want you to meet Jessie; she's gonna need our help."

Rafe looked at her and gave a half-smile.

The young girl who had been crying dried her eyes after Bidzill reassured her that everything would be all right.

Aggie and Annie Mae accepted Jessie with open arms after hearing the tragic details of her father's death. At the time, it seemed the neighborly thing to do, however, they had no idea what was about to happen. They waited all that day and into the next day, but Margie Conway never returned.

"Bidzill, don't you think it's time we find out what's going on? I have a feeling that Margie Conway is either in trouble, or she's left town," Aggie said.

"Something ain't right! I'm going to find out what's happened."

Taking Jessie with him, they drove out near the Lawson place where they found nothing left of the house except a pile of black rubble. Anything that wouldn't burn was twisted and charred. Bidzill got out and walked around until a man walked up who generously offered information concerning the fire.

"The body was burned so bad they took him over to the Whittling Shop and buried him in a homemade coffin right quick," Mr. Jenkins said. "Mrs. Conway didn't have no money for burial, so they put him in the Old Town Cemetery. She said she needed to git' back home to pack and go to Georgia where she was raised," he explained.

"You mean she buried her husband before his daughter could pay her respects? Bidzill asked with a puzzled look...

He was glad he had left Jessie in the car, so she wasn't hearing these bad things about her step-mother.

"We didn't know nothin' 'bout no daughter. All she said was she had to leave and go back to Georgia. I reckon Mr. Conway was a good man 'cause he ran into a burning house to rescue Mrs. Lawson, but they both died in the fire and there wasn't a dang thing nobody could do about it. By the time he got inside it turned into a dad-burned blazing inferno."

All Bidzill could think about was Jessie and having to tell her that her daddy had already been buried and her stepmom left town without her.

"I want to thank you for the information, but right now I gotta figure out what Jessie's gonna do since she's left without a family."

"Poor girl, I spec' she'll be a ward of the state," Mr. Jenkins presumed.

"We'll see. I need to talk to my wife first," Bidzill countered.

With a heavy heart, he drove Jessie back home to deliver the news to Aggie that Margie had already buried Jessie's Pa and left town.

The girl didn't even get to see her daddy be buried, he lamented.

It had been a long time since Jessie felt someone cared for her, and the kindness and comfort Aggie and Annie Mae had given her meant a great deal to her. So, when she heard the news about her Pa, and what Margie had done, she took it much easier since it came from Bidzill and Aggie. They made her feel at home and there was no way any one of them would turn her away.

Annie Mae had already taken an interest in Jessie, and assumed that the girl had been abandoned. Aggie remembered how alone she was after she falsified her death.

"Annie Mae, if it hadn't been for you, I don't know what I would have done. I was all alone, but you made up for it."

"That's how it works, and now you and Bidzill are taking me in and young Jessie," Annie Mae replied.

"Don't be silly, you are as much a part of this family as any one of us and don't forget it," Aggie stressed.

Annie Mae insisted that Jessie stay with her, for she knew how important it was for Aggie and Bidzill to give Rafe all their attention.

After waiting a reasonable time, they adopted Jessie and gave her the family name. She was such a lovely sweet girl, and two years later she graduated from high school with honors.

The relationship between Aggie and Jessie grew and it was foreseeable that this young beauty had a mind of her own. She adored her new mother, for they had a lot in common.

When Jessie spoke of writing, they encouraged her to become a writer. In no time at all she earned a part-time job with a local paper dealing with life-and-death stories. As she advanced, her experience landed her a position with a credible newspaper.

Expressing her independence, she planned to move to Beaumont, which seemed to be calling her name.

The town's growth was due to the oil boom and became a melting pot for writers. Crime was not a big issue but mostly because the town handled its growth well. Although she missed her family, she filled her time calling on businesses and gaining their trust.

Chapter 25

After murdering Sebastian Parker and Lee Tompkins, the case grew cold after the years of no solid leads. Sonny had gone on with his life after losing his enthusiasm for the oil business. The thought of having a brush with the law and facing the probability of being incarcerated scared the heck out of him. Keeping a low profile and minding his own business seemed to be the only thing that made sense if he wanted to continue his charade and enjoy the fruits of his crimes.

This also included staying away from Jared and the Porters, just in case the boy suddenly remembered that he was the one who tried to kill him.

Money was no problem since he had the fortune he had stolen from Lucy. His wealth afforded him a different lifestyle, but money wasn't enough, for something else was missing and the loneliness began to drive him crazy.

I need a cook and the company of a woman full time, he thought.

Most of his time was spent hanging out in saloons and chasing after women, until he met Mable Fontenot whom had just moved to Woodville. She was rather plain, some might even say homely, but she was available, and very vulnerable. She was "easy pickings" for a guy like Sonny. She had a hard life of poverty prior to her divorcing her abusive husband. It appeared that Sonny was a step-up from what she had, especially since he had money and a nice home. There was only one problem; Mable chatted incessantly.

Soon after meeting Sonny, she moved in with him and became his common law wife.

One evening, after having too much to drink, Sonny began talking. After hours of bingeing, loose lips began to tell secrets that he had never planned to share with anyone.

He spoke of the Porters and their self-righteous behavior.

"Them Porters ain't no better than me. They're a bunch of bank robbers and murderers. They poisoned them two businessmen from San Augustine and got rid of their bodies."

"Why would they do that?" Mable asked.

"Because they were all in cahoots robbing that bank in Carthage."

"Seth, how do you know this?"

"Before them two men were murdered, they come by and wanted to buy my land. That's when they started throwing their weight around. They heard I was 'bout to start drilling and they thought they would buy me out, but I fooled 'em. Ain't nobody messes with me and lives to talk about it."

Mable thought Sonny was talking crazy but there was something about his last remark that made her think that he might have murdered those two bankers.

The next morning Mable remembered everything from the night before, but Sonny acted as if nothing had happened. She was sure he didn't remember a thing. For the first time, she began observing flaws in him that she had not seen before. There's something about him that's not right, she concluded. I've misjudged him, she thought. She grew concerned about her own safety if she chose to stay with him.

As the weeks turned into months she became consumed with what kind of man Seth really was. One evening, after he began his usual drinking, she decided to try again.

"Seth, why do you believe the Porters are bank robbers? Do you mind explaining?"

"That ain't none of your business. Why you keep flapping your jaws about them Porters? They're the scum of the earth. That's all you need to know."

"I didn't mean to upset you, I'm just trying to find out what kinda' neighbors we are living by," she responded.

Sonny tried to remember what he might have said to her about the Porters. *What could I have told her?* he thought.

Mable knew not to argue, but she couldn't control the habit she had of talking.

"Seth, I'm sorry, but you scared me when you said the two businessmen came by to make an offer about buying this place."

"Lady, I told ya' we ain't talkin' 'bout that!

Some things a man needs to keep private," Sonny replied.

"Well, you know you can tell me anything, don'tcha?" She tried to sooth things with her sweetness.

"I don't know about you! You sure are full of questions asking about them Porters, kinda' makes me wonder what you trying to find out."

"Seth, I didn't mean to make you mad!" she cried out.

He gave Mable a look that would kill, then walked to the pantry, pulled out a whiskey bottle and headed out the door.

He's hiding something, she thought assuredly.

Sonny walked into the barn and crawled up onto a bed of hay. Finally, I have some peace. He took a big slug of whiskey, feeling the warm soothing flow as it trickled down his throat. It took only a few slugs before he began to have a false sense of security. "I did what I had to do when I killed them crooks." He tried to justify committing the murder as he relived it over again.

Mable who normally couldn't care less about reading the newspaper, began to read the headlines whenever she was in town. On one such day, she read of Lee Tompkins, banker and Sebastian Parker who had been missing for years. She recalled Sonny making claims that the Porters murdered the two men. *Something don't make sense,* she thought.

Noticing a change in Mable, Sonny became suspicious. He wondered why she was going into town so much. I'm gonna get some answers today, he planned.

While in town, she ran into Lucy Porter who stopped to speak to her.

"Miss, could I talk to you a minute?" She noticed that Mable was trying to hide her eyes to keep from looking at her.

Mable was embarrassed, for she had been nursing a black eye, which Sonny had given her.

Lucy paid no attention to Mable's shyness and pushed a meeting on her.

"I've been wanting to get over to meet you. My name is Lucy Porter."

Mable was very uncomfortable, but she remained cordial. She thought that Lucy was just the opposite of what Seth had mentioned. She felt her compassion and Mable was convinced that she was a good woman.

Perhaps she needs a friend, Lucy thought. *How could anyone live with Seth and be okay?*

After several attempts, Lucy finally broke the ice.

"How do you like your place?" Lucy asked.

"Oh, it's nice," she said.

"How is Seth doing? We haven't seen him around."

"I'll tell him you asked about him. We're pretty much sticklers for stayin' around the house."

"I'm sorry, I didn't get your name..."

"Mable Fontenot, I'm from a little town in Louisiana called Merryville. Me and Seth hit it off right away and now we gonna get married," Mable lied, sensing Lucy's refinement. She was just the opposite living with a man out of wedlock.

"Well, congratulations, I'm sure we'll be seeing you from time to time. If there's anything I can do for you please let me know. It gets lonely when you don't know anyone." Lucy figured that Seth gave Mabel the black eye. Poor thing, she thought.

Mable was not used to people being so nice, and when Lucy reached out to her she felt uneasy. Seth wouldn't approve of her being friends with Lucy.

"I need to go, but it was nice meeting you Mrs. Porter," Mable said.

"Oh, please call me Lucy."

Mable never answered as she walked away.

She's a strange one, Lucy thought.

Mable was physically and emotionally distressed when she drove back home, knowing that Seth had lied. Things were not matching up, for there was no way he could convince her that Lucy was involved with a bank robbery, much less murder.

One thing for sure, he didn't lie when he said something happened to the two investors. The papers had confirmed that.

Mable tried to put on a happy face as she walked up the steps to the house, but when she saw Sonny standing there, her face gave her away.

"Where you been? You're late!" he shouted.

"Time just got away from me," she answered. She tried to change the subject.

"I didn't mean to keep you waiting, whatcha' been doing?" she asked.

"I ain't been doing nothing but sittin' and waitin' on you to get back ta feed me! Ain't no food here...no nothin'...so whatcha cookin' for supper?"

"Ya ain't missed a meal yet, have ya?" she asked.

"Don'tcha be talkin' to me like that, woman!" Sonny lifted his hand to slap her and swung awkwardly, but she ducked.

Mable knew that provoking him while he was drinking was not good.

"Not to worry, I have something in mind," she reassured him.

Sonny, clearly intoxicated from the whiskey, stumbled off in the direction of the barn, which was becoming his escape from the world-—and her.

"Call me when it's ready!" he said as he stormed out.

After he left, Mable began looking for anything to convince her that he was guilty of murder. *There must be something in this house that I can use against him*, she thought.

Room after room she searched, rummaging through things she had never had cause to bother with, until she uncovered a heavy load of clothing in a small closet. For the first time, she noticed how oddly they were positioned, just right to cover up two large suitcases. She quickly removed the clothing and took one suitcase out to look inside. There were a few books covering what was beneath and a small pillowcase covering the rest of the contents. When she removed it she gasped, for there were thousands of dollars bound together in currency straps with the name "Carthage Bank" stamped on them.

"Oh my, oh my," she kept saying aloud. "Seth is the one who robbed that bank." Her thoughts were whirling as she imagined him poisoning the two missing investors. She quickly replaced the suitcase and rummaged through the cabinets where she found the poison. This must have been what he used to kill those men. She quickly poured it down the drain and replaced it with tea. "He ain't poisoning me—not yet anyway," she said under her breath.

"I gotta get out of here—and quick."

Before she could begin supper, Sonny came in from the barn.

"Woman, you ain't even heated a pot! Whatcha been doin'?"

"I started ta get them taters together when I got this terrible headache and had ta lay down. I ain't feelin' a bit like cookin'."

Sonny walked toward her and Mable began to shake uncontrollably.

"Woman, what's wrong with you. You acting like I'm gonna hurtcha'."

"Naw, it ain't that, it's my nerves caused from my headache. Have you ever had a headache like mine?"

"Don't reckon I have since I ain't you." Sonny began laughing, making fun of her. "You scared of me, ain'tcha'!"

"She knew he was unpredictable and feared that he was up to something."

"Seth, please—I need to go git' me some medicine. I'll cook for ya' when I git back."

"You ain't goin' nowhere 'cause I gotta' cure that'll stop your pain."

She saw him walking toward the sink where she had thrown out the poison.

He positioned himself so she couldn't see what he was mixing together, but she knew.

"Seth, don't worry about me, I'm beginning to feel better now," she said.

"This is gonna make you feel a lot better, it's a real cure. My momma used to give it to me any time I was sick." He turned and walked toward her holding the glass.

Mable didn't have a choice as he forced it down her throat. She didn't really resist since she knew it was tea.

"Now, you gonna feel better." He looked at her with the most deviously hate-filled eyes as he waited for her to show the first signs of impending death. "Now, let me sit you down where you can rest. It won't take long before all your troubles will go away."

Mable knew what she had to do. I've gotta' git outta here, she anguished.

Sonny started toward her thinking she would keel over, but instead she jumped up and ran past him and out the door.

"Whatcha doin'?" he yelled. It took a moment for him to realize that the poison hadn't affected her. She was already in the road running toward the Porters' place when Sonny caught up with her in his car. Mable did not stop until Sonny opened the door of the car and hit her when he drove by. He stopped and picked her up by the hair of the head.

"Gal, where you think you goin'?" he asked.

Mable was in a daze after being knocked down with the car door. She tried to speak but she couldn't.

"The cat finally got your tongue?" Sonny asked and then laughed.

"Me and you coulda' made it jest fine if you woulda' kept that mouth of yers shut. Now, you tell me what's got you so spooked."

He figured she had found the poison and dumped it.

"I think it's time for us to take a little ride," he said.

All Mable could do was move her mouth, but no words would come out.

"Do you know how many times I pictured you with your mouth shut and finally, jest when me and you are about to part ways, yer' at a loss for words. Ain't that somethin'?"

Mable tried to sit up but she was too weak.

"Seth," she whispered, give us a chance, I love you."

"Who's Seth?" Sonny asked. "I guess it's time I introduce myself. I'm Sonny Bilbo."

Mable was trying to make sense of what he was saying.

"Seth?—I don't understand." Mable quietly asked.

"I'm jest itchin' ta tell ya' who I am 'cause it's been a long time since I've heard my name. I'm Sonny Bilbo, don'tcha like the ring of that?"

"Who's Sonny Bilbo? she asked.

"Me—I was a guard in the Huntsville Prison and Seth was my prisoner. When he got that letter about his dead wife and his place sittin' on a lake of oil—well— that's when I thought I'd make a purdy' good Seth!"

254

"What did you do to 'em?" She asked

"I did the same thing that I'm fixin' to do to you! In about five minutes you're gonna be meeting 'em."

"Please don't hurt me. I don't care who you are— I love you."

Sonny turned and drove on the Porter's land, through the woods where he buried Lee and Sebastian inside their car at the bottom of a lake. "You about to meet Mr. Tompkins and Mr. Parker.

Mable began to fight but Sonny overpowered her. "You want to fight, huh?" He took his fist and knocked her unconscious and then sat there for a time looking at her limp body.

When he was sure she was unconscious, he took her out by the lake and shoved her adrift watching as she slowly sank beneath the murky water.

That'll teach her, he thought. Sonny stood there for a time and then walked away.

Mable's body did not sink to the bottom, but instead landed atop the sunken car. The jolt, along with the cold water at that depth helped her regain consciousness. Being a good swimmer, and knowing she was fighting for her life, she did not immediately surface, but instead swam underwater as far as she could until she had to surface for air. Luckily, she was swimming in the right direction away from the bank where Sonny was. He was turned away and walking to his car when her head bobbed up like a fishing cork, taking in a gulp of air to fill her lungs that were fighting for oxygen. Again, she swam underwater until it was time to come up for air again. After repeating the process several more times, she finally reached the bank on the other side of the lake. Climbing out, she crawled into the bushes to hide herself, not knowing if Sonny had seen her or not. As she coughed the water from her lungs, she remembered what Sonny had said about the two men he killed, and figured the car that she hit belonged to them. Sonny's drunkenness and her will to live saved her life that day. She laid there with only one thought in mind, I've got to get away! Mable who became panic stricken planned to return to Louisiana where she had spent most of her youth.

Chapter 26

It took several years but eventually Lucy lost interest in Pecan Plantation and the accounting books. *Perhaps it's just as well,* she thought. Little good it did to try to regain legal right to the Plantation when Sebastian Parker and Lee Tompkins were still missing, along with the accounting books. Without their presence, nothing could be done to settle the controversy of who the real owners of the estate were.

Foul play was still the probability of their death and there was no new evidence to determine who might have killed them. But doubt still prevailed, since rumors circulated from town to town of reports that the two men had been seen. No one could say for sure what happened to the men except for Mable Fontenot, who was too traumatized to return to Texas. Even though she knew Sonny Bilbo was impersonating Seth Jackson, she was afraid to blow the whistle on him for it would surely lead him to her. If she remained silent, she knew he would continue his carnage. Yet, the thought of him getting away with murder continued to eat away at her. He's the devil in disguise and I intend to stay as far away as possible from that evil man with no conscience, she thought.

Several times she felt brave enough to return to Texas to make sure Sonny got what he deserved. But each time, she gave in to her fear of him.

The Porters were happy and they settled into a comfortable lifestyle watching Jared grow and mature into a young man as he ventured into making a life for himself.

Business was good for the Porters and they lacked for nothing.

∼

When World War I ensued, creating a new life for the Porters as well as all Americans, all ships, including steamboats, were used to facilitate the war effort, and to take pressure from the railway. It was during this time that the High Stepper met its demise.

It happened in the early morning hours while carrying a heavy load of artillery, when an inexperienced stern crew ventured too close to shore and snagged a large object. In a matter of hours, the vessel, with all its cargo, (along with years of memories), sank to the bottom of the river.

Now that the Porters were out of the steamboat business, they purchased a tugboat for transporting.

At the time Cain and Vick got the news that they had lost the Stepper, they were already seasoned and experienced in water transportation, and within the month they had purchased a brand-new tugboat they named the Little Stepper.

Vick and Cain were surprised to see how many people came to visit the waterway just to see the little tug with the name similar to the High Stepper, which soon became a novelty. The Little Stepper reminded them of the High Stepper that had given their small town so much prominence.

As the novelty wore off, the Little Stepper became just like all other working vessels as it continued to carry cargo from Beaumont to Galveston.

∼

One late afternoon, while returning from Woodville, Jared and Hop stopped at the corral to watch Vick who was trying to break in a new horse.

Seeing his grandfather being tossed around like a rag doll was very unsettling to Jared.

They watched in awe as Vick fought valiantly to tame the young mare. The horse was plenty wild as it reared, bucked, and twisted in midair. Inevitably, the horse won, and Vick was thrown over the fence onto a small tractor.

It took a moment for everyone to realize what had happened, but it soon became obvious that Vick was hurt, as he lay in a near fetal position on the ground. Hop jumped from the fence and rushed to Vick's side, propping his head on his lap. "Jared, you run and get your grandma, I think your Pa's hurt—bad."

Alarmed with concern, Jared sought help.

Lucy saw her son coming from the corral and met him at the door. "Jared, is something wrong?"

"It's Grandpa! He's been hurt."

"Oh no," I'll get Elizabeth!"

"Elizabeth, please come quick, something has happened to Vick!" She shouted.

Elizabeth hurried to the kitchen, filled a pan with water and grabbed a towel, then hurried out the door.

Tending to her husband, she bathed his face as she questioned Hop.

"How bad is he?"

"I don't know—but I think we should move him into the house."

"What if he's hurt too bad to move?" She tried to lift his head. "Vick, I'm here—can you hear me? We're moving you into the house." It was apparent he was unconscious. "Hop, do you mind rounding up the workers, so we can move him? We must keep him in this position in case his back is hurt."

"I'll be right back," he said. Hop jumped on the tractor and drove toward the fields.

Within minutes, he and Cain rounded up several men who helped lift Vick onto a gurney, then moved him into the house.

"Be careful with him—we don't know if anything is broken," Elizabeth pled.

"Grandma, I'll be in as soon as I put the horse away," Jared said.

Elizabeth anticipated that Vick would regain consciousness but when he didn't, they decided to take him to the doctor.

The next day, he regained consciousness on the ride to the doctor's house. By mid-morning, they arrived at the little blue house that functioned not only as a hospital but the residence of the town doctor.

Lucid enough to move, Vick was led into a hospital room and helped onto the examining table.

Doctor Jacks asked Cain to stay while he examined Vick. After a thorough examination, and unable to find any major injury, Doctor Jacks came up with an unexpected diagnosis.

"Son, I didn't want to be the one to tell your Ma, but your Pa had a stroke. You may want to wait until you get home and explain to her that it might be a long time before your Pa is his old self again. I don't have any cures for this, just some medicine that'll help him relax. I don't want him to get all worked up."

He handed Cain a little brown bag filled with all kinds of herbs.

"You make sure he takes this with a little tea."

"Are you sure Pa had a stroke?" Cain asked.

"I reckon so. Ain't no one wants to believe their loved one had a stroke—but I think your Pa did."

Cain waited until he and Elizabeth were alone before he told her.

"Ma, the doctor said Pa had a stroke and it's gonna take some time before he's back to being himself."

She developed a lump in her throat hearing the word "stroke". He was the love of her life, and she had waited years for them to be together, and now the thought of him being an invalid brought tears to her eyes. It broke her heart to see him this way.

Cain noticed her reaction and put his arms around her.

"Ma, you know Pa— he's strong as an ox. He'll come back from this. It's just gonna take time."

"Is that supposed to make me feel better—when the Doctor said he suffered a stroke?" she asked.

It was apparent with Vick's struggle to walk and express himself that Dr. Jacks' diagnosis was correct.

Elizabeth took care of him night and day as if it would be his last.

His language skills were affected as well as his right leg and because of that, Cain began to worry that it may have affected his memory. I wonder if he remembers the diamonds that were left at Panther Holler? If only Vick could have communicated that his memory was intact and as good as ever. Frustrated with his inability to speak caused him to withdraw from Elizabeth, which added to their problems.

Cain was devoted to his Pa and every chance they had he would saddle up and take him on short rides around the property. As Vick showed signs of improvement, Cain took him on longer rides, which gave his Pa confidence that he was getting better.

On one such day, Sonny saw the men out for a ride and decided to follow them. Well, ain't that a sight! Sonny thought. Occasionally, Cain would stop and help his Pa from the saddle, which stirred Sonny's curiosity even more. Something ain't right with Vick—he ain't walking too good, he observed.

Cain helped his Pa underneath a rain shelter, while they overlooked a small lake on the property, which coincidentally contained the bodies of Lee Tompkins and Sebastian Parker. It was the perfect place for Sonny to eavesdrop.

Sonny tied his horse to a tree and walked quietly toward the rain shed. There he was, close enough that he could hear pieces of conversation. Cain was doing most of the talking.

"Pa, we ain't talked about the diamonds in a long time. I think it's time we go back to Panther Holler and see if they're still there."

For the first time since his stroke, Vick sounded interested, but it wasn't for the reason Cain assumed. Vick knew his declining health was an issue and if it was his responsibility to deliver the diamonds to the descendants of the Original people, it had to be before he took his last breath.

"Cain—maybe before long," Vick said.

Hearing Vick form words was music to his ears and left no doubt that his Pa was hopefully on his way to a full recovery.

Sonny heard just enough to get the picture that there were diamonds hidden in a place called Panther Holler. *Where in the hell is Panther Holler?* he wondered. He waited for them to continue the conversation, but Cain was satisfied that he had heard enough.

Afraid of being seen, Sonny crept back to his horse and waited in the shadows of the bush to see what Cain and Vick would do next.

Vick felt good after the long ride but by the time he got home Cain had to help him into the house.

"Pa, I hope we didn't overdo it today!"

Vick walked to the bed to lay down. "Son, do you mind helping me with my boots? Cain smiled, "Anything else, Pa?"

"No, I'm just gonna rest my eyes a bit."

Elizabeth and Lucy were cooking when Cain walked in from Vick's bedroom.

"Ma, Pa's getting better 'cause he talked up a storm on the way home from our ride."

"Where did y'all ride?"

"Out to the old rain shed by the lake. This is the first time I've noticed him getting better. I hope we didn't do too much though, he wasn't feeling very good when we got back."

Elizabeth went into their bedroom to check on Vick.

She found him sleeping. He must be dreaming, she thought. She noticed his eyelids fluttering and how deeply he was breathing. I don't have the heart to disturb him, she thought.

During Vick's sleep, he was swept away as part of a foreboding vision. In his dream, he was young again—riding horses—then his dream changed. Suddenly, before him stood Hawk, beckoning him to follow—he felt invigorated and agile.

As before, Hawk only visited when an important change in his life was about to occur. Unable to speak, Vick saw a small town that he had never seen before. He felt calm as he rode along a dirt road before entering a drive that led to a stately house. Without hesitation, he stopped, dismounted and walked to the door.

What is the significance of this house? he wondered. Without knocking or any warning, the door opened and there stood before him the Indian whom he had met years earlier aboard the High Stepper. Vick stood waiting, until he heard a voice whisper— "Bidzill Franklin." Vick awoke and remembered the Indian whom he had not seen in years. If Bidzill hadn't had the skill of a doctor my grandson would have died. As he lay thinking about his dream and its significance, an overwhelming urge to find Bidzill came over him. He was deeply stirred by the dream and uncertain of its meaning, but he knew he had to see the Indian again. Vick was in no shape to find Bidzill, but over time, he knew that his dreams meant something; and like always, there would be a way provided for him.

Several weeks' later, Vick's health changed for the better and he remembered the intensity of his dream. I must try and find this Indian, he thought. Perhaps someone at the ship channel would know Bidzill's whereabouts. He was thinking about the time Bidzill owned the High Stepper.

Vick sensed finding him would be like finding a needle in a haystack, but he had to do this. Jared, who had been piloting the Little Stepper, asked Vick if he would take a trip on the tugboat with him just to get away and smell the fresh gulf air. He also wanted to have time with his Grandpa now that Vick was in full recovery.

The day before they were to begin their trip, a big storm blew in and caused extensive damage among some of the ships anchored in the ship channel. Jared was concerned for his tugboat, since it had been left in open water with only a lightweight anchor to secure it. "Grandpa, no telling what shape we're going to find her in! I'd like to leave in the morning."

The next day, Jared and his grandpa arrived at the ship channel to survey the damage. Vick watched with pride as Jared interacted with the workmen concerning the "tug". Seeing his grandson all grown up, he remembered how troubled they were when Jared went missing years ago. He's grown into a fine-looking man, Vick thought.

Three generations of Porters, and Jared had acquired the same handsome traits and penetrable blue eyes as his father and grandfather. The only difference was he stood a head taller than them and in place of dark hair, he had dark blonde, wavy and a bit longer. He was a looker, and the girls liked him, but he was more focused on developing his transport business than looking for a woman who would want to get her hooks into him. Seemingly, his only love was his tugboat, and it took priority over everything—even college. One day, Jared will settle down long enough to have a life, Vick thought.

Many times, sailing up and down the shoreline, Jared would tip his hat at the ladies, but that was the extent of his interest. Sometimes, no matter how intent one is, fate intercedes—and life can change like the wind.

After surveying the damage, they walked into the shipping office where a beautiful young girl caught Jared's eye. She had a glow about her that was refreshing and different. Dressed in a black ankle length suit with a white blouse, she looked very businesslike with her ivory complexion and her long auburn hair pulled back. Within seconds, he imagined her with her hair flowing around her shoulders and her soft lips brushed against his. Her voice was melodic, and he examined her from head to toe, admiring everything about her. She had the most perfect sculptured face with flawless skin. He couldn't keep his eyes off her. Vick, too, could not help but gaze at such a beauty. This young lady drew the attention of every man who saw her, regardless of their age or status. As the two waited, they wondered what a girl like her was doing at a ship channel.

The young woman noticed Jared in his Captain's hat and assumed he was the skipper of the damaged cargo ship that she had been sent to investigate.

She immediately turned to him and introduced herself.

"Sir, I'm Jessie Franklin from the paper, and I'm here to talk with you about the storm damage to your ship."

"We were lucky that we did not incur any damage," Jared responded.

"I understood you not only lost your cargo, but also had serious impairment to your boat?"

"Ma'am, I think you have me mixed up with someone else. I'm the Captain of the Little Stepper, the tugboat in the harbor."

"Oh, I'm so sorry, I just assumed you were the Captain of the cargo ship."

Jared could hardly speak, for he was lost in her eyes. "Yeah, I guess it's the hat," he said with a shy grin.

Vick could read his grandson's demeanor, and it was apparent that the newswoman had his grandson a little tripped up. At one point, Jared's and Jessie's eyes locked, but it was only for a moment. Before she left, she asked Jared if he would take her name and inform her if there were any other newsworthy stories that might have developed because of the storm.

As the three of them were about to walk out of the clerk's office, she remembered the steamboat she had heard her parents talk about.

"Your tugboat reminds me of a steamboat called the High Stepper!" she said.

Jessie's statement grew Vick's interest. *I wonder what she knows about the High Stepper?*

He called out to her, "Mrs. Franklin, I have a question for you. I'm curious— what do you know about the High Stepper?"

"I don't know much. Only what I've heard from my parents when they owned the steamboat," Jessie stated.

A shock went through Vick's body when he heard that Jessie's parents owned the steamboat at one time. *Once again, the Great Spirit has shown me that He is in control of my destiny*, Vick thought.

Athough he remembered Bidzill did not have children, he thought this must be the Indian.

"So, why did your father give the High Stepper up?" Vick asked.

"Steamboats were not a good place to raise children. My parents live in Tyler now, where my father practices medicine."

"So, you're here and your family is in Tyler?"

"Yes, I've been here for quite some time. Have you ever been to Tyler?"

"No, I haven't," he answered.

"You should go—it's a nice town."

He had the strangest feeling when she mentioned Tyler.

"Ma'am, one other thing—you said your father was a doctor. Do you mind telling me his name?"

"Of course, his name is Bidzill Franklin," she replied. Vick could not believe his luck. *It's just as I thought. If I need to know, there's a way provided.* He now knew how to find Bidzill.

The information was dropped in my lap. He wondered if it could be an omen?

Jared had no inkling of why Vick was asking so many questions.

Jessie finished her business with the clerk and excused herself, but Jared wasn't ready to say goodbye. Being a gentleman, he walked with her to her car. He was careful not to give the impression of being presumptuous, so they said their goodbyes and she drove away.

That wasn't too smart, he thought. There was no doubt that Jessie had Jared completely flustered, just by her mere presence—he was smitten.

Vick was still inside the office and questioning the clerk.

"Sir, I wonder if you knew the original owner of the High Stepper?"

"I can't rightly remember because that boat was here before I hired on. But what I recall is a woman owned the High Stepper. She had her car stored here for a long time, but then she sold the steamboat and moved to Tyler."

"Do you remember her name?"

"Jest a minute and I'll find out."

The clerk left his desk and went to a bookcase where he found a folder on the High Stepper. He spent a little time thumbing through the papers and then looked up to Vick and said, "The last owners were the Porters. I think the Porter's bought the boat from Aggie Dawson Jackson, but when she married, it shows she changed her name to Aggie Franklin." Wait! said Vick. "Would you repeat that lady's name again!"

"Aggie Dawson Jackson, he said." Vick could hardly believe his ears. That was a name from the past he would never forget. The clerk continued, "I remember them 'cause the woman never left the boat. Her husband used to handle all the business transactions as I recall. I thought it was strange. It says here her husband's name is Bidzill Franklin. Ain't no people I ever heard with that name—it's a mouth full," the clerk chuckled.

Reading on, the clerk said, "If you want to know who owned the boat before Mrs. Jackson, the man's name was Packer Rover, who killed himself. Mrs. Jackson acquired the boat after Mr. Rover died and co-owned it with Packer Rover's nephew, Kyle Rover. When Kyle was killed that's when Aggie Jackson took over as the primary owner. Do you want me to go on?"

"No, that's all I need to know. I want to thank you for the information," Vick said.

"Mister, you sure look familiar, I've been trying to figure out how I know you. It'll come to me later." Vick smiled, never letting on that he remembered him from years ago when he and Cain owned the High Stepper.

Vick walked away in a daze. I can't believe Aggie is alive and married to the man I have been trying to find. Could it be someone else with the same name? But it's not a common name. He remembered the night aboard the High Stepper when a woman came into their room to tell Jared goodbye. *That must have been Aggie*, he thought.

Vick's face must have been an open book, for Jared noticed something wrong.

"Grandpa--are you okay?"

"Everything's good," Vick lied. His thoughts were consumed with Aggie and how finding out she is alive might affect Cain.

It didn't take Vick five minutes to reconsider, for if Cain found out there could be irreparable damage— and lives could be ruined.

～

Jared was extremely lucky that the Little Stepper survived the storm and did not affect his work load hauling rice to Galveston.

～

It was a picturesque, sunny day when Jared docked his tug in the Beaumont Ship Channel and noticed a familiar figure walking out of the dispatch office. It was Jessie, the same stunning girl he had seen weeks before. He sounded the foghorn, which echoed in the harbor like a moose call. She looked up just in time to see the handsome Captain standing at the wheel of his tug, tipping his hat. She walked toward the edge of the dock to meet him—it seemed the natural thing to do since they had already been properly introduced. She remembered how handsome he was and that he had left a lasting impression. So, lasting that she was unable to quit thinking about him.

After anchoring the tug, he climbed up the ladder that led to the dock.

"Jessie, how are you?" He smiled and touched her shoulder. That simple touch caused goose bumps to run up and down her spine.

"Well, I didn't expect to see you here today!" she said.

"Good to see you too. What are you doing out here?" he asked.

"I came to deliver the paper that had the story I wrote."

"Perfect timing," he laughed. "Did you save a copy for me?"

"I have some extra if you care to walk me to my car?"

"Why don't you sit with me while I read it over coffee?" Jared asked.

"Great! I'd like to know what you think?"

The two of them walked into the coffee shop and sat in a booth with a view of the harbor.

"This is a nice surprise, meeting you here today," he offered.

"Thank you. Don't you get lonely all alone on your boat?"

"I wouldn't if I had a pretty girl like you sailing along with me."

He worried that he had come on too strong. *I can't believe I said that*, he thought.

She smiled with approval.

"I've always wanted to sail on a big boat like yours."

"It's not so big, at least not like the High Stepper," Jared said.

"I've only heard stories about that steamboat," Jessie offered.

"I bet there's one story you don't know about," Jared challenged.

"You've got me curious. Don't tell me you were a passenger on the steamer."

"As a matter of fact, I was—when I was very young. It involves your father, and possibly your mother. This is a coincidence that we've met," he said.

"What happened on the steamer?" she asked.

"When I was very young, my folks thought I was kidnapped. I later learned that your father was the one who rescued and treated me for my injuries. When your father found me, he had no idea who I was. You can't imagine the times I've thought of thanking him and your mother for saving me. If it wasn't for your mother and father, I might not be alive today."

"This is very strange. I would never have imagined we have my parents in common," she said. "You know, my father is a doctor in Tyler and my mother takes care of my brother. Now that I think about it, you and my brother favor a bit."

"I suppose I have one of those faces," Jared said.

"Jessie, before you leave I want to ask if you think it's okay if I meet your parents? I know it was years ago, but I would like to thank them for taking care of me."

"I'm sure they would like to know what happened to you. Just in case we lose contact with each other, let me draw you a map." She was careful to explain how to find her home. "Now—if you follow these directions you won't have any trouble at all."

"Will you be there when I come for a visit?"

"It depends on the weekend. Why don't you call the paper and we'll plan to meet on one of my weekends off?"

Chapter 27

Sonny had become obsessed after learning that Vick and Cain knew of a treasure of diamonds hidden at Panther Holler.

He tried, to find out where Panther Holler was but he couldn't. Only Vick and Cain knew Panther Holler existed and consisted of just one small cabin and Sam's grave deep in the forests of Arkansas.

Sonny was frustrated without a map, and needed more information about Panther Holler. *How am I gonna find the place unless they lead me to it? Without following every move, they make that's nearly impossible*, he thought. But that did not dissuade him.

After time passed, he began doubting his own mind, questioning himself on what he had overheard. Maybe it was just my imagination, he considered. But maybe I heard right after all. The possibility that he was right about the diamonds kept gnawing at him inside, motivating him to find out more.

He would stay awake at night plotting how he would force Vick and Cain to take him to the diamonds, but he couldn't muster the courage to make it happen.

One afternoon, he followed Vick and Cain back to the lake where he dumped the bodies of Lee and Sebastian. As usual, Cain brought up the subject of the diamonds again, asking if Vick considered drawing a map in case they forgot where the cave was located. Cain was always testing Vick's memory since the accident.

Sonny dismounted over a hundred yards away and sneaked up as quietly as possible, so he could hear. *I may get caught, but it's worth the risk.* Sonny listened intently, for this was the break he had been waiting for. *A map is exactly what I need*, he thought. Cain asked his Pa if they should go for the diamonds soon.

"Son, I don't know."

"But Pa, don't you think you should at least jot down the directions. You know, landscape changes and if that happens we could be days finding our way."

"I hadn't given it much thought, but you may be right, since my health ain't as good as it used to be. He knew that Cain had become important to their mission, and his boy had made a good point.

"I'm not good at drawing, so you might have to help me out," Vick chuckled.

When Sonny heard that they were drawing a map, he slowly eased away.

A map ain't no good if I can't have it! he thought.

Soon after returning home, Vick and Cain noticed the clear sunny day had evaporated almost before their eyes. Ominous storm clouds suddenly appeared, changing the sky to steely dark grey. In the distance Vick heard the crackling of thunder as tiny raindrops fell, then quickly developed into a hard downpour. The clouds overhead were now blackened by the tremendous amount of moisture they held. It wasn't long before those clouds released every bit of rain they had. The soil was soaking up the rain like a sponge, and the ground quickly turned to mush. The strong wind accompanying the rain seemed to be blowing in all directions, making it impossible to walk in a normal pattern. As they approached their property, Vick remembered that one of his special heifers was ready to give birth any day.

"I've got to find her," he said.

"Pa, it ain't safe for you going out in a storm like this. You could be hit by lightning."

"You don't worry about me, I ain't afraid of a little rain."

Storms always brought back bad memories of what happened to his brother, who fell victim to a storm when he was a boy. Vick was worried about history repeating itself.

There was no one to blame for the intensity and ferocity of an approaching storm. It had been raining for two days further north and properties that usually survived heavy rainfall began showing signs of weakness.

There was no way this small town could have prepared for what was about to happen. Creeks began to overflow their banks, and homes which were once considered safe from floodwaters, were suddenly threatened. Those in low-lying areas and in small valleys were soon underwater and crumbled in the path of rushing waters.

Vick watched as the enormous power of the wind peeled back the tin roof of his barn like an orange peel. It was too late to go back now, he whispered under his breath. He walked bent over, pulling the flap of his coat over his face, but little good it did, for Mother Nature was not to be ignored. All he could think about was his heifer that might be drowning somewhere. He was tender like that, thinking of a newborn calf and its mother struggling to give birth.

The storm was in full progress before Elizabeth noticed that Vick was not there.

"Cain, where's your Pa?" she asked.

"He's gone to find that pregnant heifer who's about to deliver."

"Why didn't you stop him. Haven't you taken a good look outside? Your Pa is still recovering. I can't believe you let him take off in this rain."

"Ma, have you ever tried to stop Vick Porter from doing something? He's as hard headed as Orson Cargill was."

"Well, you should have gone with him to help."

Elizabeth started pacing the floor and after a considerable time she walked into her bedroom and changed into her riding clothes and heavy range coat. I'm not leaving him to die alone, she thought.

When Cain saw his mother wrapped up in her coat and riding gear he hurriedly changed into his. "Ma, I'm not letting you go out in this storm by yourself. You're going to have to wait until I bring the horses around, there ain't no way a car can make it through the mud—the ground is too soft. So, wait until I get back."

"Well, don't take long!" Elizabeth said.

When Cain returned, she mounted her favorite mare and followed him. It was difficult pushing through the rain as they dodged brush and other debris flying. The destruction was overwhelming as they passed by Seth's place. His house was destroyed and trees were down, with their roots giving way in the softened earth. All that was left was the small cabin that was used by the ranch hands. Unfortunately, the main house, which sat on lower property than the Porters', was floating away in a sea of broken lumber. It was if the house had first been victimized by an isolated tornado.

"Cain look, I wonder if Seth survived?" Before he could answer, lightning hit a tree, and a moment later the crack of thunder caused the horses to rear up. Elizabeth fell backwards off her horse onto the road.

"Ma, are you alright?" Cain held on to his horse but when he saw his mother on the ground he let go and jumped down to help her. There was another rumble and flashes of lightning lit up the sky. Both horses became frightened and ran away, leaving them stranded. Cain bent down to help Elizabeth, but she stood up by herself.

"Ma, I need to take you back home—you're covered with mud."

"No, we need to find your Pa!"

Elizabeth followed Cain as they walked through the blinding rain in the direction of the pasture.

"Ma, has anyone ever told you that you're as hard-headed as Pa?" She gave him a half smile.

It was tough going, but they soon found Vick amid helping his heifer deliver her calf. They ran toward Vick to help.

"What took you so long?" Vick asked.

Elizabeth shook her head. "You're in trouble, so don't forget it!" she admonished.

"Here, comes help deliver this calf!" Vick shouted.

They hurried over and assisted a helpless creature that without the three of them would have surely died.

The rain was streaming down their faces, but they managed a smile of gratitude for being able to save the heifer and her calf. No matter what conditions surrounded them; it was an amazing sight to see the newborn struggle to stand as her mother licked her clean. With a little help, Cain lifted the calf in his arms and carried her the rest of the way home.

~

Once the storm had passed, the Porters surveyed the damage. Many homes were destroyed. The ones not flooded were hit with high winds that ripped the roofs off any kind of building. But one of the worst was Aggie's old house that Sonny was staying in. He planned to continue his ruse impersonating Seth, but after losing the home that he and Jared shared as co-owners, there was little left—not even the stolen money from the Carthage Bank. Now Sonny felt jinxed. *What now?* he asked himself. If it hadn't been for Lee Tompkins and Sabastian Parker, I would have already struck oil.

Sonny became paranoid and blamed his hard luck on Sebastian Parker and Lee Tompkins—*if only they hadn't dug into my past and meddled in my business.* He convinced himself that he would do whatever it took to survive.

He was now more desperate than ever to get his hands on the map to the diamonds.

Sonny had always been shady and unpredictable, but now after killing five people the beast was released within him. He changed from what normalcy he had to being completely evil and malicious. Soon, he regressed back to the old days when he felt worthless. At least money made him feel like he was somebody. Now, that all his efforts had failed, and he was back to being the same old Sonny, he planned to do whatever possible to continue his deception. Deep down, he knew that wearing the name of Seth Jackson would not help if he couldn't find a way out of the hole he had dug for himself.

In the days following the storm, Sonny checked out the losses of the Porters who had apparently not suffered much damage at all.

"Ain't that jest'my luck! They go unscathed, and the poor folks like me lose it all." He grew angrier thinking how difficult his life had become.

Luckily, his garden survived for if not, he would have been forced to take handouts from his neighbors.

The destruction of the storm brought most people together——all except Sonny, who held bitter contempt for anyone who was spared. *At least I've got the worker's shack to live in,* he thought.

The Porters, who had braved the storm, were ready to help whomever was in need—even if it meant helping the imposter they thought was Seth.

After a harsh winter and unseasonably warm spring, many newborn Hereford calves were plentiful. The herd was growing at a good pace. Vick and Cain occasionally opened the gates to the pastures to let the cattle fatten up before taken to auction, when suddenly Vick noticed the count was off.

At first, he figured some had wandered into the brush and he had missed them—until he noticed the number had shriveled.

"Cain, I want you to take a count 'cause some of our heifers are missing."

"I've been riding through the herd and there's a lot unaccounted for. Something's wrong," Vick said. Cain agreed.

Vick jumped from his horse and began going through the herd examining and making a mental note of all the livestock missing.

"Pa, come look!" He walked over and saw what looked like a bullet graze. "Yeah, it's a bullet graze alright." He took his hat off and scratched his head.

"Need I ask who might have done this?" Vick asked.

"It's probably our friend Seth. I bet he's selling my herd for the meat and keeping some for himself. I can't believe he killed some of my best calves."

"Pa, we can't accuse Seth without proof."

"It has to be him because he's the one who always makes trouble."

"What do you think we should do?"

"We're not planning on doing anything right now, but come morning, I'm gonna to be knocking on his door," Vick said.

The next day, they decided to report their rustling problem to the Sheriff before confronting Seth.

They drove like a bat out of hell to report who they thought might be stealing their cattle.

The Sheriff followed them back home in his truck to question Seth.

Sonny was coming from the barn right when Vick and Cain drove up with the Sheriff, just in time to see two of the Porters' calves being slaughtered before their eyes.

Nervous for being caught red-handed, Sonny had to face the Porters.

When the Sheriff asked Seth to explain himself, he lied and said, "I caught them cows eating my garden."

The Sheriff turned to Vick. "What do you want to do about this, Mr. Porter?"

Vick reflected back to his childhood when he and his brother were left hungry by an alcoholic father. He wanted to tear into Sonny, but he couldn't.

"Pa, you have every legal right to send Seth to jail—so what's stopping you?" Cain asked.

"Not now, we'll talk about it later" Vick gave Sonny a stern cold look and presumed, with the sheepishly cowardly look he got back, that Sonny would not bother his herd again.

"Mr. Porter, you ain't pressing charges?" asked the Sheriff.

"Not this time," Vick answered.

The Sheriff got in Sonny's face. "You better be glad you got some good neighbors 'cause if it was me you'd be hanging on one of them trees ya' got planted in 'yer yard. Now, don't give the Porters no more trouble, you hear?"

Sonny stood there looking down at his boots and then shook his head "yes".

"I don't like that sonofabitch. *I sure wish them Porters would have let me have him*, thought the Sheriff.

"Mr. Porter, you let me know if that man deals ya' more trouble—you hear?"

"Don't worry, he ain't messing with us again. I want to thank you for coming out and talking to him."

"Yes sir, anytime." After the Sheriff left, Cain confronted his dad one more time. "I don't understand. Why did you let him off?"

"I reckon 'cause I remember what it's like to be hungry."

"That doesn't give him the right to shoot our herd."

"I take it you ain't ever been hungry?"

Cain had no more words, for there were recesses in Vick's mind that no one, not even his son, knew about.

A week later Sonny was up to his old tricks again— stealing and killing livestock from the Porters. Cain and Vick were coming home from Woodville when they heard more shots ring out near their ranch.

"Pa, you reckon that's Seth shooting our cattle again?"

"I don't know, but I intend to find out and this time I don't give a damn whether he's hungry or not. I can't let him shoot up my herd. Step on it, son. I need to get there before he kills everyone of 'em."

Cain floor-boarded the accelerator and as he was coming out of a curve he slid off the road into a heavily wooded area. They plowed through briars and brush until they hit a tree and stopped. The car came to rest with both doors open, and Vick was hanging out of the passenger side of the car. Cain rolled out of the car okay, but Vick sustained the major impact from the wreck. "Pa," Cain cried. He worked to get the rest of Vick's limp body from the car. Regaining consciousness momentarily, he then lapsed into a coma. Cain sat and lifted Vick's head on his lap. I've got to get help! he thought.

As he sat there helplessly waiting; out of nowhere appeared Sonny on his horse.

"Looks like ya' got yerself in a little trouble. Is yer Pa gonna be okay?"

"I don't know, but I need you to help me bring him home. That's the least you can do, since you been killing our herd."

"Well then, this will make us even. Help me git 'em on my horse."

After Cain and Sonny loaded Vick, Cain watched as Sonny rode in the direction of home.

Cain ran most of the way to make it in time to help unload and carry Vick to bed.

Elizabeth was upset when she saw Vick brought into the house.

"Cain, what on earth happened?"

"We had a bad accident. I was driving when I missed the curve right before we got to Seth's place. I think Pa's hurt pretty bad."

"What should we do?" Elizabeth asked.

"Right now, we need to take care of him the best we can until we can get a doctor."

"There's no doctors around that knows any more than we do," Elizabeth stated.

"I know, but let's see how Pa does tonight."

"Jared's supposed to be here by lunchtime tomorrow, maybe he can help us," Lucy offered.

The next morning, everyone was anxiously waiting for Jared to get home, for they felt Vick was not any better.

When Jared walked through the door and saw his Grandpa unconscious, he did not waste a minute.

"Ma, I know a doctor in Tyler. Don't move Grandpa until I get back."

"Who do you know in Tyler?"

"I'll explain when I get back." Jared grabbed his hat to leave when Elizabeth followed him with a small sack of food.

"Son, take this so you won't have to stop."

"Grandma, don't worry it's about a 6-hour round trip, and I'll be back as soon as I can," he said.

It was mid-afternoon when Jared arrived in Tyler. The thought never entered his mind that it was an inconvenient time for him to call. His Grandpa needed a doctor and that was all that mattered.

When Jared knocked, Jessie answered the door totally surprised to see him.

"Jared— I thought it would be a couple of weeks. Is something wrong?"

"I'm sorry to show up like this but I don't have time to explain. Is your father here? I need to see him."

"Of course, wait here!"

Jared stood there waiting when Aggie walked in

"I heard someone at the door, can I help you?"

"You must be Mrs. Franklin. I'm Jared Porter, a friend of your daughters. You may not remember but years ago you and your husband saved my life. It was aboard the High Stepper."

Aggie stood there in shock. Before she could speak Dr., Franklin and Jessie walked into the room.

"Mother, I want you to meet a friend of mine, Jared Porter, and of course this is my father Doctor Franklin."

"How do you do, Jared. Jessie tells me you have a crisis of sorts."

For a second Aggie thought she would faint.

"Bidzill, this is Jared the young boy we took care of on the High Stepper when his father thought he was kidnapped."

Bidzill was very confused but didn't let on.

"Mam, I'm so sorry to barge in on you and Dr. Franklin but my Grandpa had a bad accident and he needs a good doctor. Sir, is there any way you can come and look after him until we know if he's going to be alright? There's not a doctor around that can help him, and we'll see that you're well paid for your time."

Bidzill knew he would have to make it okay with Aggie.

"Of course, Bidzill will go with you," Aggie spoke up. She turned to Bidzill and nodded. "Please go with Jared." She almost said, "my son," but caught herself.

"Aggie, are you sure?" Bidzill asked.

Jessie was standing there taking it all in when she noticed something about Aggie that was very strange. Her countenance and interest in helping Jared was very perplexing. *It's probably nothing*, she thought.

After the men left, Jessie invited Aggie to have tea. They were making idle chit-chat when unbeknown to them Rafe came in from school. He was about to walk into the kitchen when he heard his mother share something about Jared, which caught his attention.

Jessie had spoken with Rafe in confidence and told him she had met someone she was fond of.

Eavesdropping on the conversation, he noticed how distressed his mother and Jessie were. He imagined it was because of Jessie's new friend—Jared.

Interested to hear the details, he stood on the other side of the wall listening.

Rafe heard everything including where the Porters lived.

"Aggie, are you sure you're feeling well? There's something going on—is there something I can help you with?"

Aggie took a drink of tea as if she needed time to answer. "Thank you, the tea's good," she said. Her eyes began to water, and Jessie knew she struck a nerve.

"Aggie, are you alright?"

For the first time, with little thought, she began the story of her life, as her son stood only a few feet away listening to every detail. She left nothing out and with deep emotion she shared how and why she falsified her death.

She defended her motives by explaining that her siblings had threatened to kill both Jared and her because she was one of the heirs to the Petty fortune.

"Aggie, I don't understand about the Petty's."

"I'm sorry, they were cotton farmers, and at one time the richest family in the state of Texas. Hamp Petty was my real father. The man I was raised to believe was my daddy was hired by Hamp to take care of my mother and me. I learned later, before daddy died, that I was Hamp Petty's illegitimate daughter. My brothers and I were all left an equal share of the Petty fortune, but I was never able to claim mine, because my brothers did not accept me. Since then, there's been nothing but lies and deceit—mainly to protect Jared, Rafe and me. So now, since it's out in the open, I'll take it as it comes."

"Aggie, I can't believe what you and Jared must have gone through. No one would blame you for what you did to protect your son. Your secret is safe with me—so please don't worry."

"I think as long as my brothers think I'm dead, I'm okay. I can't afford to have them hunting me down and killing my children and me," Aggie said.

Rafe lost all perspective after listening to his mother's confession. The story was too unbelievable for him to comprehend. *Why would she keep the truth from me about my brother?* He was immediately upset with her for not telling him he had a brother.

How could she? he thought. His thinking was irrational, for he somehow discerned that his mother's confession was all about him.

Rafe was young and never had experienced real disappointment. His instinct was to run away, much like his mother had done rather than facing the problem. Pure adrenalin drove him to pack his things and leave to find Jared.

Given little concern for the complications that might result, he went into his room and pulled out a small leather tote, then filled it with some clothing for his trip. There was only one mode of travel, and that was horseback, since Rafe did not own a car.

It took several days of travel but when Rafe arrived at the Porter home he panicked. His mission was to see Jared, and destroying lives was of little consequence.

Rafe needed Jared to experience what he was going through since they were both in this together. Soon he would be facing his father, whom he blamed as much as his mother. *Pa should have told me that I had a brother,* he thought.

It did not take long for Aggie and Jessie to figure out why Rafe had run away.

"Aggie, do you think Rafe heard us?"

"Apparently so, look at this mess! I should have been more careful," she said.

Jessie tried to console her. "You can't blame yourself—he had to know, and if you had waited, you may have decided to never tell him."

"What about Jared?"

"Aggie, if Rafe tells Jared, it might be best that he hear it from his brother, than from you. Try not to second guess what will happen."

"How could I have been so careless? I don't even know if lying about my death is a crime."

"I wouldn't worry about that now. When they hear your story, there's no way anyone will hold you accountable."

"It's shameful that I've put my family through this, but I was frightened, and I wanted to spare my children. I'm sure by this time tomorrow the Porters will know. They'll think I need to be put in an insane asylum somewhere."

~

Rafe hesitated when he walked to the door of the Porters. He was standing with his hat in his hand when Elizabeth came to the door. There before her stood a nice looking young man who reminded her of Jared. Rafe had the same sandy brown hair and blue eyes, but there was nothing to attribute to the young men being brothers. She was caught completely off guard, for she had no idea who this young man was.

Within seconds she noticed everything about him from his blonde wavy hair to the nice shiny belt buckle that cowboys often wore. She thought he was well dressed in a nice pair of trousers, white shirt, and brown dusty boots that showed their wear.

"May we help you?" she asked.

"Yes mam, I'm looking for my Pa. I think he's here to see after Jared's grandpa. My names Rafe, and I'm from Tyler."

"Oh, you're Dr. Franklin's son, so, nice to meet you. Won't you come in? I'll get your father," Elizabeth said.

Elizabeth told Jared that the doctor's son Rafe was there to see him. He couldn't imagine why a young man whom he had never met would travel so far to meet him. Cain walked into the room and tried to put his guest at ease. "Hey Rafe, I didn't know you were coming. Is something wrong?" Jared asked.

"No —well, —yes there is something. Do you have some time I can talk to you alone?"

Jared had no idea what was about to happen.

"Rafe, I was about to ride into to town to get something to eat. Are you hungry?"

He shook his head "yes". "I'm on my horse, so I hope you don't mind driving."

Walking out the door, Bidzill caught a glimpse of Rafe and ran after him.

"Son, what are you doing here? Is your mother okay?"

Tears welled up in Bidzill's eyes, for the look on Rafe's face said it all.

"Pa, how could you lie to me? All this time you've known and didn't tell me."

Jared thought this was a personal issue between Rafe and his Pa and wanted to excuse himself. It was all so strange to hear the doctor and his son have differences before him.

"Son, please wait until we get home, so we can talk about this as a family."

"Family?" Rafe asked.

By this time, Jared sensed something very serious was going on, but with still no inkling of what it was.

"Pa, I'll talk to you later, but right now I need to talk to Jared."

What is Rafe talking about? Jared thought.

Driving away, he couldn't wait to ask. "Do you mind telling me what's going on? It must be serious for you to ride your horse all the way from Tyler just for the heck of it."

"Can we wait until we get to where we're going? At least the boy had the good sense to wait, and not take a chance that the news of Rafe being his brother would cause a wreck.

"Okay, if that's what you want."

The kid's upset, but what can I do about it? Jared continued to wonder why he was brought into a problem that the boy was having with his father.

Pulling into his favorite café, the two of them got out of the car and went in to talk.

The two of them sat for a moment studying each other.

"We're here now, so what has you so upset?" Jared asked.

"I've been lied to by both my parents."

"Rafe, you're young and I've been through some of the same stuff. Sometimes they want to protect us. Try not to be so hard on them," Jared explained.

Rafe had relived this moment a thousand times on his ride to Woodville, but now that he was about to change Jared's life, he decided to do so with a little more diplomacy.

"Jared, what I'm about to tell you concerns me and you."

"I'm afraid I don't understand."

Jared sat back abruptly for he had no idea what Rafe was talking about. For a moment, he thought it was about him and Jessie. Maybe they don't approve of me, he thought.

"Rafe, why don't you tell me what's going on?"

"First, let me ask you something. Have you ever thought you might have a brother running around someplace that you don't know about?"

"Jared wanted to laugh but he smiled. *What a stupid question.* he thought.

"Rafe, I have to be honest, I haven't given it much thought. Is this something you've thought about?"

"What if I told you that you have a brother and that brother is me?"

So much for diplomacy. The information hit Jared like a ton of bricks.

He was stunned and thought Rafe must be playing some kind of game. Somehow what Rafe said didn't make any sense.

"I'm afraid I don't understand," Jared said.

"I know you don't understand, but I heard mama tell Jessie that you're her son, and she had to give you to your Pa to save you from her half-brothers who wanted you and her dead. I only heard bits and pieces, but I heard enough to know we're brothers."

Jared felt he was in a fog, but then there was a ripple of memory that came pouring in as he tried to grasp what this kid was saying. He recalled hearing the name Petty before from his parents. And for Miss Aggie to have the same name as his mother, he was sure some of what Rafe was telling him was true.

How would Rafe know of the Petty's? Jared listened to the rest of the story, but it was difficult for him to believe this kid, whom he had just met, would turn out to be a long-lost brother. Hearing a story that he was the son of Aggie Franklin might have humiliated some people, but Jared felt there was a piece of his life's puzzle that finally fit. It was like a revelation of her love and its abounding connection to him. Even though these feelings were made known to him, he had a hard time grasping the truth, for he had been told all his life that his mother was deceased. Even though he knew this had to be true, there was part of him that needed more confirmation.

"Rafe, I'm sure you must have misunderstood, because my mother died when I was a little boy. My Pa received a letter that she was dead—and it came from her. You know, she sent the same letter to her husband she was married to at the time. So, I don't know what you heard but it's not possible that your Ma is my mother.

"No, you don't understand. I heard Ma say she lied when she sent those two letters. I was listening to her from the next room."

Jared turned white as a ghost as he heard more details come from this young man he hardly knew.

"Rafe, I don't know— this is hard to believe."

"Well, if I hadn't heard it with my own ears I would be skeptical just like you! I've been riding for two days thinking about nothing else, and I know what I heard. Rafe changed the subject. "Don't you think we kinda walk alike?"

Jared smiled, for he had always been told he had a swagger.

"I can't take credit for my walk, cause that came from Vick Porter—my grandpa. There were a lot of questions running through Jared's mind, but he couldn't think clearly enough to ask. There was something about Aggie's voice that had a special ring to it and now that he knew the truth, it was rather poignant. As bad as he wanted to disbelieve Rafe, he knew deep in his gut that Aggie was his real mother. *It's true*, he kept saying over and over in his mind.

Jared felt the necklace around his neck that he had worn since he was a kid. It must have been my mother who gave me this necklace to wear. He remembered he received the necklace from the lady who took care of him aboard the steamboat. Now it makes sense. he thought.

"Rafe, does your mother know you're here?"

"No, she doesn't. As soon as I heard that you were my brother I had to come see you. Now that you know, I guess I don't have any reason to stay."

"Well, I hate for you to put your Ma through this."

"I reckon that's so, but I wanted to come tell you that we've both been lied to."

"Rafe, I want to make something very clear. Parents sometimes keep secrets. If you think I'm going to join you in making your parents feel bad—I'm not. You should listen to me about this. Nothing is ever going to change in the way I feel about your parents. They are good people and whatever they did they did for a reason, and from what you said, they wanted to protect the family. Rafe, why don't we go and you clear the air with your Pa."

"I don't know if that's possible, but I don't want to cause trouble between you and your family." Rafe said.

"There's not going to be any trouble, but we need to be careful how we handle this," Jared explained.

Chapter 28

BACK AT THE RANCH, CAIN AND BIDZILL STEPPED OUTSIDE TO DISCUSS what was happening with Rafe.

"Dr. Franklin, was it my imagination or was your son upset?"

"Please, call me Bidzill."

"Okay, if that's how you want it."

"Cain, I hadn't planned to get into this, but I have to talk to you about something that I'm not sure you'll understand. At this time, I'm sure Jared already knows what I am about to tell you."

Cain immediately thought of Vick. I hope he's not going to die."

"No, that's not it at all. I'm sure as we speak that my son is explaining a secret to Jared that we've had in our family for many years."

Cain thought, *what's this to me?*

"I know this is going to come as a shock, but I want you to have an open mind."

"Okay, please continue." Cain instructed.

"Many years ago, my wife sent you a letter claiming that she had died of a mysterious illness. She also sent her husband of that time the same letter. She sent it to Seth Jackson who was in the Huntsville Prison after they were divorced.

"Wait, how do you know this?" Cain asked.

"Just hear me out." Bidzill asserted. "The same Aggie Dawson, who is the mother of your son Jared, is my wife, and that means our two sons are brothers," he explained.

"My wife is Aggie Dawson Jackson, Jared's biological mother."

"No, that can't be. Aggie would never fake her death and do this to her own son."

"Cain, if you'll think back to the conversation you had when you found out you had a son, you'll know why. She did this to save Jared's life and hers. This is the only reason she gave Jared to you to raise and protect. Do you remember now?"

"I know she was afraid of her two brothers, but I didn't think she was so desperate as to fake her own death."

"Yes, she gave you Jared because she knew he would be safe from her two brothers."

Cain was having great difficulty understanding. "Things don't add up, and now that I think about it, I remember Vick telling me that you said your wife owned the High Stepper."

"When was that?" Bidzill asked.

"That's when we found Jared aboard the High Stepper. I can assure you that Aggie never owned a steamboat."

"But she did! She owned the High Stepper and I worked for her as her Captain. That is another story, and I won't get into how she acquired the steamboat, but she did own it. We married during that time, and after we found out the steamboat belonged to the Carthage Bank and was not legally hers, she gave it up and we moved away. Shortly thereafter, we left Beaumont and settled in my father's home near Tyler. Rafe was born to us, but we never told him that he had a half-brother—mainly to protect Aggie from someone finding out that she was alive. I suspect Rafe found out the truth and that's the reason he's here to tell Jared. I for one, never meant for this to happen."

As the story unfolded, Cain was in such shock that he had to find a place to sit. A cool breeze swept over him, but it did little good, for he was at a boiling point that was indescribable. He sat there nervously running his fingers through his hair while he tried to make sense of what he'd just heard.

"Bidzill, what you've shared with me has proven one thing—and that's how drastically a man's life can change within a moment's time.

When you asked to speak with me in private, I had no idea that you were going to drop something like this on me."

"Cain, I want you to know that I love Aggie very much and she doesn't deserve any condemnation for what she's been through. It took great courage and a strong love for her to deprive herself of her only child at the time to protect him."

Cain sat there trying to absorb that Aggie was alive.

"What she's been through is quite clear, but I don't understand why she wouldn't reach out to me before she wrote those letters. I could have told her that her brothers and everyone she considered a threat were all dead. Had she come to me I could have spared her."

"You're telling me that Aggie's brothers are dead?"

"Yes, Aggie has been running when there was no need to run, and not only that, she's an heir to Pecan Plantation. At least she will be if we ever find the accounting books that can prove that Lee Tompkins and Sebastian Parker swindled us out of the plantation. If Aggie would have let me know she was alive, all the Petty wealth would have been awarded to her, with only a portion going to me because I was married to her sister when she died. I would imagine Lee Tompkins thought it would be easy to manipulate Aggie's half-brother Jonathan 'cause he was crazy and didn't have the sense to know what was happening. His death made me the only living heir, and for a time it was all mine until, the Bank of San Augustine notified me and Lucy that they had foreclosed on the property. When this happened, my family was forced from the property, which was then sold to Sebastian Parker. We need to find those books so we can get this straightened out. I'm sure Aggie would want to be informed that the plantation is hers."

Bidzill was silent and did not tell Cain that Aggie had the accounting books. *Now is not the right time*, Bidzill thought.

Cain's main concern was not for Aggie, but for his family; especially Lucy, who would be devastated to know that Jared's mother was alive and living only a short distance away. *Lucy's not going to be as understanding*, he thought. *Hell, I don't even understand! She might have lied to Bidzill, so he would marry her. Aggie is not only a liar, but she's also a bigamist. This is getting deeper and deeper.*

"Cain, I'm going to need your help. I don't know what to do about this. I don't even know if she's committed a crime."

"You can rest easy. I don't think there's a crime for her faking her death if she didn't commit a crime covering it up. Usually, when you tell one lie you must cover it up with another lie, it could be she's done something illegal with her business, but that's only speculation. I'm not concerned with the possibility of her having legal problems at this point, but if something comes up, she might be in hot water. I figure if the government hasn't inquired before now, they probably won't. However, there is another problem of bigamy. Aggie's husband, who was in prison, is still legally married to her—and bigamy, as I recall, is still a crime."

"I had heard he filed for divorce since he was in prison."

Bidzill thought he was the one delivering the blow, but when he heard that Aggie's husband was alive and released from prison, he wasn't prepared to reckon with that. Aggie assumed her husband had filed for a divorce and that they were no longer married. Of course, there was no way they knew if the real Seth divorced her, or had later known if he had been released from prison. Bidzill also assumed that Seth Jackson was divorced from Aggie and was still in prison serving out his life's sentence.

The two men sat in silence until Jared and Rafe drove up, but before the boys got out of the car, Bidzill asked that Cain keep the bigamy charge to himself.

The two boys walked over to their fathers and sat together, waiting for a response. Finally, Jared spoke to Dr. Franklin.

"How is Grandpa doing?"

"Your grandfather is doing much better, and I expect he'll make a full recovery if he takes it easy. Tomorrow, Rafe and I will be leaving. But in the meantime, I'll leave some medicine for Vick until he's up and about. Rafe and I need some time together so I'll be returning home with him."

Rafe contested his father's demand.

"Pa, I don't think I should be leaving just yet."

"Son, tomorrow morning, I want you to be packed and ready to leave. We'll plan on picking up your horse later, or if Cain has a buyer for it, perhaps he'll sell it for us."

"I might be interested in the horse for myself," Cain said. "Just tell me how much and I'll pay you before you leave."

"That's mighty kind of you Mr. Porter. I think she's worth twenty-five dollars. I been aiming to sell her," Rafe said.

"Sounds good to me," Cain agreed.

"Jared, I know you and my son talked and I hope if you need to discuss this, I'll do my best to explain."

"At some point I will, but for now I need to think how this is going to affect our family."

Cain hated to see this bit of information create problems with Jared's relationship with his biological mother, but he knew his son needed time to clear his head.

"Bidzill, why don't we take the horses and go for a ride! I haven't shown you around the property." Bidzill took the hint.

"Son, are you going to be alright if I leave?" Bidzill asked.

Jared answered for him.

"Don't worry Doctor Franklin, Rafe will be just fine."

Rafe, looked at Jared and smiled. *I think I like having a big brother,* he thought.

⁓

Cain went into the house and brought out a small bottle of whiskey, then escorted Dr. Franklin out to their favorite place, with Sonny secretly following. At first, Sonny thought Vick was riding with Cain, but when he got closer he was with a very distinguished looking stranger; which made him a bit nervous since they were headed to the lake where two bodies and a car lay at the bottom of the lake. With Sonny's paranoia, he thought the worst. Could it be they're looking for evidence that the Banker's bodies might be there? He was especially cautious since the lake was at an all-time low. Everything was happening too fast, he thought. When the men arrived, he positioned himself close enough, so he could hear Bidzill speak.

"So–what is this place?" asked Bidzill.

"It's just a quiet place where me and Pa come to talk about things–nothing special. But it's a good place to get away and clear our head. I hope you don't mind my presumptuousness, but I think we could use a drink." Bidzill was not a big drinker nor was Cain, but after all that had happened, he took a big swig from the bottle. "Wow, this is powerful stuff! What proof is it?" he asked.

"I don't know—I grabbed the first thing I saw. Whiskey is whiskey to me. Would you like to take a break and walk around the lake? The water level is low this time of the year, but it's still beautiful," Cain explained.

Sonny cringed, for he did not like the idea that they were moving about.

Cain went to the shoreline and picked up some pebbles.

"This reminds me of when I was a kid back in Arkansas. The only difference is the lakes in the Ozarks are clear and this lake is always murky due to the muddy bottom."

He watched as the pebbles skipped across the water, creating a shimmer and ripple effect.

Sonny noticed that he was throwing pebbles in the same location where the bodies were.

"Why don't you give it a try? It'll take you back to another time when life was less complicated."

Bidzill chuckled. "You think?" He walked over to the edge and reached down for several large pebbles.

"I'm surprised I never took the time to do this with my boy." He stepped closer to the lake and tried his luck at skipping the stones.

The first one was thrust across the water creating a long shimmering ripple. When the water parted they saw something shiny.

"What's that shiny thing sticking out of the water? It looks like part of a car!"

"Yeah——but what would a car be doing this far off the main road? It's probably something else," Cain offered.

They continued to walk, which made it hard for Sonny to keep up. Finally, Cain mentioned that he couldn't believe that Aggie was alive and living in Tyler. "All this time she's been living only a hundred miles away."

Sonny cringed! He was sure he overheard that Aggie was alive and living in Tyler. Hearing all the bits and pieces of their conversation, which explained a lot, finally it began coming together. This news meant she was still married to Seth Jackson. So, she's been running from her past and that's why she wrote those letters about being dead. Sonny gathered. I'm in trouble, 'cause now she's gonna know I'm alive.

Cain and Bidzill talked about the legality of what they were facing if the public knew that she was still married to Seth. "How are we going to keep this quiet?" Bidzill asked. By now Sonny was wondering how he was going to get out of the mess he was in.

Cain tried to understand, "I wish I knew how to advise you. It's a lot at stake here——especially since we all have family involved."

"I think the worst will be when Aggie finds out that her husband never divorced her," Bidzill remarked. "I know my wife, and I'm sure she never thought she would be committing bigamy."

Hearing the words that the Porters could prove Seth was alive had a sting about it that brought out the beast in Sonny. I have to find Aggie and shut her up for good before they all learn that I'm not Seth Jackson. It's her or me, and at this point it's gonna be me if I don't strike first! He thought. He remembered how he believed killing the real Seth would mean the end to all his problems, but somehow his problems multiplied. Now I have nothing, not even the little tack house that belonged to Aggie. He thought about Jared and how being tied to him screwed up everything for him. If only that bastard son of theirs was dead. At least I'd be able to sell my land. He was in an uncompromising position with no way to get out unless he eliminated Aggie, Jared and all those who stood in his way.

Sonny had become too careless with his snooping. As he quietly walked away, his horse snickered. Dang it, I bet they heard me, Sonny thought.

"Doc, did you hear that?" asked Cain.

"Yes—I think it came from that grove of trees!"

"Do you think we have company?"

"I don't know, but just in case, let's ride on back to the house."

Jared and Rafe kept their distance from Lucy and Elizabeth as they waited for Cain and Bidzill to return from the lake. I'm glad Pa's the one to explain to mother and not me.

Rafe was puzzled that Jared showed very little emotion after learning that Aggie was his mother. Perhaps if Rafe comprehended that Jared already knew he was adopted, and that he was the son of Aggie, he would have understood how Jared felt. Rather than being traumatized, he was eager to learn more about her.

Jared knew they had some things in common because he and Aggie both loved boats. He was impressed that his mother had owned the High Stepper and that she had been the sole owner of a steamboat which she successfully operated and ran as a business.

Chapter 29

AFTER BIDZILL AND RAFE ARRIVED HOME IT WAS A HAPPY BUT SORROWFUL reunion. Aggie was proud of Rafe for apologizing to her, but it was Jared she was most concerned about. I wonder if he will choose to see me again, she thought. And what about Jessie's relationship with Jared? What will he do about that? There were so many uncertainties.

Aggie cried in Bidzill's arms as he explained why he could not come home right away. "Please Aggie—don't cry. Let's give it time, everything will work out."

"Do you think Jared and Rafe will ever forgive me?"

"Of course, they will. Both boys are so much like you. I think if you had seen them after Rafe told Jared you were alive, you would have been proud of both your sons."

"I've waited so long for him to know the truth, but I wanted him to hear me, not Rafe. I wanted to be the one to tell him," she explained.

"It doesn't matter who told him. It would have been the same results. It may take a little time, but he'll come around," Bidzill tried to comfort her, and thought it best not to tell her that she might still be legally married to Seth. But there was other important news that he shared with her.

"Aggie, at least you're safe now and no one will ever hurt you again."

"What do you mean?" she asked.

"Cain told me that the entire Petty family is dead. Jonathan was the last to die, and when he died this made you the heir to Pecan

Plantation. Of course, you didn't know, but Cain was married to Eileen before she died; which made him heir to her portion of the estate, but otherwise you and your sons own all of the Petty estate which is worth a fortune."

"So, my brothers and sister are all dead? Are you sure about that?"

"Yes, Cain told me before I left. I didn't tell him that you had the accounting books."

"I'll have to tell him now that I know that the family is dead. What about Lee Tompkins and Sebastian Parker who own the Plantation?"

"As you know, Lee and Sebastian are no longer with us. The accounting books will clear that up when we turn them over for examination."

"I had no idea that Eileen was dead. That must have been difficult for Cain when he lost his wife."

"I wouldn't know. Cain seemed very much in love with Lucy. In case you are wondering, Lucy doesn't know that you're alive. I don't think Cain wants her to know, just yet."

~

After Bidzill left, Vick made a full recovery, and within the week he and Cain were involved in harvesting their crops.

Although he was not one hundred percent well, he knew he had to step up and help Cain or they would have to go to the expense of hiring someone.

One afternoon late, Cain asked his Pa if he would take a ride with him. They purposely rode past Seth's place on the way to the lake to see if he would follow them. As they meandered along, sure enough, Cain caught Seth out of the corner of his eye following them.

"Pa—I think we have company, Seth's right behind us."

"I wonder what's going on with him? Do you know?"

"I have an idea. He's curious about something in the lake."

"Something in the lake?" Vick asked.

"I'll show you when we get there."

After the men arrived, Cain walked close to the water and noticed the lake had receded even more since his last visit.

"Pa—you see that piece of metal protruding out of the water?" Cain pointed toward the shiny object.

"Yeah, it looks like part of a car," Vick responded.

"That's what it looks like to me, too. I wonder what a car would be doing in our lake? Better yet, this far off the road?"

"Maybe someone put it there on purpose!" Vick suggested.

"That's what I'm thinking. Perhaps we need to get the Sheriff and check it out!"

Sonny overheard their entire conversation. He eased his way back to his horse, which was tied up in the bushes, and then headed back to his place.

It's just a matter of time before they find the Bankers," Sonny fretted.

His first thought, when he returned, was to start packing if he wanted to keep from being caught. Then it hit him that the Porters would be the primary suspects since the lake was on their property. With that thought in mind, he went to the cabinet and picked up a jug of his favorite whiskey. All I need is my jug to settle my nerves. Why worry! Anyone could have killed the Bankers and it would be my word against my accusers," he rationalized.

The next day, Sonny watched the Sheriff, with a team of mules, pull the Banker's car from the lake.

They're gonna know about the Banker's and maybe even Mable before day's end, Sonny imagined.

As they scraped the mud from the windows they could see what looked to be human remains.

"Holy cow!" The Sheriff shouted as he backed away from the window.

"What's wrong?" asked Cain.

"It ain't good!" Sheriff Logan replied. "This car ain't in any shape for us to find clues. What I'm wondering is how this car came to be in your lake without some help.

The Sheriff turned toward Vick and Cain, glaring at them in an accusatory manner.

"After we pull the car out to the main road it's gonna have to stay put until I can get a truck. We'll leave as is for the time being. Cain... what do you know about anyone gone missing?" Sheriff Logan asked.

"It seems like I heard of a couple of men who went missing from San Augustine, but it was a long time ago," Cain said. The Sheriff's eyes darted toward Vick.

"And what about you, what do you know?"

"Sheriff, this is as much a shock to us as it is to you," Vick said.

"Well, while you're thinking about it, I'll go through some old wanted posters and see if I come up with anything," the Sheriff replied.

It took a few weeks for the word to travel to San Augustine, but as soon as the Sheriff got word of two men missing, it was easily determined that the bodies were probably that of Lee Tompkins and Sebastian Parker. This came as a shock to Cain and Vick since they had a history that tied them to the men. Their first thought was if they should report their connection of the two dead men. The Sheriff was already showing signs of suspecting them.

"Pa—this ain't a good idea if the Sheriff learns we had an ax to grind with these two men. We'll have a lot of explaining to do."

For a small town in East Texas there was a great deal of speculation about how the car got into the Porters' lake. Even Elizabeth and Lucy noticed the sneers and whispers behind their back. Obviously, assumptions were being made that the Porters had something to do with the death of the Bankers. Then they worried about Vick's prison background being known.

Cain grew increasingly concerned that the Sheriff might find out that Tompkins and Parker were the two who foreclosed on their plantation home in San Augustine. Then there was the money that Lucy stole from Lee and Sebastian, which belonged to the Carthage Bank.

They were afraid if they slipped up and someone began putting two and two together the whole bunch of them would be hauled in to answer questions that would make any one of them look guilty. "The Sheriff could build a strong case against us if he knew all the facts," explained Cain.

"Pa—who could have done this?"

"If I had to guess, I would say it's Seth! He's the one that's always causing trouble around here. It must be him! Who else could it be?"

The small town of Woodville had never been the center of publicity until now. People of every country were all abuzz with conjecture of who might have murdered the two men.

It was mid-day when Vick and Cain finished work and went for a dipper of cool water. They were just finishing up when they noticed a rider in the distance. Lucy was the only one who could make him out.

"Cain, that looks like Caleb. You remember Caleb who worked for Lee Tompkins in San Augustine? That's him."

"He's been gone a long time. I wonder why he decided to come back?" Cain asked.

"Probably because Lee and Sebastian are dead! You remember me telling you that Caleb worked for Lee Tompkins at the bank in San Augustine? He knew their shady past, and after he warned me about them, he never felt safe.

"You don't reckon Caleb would be the one who killed Lee and Sebastian, do you?"

"No—Caleb wouldn't hurt a flea," Lucy stated.

"I hope he's here to work. We can use some extra men," Cain said.

They all walked out to meet Caleb as he dismounted.

"Well, if you ain't a sight for sore eyes. We wondered what happened to you," Cain said.

"Howdy to you, too, Mr. Cain. I come back to see if y'all might be hiring."

"We can use another man to help us with our sweet potato crop."

"Then consider me hired," Caleb said.

Elizabeth was curious, for she had remembered Caleb mention that Seth was an imposter.

"Caleb, did you have a chance to stop by and see your friend Seth Jackson?"

"Ma'am—like I told y'all before, the man claiming to be Seth is trying to fool everybody. That ain't the Seth I know."

This was the first time Vick had heard Caleb make such a claim that Seth was an imposter.

"Caleb—I wonder, would you be willing to testify that the man claiming to be Seth Jackson ain't who he says he is?" asked Cain.

"I'd have to be sure, 'cause it's been a long time since I've seen the man. I'm sure that he ain't the Seth Jackson I knew as a kid. Do you mind me asking why y'all want me to testify?"

"Caleb, did you hear they found the bodies of your former boss and Sebastian Parker in our lake?"

"I heard about that, and that's another reason I came back."

"Do you have a mind to tell the Sheriff about your suspicions?" Cain asked.

"I reckon I can do that."

"I have an idea. How about we pay Seth a visit tomorrow on our way to town. We'll see how he reacts when I introduce you to him. If he doesn't know you, we'll know he's been lying."

After breakfast the next morning, the three men rode up to Seth's place and waited for Vick to go to the door. After he dismounted, the door opened unexpectedly and out came Seth who was thrown completely off guard seeing the Porters and Caleb facing him.

"What the hell are y'all doing here?" Sonny asked.

Vick hadn't planned on offering him a job, but before he knew it, he was asking.

"Seth, I'm gonna need some help with my sweet potato crop. Are you interested?"

"Hell no! I got my own work to do."

Sonny kept looking at Caleb, mainly because he was suspicious.

"Seth—this is Caleb. He'll be working with us too if you decide to help out!"

"I told ya——I got my own work!"

"We just trying to be neighborly," Vick said.

Sonny scooted past them and hurried out to the barn.

Vick looked at Caleb and smiled. "I reckon we got our answer."

"That's for sure," said Caleb. " 'Cause that ain't Seth Jackson. Seth and I go back a long way, and there ain't no way he would forget me. He doesn't even resemble Seth, and the Seth I knew didn't have a limp."

"Pa, who do you think he is?"

"I think we need to let the Sheriff figure that one out! If he ain't Seth, then I suspect the Seth we know is still in the Huntsville Prison."

After Sonny walked away, it took a few minutes before it occurred to him that Cain and Vick were fishing for something— and then it registered. How stupid of me not to know, he thought. That man was here to identify Seth, and I fell for it.

Sheriff Logan hated to believe it was one of the Porters who killed Lee and Sebastian, but since the lake was on their land, his obvious suspects were the Porters.

After arriving at the Sheriff's office, Vick was eager to shift the suspicion from them onto Seth.

"Sheriff—you don't really think my son and I had anything to do with killing Sebastian and Lee, do you?"

"It's hard to think it's anyone else, when the car with two men were found in your lake!"

"I believe it was me and Cain who asked you to find out what was in our lake. We were as surprised as you to find the remains of those two bankers in that car!" Vick pointed out.

"That's right, Sheriff. What you're saying doesn't make sense." Cain said.

"Okay then, why are y'all here?" the Sheriff responded.

"We have something that might interest you! It's about Seth Jackson!"

"What's he up to now?" asked the Sheriff.

Caleb broke in and explained.

"Sir, I been knowing Seth Jackson since I was a kid, and the man who calls himself Seth, ain't Seth. He's an imposter."

"Maybe he's changed since you knew him," Sheriff Logan stated.

"Naw, it ain't that! There's things about a man that never change. I guarantee you—he ain't Seth Jackson!"

"So, what do you want me to do—arrest him? Remember, without proof it'll be your word against his."

"Sheriff Logan, if you don't mind, would you check with the Huntsville Prison and see if Seth was released? That could make it a whole lot easier in finding out who this man really is," Vick suggested.

"Now y'all got me curious. I'll have my Deputy contact the prison, and when I find out I'll give y'all a holler!".

~

Sonny grew very suspicious of the Porters' stopping by his place unexpectedly. He had a gut feeling that something wasn't right. Judging from his luck, his instinct told him to pack up and get the hell out. It's just a matter of time before the Sheriff comes calling, he figured.

That night, Sonny packed him a bag with a few pieces of jerky and planned to leave the following morning.

As he headed east, he had only one place in mind, and that was the little east Texas town called Lufkin; where he planned to join up with the Morrison brothers with whom he had a history. It was a long ride through small trails and forests as the flickering sunlight shown through the tall pine trees. Some things don't change, he thought.

Traveling to Lufkin he saw the sun come up and go down more than once. Plenty of cool streams and lush green vegetation made the trek easy by horse. However, sometimes the thickets were more a problem than he remembered. On his last evening of travel, after he feasted on the last bit of jerky, he remembered how he framed Gill Morrison for murdering Seth Jackson. *Those brothers of Gill's are as stupid as he was, and it ain't likely they know that I'm the one who had their brother hung. I may as well have placed the noose around ol' Gill's neck. But they ain't gonna find out.*

His next stop would be the Morrison cabin.

Although it had been years since Sonny had been to Lufkin, he would never forget the little two-room shack that the Morrison's called home. He wondered if Clifford and Barry were still alive, since they no longer had their brother Gill to call the shots. The boys shared the same family resemblance, with wide faces and a defined crease in their chins. They were unsavory characters with tendrils that grew out of the side of their eyebrows. But what was most noticeable about them was their body odor, which was a sweet, musky, sickening smell that permeated the cabin. I'm sure they haven't changed a bit. There was never a doubt that these men were brothers, for they both had the same idiosyncratic mannerisms, along with an annoying snort when they laughed.

Before the turn of the century, the Morrison's were at the top of their game robbing mostly banks, but that changed over time when the banks developed ways to protect themselves. Now, since Sonny had lost everything and the Morrison's were on the lamb again, it seemed only right that he would try to return to the people he knew for support. Sonny never quite fit in with these dregs of the earth, but it didn't matter—for they shared the same evil.

On the third day of his travel he arrived at the Morrison's only to find no one home. He peeped through the cabin window and saw signs that someone living there, but he wasn't sure it was still the Morrison's. Until, he got a whiff from a small crack around the window frame. That unmistakably disgusting odor coming from the two- room shack confirmed that the Morrison's still lived there. It's them alright, I'd recognize that smell anywhere," he said.

It was dark when Clifford and Barry rode up to the cabin and saw a dim light through the window. "Barry, we got company!" They dismounted and went around to the side of the house with their guns drawn. There was a man sitting before their fireplace. "You reckon he's a squatter?" Clifford asked.

"Ain't but one way ta' find out," Barry replied.

"We gonna bust in when I count to three!"

"One-two-three," Clifford said.

Without any hesitation, the two men charged in and pointed their guns at Sonny.

"Wait, Wait—-don't shoot--I'm Sonny Bilbo—remember me?"

Clifford thought the name rang a bell. "You sure you Sonny Bilbo?"

The men walked around in front of Sonny who was hugging the back of his chair. "Yes, I'm sure. I'm Sonny. Remember when we used to ride together?" Sonny didn't recognize the two men at first, as many years had passed. But he knew their smell. Their beards covered their entire faces with only their beady eyes showing through their extra-bushy eyebrows.

"Yeah, I 'member we used to ride together—but we ain't heard from ya in a long time!" Sonny took his hat off and scratched his head. "Well, you're hearing from me now," Sonny emphasized.

"Well I be, I guess it is you——ain't it?"

"It's me in the flesh, and I came to see ya!" Sonny said.

"Barry, why don't ya' be neighborly and git the jug? We got some home brew that'll knock ya mama down. We ain't seen you in a coon's age," Clifford said. Clifford was the brains in his family and Barry was the introverted quiet one who (according to Clifford) spoke only on occasion just to let you know he was still alive.

"I got something I want to run by ya' and see if y'all are interested. I think I know a way to make us rich, but I can't do it without y'all's help," Sonny explained.

"Don't tell me it's robbin' a bank, 'cause it ain't like it used to be," Clifford said.

"It ain't no bank robbery—it's diamonds——you know, a treasure, maybe some jewels, like rubies and pearls."

"Diamonds? That's somethin' we ain't heard much about."

"Ain't y'all heard of jewels and rubies?"

"Yeah, but ya said, diamonds and that ain't nothin' we know much about."

Where them diamonds at anyway?"

"They in a place called "Panther Holler, Arkansas!"

"Arkansas? That's a hellava long way!" Clifford responded.

"I didn't say it was across the street. But I gotta' a map."

Sonny explained about the Porters and what he had heard about the diamonds. Once we get Vick and Cain together, they won't have a choice but lead us to the diamonds—even if it means killing somebody."

"Do y'all feel like making a little trip to Tyler first?"

"Why Tyler? I thought we were going to Arkansas."

"There's something I need take care of in Tyler before we go. There's a woman by the name of Aggie is threatening to go to the Sheriff, and if that happens we can kiss the diamonds goodbye. She's got the goods on me and it ain't likely we can go if we have the Sheriff and his posse tailing us. This could blow our plan if we don't kill her before she identifies me to the Sheriff."

"Where does she live?" asked Clifford.

"All I know is someplace in Tyler."

"That ain't as far as Arkansas!" Clifford remarked.

~

It was late afternoon when the Sheriff received information from the prison regarding Sonny. "I reckon them Porters are gonna be happy to have their name cleared. James Adams, do you want to ride out to the Porters with me to break the news?"

Gathering the paperwork that had been delivered to them by courier, the Sheriff and his Deputy rode out to the Porters' just before supper to break the news.

Everything was quiet when he walked up to the door and knocked. He waited until Elizabeth answered.

"Vick and Cain are working out in the field somewhere. Why don't you come in and have some coffee and wait until they come in for supper?" Elizabeth offered.

"I reckon I can do that!" The Sheriff and James Adams took off their hats and sat in the parlor and waited until Vick and Cain came in. They had not waited long when Elizabeth saw the men riding toward the house. The Sheriff and James stepped outside so they could meet the men in private.

When the men rounded the corner, they could see they had visitors.

"Pa—it's the Sheriff and his Deputy," Cain said.

"I sure hope he has some good news. I'm tired of waiting!" Cain and Vick dismounted and shook hands with the two men.

"Well, did you hear back from the Prison? Vick asked.

"I reckon Caleb was right all along. The man couldn't be Seth 'cause 'ol Seth's been dead for years. They checked the records and what they found was an inmate killed Seth. After his death, a prison guard by the name of Sonny Bilbo left the prison unexpectedly. Word got out that Sonny had the inmate kill Seth and for what reason they didn't know."

"Maybe the man claiming to be Seth is Sonny Bilbo," Cain said.

"That's the only thing that makes sense," the Sheriff stated.

"Judging from what I know, I think if you arrest the man pretending to be Seth, you'll be arresting the killer who murdered the two men who were found at the bottom of our lake. I'm betting the man who did the killing is Sonny Bilbo."

"We need to be careful and not let him know we're on to 'em until we're ready to bring 'em in." Sheriff Logan stated.

"Thank you, Sheriff. From the first time, I met Sonny I thought something was off. I suspect we know the reason now. There's one other thing."

"And what would that be?" Sheriff Logan asked.

It's about a letter that was sent to both Seth and me explaining about oil on the old Dawson place. Somehow, Sonny got his hands-on Seth's letter and decided that he could carry out his charade until he became wealthy," Vick offered.

"I imagine there's a lot we won't know until we bring him in. Just one word of advice—don't go taking the law into yer own hands," the Sheriff advised.

"Sheriff, do you know the name of the inmate that killed Seth?"

The Sheriff took out a paper from his shirt pocket and unfolded it.

"It says that Sonny Bilbo identified Gill Morrison as the killer of Seth Jackson, and after a trial Gill was found guilty, and hung in the Huntsville Prison. But that's not all, the letter also mentions that a guard confessed that Sonny Bilbo arranged for Gill Morrison to kill Seth Jackson."

"Vick, if that's true, I suggest y'all keep your distance from Sonny and let us deal with 'em. If he knows we're on to him he might kill again. Understand?"

Vick and Cain agreed, and thanked the Sheriff for clearing them.

After the Sheriff left, Cain and Vick went to warn Elizabeth and Lucy to watch out for Sonny.

Chapter 30

J̶ESSIE WAS STANDING OUTSIDE THE DOOR AS SHE OVERHEARD AGGIE AND Bidzill's conversation. *I hope Jared still thinks the same about me,* she thought.

For the next few days she tried to avoid conversations that reminded Aggie of Jared. Perhaps it's time for me to go back to Beaumont, she thought. I need a change of scenery. The real reason for her return would be to find out if Jared had feelings for her.

Bright and early the next morning, Jessie drove back to Beaumont to take up with the paper where she left off. She was excited to be back to work and away from the drama back home, but it was eating her alive not knowing if Jared will respond to her. She waited over a week before she had the courage to do something about it. When she couldn't stand it any longer she went to the ship channel to see if Jared was running his tugboat. The shipping clerk was very helpful when she inquired. "He usually signs in about 4:00 o'clock in the afternoon. I think if you come back later you might catch him," the clerk said.

Jessie thanked him and left. As she walked back to her car, the thought of seeing Jared gave her a rush of excitement. It had been too long. She hoped it would not look obvious that she was checking up on him. *After all, he should be the pursuer and not me,* she thought. What attracted her most about Jared was his broad shoulders, blue eyes and of course, his boyish smile, which melted her heart.

I can't wait to see him, she thought.

That afternoon, she had so many butterflies; the thought of cancelling ran through her mind, but she had to know if there could be anything between them. I don't want to turn him off if he thinks I'm running after him. She was in such a quandary about her aggressive behavior, which was not normally like her. I hope it doesn't show, she thought. As the tug entered the channel she quickly walked to the shipping office as if that was her main mission. The timing could not have been more perfect, as they nearly collided with Jared as she was walking out of the office He instinctively said, "Oh, pardon me ma'am. I should be more careful." That's all he said before he realized it was Jessie.

"We meet again! What are you doing at the ship channel?" She quickly changed into her prepared performance. "Jared, I had no idea that I would see you today. I had some brochures to deliver and thought I would drop them off on the way home," she lied.

"Oh, I thought you were here just to meet me," he kidded.

"I wouldn't want you to think I was running after you," she said.

"Well, I'm glad you caught me. Do you have time to catch supper– somewhere?"

She looked at her watch just to throw him off. "Ohhh…I don't know, it is a little late!"

"Come on Jessie, everyone needs to eat supper! However, if you don't have time, I understand," he said.

"That's okay, I was headed to the office to pick up some contracts, but that can wait." She hated she lied, since there were no such contracts to be picked up.

"You wait here! Don't go anywhere! Let me sign out and I'll be right out," he said.

"Take your time—I'll be here." She chuckled seeing her charade had worked.

She shuddered with excitement as she watched Jared walk off with his jacket thrown over his shoulder.

When he entered the clerk's office, a very talkative clerk met him. "I see you made it about the right time. A lady friend of yours was out here this morning and wanted to know what time you would be in today. I told her about 4 in the afternoon—and you're here right on the dot. I guess you saw her; she was just here. Jared smiled as he listened to the clerk. I wonder why Jessie lied. He chuckled and then thought, *two can play this game.* Jared decided to play along, and she would she would do.

He was very smooth. "Jessie, I'll follow you to your office, so you can pick up your contracts," he said.

"That's all right; they'll be there tomorrow," she said.

He was very serious. "Oh no, I'm not going to be the 'cause of you not picking up your contracts," he replied.

Jessie was not happy with the idea of having to drive a distance out of the way to pick up contracts she never had in the first place. I shouldn't have lied—serves me right, she almost whispered under her breath.

Finally, after being backed into the corner, she felt guilty and confessed.

"Jared, I'm sorry. I really don't have any contracts to pick up. I came out here to meet you because I wanted to make sure you were alright." Jared couldn't help but laugh.

"Why are you laughing?" she asked.

"Oh, just maybe it's because the shipping clerk told me all about you asking about me."

"Oh, you!" she said, and punched him softly on the arm.

His voice turned very serious as he pulled her toward him. "I'm glad you're here. I needed to see you."

There was something about Jessie that touched his heart. *She's the one—I just know it!* he thought. *I know we haven't known each other that long, but time has a way of moving on and I don't want to live another day without Jessie,* he thought.

After sharing a wonderful evening together, he took her home. He had been thinking of her constantly, and he was not ready for the night to end. *Tonight, will be the best opportunity I have*, he thought.

Jessie made it easy for them to talk about their dreams and aspirations, but she had no idea the conversation would become serious.

Jared became lost in her eyes and before he knew it, he was sharing his feelings for her.

"Jessie, I hope you will indulge me for a moment."

She was feeling the same as him. "Of course, you can talk to me about anything."

He hesitated a moment and then went on. "I know this is happening rather fast, but I have never met anyone like you. You are all I can think about. I know this is sudden, but the way I feel, I have to tell you that I'm falling for you."

Jessie was stunned, for she had no idea her date with Jared would lead to him declaring his love. She had several close calls with other hopefuls but Jared, was different.

Jessie had become lonely and whenever Aggie included her in the secret she had been carrying for years, things changed for Jessie.

"Jared...are you sure? Please don't say you love me unless you really mean it."

"I mean it–I've fallen for you. I've never told any other woman I love her....You are the first."

She couldn't believe this was happening. She reached for him and that was all it took. They kissed until the heat of passion became so great they had to stop. "I'm sorry, Jessie. We should wait——I have too much respect for you." They both pulled away to cool off.

"Jessie, I've been thinking, when I meet you in Tyler tomorrow, I'm going to ask your mother and father for your hand in marriage." Before she had a chance to think of what he'd said, he went down on one knee.

The only thing missing was the ring, for he had not expected to ask her to marry him.

"Jared, I can't believe this is happening. Are you sure we're not rushing into this?"

"Yes—I mean, no. I don't want to wait a second longer." Jared looked into her eyes and took a long pause— and then said, "Jessie Franklin, will you marry me?"

Her eyes filled with tears and trickled down her cheeks. She had never been happier.

"I didn't mean to make you cry!" he said.

"It's just that I'm overwhelmed, but I feel the same way about you." Before he knew it she had her arms around him kissing him again.

"The minute I heard those words, I knew in my heart that we are meant to be together. Jared Porter, I promise that I will always love you and be there when you need me," she whispered in his ear.

The two lovers talked for hours about their plans and places where they would like to live and when it was time to leave it was difficult to say goodbye.

Before the evening ended, Jessie suggested she go home ahead of Jared and feel out what would be the best way to tell Bidzill and Aggie about their plans to marry. She wanted everything to be perfect, for this would be the first time Jared would visit with Aggie as his mother.

She knew Jared was still dealing with the unexpected news that his mother was alive. She couldn't take the chance of an emotional outburst putting a damper on her engagement to Jared——nor did she want to upstage the reunion of a mother and her son.

The couple agreed that she would arrive a day earlier, and that Jared would come the next day. This should be plenty of time for her to make things right with Bidzill and Aggie before Jared's arrival.

The next morning, Jessie drove to Tyler dreaming of her wedding day and what it would be like being Mrs. Jared Porter. This is too good to be true, she thought.

After she arrived home, she noticed everyone was back to their normal selves, but no one expected her back so soon. Aggie had settled down a bit and Rafe was talking about going to Beaumont to have Jared take him out on his boat.

"Jessie, do you think Jared will take me for a ride on his boat?" Rafe asked.

"I'm sure he would like that. You'll have to ask him when he comes, which reminds me—he'll be here tomorrow morning." Aggie turned her attention to Jessie. "Dear, did you say he was coming tomorrow?"

"Yes, he'll be here tomorrow."

Aggie immediately began planning.

"I have to make everything perfect. I can't believe he is coming to see me so soon. I want to make a perfect meal for him," she said.

Jessie had planned to tell them Jared was coming to ask for her hand in marriage, but after hearing Aggie, she thought it would be upsetting to announce her engagement at the same time Aggie was planning for the reunion with her Jared. She did not want to take anything away from Aggie and Jared's reunion. *The engagement has got to wait, she thought. I must warn him before he gets here.*

The next morning Aggie was on pins and needles waiting for Jared. As time passed, she was growing more and more intense until it occurred to her that she had forgotten something from the store.

"Jessie, I have a list of things—would you mind going to the store for me?" Jessie thought about asking Rafe, but then she considered that she might run into Jared and forewarn him about announcing their wedding plans.

Chapter 31

THE HOOVES OF THE HORSES MADE A CLATTERING NOISE ON THE BRICK road as Sonny and the Morrison's rode into Tyler at mid-day. Sonny was a bit nervous and had chewed his cigar down to a nub. It won't be long now, he thought, as he plotted how they would kidnap Aggie Jackson.

Passing several businesses, he pointed toward a country store where he hoped to obtain directions to Aggie's home.

"Clifford, let's stop at that store. Maybe them people know Aggie Jackson," Sonny said.

Walking into the store with the two shabbily dressed brothers, the clerk grew suspicious right away. She wasn't used to having that kind of filth enter her store. They were not only dirty, but had a stench about them that she wasn't likely to forget. Sonny must have sensed her fright and gave a half smile, with the butt end of his cigar planted firmly between his lips. The proprietor thought, I hope this ain't trouble. I want them out of here quickly as possible!

When they asked about Aggie Jackson she quickly gave them directions to Aggie Franklin's house, which was only a short distance away. Although the clerk wondered what their type would have in common with a doctor and his wife, she presumed it was someone in need of medical attention.

After the men left the store, she ran to the window to take a good look. She noticed the brothers had their rifles in makeshift scabbards attached to the pommels of their saddles. That can mean trouble— but it ain't my business, she thought.

Jessie was leaving the entrance to the Franklin place when Jared drove up. Timing could not have been more perfect, she thought. They were excited to see each other and embraced. She was amid telling him why they should wait before announcing their wedding when she saw three men riding toward them. It was Sonny and the Morrison's. Jared had no knowledge that Sonny Bilbo was an imposter, so naturally he assumed it was Seth.

Somewhat confused, he watched as the men stopped their horses in front of the cars as if to prevent them from moving.

"Seth, what do you think you're doing?" Jared shouted.

"Well, if this ain't my lucky day. I got me two birds with one stone," Sonny said wryly.

Jessie looked to Jared for answers.

The two Morrison's placed their hands on their rifles to make sure Jared and Jessie knew they meant business.

"Seth, what's going on?" Jared demanded.

"It's yer Pa. He wants you to come with us!"

Jessie walked closer to Jared and grabbed his arm for comfort and protection.

Something is not measuring up! Why would Pa be with Seth? Jared thought.

"Seth, why don't you tell me what's really going on?" Jared asked

"Why in the hell is he calling ya Seth?" Clifford asked.

"Awww, Sonny—or Seth—what the hell does it matter?" Sonny replied.

"Well, if you have to know, your Pa is waiting for you to sign your half of the property over to me!"

"We can do that." Jared said. He turned to Jessie, and to protect her, he insisted that she go back home.

"Wait a minute, y'all ain't going nowhere, so git your ass in the car—both of ya!" Sonny yelled.

Jessie whispered, "Jared, who are these men?"

"Seth's my neighbor, but the other men I've never seen before."

Sonny smiled at Jessie. "Nice to make yer acquaintance. You're a mighty pretty little thing."

Barry, who was scarier of the two brothers, stared at Jessie so long that it frightened her. She had never seen anyone who looked and smelled like those men. Jared thought they might be part of a clan his mother had told him about. He remembered her telling him of a band of illiterates who were descendants of a group of interbred people.

A likewise group kidnapped his mother before she married his Pa. This was something Lucy never chose to talk about, he remembered. One common trait shared between these two men were their constant staring, which was very unsettling to Jessie.

Barry pulled out a chew of tobacco and tongued it into his cheek.

All they did was chew, spit, and stare at Jessie. She shivered with the thought of either of them touching her. "Where are you taking us?" she asked timidly. They ignored her as they continued to stare.

"I asked you where you were taking us?" she asked a bit more forcefully.

Sonny finally gave her a ray of hope.

"Don't worry Missy, when Jared signs my land over ta me, y'all can go free." Anything to keep her calm, Sonny contrived to himself.

After Jared and Jessie were in the backseat of their car, they watched as the men talked among themselves.

"What about that Aggie woman?" Clifford asked.

"She ain't my worry just yet," Sonny explained.

Jared and Jessie overheard them and wondered why they were talking about Aggie. No one had mentioned her up until now.

Sonny retrieved a pencil and paper from his saddlebag and gave it to Jessie.

"Missy, you're going to write me a letter!"

She looked at Jared for his approval.

"Jessie, go ahead and do as they say."

Sonny pulled Jared aside. "We need to talk," he said.

"Please let us go." Jessie begged.

Sonny ignored her and pushed Jared into the other car to begin his questioning.

"We ain't got time ta stay here all day, so let's make this quick. Where 'bouts in Arkansas did yer folks live?"

"Why would you want to know about Arkansas?" Jared asked.

"Just answer the question!" Sonny stressed.

"They lived in Jonesboro."

"Where 'bouts in Jonesboro?"

"They lived in my grandmother's place called 'the manor'!"

"What in the hell is 'the manor'?"

"It was my grandmother's old home-place."

"Do people in Jonesboro know where this manor place is located?"

"I expect that everyone knows," Jared responded.

"What about Panther Holler—where's that?"

"I don't understand why you're asking me all these questions about places I've never even been before. This ain't about signing over the land to you, is it?"

Sonny jabbed Jared in the gut with his gun.

"You keep jabbing me with that gun and I might decide to leave something out," Jared responded.

"Well then, maybe I need to visit with your girlfriend," Sonny said.

"Jonesboro is where my parents were raised—that's all I know. I've never even been there," Jared spoke frantically. *This is crazy!* Jared thought.

"Where is Panther Holler?" Sonny asked.

"It's not a town—it's a damn cabin in the woods somewhere. Now, what does that have to do with anything?"

"A cabin? Boy, ya' better not be lying ta me!"

"No, I'm telling you the truth! The cabin was named Panther Holler."

"Who in Aggie's house can take a note to Vick Porter in Woodville?"

Jared knew he better cooperate for fear they would hurt Jessie.

"Doctor Franklin lives there. Maybe he can take the note."

Sonny poked Jared with his gun again to make his point and then walked over to Jessie. He held the paper against the window.

She took the pencil and nodded for Sonny to begin. He cleared his throat and then spoke.

"If you want to see Jessie and Jared alive, you better do as I say. Get this note to Vick Porter. Meet us in Jonesboro at the manor in two days to take us to Panther Holler. No Sheriff—or they die. Seth Jackson."

Jessie started to cry with the thought of the men killing Jared's family and hers.

Sonny took her chin and looked into her eyes. "Listen up—if you don't want us hurtin' Jared, it's best you dry your eyes." Jessie gave a couple of sobs and then regained her composure.

After the note was written, Sonny attached the letter to a rock, but before he rode up to the Franklin place, he had to make certain that one of the Morrison's could drive Jessie's car before they began their trip to Jonesboro.

Jared imagined the letter would frighten the Franklins enough that Bidzill would travel to Woodville and warn Vick and Cain that Seth had kidnapped them.

Sonny talked to the brothers and asked Clifford if either of them could drive a car. "I ain't drivin' no car," said Clifford. Neither of the brothers had ever owned a car.

He took a good look at Barry. He looks like a dead man walking. Ain't no way he can figure out how to drive, he assumed. Sonny needed Clifford to keep an eye on Jared and Jessie as he drove. That would mean Barry would stay behind and kill Aggie.

Jared tried to comfort Jessie by holding her.

"I'm afraid for Aggie," she whispered.

"Keep an eye one 'em while I'm gone," Sonny commanded.

Sonny mounted his horse and rode like a madman down the road to the Franklins house in a cloud of self-imposed euphoria. It's about time I staked a claim. If I want that treasure, I gotta make it happen, he fantasized. He sent the rock, containing the note, crashing through a window, then quickly rode away like the coward he was.

Aggie and Bidzill were already concerned about the whereabouts of Jessie and Jared, and after they heard what sounded like glass breaking it occurred to them that something was very wrong.

Rafe reached the rock before his parents and quickly detached the paper and gave it to his Pa.

Aggie was terrified, and placed her hand over her mouth to keep from screaming. Bidzill took the note and read it aloud so Aggie and Rafe could hear every word. "They're not getting away with this—I'll find them!"

"No, there's got to be some mistake!" She shook her head and then took the note. "I have no idea what this means—damn that Seth!"

Bidzill took Aggie in his arms and tried to console her, but there were no words, nor gestures on earth that could give her comfort under those kinds of circumstances.

"Aggie, they've been kidnapped and the men who have them are not going to let them go until the Porters carry out their demands. I have to go and deliver this letter to them."

"What demands?" she asked.

"Aggie, I don't know who these men are or what they're talking about."

She reread the letter and tried to calm herself, but inwardly she was panicking. It was the same fear she had experienced when her brothers were alive and wanted her dead. *I thought it was over, and now we have men who want to kill Jared and Jessie.*

"Bidzill, what are we going to do? These men have our children!"

He had no words, he just stood at the window trying to think.

"You have to say something—we have to protect them!" Aggie stressed.

He finally spoke.

"Aggie, I don't have much time. Could you help me get my things together?"

"You can't go without me!" she said.

"Aggie, it's not a good idea! I'm going to the Porters, and it's best that you stay here! I want to make sure Rafe is safe—and you too," he said.

"What do you think the Porters are going to do?" Aggie asked.

"They have all the answers. I don't know why these people want to meet up in Jonesboro, Arkansas of all places. Nothing makes sense, and now I have to leave you and Rafe by yourselves which is killing me inside."

"Don't worry about us, just take the car and go. We'll manage just like we've always done!" Aggie said.

Bidzill went to the gun cabinet, taking out two shotguns with boxes of ammunition.

"I'm leaving one of the guns and shells for your protection. Rafe, you know how to use it so, if there's trouble, don't hesitate to shoot. In the meantime, I want you both to believe that we'll find Jessie and Jared."

Aggie followed him around until he threw enough clothing together for the trip.

He hated to leave her and his son, but he knew what he had to do. After they loaded the car they embraced, and for a time he wanted to take her with him, but he knew it might cause problems for the Porters.

"Bidzill, please take care of yourself. If anything happened to you, I don't know what we'd do. I love you."

Tears began to flow as she and Rafe followed him out to the car to say their goodbye. "Rafe, take care of your mother!" Bidzill said.

"Don't worry Pa, just find Jessie and Jared." For a moment, Bidzill thought how grown his son was to answer as he did. *I've never heard Rafe talk with that kind of confidence.*

Fearing that he might run into trouble, he drove out the south exit to the ranch. He had no idea how many men he might encounter, so to be safe he took a private exit that was seldom used.

After the car was out of sight, Aggie walked away unable to contain her composure. *I can't allow Rafe to see me like this.*

Sonny was inundated with concern since he had to depend on two idiots to help him do his dirty work.

"Say Clifford, you know your brother better than me——do you think he can kill Aggie?" Sonny asked.

"He's mean enough!" Clifford responded.

"I'm counting on him!" Sonny emphasized.

"Barry, it's up to you! Think you can take care of that woman?" Sonny asked.

Barry stood there looking at him and then shook his head yes. Sonny noticed how Barry kept looking at the car that had belonged to Jessie.

"We can't afford to make any mistakes if you want your share of the treasure, do you understand?"

Barry went over and looked inside the car.

"Ya better leave me the keys," he said. That was the most Barry had said since they left Lufkin.

After the men left with Jessie and Jared, Barry came alive like a sleeping bear who suddenly awoke from a long nap. He looked more alert and twice as mean as he examined the car that was left behind. He rotated the steering wheel as he tried it out, and then pushed on the brakes as he studied the machinery. Once he gained a little confidence, he turned the key and started the motor.

"Hot dang," he said, as the motor continued to run.

He turned the car off and then walked around to the back of the car to open the trunk. Inside the trunk was a gas can, which he took out. Without any hesitation, he got into the car and cranked it again. When he stepped on the gas the car jumped and jerked a bit, but he managed to make it to the store, which was only short distance away. While at the store, he put gas in the car and filled the gas can.

Once back to the entrance of Aggie's place, Barry drove carefully down the path leading up to the house. Hearing an approaching car Aggie ran to the window thinking it was Bidzill. "Perhaps he has news about Jessie and Jared," she said to Rafe. As the rattle of the Model T came closer, her excitement turned to fear as she came face to face with what appeared to be a mountain man. Barry was out of the car and not saying a word. He simply stood there staring at her. He was filthy and reeked of a smell she found disturbing.

"Who are you, and what are you doing with my daughter's car?" Aggie asked.

The stranger ignored her as he reached into the back of the car and brought out a short rope, just long enough to strangle someone with. Barry began flexing the rope as he walked toward her. Fearing for her life, she screamed at the top of her lungs. Rafe heard her and suddenly swung open the door to see what was wrong. He had not heard the car come up. Upon seeing this strange man, he too became frightened.

"Rafe, go back into the house," Aggie shouted. Barry continued to walk closer but she was much faster and ran inside the house, locking the door behind her. Standing behind the locked door, she shouted, "What do you want?" She could tell that he had a mouth full of tobacco, for one jaw was protruding. He stood there tongue-tied or just too plain ignorant to speak. Finally, he spat and began to talk.

She noticed the bullet hole scar on his neck and knew she and Rafe were in trouble.

"You are coming out or do I have to come in after ya'" he said. She wondered about his accent for she had never heard such a strange dialect.

"Please go away. If you want the car you can have it—just go!" she commanded.

"Either you comin' out, or I'm comin' in," Barry said.

Rafe was in the background listening. "Mama, what are we gonna do?" They knew they had the gun but neither of them wanted to go to that extreme if they could talk their way into making the man leave.

No sooner had Rafe spoke when Barry grabbed the door and began trying to force it open. Aggie screamed, "Rafe, get the gun."

He grabbed the gun but forgot the box of ammunition. "Mama, what are we gonna do now?" They both ran for the upstairs but had no place to run unless they opened the window and climbed onto the roof. *This may be our only option*, Aggie thought. She knew they could both jump from the roof if they had to, but even if they jumped they stood a chance of hurting themselves. "Rafe, go into our bedroom and use the gun if you have to!"

"Ma, I forgot the ammunition downstairs."

"Then do what you must to survive, even if you have to climb out the window and jump. Just remember to jump and then fall into a roll. This will help deflect the blow. Understand?"

"Okay, but what about you?" Rafe asked While they were upstairs Aggie saw Barry with a gas can pouring it around the exterior of the house.

"Rafe, we've got to jump! He's planning on burning us alive if we don't!"

The determined young man ran to his mother and started taking control just like his Pa would expect him to do. "Ma, when he walks to the other side of the house we are going to jump and run. When we get to the front of the house we'll make a run for Jessie's car and drive off."

"What if there are no keys?" she asked.

"Don't think like that!" he shouted.

They stood watch and when the coast was clear, Rafe opened the window and helped his Ma out onto a slanted roof. "Ma, be careful and don't slip," he said. He was very attentive as he helped her down to the edge of the roof. "Son, I don't know if I can do this! It's so high––I'm afraid."

"Ma, please, you have to do this. If we don't jump, we're as good as dead. You must think we're going to get out of this. Remember as soon as I jump, I want you to bail out behind me. When you jump, I'll be there to break your fall."

Aggie knew that it would be a matter of moments before Barry came back around the house. "Son, be careful," she whispered.

Rafe was ready to make his move but just as he jumped they heard Barry coming around the end of the house. Rafe hit the ground and looked up at his mother just in time to see her motion for him to run. She wanted to scream but Barry was just a few steps away from being able to see Rafe. Being young and tough, the boy jumped to his feet and ran toward a tree that had a flatbed trailer positioned in front of it. At that very moment Barry was dousing gas on the back of the house with Aggie lying flat on the roof as she waited for her time to jump.

Midway behind the house, Barry ran out of gas and stopped to light it. Rafe saw him take the matches from his pocket and get ready to strike when suddenly Barry stopped. Maybe they gonna come out the front door and get away, he thought. He ran to the front of the house to check out his suspicions, which was the perfect time for Aggie to jump, but the timing was not right for her son to catch her and break her fall. When she hit the ground, she landed on her side and hip, seriously injuring herself. Rafe ran toward her after seeing her fall. "Mom, are you okay?" Aggie was in terrible pain, but she refused to make a sound. "Ma, you're hurt— are you okay?"

"I will be when we get away from this place. He's going to burn our house down."

Barry was sure Rafe and Aggie were in the house and he decided that burning them alive was much easier than having to fight off Rafe, who looked plenty tough. Rafe picked up his mother and carried her to safety where they hid behind a small storage shed. They peeked around the edge of the shed and watched as Barry lit the gasoline that surrounded the house. It quickly caught fire and was soon totally ablaze.

Rafe held his mother as she cried while watching their home burn all their belongings and memories to the ground. The crackling noise of the rafters falling was a sound she would never forget. After her home turned into a smoldering pile of rubble, she looked at Rafe as if all their memories were now gone. She was consumed with pain from the fall and could hardly stand on her own two feet.

"Rafe, this is too much! What are we going to do?"

"We have to leave before that man comes back."

"Son, you're going to have to do the best you can, I'm in too much pain to even talk."

"Ma, you may have a broken hip, so when I lift you put your arms around my neck." Carrying her to the car, he carefully helped her into the back seat, so she could rest.

"Thank you, son, I don't know if I can make it all the way to Woodville." Rafe could tell his mother was going into shock. She needs a proper place to rest, he thought. He knew where his father went and how long it would take to get there, but he was thinking about his mother.

"Ma, maybe we can catch Pa!"

Rafe planned to drive straight through, but by the time they got to Lufkin Aggie was in such pain they had to stop and rest.

"Rafe, I want to thank you for what you did today. Your father is going to be so proud you."

He could tell she was in shock for she kept repeating herself.

His only concern was making it to Woodville in time for his Pa to take care of his mother.

Chapter 32

IT WAS MID-AFTERNOON WHEN BIDZILL ARRIVED JUST IN TIME TO SEE
Cain close the barn doors for the night.

Recognizing Bidzill's car, Cain wondered what would bring the
doctor back to Woodville. After what all had happened with Jared and
Rafe, he knew it couldn't be good.

"Sorry for just showing up like this Cain, but I have to talk to you
and Vick."

"Is there a problem? It's not about Vick's health, is it?"

"No, it's not that, but I need to talk to you and him, now! It's
about Jared and my daughter, Jessie."

Cain had no idea there was a relationship between Bidzill's daughter and Jared, which left him puzzled. He first thought that it might
be something pertaining to Aggie, since he had not yet told Lucy
or Elizabeth that she was alive. Cain assumed Jared had met Jessie
through Aggie.

"What about Jared?" Cain asked.

"A man kidnapped your son and my daughter, Jessie. I have a letter here that I hope you can explain."

"Oh my God, when did this happen and who has them?" Cain
asked.

"It's all in the letter. The man's name is Seth!"

"Seth? To make this clear, the Seth I know is no friend of mine.
He's an imposter who calls himself Seth, but his real name is Sonny
Bilbo. It's a long story. You say you have a letter?"

Cain was expressionless as Bidzill gave him the letter.

"Is this all you have?" Cain asked.

"That's it, I have no idea what this letter means, and Aggie's beside herself with worry. We need to find the kids before something bad happens to them."

Cain read the letter again, thinking he may have missed something.

"What do you think? asked Bidzill.

"It looks like we're going to Jonesboro. That's all I can say for now," Cain said.

"What about Panther Holler?" Bidzill quizzed.

"Pa can tell you about Panther Holler. One other thing——Lucy and Mother still don't know about Aggie being alive, and now is not the time to tell her. If you'll wait here, I'll get Vick."

"If you don't mind, I think I'll camp out in the barn until we leave in the morning. It might raise a few questions and I don't want to have to lie."

"I'll see you get some blankets," Cain said.

"Don't worry about me, I'm prepared. Where do you want me to park my car?"

"Perhaps you should park on the other side of the barn, so it won't be seen. That'll just raise questions," Cain advised.

Once inside the house, Cain motioned for Vick to come with him.

"Pa, we have a sick cow in the barn," Cain lied.

Vick followed him outside. "Now tell me the real reason you lied."

"We got a visitor in the barn."

"Who?" Vick asked.

When they opened the barn door Bidzill was standing there with the note.

"What's this?" Vick asked.

"Pa, he's here because someone kidnapped Jared and Jessie. You don't know but Jared has been seeing Jessie who is Aggie's and Bidzill's daughter."

329

"Well, don't just stand there, read it!" Vick said. All he could think about was Jared and if he was safe.

Vick was livid when Cain read the letter, but he was confused how Sonny knew about Jonesboro and Panther Holler. *It must be about the diamonds,* he thought. That was his first inclination, but he kept his suspicions to himself.

Vick explained as much as he could about Jonesboro and Panther Holler, but he wasn't ready to share the mystery surrounding the diamonds.

"Bidzill, sorry about your daughter and my grandson. We'll plan to leave in the morning at first light," Vick said. "I think it's best we not mention any of this to the women. Let's see what's going on before we alarm the entire family."

"I'll be ready early," Bidzill said. He had a feeling there was much more that Vick did not share with him but now was not the time to press.

Vick needed time before he explained about the diamonds.

"See you in the morning," Vick said.

Cain realized the spot Vick was in; having to protect a secret he had carried with him for many years.

After the men said their goodnights, Vick and Cain walked back to the house and talked privately before going inside. "Pa, I want to know if you're going to tell Dr. Franklin about the diamonds?"

"I don't know just yet! I might be forced into telling him to keep him satisfied. First, we need to talk about Sonny. There's a good chance he knows about the diamonds. My question is how much does he know, and how did he hear?" Vick asked.

"Pa, remember the time we went to the lake and talked about the diamonds?"

"Yes, you think that's when he overheard us talking?"

"I asked if you would draw a map to the cave where the diamonds were hidden! I remember hearing a noise that day and it had to be Sonny," Cain offered.

"It has to be, that's the only thing that makes sense. There was also another time when we thought we overheard someone eavesdropping on us. I remember we saw Sonny following us," Vick replied.

"I think we can agree that it has to be Sonny."

"Pa, how are we going to explain this to Ma?"

"I hate to lie to your Mother, but I don't want her stressing about Jared until we have a chance to bring him home. I'll tell her we're going to Beaumont to see Jared and take a trip with him. She'll be glad we're having some time to spend with her grandson."

"What about Bidzill. He'll have to know where and why we're going to Panther Holler."

"I'll think about it. Right now, we need sleep if we're going to drive to Jonesboro in one day."

Cain was beside himself with worry, but he made up his mind that Lucy should not know about any of this until they took care of Sonny and brought Jared and Jessie home.

"Pa, I ain't gonna be able to sleep a wink. Do you think they'll hurt the kids?"

"I don't know, but if they lay a finger on either one of them I'll hunt 'em down and kill 'em."

That night Vick lied to Elizabeth for the first time. He tried to act normal as he lay across the bed watching her comb her long auburn hair. She wondered what he was thinking.

Vick learned to keep a stoic face over a hand of cards, and as far as Elizabeth knew, there was nothing going on.

I want to kiss and hold her, he thought. Seeing her sitting there looking so ravishing revived the same passion he felt for her from the very beginning. *She's as beautiful now as the first time I saw her*, he thought. *He remembered when he was a boy riding with his father on their old wagon. We were poor and from the wrong side of town, but I remember Lizzie, who was rich and several years younger. She saw me shabbily dressed, but she smiled at me, even though her rich father was trying to shield her from someone whom he considered white trash and unfit for his daughter.*

There was a connection even then. It had been a long time since he had thought about those years, and it brought back memories of his brother Sam and how he died. Soon I'll be back in Panther Holler. *I can't share much, for any sane man would think I'm crazy. Bidzill will have to see with his own eyes, and then I'll answer his questions.*

Elizabeth could see he was studying her. "Vick, are you okay?" She walked over to the side of the bed, kissed his forehead and sat down. He wanted to be near her, so he laid his head in her lap. "You're very quiet," she said.

"It's just one of those days. Cain and I are going to spend some time with Jared. I hope you don't mind. That's what we talked about when I went out to the barn. We plan to leave before daybreak in the morning."

"I'm glad you're going, I think it will do you and Cain some good to visit with our grandson."

"You'll still be sleeping, so don't bother to get up when we leave. But before I go–I want to tell you something."

"What is it?" she asked

Vick looked her in the eyes and paused, then in Vick fashion, he said,

"You're still my girlfriend." Vick broke into one of his big grins that could charm anyone.

"Oh you!" Elizabeth said. She loved how playful he was when she thought he was being serious. "I never know about you," she remarked.

How right she is, he thought.

At daybreak the next morning, Cain and Vick slid their two bags in the back of their car. It was a tad cool, so they brought along their long dusters and rifle coats they planned to wear to conceal any weapons they might need— just in case. Both Vick and Bidzill drove their own cars to make room for Jared and Jessie when they were found.

Driving separately was all good, for this gave Vick and Cain time to decide what they would share with Bidzill when it came time to share what they knew about the diamonds.

⁓

After giving Aggie a rest, it was time to move on again. Rafe was beside himself with worry when it came time to leave.

"Ma, are you sure you can travel?"

It was mid-afternoon before they got to Woodville and not a moment too soon. Aggie had already slipped into a coma. Pa will know what to do, Rafe thought. *Oh Ma, please be okay.*

It was very unsettling when he drove up to the Porters' and did not see his father's car. I need to get Ma into bed. Rafe was beside himself when he went to the door of the Porters.

Lucy welcomed him, but it took her a moment to recognize him.

"Oh Rafe, I didn't recognize you at first. I wasn't expecting you."

"Miss Lucy, have you seen my Pa? My mother is in the car and she's unconscious."

"Your mother is what—she's with you?" She didn't understand why they were at her door. "What seems to be the problem?" she asked.

"Miss Lucy, I'm sorry, but I thought my Pa would be here."

"No, I haven't seen your Pa. Do you want to bring your mother in the house?" Lucy asked.

"Rafe, you wait here! I'll get one of my workers to bring her in. Lucy ran to the corral and asked Caleb if he would come and help Rafe lift his mother and bring her in the house."

"All I know is she's unconscious, I don't know what's wrong," she said. Caleb ran to the car to help bring Aggie in. As he approached the car, Rafe was waiting to help.

"Son, you step out of the way—I can carry her."

Caleb was careful as Lucy led him down a long hallway to a bedroom. Lucy noticed Aggie's long flowing red hair and how pretty she was. *Her skin is like ivory, so smooth and soft. So, this is Rafe's mother?* She should have guessed that Dr. Franklin's wife would be a beauty, for she remembered the handsome features of the Doctor and surprisingly, Rafe reminded her so much of Jared. Lucy had no reason to suspect that secrets were being kept from her.

"Caleb, just a minute while I pull back the spread," Lucy said.

He carefully laid the unconscious woman down and stepped aside.

"Thank you, Caleb…I need you to go into town and get Doctor Pete."

"Ma'am, I ain't got no car, so it'll take a little time." he said. Rafe spoke up, "Here is the key to our car, you can take it."

"Much obliged," answered Caleb.

Lucy could see how worried Rafe was about his mother, as he hovered over her.

"Rafe, do you want to tell me what happened to your mother?" Lucy asked.

"It was all so awful. There was a man who tried to break into our house. Ma and I were afraid, so we ran upstairs. When we saw him pouring gasoline around our house we knew we had to get out. When he got out of sight, that's when we jumped. I made it okay, but Ma hit sideways on her hip. I don't know, but she could have injured herself internally." While Rafe was telling his story, he sensed that Lucy knew nothing about his father being there to explain to them what happened with Jared and Jessie.

"Rafe, there's something I don't understand; why did you come here?"

"Miss Lucy, is Mr. Cain here?"

"No, Cain and his father left for Beaumont early this morning. They're gone to visit Jared."

"You mean my Pa hadn't been here?"

"I'm afraid not. Was he supposed to be here?"

Rafe was very confused, for he did not know what to think. He was in a terrible dilemma; with his mother unconscious and needing a doctor, and his Pa not being where he thought he would be.

"Miss Lucy, my Pa left mid-afternoon yesterday coming to see Mr. Cain and you about Jared."

"Jared? Why would he be coming here to talk about Jared?"

Pieces of what happened last night started to present questions for her. She was frantic when she said, "Tell me about Jared."

"My sister Jessie was with Jared when they were both kidnapped by a man named Seth, and my Pa was supposed to come here and tell you that something might happen to my sister and Jared if Mr. Cain didn't meet Seth's demands. My Pa ain't been here?" he asked again.

Lucy sat on the side of the bed to keep from falling. She remembered how somber Cain was the night before and things were beginning to make sense.

"Rafe, I'll talk to Caleb when he comes back with the doctor, maybe he knows if your Pa was here. In the meantime, please tell me what you know of Seth kidnapping Cain and this girl. You did say her name was Jessie, didn't you?"

"Yes mam, Jessie is my sister. Finally, after several more questions, Rafe told Lucy about the note and what it said."

She could hardly wait until Caleb returned so she could have answers. She and Elizabeth watched over Aggie until the doctor came, but all they knew was the woman was Rafe's mother and Doctor Franklin's wife.

Elizabeth was outside when she saw Dr. Pete drive up. "Howdy Elizabeth. I understand there's woman here unconscious."

"Yes, please follow me," said Elizabeth. The doctor grabbed his kit and walked into the room where Aggie lay sleeping.

"Y'all might want to step outside while I examine this lady," Doctor Pete said.

"Miss Lucy, do you think my Ma is gonna die?" Rafe asked.

"No, of course not. Your Mother is going to be just fine. The doctor will see to that!" Lucy was still frustrated with the unknown and walked outside to wait for Caleb. She began pacing back and forth until she saw him drive up.

She ran outside to meet him.

"Miss Lucy, I see the doctor made it. Is the woman still unconscious?"

"Yes, she is! Why don't you come inside, so we can talk?" They walked in together and sat at the table.

"Caleb, last evening did you know if Doctor Franklin came to see Cain and Vick?"

"Yes ma'am, I think. I did hear a car just about dark. Couldn't make out who it was, but I heard 'em talking and then the feller moved his car on the other side of the barn, for what reason I don't know. Then again, this morning I heard the two cars leave together. It wasn't even daylight when they left."

Lucy was crushed as her eyes filled with tears.

"Miss Lucy, is everything alright? I hope I didn't upset you."

"No Caleb, you answered my questions and now I know what happened."

Lucy and Elizabeth walked back into the room where Rafe was sitting. She slid on the couch beside him and took his hand. He was rather shocked that she showed that kind of sensitivity, but he liked it.

"Rafe, I need you to tell me and Miss Elizabeth everything you know. Can you do that?"

"Ma'am, all I know is Jared was coming to see Jessie at our house, but he was late. My sister had to run to the store for my Ma, and she didn't come back. Later, we heard something crash through the window and it was a note attached to a rock saying that Jessie and Jared had been taken and would die if the Porters didn't meet their demands.

"Then it said they had two days to meet them in Jonesboro, Arkansas at the manor and take them to Panther Holler—which didn't make sense to any of us. My Pa left yesterday to come meet with Mr. Cain and Mr. Vick to have them explain what the note meant. Pa wondered why they would be taking Jared and Jessie to Jonesboro, Arkansas of all places. And we ain't never heard of Panther Holler. It was all so confusing to us. After Pa left there was a man that drove up to our house and tried to kill us. We both had to jump off the roof to get away, but Ma hurt herself pretty bad. That's why we're here. I hope my Ma is gonna be okay. I think there's something serious wrong with her."

Hearing the details of what happened, Lucy and Elizabeth sat there in a trance trying to think of how they could help. Finally, the Doctor came out and asked to speak with Lucy and Elizabeth in private, while Rafe went in to see his mother.

Being that the Doctor was a country doctor mostly used to taking care of livestock and birthing babies, he had little to offer except for the patient to rest comfortably. "I think she'll be okay when she wakes up," he said.

Rafe took a wet cloth to wipe his mother's face, and when she felt the coolness, she opened her eyes briefly but didn't say anything. Even though it was just for a moment, it gave him hope.

He bent over and kissed her forehead. "Ma, we're taking good care of you 'til Pa comes back. You're gonna be all right," Rafe said.

After the doctor left, Elizabeth was visibly upset.

"Lucy, I thought when Jonathan Petty died that would be the end of Panther Holler. Now with all this, I feel like history is about to repeat itself. Here we are waiting again, but this time I have a feeling it might turn out different." Hearing Elizabeth be so negative frightened Lucy.

"Elizabeth, I know you're upset, but we have to remain positive that Vick and Cain will find Jared and Jessie and bring them back to us.

"But I don't understand...who is Jessie?" Elizabeth asked.

"Apparently, she is the daughter of Dr. Franklin." Lucy said.

"His wife is very pretty, did Rafe tell you her name?"

"No, Rafe was upset and everything happened so fast that I failed to ask."

Chapter 33

WHEN SONNY AND CLIFFORD CROSSED THE STATE LINE INTO ARKANSAS the magnificence of the land was hard to ignore for Jared and Jessie, even under their dire circumstances they appreciated its lovliness. It had everything: rugged timberland of both pines and hardwoods, crystal clear rivers and waterfalls, vast lowlands and rocky hillsides, plus thickets. A good place to become lost, thought Jared. He imagined escaping, but surviving in this wilderness would put both him and Jessie in imminent danger. But at least they would have a chance if the men turned violent.

Their only alternative was to stay put for the time being—at least until they got close to Jonesboro. Sitting in the back seat, he studied the habits of both men and devised a plan to escape.

Jared had to be careful when talking to Jessie. He would wait until Sonny seemed hypnotized by the road and Clifford showed signs of drowsiness before he whispered into her ear. "Be ready when we get closer to Jonesboro." Her eyes widened with a combination of fear and excitement as she waited for Jared's signal. *I just want it to be over*, she thought.

Since the beginning of their trip, they only stopped twice but it was impossible for them to escape with a shotgun pointed at their heads. Jessie grew discouraged. Her emotions were running up and down an imaginary scale, causing more anxiety than she had ever felt in her entire life. They hoped their psychology worked by being

cooperative and passive, to gain their trust. Jared read every sign, trying to get an idea of how far they were from Jonesboro. He kept waiting and watching for any opportunity to free themselves from their
nightmare.

Just when he and Jessie were about to give up, they got their break
about 75 miles from Jonesboro.

It had just begun raining when a big buck jumped from out of nowhere and hit their car. It made a load thud, but startled everyone as if
a stick of dynamite had gone off. It transpired so fast that no one had a
chance to understand what had just happened. All Jared remembered
was the squeal of the tires as Sonny weaved on and off the road, fighting with the brake to lessen the impact. It was a bloody sight with the
dead deer's head sticking through the shattered windshield and ending
up right in front of Sonny's face. It was as though the glassy-eyed buck
was staring right at him. Unable to see the road, Sonny took them on
a wild ride off the road, careening down a rocky hill and into a ravine.

Finally, the car twisted and turned before it came to a stop on its
side in a shallow mountain stream. The men must have had a brush
of unconsciousness, for they were dazed long enough for Jessie and
Jared to free themselves and wade to shore. They looked back and
saw Sonny shake Clifford, trying to wake him.

"Jess, we have to move fast—they're coming after us." They ran as
fast as the forest would let them, as they ran for their lives.

Sonny and Clifford instantly regained their bearings when they
saw the two of them running toward the woods. The rain had continued and was making footing extremely difficult. The men ran
through the brush—hot on their trail. Clifford kept wiping his face,
for the branches of small trees were wet and kept hitting him as he
ran through heavy terrain.

"Where in the hell did they go?" Clifford shouted.

"Go after 'em, we can't let 'em get away!" Sonny screamed. With
Jared and Jessie no longer in site, the men ended up running blindly
through the brush, losing their sense of direction in the process. It

was hard to keep up with two young people who were scared out of their wits. The men did not give up easily. They regained their bearing, then hurried back on their trail. The broken branches along the way told them they were on the right track.

Jessie and Jared continued to run, but now Jessie was having trouble keeping up; especially when they reached an area with thick and thorny groundcover.

"Jessie, you have to stay up or they're gonna kill us."

"I'm trying, but my skirt holds me back," she said.

"Where is the stream we saw before?" she asked.

"We'll find it if we can keep moving," Jared assured her.

She lifted her skirt, exposing her white stockings which allowed her legs to take the brunt of the thorns. She tried her best to ignore the pain.

At one point, Clifford was very close. They couldn't see him but they could smell him. His body odor was undeniable, and the slight breeze brought it to them as an invisible warning—much like animals sense humans.

"Jessie, quick—behind this tree!" A tall round oak that must have been a thousand years old shielded them as they edged around to keep from being seen. Clifford was within a stone's throw from Jessie and she could see him as he maneuvered along, shoving the barrel of his gun through the underbrush in attempt to hit one of them. She trembled knowing that the men were angry and so close. Jared stood frozen, but he managed to put his finger to his lips and signal that he could hear her heavy breathing—mostly brought on by panic.

While they waited, they listened intently and occasionally could hear the men talking, indicating they were getting closer, but then—their voices began to fade.

Sonny and Clifford were frustrated by their failure to track them. "What we gonna do now? There ain't no hide nor hair of 'em," Clifford said, "and it's getting dark!"

"We can't give up," Sonny shouted.

Finally, as the sun faded and the shadows crept in, the men realized all was lost. Without Jared and Jessie, Sonny knew he would have to convince Vick and Cain that they left the kids with Clifford's brother, Barry.

"You know—them Porters are gonna want to see them kids."

"We'll tell 'em they're stashed someplace. They don't need to know what happened."

"It's gettin' late and them skeeters are abitin' me," Clifford said.

"Damn that buck—we were almost to Jonesboro. No tellin' where them kids are now. Let's just hope they don't show up before we do," Sonny lamented.

"What if they do? What then?" Clifford asked.

"Don't think about that! I'm overdue for a lucky day," Sonny said.

"All we want are the diamonds and after that, the Porters will get what's coming to 'em."

Jared and Jessie were hidden in the deep wet underbrush—afraid to move, fearing that any sound they made would endanger them. They knew they were quite a distance from the road.

Jessie shook with fear knowing they could still be found. They stayed there for what seemed to be hours, and finally Jared made the decision to move.

"Jessie, we have to take the chance that they have moved on. If we find the stream, we'll find the road." They were lucky, for they had just enough moonlight to see the winding stream as it glistened in the night. The only problem they were going away from the road instead of toward it.

After wading what they considered to be a mile or two, they became tired and confused, for the stream winded around causing them to lose their sense of direction. They didn't know if they were going north, east, south or west. It was frightening, but at least they were safe. They eventually came upon a small shack not far from the water's edge. It had a nice size shed that could be a refuge for them for the night. He pointed in the direction of the shed, but Jessie hesitated.

"Jared, I don't know. People living in the backwoods without any neighbors could be dangerous. This place looks spooky to me," she said.

As they got closer, they could see beaver skins hanging on a line curing. Jared was concerned, but figured the shed would offer protection from the night.

"At least we will be out of the mud and water," he replied.

While running toward the shed they caught glimpse of two horses in a makeshift corral. When Jared opened the door to the shed the smell of a skunk was stifling. The ensuing odor took the shed off their list of possible places to bed down.

"What now?" Jessie asked.

They walked a distance away from the cabin and watched to see if there were any signs of life. Not only were the two exhausted—they were hungry.

"Jess, I don't think anyone is at home; I'm going to look through the window and see. You stay put until I motion for you." She nodded as Jared walked toward the cabin. He was very careful as he moved forward. Once he got to the window, he peeked through and saw a fireplace with a faint fire and two rockers. He guessed two people were living there.

Jessie watched from afar and had more of a peripheral view than Jared. When she saw two men approaching with shotguns she thought it might be Sonny and Clifford. She wanted to scream, but she knew if she did it would put both Jared and her in danger. She knew if it was Sonny that he would not harm Jared without knowing where she was. Watching the events unfold, everything turned into slow motion as the two mountain men sneaked up behind Jared and hit him with the butt end of the gun. She saw the impact and watched helplessly as Jared's body folded and crumbled to the ground. She placed her hand over her mouth to keep from screaming. She stood frozen with fear as the two strange men took Jared's arms and pulled him into the cabin.

It was now up to her, she thought.

~

It had been many years since Bidzill had been to Arkansas, but he remembered the mountains and lush greenery of the landscape. It was with his father, Dr. Earnest Franklin, who took him to his first Indian Village. At an early age, he taught his son to respect his culture.

Driving alone Bidzill's mind was all over the place thinking of his mother, of whom he remembered very little. As he passed through the small towns, he felt a connection with the Indians, especially those dressed in their tribal clothing. His adopted father had taught him that he should never feel ashamed of his people and he should be proud. He also explained that the mysterious spiritualism among the Indians was often considered nothing more than folklore by the white man. They grossly misunderstood and underestimated the strong spiritual power of the Indians.

As he traveled he was sure he heard the voice of his deceased grandfather, Chief Asta who was the Chief of the Navajo.

"Son, the power is within you." The voice was very firm and assuring, and for once, Bidzill was comforted.

I need that power now more than ever, he thought.

Bidzill hated leaving behind Aggie and Rafe, but he knew how important Jared and Jessie were to both of them.

Finally, after hours of traveling, Vick found a good place to stop and take a break. Bidzill pulled in behind them and they all walked to the edge of a bluff overlooking a stunningly vast green valley with hundreds of pine trees.

Bidzill thought, this is the land of the Gods.

"How much farther do we have to go?" Cain asked.

"Not too far—maybe a couple of hours," Vick offered.

"If you don't mind I'm going to ride the rest of the way with Bidzill."

Vick agreed, for he was glad to have the peace and quiet from Cain's incessant talking.

Cain thought his father was too intense. *He's focused on one thing and whatever that one thing is— he's not sharing.*

"Bidzill and Vick shared many of the same traits and understood each other—unlike Cain. They didn't need to have conversation to know they were one in purpose. That was the Indian way.

On one occasion Cain talked about Aggie and Lucy.

"Bidzill, you haven't asked, but Lucy still doesn't know about Aggie.

"Try not to think about it. Things have a way of working out," Bidzill said.

Cain thought Vick would have given the same answer.

Secluded with only his thoughts, Cain remembered the time Sonny tried to kill his son. *I should have signed the land over to him way back then, and none of this would be happening. If it's diamonds they want—I don't care. They can have 'em—they can have everything. I just want my son!*

~

It had been years since Vick had seen the manor, and if he was traveling under different circumstances it would be like going home.

Bidzill, who had been following close behind, was impressed when he saw the majesties of the manor. *This is like a shrine. Why would the Porters want to live on a ranch in Texas when they have a mansion and thousands of acres to take care of!* It was more fascinating than anything Bidzill had ever expected. When he drove through the iron gates that led up to the mansion, he followed the brick road that led him through what reminded him of a tropical forest. He was first touched by a rich scent of honeysuckle vines that were in abundance scattered about the property, with large climbing rose bushes, which wound themselves around the trees. It was a magnificent sight to behold.

Finally, he stopped the car closely behind Vick's and walked over to shake hands.

"You don't stop for anything, do you?" Bidzill said.

Vick smiled, and the men walked up to the front porch.

"I didn't know how much I missed the old place," Vick said. "Come on let's see if Hop's around."

"So, this is the manor!" Bidzill said. "I don't know what I expected, but I never expected this."

"This is my wife's childhood home," Vick replied.

"When the time's right, you can tell me why you left this to live in Texas."

"I've been asking the same thing," Vick said. "Who knows--after this is all over I might bring Elizabeth back home."

This was news to Cain, for he had never heard his Pa say anything about moving back to Arkansas.

Maybe it wouldn't be such a bad to move back home, Cain thought.

Vick led them up the steps into the foyer. "Come on in and make yourself at home."

He was looking for the caretaker when he walked through the house to the back door. A few minutes later Smitty showed up.

"Mister Vick...I didn't know you were coming, Hop ain't here right now. He left yesterday to go hunting and I don't look for him to be back for a couple of days."

"Then maybe you can help gather me some horses. I need about seven of 'em to get ready to ride." Smitty wondered why so many horses, but his job was not to ask.

"I might have to lend you a couple of mine, but we've got enough saddles. Remember that high spirited little gelding? He's not so little anymore and he's settled down a whole lot. I spec' somebody's gonna have a good ride if you take him."

"I'm gonna need 'em by morning." Vick instructed.

"Anything else I can do for you?"

"You can tell Maggie I need some food for a week, cooked up for our trip."

"Yes sir, Mr. Vick." They shook hands and all three men left.

That evening, Bidzill, once again asked questions about Panther Holler.

"Vick, you want to tell me about Panther Holler and what it's all about? I think I've been patient long enough!" He said.

Vick nodded to Cain that the time had come to tell Bidzill.

"Not too long ago, Sonny overhead Cain and me talking about diamonds that are hidden in a cave near Panther Holler. When I was a kid, I lived in Panther Holler for over four years, and I know where the diamonds are hidden. These diamonds are an ancient treasure, which belonged to the 'first people'—our people. This is all I can tell you for now. You have to trust me."

"Pa's telling the truth—you have to believe him," Cain reassured.

Bidzill and Vick's eyes locked and Bidzill knew that in time he would understand what he needed to know.

~

Sonny and Clifford were angry for letting Jared and Jessie escape. After accepting their defeat there was nothing more they could do but secure their supplies and find a means of transportation to take them to Jonesboro.

They walked for hours until a chicken farmer with an old truck drove up and stopped to help them.

"Mister, we need a ride to Jonesboro!" Sonny said.

After the farmer took a good look at Clifford, he started to pull away when Sonny pulled out his .45 pistol and stopped him with a bullet to the head. The man's body slumped forward on the steering wheel as his bloody head came to rest on the front window of the car door. Sonny got a good look at the gaping hole with blood gushing out of the side of the man's head. Although he had murdered before, he had never been close enough to observe raw tissue come from a bullet wound. It was a gruesome sight!

"When I say we need a ride—you're supposed to stop!" Sonny nervously taunted. Careful not to get the man's blood on them, they opened the truck door, rolled the man out, then dragged his body to the side of the road.

"What we gonna do if we get to the manor and them kids are already there?" Clifford asked.

"I ain't ready to cross that bridge yet!" Sonny retorted.

Sonny and Clifford arrived in Jonesboro late in the evening and found only one boarding house that had a room to accommodate them for the night. By now, Sonny had gotten used to Clifford's stench, at least to the point where he could endure bunking with him for one night.

Early the next morning, they spent a portion of their time looking for Jared and Jessie, but when they came up with nothing, they decided to make their way to the manor. Concerned that someone might recognize the farmer's truck, they carefully hid it in a wooded area outside the gates of the manor. The truck would come in handy when it came time to transport the treasure, Sonny planned.

Walking through the iron gates, they followed the brick road that led to the very large estate.

"Holy smoke—you supposin' this is the place?" Clifford asked.

"That's a mighty big house—whew-wee! Them Porters must have more money than you can shake a stick at," Sonny said.

When they stopped behind an evergreen tree to regroup, they saw from a distance, three men outside drinking coffee. It was time for them to make their move.

Approaching the manor, Vick noticed what looked like two vagabonds walking up on foot. Looking more closely, he recognized

348

Sonny as he limped up carrying his shotgun and large empty sacks they imagined were for the diamonds.

Vick and Cain walked toward them.

"Well, who are you today? Seth or Sonny?" Vick demanded sarcastically.

Hearing him called by his real name, he knew that his past had finally caught up with him. It was apparent the Porters knew something about him, but he didn't know how much. In a flick of a second he thought back to when he had Clifford's brother hung. *If Clifford learns I'm the one responsible for his brother's death, this could ruin my plans*, he thought.

"Where are Jared and Jessie?" Cain demanded.

"You'll see 'em when we get the diamonds—so don't go gettin' all riled up. If ya do what we say, they'll be safe, but if we ain't back home in due time, my friend here, has a brother who'll take care of 'em—understand?"

Vick looked at Clifford and noticed he had a gun.

"You're gonna need that gun where we're going," Vick stated.

"We ain't gonna need 'em unless y'all start givin' us trouble," Sonny said.

"Have you hurt our kids?" asked Bidzill.

"I told ya'll they're safe until we get back!"

Bidzill's main concern was Jessie after seeing the likes of Clifford. I pray to God they're okay, he thought.

Cain studied Clifford who was chewing his tobacco, and spitting profusely. He's nervous, Cain thought.

Sonny noticed Smitty bringing up seven horses.

"Are y'all ready to ride?" Vick asked.

"Thanks, Smitty, but we won't need but five."

Sonny was irritated when he saw the horses.

"We ain't planned on no damn horse—that's gonna take a lot of time! We supposed to be going to Panther Holler!" Sonny said.

"There's no road to the Holler. If you want the diamonds, the only way is by horse. As soon as we step off the main road we'll be entering dangerous country. And I must warn you, the place we're going is a very mysterious where unexplained things happen."

"Are you talking about Panther Holler?"

"I'm afraid so," Vick answered.

This was all part of Vick's plan. Just as before, Sonny and Clifford would have to deal with the Panther. At least, Vick was counting on it to be so. There was no way for even Vick to know what goes on in the mind of a wild animal.

Clifford, who had been silent for the most part, responded, "Whatcha mean—unexplained thangs?"

"People die!" Vick said emphatically.

"Y'all better not be pulling no fast one," Sonny said. "Whatcha mean people die?"

"If I could explain I would," Vick stated. "Just don't lag too far behind."

Clifford and Sonny thought, *what in the hell is he talking about!*

"How long is this trip going to take?" Sonny asked.

"If we have good luck, we're looking at no more than a week's travel— depending on the trail," Vick offered.

"Well, what are we waiting for? The sooner we get going, the sooner this is over with," Sonny said. All the time he was holding his breath that Jared and Jessie would not walk up.

Before they finished packing, Maggie brought out several sacks of food and placed them over Vick and Cain's horses. "Mr. Vick, y'all got enough food for a whole week," she said.

"Thank you, Maggie," Vick answered.

Sonny sat in his saddle rubbing his unshaven face and thinking about what Vick told him. The way he said, "people die," got under his skin.

Sonny hadn't ridden a mile when he began grumbling. "I ain't likin' this!"

Chapter 34

LUCY PACED BACK AND FORTH AS SHE TRIED TO SORT OUT HER TROUBLED feelings. On the one hand she felt fear, and on the other hand she dared to hope. For what—she wasn't certain. Something was gnawing at her, but she couldn't put her finger on it. She kept looking at the young man who was so concerned about his mother that he hardly acknowledged her presence. His steely blue eyes constantly distracted her, for they reminded her of Jared.

All the while, Lucy and Elizabeth referred to Aggie as: "Mrs. Franklin," "Doctor Franklin's wife," or sometimes, "Rafe's mother." They had no idea it was Aggie, Jared's biological mother. It was all so innocent, for Rafe would never have an occasion to address his mother by her first name.

Each day that passed they were hopeful that Aggie would open her eyes, but her condition remained the same. There was nothing they could do but wait for the men to return.

Elizabeth was very concerned and desperately needed to contact someone to find out if Cain and Vick were at the manor. There were very few telephones, but Elizabeth knew the lumber company she used to own would certainly have one. And, it was only a short distance away from the manor. She rang up the operator and placed a long-distance call to Mason, one of the owners. She got through to him and asked, among other things, if he would have someone go to the manor to see if Vick and Cain had been there.

They waited all that day until late evening when she received answers to most of her questions. She learned that Vick and Cain were with a friend when two nasty looking men showed up to ride with them. She also learned that they were going to a place called Panther Holler.

After she hung up, Lucy and Elizabeth broke down in tears from worry after learning that Jared and Jessie were not with them.

"Why wouldn't Jared be with the men who kidnapped him?" Lucy asked rhetorically.

"Perhaps someone else has them," Elizabeth said. "Neither Cain nor Vick would go with those men if they thought Jared and Jessie were not alive. We have to be strong for that young man sitting with his mother," Elizabeth said.

Lucy wiped her eyes with her apron and set about preparing broth for Aggie. Perhaps Mrs. Franklin will eat this time, she hoped.

~

Jessie stood paralyzed with fear as she watched helplessly as two mountain men dragged Jared's limp body into their cabin. She had no idea how she could go up against two of them. I'm in God knows where, all alone, cold, hungry, and afraid, she thought. She had no idea what type of men had Jared or if he would be still be alive the next morning.

Jared was stretched out on the floor of the cabin when he opened his eyes to see one of the men bent over him, poking him with a gun. They toyed with him like an animal instead of a human being. He had heard of what mountain men do and it frightened the heck out of him. I can't show weakness, he thought, as he tried to stare the men down.

Curly was the name of the other man, who had made his way to a shelf where he grabbed a jug of moonshine. The jug was open, and it dangled from the man's finger while he stood over Jared to get a closer look at him.

The man called Skidder was the one who drew Jared's attention after his initial shock. He had narrowed eyes and an evil grin that spread over his face, while Curly seemed more menacing with his dark eyes and a large wide nose that showed too much nostril hair. When they spoke, their decayed teeth and diseased gums were evident. They were an appalling sight for Jared.

"We got us a prisoner!" Curly growled.

These two men looked more vicious than Sonny and Clifford. His thoughts were of Jessie and what she would do all alone and lost in the forest.

Curly handed his bottle of moonshine to Skidder. The husky man took a slug and gave it back to his friend.

"Boy, whatcha doin' nosing around here? We ain't seen sign of nobody in a coon's age."

At least they can talk, Jared thought.

"I came up to your place for help and this is a fine how-do-you-do, I might say." The men looked at each other and let out a cackle. Jared hardly recognized his own voice as he continued to look at the men. "You see, I was driving to Jonesboro when a deer came out of nowhere and caused me to run off the road. My car is stuck in a stream with no way to pull it out and I came here to ask your help.

"Ya' got a car in a stream someplace 'round here?" Curly asked.

"Yes, it's a good five or six miles where we went off the road and down an embankment into a stream."

"We? Who's we?" Curly asked.

Jared chided himself for the mention of someone with him. "I picked up a man hitching a ride but the minute my car went off the road he didn't stay around to help."

Curly and Skidder looked at each other and then let out a stream of profanities that no one would have been able to make out. It was like their own private language--coarse rough words that made no sense to anyone but them. Then they would laugh like they just heard the best joke ever told. Jared wondered what was so funny, thinking maybe their laughter was alcohol induced. They appeared to be in their own little world, totally amused at him being there.

The rugged woodsmen kept drinking and talking among themselves until Skidder went over to the oven and pulled out some meat.

"I reckon yer hungry, ain't cha?"

The meat had that rich smoky smell that would make anyone hungry. Jared felt guilty thinking of Jessie, but he knew he needed to keep up his strength if he had a chance to escape.

"Yes, I'm hungry if you have enough to spare."

"Nah, we ain't got none fer ya'," barked Curley.

Before the men settled down for the night, Curly hogtied Jared, which made it impossible for him to free himself. Skidder and Curly were both drunk and fell on their cots and went sound to sleep. Jared needed time to figure things out, but for now, he needed rest so when it came time to make a move, he would be ready.

Jessie had lived a different life than Jared, and her life had been full of hardships before the Franklin's adopted her. It took time for her to focus, but when she gathered her senses, she found a small cave in a mountainside where she could dry out and sleep through the night. She prayed that Jared would find a way to free himself. There were so many uncertainties, but for now there was nothing she could do.

Jared tried to sleep, and finally exhaustion took over and he fell fast asleep. Just before daybreak, he awoke from a nightmare. He lay there and watched the open flame from the fire cast eerie shadows on the cabin walls. *I've gotta get out of here—Jessie, I hope you know I'm thinking about you.* This was the first time Jared cried and showed emotion. *I'm so afraid for her*, he worried.

The next morning, Jared was startled at the most grueling sound of coughing. He thought the men were going to choke as they cleared their throats.

Jared waited patiently, then told the men he had to relieve himself. "Skidder, you untie 'em and take him to the outhouse," Curly said.

Skidder looked to be submissive to Curley, for when he said "jump", he jumped.

Walking to the outhouse was Jessie's first sighting of Jared since his capture. I'll be ready if he has a plan, she thought.

Walking back to the house Jared stopped and acted like he hurt his ankle then looked in the direction of the woods hoping she was watching him. He thought, Somehow, I must get away. At some point Jessie has got to go for help if I fail to outsmart these bums. He was already afraid that Skidder may make a move on him by the way he was eyeing him, which made it imperative to get a plan into action.

Jared thought if he offered the car to them, they might free him. It was worth a try. When he and Skidder returned to the house he posed the question.

"Skidder, tie 'em up." Curly instructed.

"Jared began talking about his car and asked if they knew anything about pulling a car out of the stream. "I don't think it would be difficult if I had some help," Jared said. The men just stared at him while they tore into the leftover meat from the previous night.

What Jared didn't know was the men had a plan of their own. Somehow, they communicated their plan through their bizarre conversation that Jared could not understand. They aimed to kill him as soon as Jared helped them pull the car out of the stream.

"We gonna help ya' after breakfast," Curly said.

"Could y'all untie me now, since we're working together?" Jared pled.

"No!" Curly said.

They kept looking at him in such a way that Jared was afraid for his life. They're not going to free me, he thought. Somehow, I must escape before we get to the car.

355

While Jessie waited she devised a plan for when the men left the cabin. She saw the smoke from the chimney and wondered how warm it was inside. It was nippy outside but not that cold, she thought. She knew when they threw a log on the fire for a puff of black smoke would trail from the chimney upward into the sky.

Jared waited a couple of hours and then he had to relieve himself again. "Sorry, but I need to go again," he said.

"Ain't goin' till we ready," Curly responded.

"We might as well walk 'em to the toilet when we go for the car," Skidder offered.

"Guess we ought to get it over with," Curly said.

Skidder and Curly led Jared to the outhouse and waited until he got through. He took more time than needed as he enjoyed the moments of freedom. It was a cool day, but he was sweating profusely from being fearful of how this was going to play out. If I get out of this one, I'll never leave home again, he thought. Curly knocked on the door.

"Hurry it up, we ain't got all day!"

"Just a few more minutes," Jared said.

Skidder was waiting to give him a rap on the head when Jared opened the door. Jessie had now positioned herself in the perfect place for what she was about to do.

She had been eyeing all the beaver skins that were curing on the line, and as the mountain men had their back towards her she quietly took all the skins off the line and placed them in the shed where the skunk had been. The skins would never be of any worth to them after the skunk smell penetrated the fur. Looking at the wasted skins it looks to be a year's worth of work with no pay. This all happened while Jared was in the outhouse. The minute after Jared stepped out, Jessie gave out a loud whistle that got the men's attention. They were sure it was a man for no woman could whistle as loud as she did. They had no idea if it was one man or two. When Curly looked toward the cabin he noticed all the beaver skins gone.

"They done got our skins," Curly shouted. Skidder turned sharply toward where the skins used to hang, and Jared took advantage of the opportunity. Again, he was running for his life. Bullets began ripping through the woods, not just in his direction, but in all directions. Curley and Skidder had no idea where the pelt thieves were nor how many of them were out there. They thought that it would take at least two people to steal that many pelts in such a short period of time.

"Check the shed," Curly shouted. Skidder ran toward the shed and stopped suddenly. "I ain't goin' in that shed, 'cause there's a skunk inside." They felt certain that no one would be in the shed with their skins, if a skunk was there.

"It's got to be two or three people to carry that many skins," Curly shouted.

They ran into their cabin to grab their rifles and more ammunition for their pistols.

Jared kept running until he came to something on the trail that was very strange. He stopped in his tracks. Lying on the ground was one of Jessie's stockings. She had stuffed it with leaves and left it with the toe pointing in the direction she wanted him to go. He picked up the stocking and ran as fast as he could until he found the other stocking pointing in the opposite direction. Where is this taking me? he wondered.

Jared had no idea where the stocking would lead him, but he trusted Jessie, for he knew she was smart and evidently had a plan.

Jared kept running until he stopped short of a grove of trees. Am I about to die? Jared thought. All this running and I'm right back near the cabin. He hid in some bushes trying to conceal himself, but it was too late. They've found me, he thought. A thousand things were running through his mind when the bushes parted and there before him stood Jessie. He couldn't believe his eyes. She looked so gorgeous to him, even in her tattered clothing and dirty face--but it was her. Yes, it's Jessie! He could smell a special fragrance about her, but it wasn't perfume—it was skunk.

"Jared, we have to hurry or they'll find us," she said. He didn't take time to question—he followed. They ran in a completely different direction, which was confusing to him because it appeared they were going back to the cabin. He stopped her, "Jessie, we're going back to the cabin."

"Yes, I know, but we're going in a different direction to the cabin. I saw which way they went," she said. Jared had no choice but to trust her. It wasn't long before she slipped behind a mound of bushes and walked into a small cave that led somewhere. It was just big enough for two people and they hid and waited there until it was safe for them to escape. After hours of waiting they heard what sounded like water. "Jared, we may have to leave."

"Why?" he said.

"Because of the rain from last night. There's a stream on the other side of the cave and it might overflow and come in on us."

Jared walked outside the cave and saw what looked like a mountain stream. "Jessie, we have to get in the stream. We'll be safer in the stream than running through the woods."

When they were sure it was safe to leave the cave, they made a run for the stream. It was cold, and there were a few rapids that carried them a long way down stream, which was better than walking. Jared tried to hold on to Jessie but it was difficult, for he was fighting with the rapids and the undercurrent that suddenly got stronger. "Jared, I can't hold on," Jessie said. They fought to get to the shoreline, but it was no use, for Jessie was ripped from Jared's hand and set on a treacherous journey bobbing up and down going to whereabouts unknown. All Jared could do was follow her. He also had no power over the stream. She tried to turn her head to see if Jared was still there, but she couldn't because the water had complete control. Her only option was to relax and go with the flow. Jared could see that Jessie had stopped fighting and he did the same. It seemed like they traveled for miles as their surroundings switched from lightness to dark as the sun flickered sporadically through the trees. Suddenly, things began slowing down as the water widened into more of a lake.

Once there, exhausted from the wild ride, they swam to shore and staggered to a place where they could lay down. "Jessie, are you okay? I thought I lost you."

She could hardly speak, for up ahead she saw the two beaver trappers they were trying to escape from.

Chapter 35

RETURNING TO PANTHER HOLLER

Throughout the day they traveled the main road from the manor until they reached the cut-off to Panther Holler. Recognizing a landmark that only Vick knew about, he pulled his horse off the road and into the shadow of a tall evergreen and slipped silently to the ground.

"This is where the riding gets tough," he said. Corralling the men together, he warned them, "It's been a long time since I've been back to the holler and there's no telling what kind of trail we're gonna find. If you're planning on questioning me about where we're going—don't!"

Sonny, who was tired and frustrated, shook his head in disgust. Worn out from riding, he hated taking orders from Vick.

"We're going to have to ride single file—so follow!" Vick ordered.

He led the pack into the lush green thicket; followed by Cain, Bidzill, Clifford, and then Sonny.

This ain't fun, but it sure will be worth it, Sonny thought.

Within a few miles the scenery changed, which provided for much smoother trekking. It was surprising to Vick that the trails were not overgrown. As the horses picked up their pace, he recognized where he was. Once again, Vick was returning to Panther Holler, but this time the trip was to try and save Jared and Jessie. All through the night and into the next day they traveled until they came to the military camp, which was still standing. The place had lost most of its roof and the windows were open from being shot out during the war. To

Vick, it still looked pretty much the same from the time he and Sam discovered it as boys.

Relieved that he had not lost his sense of direction, he slipped from his saddle and invited the others to make camp. While walking through the old camp-house, all the memories of his past flooded back. He remembered his troubled youth and his alcoholic father who abused Sam and him. The military camp had provided the run-aways with shelter.

Vick had many apprehensions about removing the diamonds before their rightful time. Without the Great Spirit's guidance, he was un-certain of what might happen.

All the men brought their gear in to make camp for the night.

Vick walked outside, expecting to see some sign of Hawk, his phantom friend who on more than one occasion had saved him. *I need your protection now more than ever,* Vick thought.

After the men had eaten a bite and settled down for the night, it turned cold as blue blazes, although it was not yet winter. Sonny and Clifford, who were unprepared for the cold were freezing their butts off.

"Ain't nobody 'round here gonna make a fire?" Sonny anguished.

"You should have brought a heavier coat," Cain replied.

"Ain't nobody told me we were going to the North Pole," he growled. "If y'all ain't building a fire, then I damn sure am." Pushing Clifford aside, he went to gathering kindling and then came back, dumping it on the floor in front of the old fireplace. Clifford sat on his saddle chewing his tobacco and spitting –watch-ing Sonny struggle to light a match. After the fire was up and go-ing Sonny barked again, "I got the damn wood, so let's make the coffee," he ordered.

Sonny bent down to the developing fire trying to warm himself.

"Why is it so damn cold here? It ain't the time of year for cold weather," he complained.

"It's because we're getting close to Panther Holler. It's just one of the mysteries surrounding the place that you wouldn't understand," Cain stated.

Sonny rolled his eyes. "Yeah, yeah…that's what y'all keep saying but I ain't buying this unexplained crap. We just got us a Northerner— that's all!"

Cain was amused with Sonny's performance, but Vick's concern was Sonny and Clifford who had no idea what they're up against when they come face to face with the panther.

Later that evening, Bidzill and Cain pulled Vick aside to talk. They sat on a downed log drinking coffee while Sonny and Clifford were all tucked in their bedroll trying to stay warm.

"Pa, what do you think?"

"I really don't know, I've been waiting for a sign. I have a feeling we're headed for trouble if we try to remove the diamonds before it's time. It may not be as easy as we think!"

Bidzill listened closely with interest.

He had no idea what Vick and Cain had gone through prior to this, and without all the facts his only interest, was to get the diamonds and win Jared and Jessie's freedom, like Vick and Cain.

After everything was quiet and the men had gone to bed, Vick lay there thinking of the terrible predicament they were in. He knew they were headed for trouble since Sonny was a known killer and wasn't likely to let them go. They're gonna kill us anyway, he thought. *Let's just hope the panther is in the right frame of mind to protect us like he did before*, Vick thought.

Laying there, he remembered the last time he traveled to the cave of diamonds— and it wasn't easy. He had received a vision back then, telling him that he should find the "road that roars", which turned out to be a waterfall over a cave that offered them passage to where the treasure was hidden. Only Vick and Cain were privileged to see the inside of the cave, which contained the diamonds and the history of the ancient Indians. The cave held many lost secrets, of how to heal the sick, what crops to plant and when, how to teach a young boy to be a warrior, and many others. Many secrets contained miraculous cures from the herbs that were discovered to save their people. One of their greatest discoveries was an anesthetic—a natural and merciful way to deaden pain.

The diamonds had a different meaning to the ancient Indians. Diamonds were tools needed for the sole purpose of advancing their knowledge to their descendants—a practice they took very seriously. They were their greatest treasures to leave for future generations, but to people like Sonny and other treasure hunters, they were only a selfish means to achieve great wealth. In Sonny's mind, he imagined the diamonds as part of a treasure.

Vick had been thinking of the cave and its carvings when he began receiving a surge of inspiration concerning Bidzill in an array of lights. Vick had never had this happen before, which was a new experience. It was made known to him that Bidzill will be celebrated as a great healer among his people, and that through him, the Indians will prosper through the contribution of his talents to the children of men. Not only will the Indians receive this gift of knowledge, but to all mankind as their secrets will be shared to the white man.

The sacred cave will become a shrine and through Bidzill's literary skill, he will share the secrets of the cave with the world, providing knowledge concerning medicine as well as other secrets.

As the night darkened, Vick lay quietly looking at the fire and listening to the soft crackle of wood, when he heard the soft beat of drums. He thought it was the heart of Mother Earth crying for Jared and Jessie who had been kidnapped.

Laying there watching the stars twinkle and hearing the hypnotic drums, he noticed the dim twinkles of the stars increase in size and become brighter. It was all consuming when a ray of light turned into a horseman. Out of a mist, he saw a warrior on a chestnut stallion riding toward him. He remembered this same warrior who appeared to him before. Vick sat straight up in his bedroll; wide-awake with only himself, the stallion and the warrior. As the vision intensified, he heard the squeal of a hawk as it flew from the sky, flapping its shimmering wings. Once again, he stood before the great hawk; who for many years was thought to be his young Indian friend who promised him that he would always be his protector. And it was so—for many times Hawk fulfilled his promise and saved him throughout his lifetime.

Years earlier, it had been made known to him that Hawk was the reincarnate mother who took care of him and Sam as young boys saving them from the abuse of their father. If it hadn't been for Hawk, (as the young Indian was called), it's possible Vick and his brother would have starved or frozen to death due to their drunken father's neglect. Once again, he watched as the Hawk discarded its glistening silver feathers and transformed into a beautiful Indian maiden. He recognized her as his mother who had died when he was just a child. She had the smile of an angel and he longed to embrace her, but he knew they were forbidden to touch. She was surrounded by a glorious light and the warrior dismounted and bowed to her, which surprised him— but his visions were always full of surprises. "My son, the warrior you see is the blood of Bidzill who represents healing. He will become a teacher among his people."

It was made known to Vick that there was a connection between Bidzill and him, but he had no idea they were direct descendants of each other. He stood before his mother with tears in his eyes, for it was such a blessing to revisit her. "Am I dreaming or is this really you?" Vick asked.

"Yes son, it is I who have come to you."

"Mother, I have longed to speak with you about Cain's son and a young woman who was taken from us by force."

She walked toward him and smiled. "My son who shares the blood of our people—you are a great warrior and the chosen one, but I cannot intercede with man's free will. I am only here to instruct you. Before you can remove the diamonds, you must find a trunk filled with ancient clothing and three pairs of moccasins. If they are not there you will know it's not the right time for you to remove the treasure. The shoes hold the power to leave the cave with the treasure of our people."

"Mother—why would I need three pairs of moccasins when it's only me."

"Because you, Cain, and Bidzill have the pure bloodline of our people, and when it's time to remove the diamonds, you must all walk out of the cave together."

It took only minutes for the manifestation to be over. He shook his head, trying to reconnect with the vision to confirm what he had just seen and heard—as if that would do any good. His mother was gone as quickly as she appeared.

The next morning, he was energized as they broke camp and scattered the ashes from the morning fire. Vick searched the sky until his eyes fell on a hawk sitting in a tall pine. "Oh! There you are," Vick said.

It was late evening when Vick and the men arrived in Panther Holler and as they got closer a hawk flew in front of Sonny and Clifford almost knocking them from their horse. The horses reared up as the two fought to hold on. "What in the heck was that?" Sonny shouted.

Vick made a point of reminding them. "I told you that unexplained things happen! You're in Panther Holler." Vick reminded.

"I reckon that was one of 'em, huh?" Sonny asked.

"I'm surprised you haven't asked about why they call this place Panther Holler?"

"Well Vick, I wouldn't want to disappoint you. Do you mind telling me? or am I supposed to guess!" Sonny mocked.

"You listen closely—you might hear them," Vick said as he looked around.

"What do you mean hear 'em?"

"The panthers, of course." He could see their concern. Vick smiled and rode on. *The plan's working so far*, he thought.

Clifford swallowed hard and stopped chewing as he looked around in all directions.

"At least I have Clifford spooked," Vick said, quietly to Cain.

"That panther better not come around me, 'cause if he does he's gonna to be one dead cat!" Sonny boasted.

Vick couldn't help but chuckle under his breath.

It was about dusk when they reached the edge of the mountain. "Just a few more miles we'll be there, but first we're going to have to either ride or lead our horses around the mountain on a very narrow trail," Vick warned. "If one of you should fall, there ain't nothing between you and the bottom but air."

Not only were Sonny and Clifford frightened, but Bidzill was also, for he had never faced such a precarious course with his horse. Each man chose to lead their horses around the mountain. When they emerged from the treacherous trail, there nestled among the evergreens was the cabin called Panther Holler.

"Pa—it looks the same!" Cain said excitedly.

After hitching their horses, they grabbed their bedrolls and hurried into the cabin.

Upon entering, Vick had mixed emotions, for it was there he spent his youth, and it was there he became a man.

～

The next morning, while the men were gathering their bedrolls, Vick and Cain visited the gravesite of Sam. Bidzill stood quietly nearby, giving the two men their privacy. He noticed a little homemade cross lying on top of the grave, and figured Vick had made the cross for his brother many years ago.

He watched as Vick took a stone and reset the cross, and then knelt to show his respect to a memory that still waxed strong in his heart. "It's been a long time little brother," he said. Even though there was no mound to indicate a grave, Vick knew it was the place Sam was laid to rest for birds had picked it bare in a perfect rectangle representing Sam's grave.

He picked up a handful of dirt from the site and let it sift through his fingers. "Sam, I'm so sorry," Vick said.

Cain bent down and placed his hand on his Pa's shoulder.

"Pa, what happened wasn't your fault— Sam knows," Cain offered.

Vick wiped his eyes, for he had a tenderness with Sam he would never have with anyone else.

"Thanks," Vick said. He tried to hold back the tears, but he couldn't.

Cain had seen his father cry over Sam before, but he could never understand why he continued to blame himself for his brother's death. His Pa had no control over that limb falling from a tree that killed his brother. However, Vick lived with the guilt of luring Sam away from their father who showed no mercy when he was drunk and out of control. *If I hadn't taken Sam away he might still be alive.* There was always that "if" that Vick struggled with. Even when it was made known to him that his brother was happy in the afterlife, Vick continued to blame himself. There was a strong tie that the two brothers had that reached far beyond the grave. What the two went through as boys would forever be an impression in Vick's heart. The brothers had a horrible childhood with Sam receiving the brunt of it.

Although Sonny and Clifford were despicable, they did not intervene with the three men who were visiting the grave. "I wonder who in the hell's buried there." Sonny asked.

"Ain't no tellin'," Clifford remarked.

After leaving the gravesite, Cain had his father's horse all packed and ready to go. "Thanks son—now let's get ready to ride."

Before leaving, Vick looked to the trees and there amongst them was the hawk, stretching her wings.

Just as before, Hawk will lead the way, he thought.

Sonny and Clifford continued to drag up the rear, but this time they were looking over their shoulders with a new concern—panthers.

Sonny rode up to Clifford and whispered, "We gonna give 'em time to find that treasure and then we're gonna kill 'em." Clifford, who rarely showed emotion gave a faint smile showing his tobacco, stained teeth from his juicy chew.

They had ridden the trail most of the morning when they reached the waterfall. It was there that Sonny saw a black panther out of the corner of his eye. Acting on impulse, he grabbed his gun and pointed toward the big cat.

"Nooooo!" Vick screamed.

He rode up beside Sonny and shouted "Stop," but the waterfall was so loud that Sonny did not hear. It was too late, for he had already lifted his rifle and fired. They watched as the black cat dodged the bullet and jumped from the ground to a ledge on the mountainside. The panther was mad as it gave a loud roar.

Vick kicked his horse in the flanks and stopped in front of Sonny.

"No more! That cat ain't doin' us no harm!" Vick recognized the old panther from his previous trip to Panther Holler.

Cain rode to his Pa's side. "Pa, is that the same panther that was here before?"

"Yes son, it is!" he said.

Sonny aimed the gun again but Vick stopped him.

"What's wrong with you? Are you crazy?" shouted Vick. "We'll need him to show us the way to the cave!"

"What the hell?" Sonny said, spinning his horse around to face Vick.

Sonny imagined Vick was the one crazy for not wanting to shoot the panther. "That cat better keep his distance or he's dead! Understand? And that's a promise!" Sonny yelled.

"You're the one who doesn't understand—the panther shows us the way!"

"You're nuts! You're plain nuts!" Sonny cried out.

The panther who was observing, jumped from the ledge a distance ahead of them and waited.

"You men follow me!" Vick said. And don't be shooting if you know what's good for you!"

Sonny and Clifford began to wonder about their own sanity for leaving Woodville on a hunch that there were diamonds in a God forsaken place that resembled a big mistake. But now, they were there, and the possibility of becoming rich was too strong of a force to deny. Reluctantly, they followed along to a spot they saw only as a dead end, for they could not see any way possible to cross over the waterfall.

It had been made known to Vick years earlier that the waterfall was the "road that roars," which offered a safe passage through a cave underneath the waterfall. Keeping their distance, Sonny and Clifford saw the panther stop at a place with heavy ground cover (made up of all types of brush and vines), when suddenly the panther jumped to another ledge of the mountain where now both the hawk and the black panther sat, waiting and watching.

"It's here!" Vick knew.

Sonny saw the big cat and hawk sitting above them and looked at Vick.

"I ought to shoot both of 'em right now!" Sonny said.

"If you want the diamonds, you won't shoot!" Vick admonished.

Sonny rode up to Vick's side to talk. "Are you tellin' me this is the place where the treasure is?"

"Yes, but there's something you don't understand. These diamonds belong to the Original People—the ancient Indians." Before he could finish explaining, Sonny interrupted, "What the hell ya talking about? You ain't talking about no damn Indians, are you?" Sonny asked.

"You might want to calm down. Our Panther friend doesn't like the sound of your voice," Vick chastised.

"I ain't listening to no more of yer made up stories about ghosts and original people, so you can cut it out— right now! If them diamonds are where you say they are—they're mine so the quicker you find 'em the better off Jared and his girlfriend will be. And if there ain't no treasure, you might as well kiss Jared and what's her name goodbye."

Vick was not afraid of Sonny, but it weighed heavily on him of what might happen if they're unable to use the diamonds for the exchange of Jared and Jessie. "C'mon, let's get this over with," commanded Vick.

They all dismounted and tied their horses outside the pathway to the cave. Vick retrieved a little can of coal oil from his saddlebag, and with a cloth, made a torch while the men watched.

"Why we need that when it's plain day light," Sonny argued.

"Remember, we'll be entering a cave," Vick said.

Clifford was spooked as hell as he stood chewing and spitting.

Vick led the men down into what looked like a ravine and then removed the first layer of brush, which was a perfect path the panther had made for them to follow. It was as though he knew they were coming.

"What if there's more than one panther out here?" Sonny asked as he followed closely behind Vick.

"You'll be safe if you listen to me and if you don't the panther attacks!"

"You act like you know what that panther will do."

Vick laughed inwardly for he knew that Sonny had no idea what could happen.

The men walked single file through the cave, following the light. It wasn't until they got to the end of the cave that Vick and Bidzill saw some of the carvings.

"Is this the place?" Sonny asked.

"Yes, but you won't be able to enter where the diamonds are," he said.

"I knew you were going to pull a fast one!" Sonny blasted.

Vick ignored him, while Cain moved a big rock that had been covering the cave where the diamonds were hidden. It was a very small passage that one had to wiggle through.

"Pa, are you going in first?"

"No, I think we should let Sonny and Clifford go first."

The two men went over and looked at the passageway, which was the size of a man's body but they had little faith in what Vick and Cain were showing them. They wondered how one could slip through an opening of that size and expect to find a treasure of diamonds. *There's something going on that I don't know about,* Sonny thought. "Is this a joke?" he asked. "Ain't no way I'm gonna slip through that place when I don't know what's on the other side. Besides it looks darker 'n hell in there."

Vick remembered there was some light in the cave, but not enough to see the carvings without a torch.

"There's enough light, so if you want the diamonds you're gonna have to go after them." He had been warned that only the pure blood of the Original People would be able to pass through the opening. To prove his point, he asked Cain if he would like to go in first.

"Both Cain and Bidzill slid inside the big rock without any problem, but when it came Sonny's turn, it was as though the hole had disappeared. In frustration, he kicked at the opening, but it was like a stone wall.

"What in the hell happened to the passage?" Sonny shouted. It wasn't obvious that the passage way had widened to allow them to slip through.

"Vick, git yer butt over here and try it," he said.

While holding the torch, Vick positioned himself exactly right and slid through the passage way until he was safe inside the cave. He heard Sonny say something to Clifford about why he couldn't squeeze through when everyone had made it through without a problem. Then he shouted, "If y'all try to escape, Jared is good as dead."

Once inside, the torch gave them the light they needed. Bidzill's jaw dropped as he examined the intricate details of the ancient carvings. They were standing on a ledge inside a massive cavern at least three stories high, which they supposed was the inside of the mountain. On one of the ledges sat the panther— guarding the treasure.

"How did the panther get in here?" Bidzill asked. The men followed Vick as he walked through another pathway leading down to the cavern's floor.

"Your guess is as good as mine. I looked the last time I was here, but I could not find any other entrance."

Bidzill was mesmerized as he noticed the walls were covered with hieroglyphics from top to bottom.

"I had no idea anything like this existed!" Bidzill said.

Taking it all in he walked over to the walls and began to chat privately, with Vick.

"How long have you known about this cave?" Bidzill asked.

"It's been a number of years. Bidzill you may find this hard to believe, but when the time is right, I'll be summoned to deliver this treasure of diamonds to the descendants of a lost tribe, and I might add, you and Cain, will be part of this excavation when it comes time to deliver the diamonds to our people."

Bidzill thought that sounded very familiar, for his father had visited him in a dream many years earlier and told him that one day he would reunite with his people who had left the reservation prior to being taken by force to Bosque Redondo. His grandfather, the great Chief Atsa had made known to him that in time, he would be a great teacher to his people. He barely remembered the dream, but being there among the carvings caused his grandfather's premonition to fill not only his mind, but his heart. Then he remembered his necklace that was given to him in the shape of a diamond. *Could this have some relevance,* he thought.

Bidzill examined all the carvings and talked with Vick, who knew many of their meanings. As they moved from one carving to the other, Bidzill could interpret for himself. As the symbols and carving were examined, he knew the Great Spirit had chosen them to deliver the diamonds to the descendants of the first people. There were no more questions, for Bidzill understood completely.

Absorbing every word that Vick shared, Bidzill tripped over a stone on the cavern floor. They nervously removed the large stone and reached into the small crevice, feeling for what they hoped were more diamonds, instead they uncovered a small trunk. Vick was excited that he had found it.

"Pa, did you know about this?"

"Yes son, I knew."

Vick gave them the details concerning his manifestation and further stated, that he was to find a trunk which contained 3 pairs of moccasins.

"This must be it, then," Cain said.

With a bit of apprehension, they pulled the trunk from its hiding place and opened it. Carefully, handling each item of clothing to Vick's disappointment, there were no moccasins but here were several pieces of clothing along with a necklace and pendant shaped like a diamond. Bidzill had just thought of his necklace and finding this one that looked very much the same reinforced to him, that he would be very much part of the excavation when it occurred. The clothing was not of celebration, silks or satins—just everyday clothing. After going through the trunk, they placed everything back in its place.

"I'm sorry that we can't remove the diamonds but without the moccasins, we are not permitted to leave the cave with the treasure," Vick said.

"Pa, without the diamonds we can't save Jared and Jessie—what are we going to do?"

"Son, I don't know." He was very disappointed realizing that Jared and Jessie were in peril—plus they had two madmen waiting to kill them as soon as they stepped out of the cave. Vick thought.

"They're not going to believe anything we tell them," Bidzill stated. "They'll kill us if we don't do as they say!"

Vick thought, *I just hope my plan works and the panther senses what is about to happen.*

Before leaving the cave, Vick took a moment and tried to reassure Cain and Bidzill that everything was going to work out and for them to trust him.

After considering their options (of which there were none) they descended from the top of the cave all the way to the bottom, then squeezed back through the passageway to face the men who were waiting. Speaking the truth, Vick explained that it was impossible to remove the diamonds before the right time. He tried to explain that the diamonds have been held for many years, waiting to be delivered to the descendants of the American Indians.

Sonny thought, *who can make up crap like that?*

"I just want to know one thing! How in the hell did y'all get through that opening? When I tried the opening disappeared!"

"We warned you about Panther Holler and you didn't believe us."

"That's a bunch of bull-crap, you're lying!" Sonny shouted.

Vick and Cain had never seen him so angry.

"Just tell me one thing, are the diamonds in there, or not!" Sonny asked.

"Yes, but you don't seem to understand that these diamonds are a treasure of an ancient people, and we're not permitted to remove them—under any circumstance. As you can see, we have a big black panther guarding them."

"Why don't you kill that damn cat! One of you gonna bring me those diamonds or I'm gonna shoot Cain!" Sonny and Clifford had them cornered and there was no way they could save Cain or escape what about to happen.

Clifford grabbed Cain and threw him on the ground and then stood astraddle him with his gun pointed straight at his heart. Cain's eyes were locked with his fathers as if to ask– now what?

He was afraid to make a wrong move with a gun pointed at his chest.

Cain listened as Vick tried to reason with Sonny. "Don't shoot my son if you want to live! The Sheriff knows all about you and who you really are-—Sonny Bilbo. I think it's about time that you tell Clifford that you worked in the Huntsville prison as a prison guard, and you're the one who had Clifford's brother hung for killing Seth Jackson."

Vick looked at Clifford who was staring at Sonny.

"I guess you didn't know that Sonny framed your brother. Ol' Sonny here, has been passing himself off as Seth Jackson, whom your brother murdered while they were in prison. Haven't you, Sonny?... Or do you prefer being called Seth Jackson?"

"Clifford, don't listen to that liar! He's full of tales!" Sonny shouted.

All the time the men were arguing the big panther was sitting on a ledge licking his paws as if he was ignoring what was going on. Vick was growing more concerned.

Clifford looked at Sonny, whom he knew from the early days when they robbed banks for a living. There was a ring of truth in what Vick said, for how would Vick know that Clifford's brother was in prison? *How would he know about my brother Gill*, Clifford wondered.

Clifford responded to Vick.

"Whatcha talkin' about Porter?" Clifford asked.

"Don'tcha pay no attention to Vick Porter. He just wants to stir up trouble between me and you, that's all!" Sonny yelled.

Clifford kept chewing and looking at Vick. "Whatcha know 'bout my brother's death?" Clifford asked again.

"The Sheriff knows all about it and so does Sonny. Ask Sonny why he's known as Seth."

Clifford looked back at Sonny. "Ya want ta tell me why that boy of theirs called you Seth?"

"I been called Seth before. Guess you never knew."

"I reckon there's a bunch I don't know, and maybe ya' ought to start talkin'."

Sonny just stood there and grinned.

"The prison told me my brother was hung for killin' a man, but I don't remember his name." Clifford looked at Sonny and knew he was lying.

"Is Porter tellin' the truth? Was that man who my brother killed named Seth?" Vick could hardly make out what Clifford was saying in his strange dialect, but he knew Sonny knew and didn't like it.

Cain lay on the ground watching his Pa try to save him by making trouble between Sonny and Clifford.

"Can't ya' tell Vick's a lyin' to ya'?" Sonny said to Clifford.

Now convinced that Sonny was responsible for his brother's death, Clifford raised his gun ready to shoot when something very quiet and fast came out of nowhere and knocked Sonny and Clifford to the ground. They were dazed and confused, until they raised their eyes and saw the black panther pawing in the dirt. They struggled to stand, and when they did, they were peering into the black eyes of a very large and powerful predator that was walking slowly toward them snorting as he breathed. They knew this wasn't good.

"Vick, don't just stand there shoot 'em!" Sonny yelled.

By this time Cain had scooted out of the way.

Vick just smiled and shook his head no—very slowly back and forth— taunting him.

"Ya'll jest gonna stand there and let us die?" Sonny pleaded. His wet eye's showed traces of dirt around them.

Clifford began slowly backing up with his hands in front of him trying to desperately calm the cat, but the predator just kept coming. Clifford had brown juice from tobacco running down his cheek as he locked eyes with the beast. The cat kept moving as though he was taunting them—and then he struck fast as lightning. Bam! Bam! With a couple of hard slaps, in a flash they were knocked a distance away into a ravine. They winced as they heard Sonny scream going down. All they heard from

Clifford was the muffled sound of ugh!

"Pa, the panther can't kill them!" Cain shouted. "Pa, without Sonny and Clifford, we don't stand a chance of saving Jared and Jessie."

Vick walked over to Cain who was panic stricken from his ordeal. He was even more distraught because the men who could free Jared and Jessie were most likely dead.

"Pa, admit it! That was your plan all along wasn't it? You knew the panther would kill the only two people who could take us to Jared and Jessie. You knew, and didn't tell us."

"Cain, what did you want me to do? Certainly, I knew the panther would kill the men. It's better than have them kill you. What good would that have done? I'm sorry, but there was nothing anyone of us could have done to make this work! We must leave it up to a Higher Power. God Almighty is the only one who can help Jared and Jessie."

Bidzill took his hat off and bowed his head.

"Pa, Jared and Jessie are going to die and there's nothing I can do about it."

"I know son, but neither of us know how this will end. You must not give up!"

Cain walked away to grieve alone.

Vick and Bidzill knew to let Cain be, for there was nothing they could say or do to comfort him. They stood by silently and let him cry it out.

Suddenly the silence was broken with the sounds of crushing bones and the tearing of human flesh.

Hearing those awful sounds, they grew concerned for their own safety.

"Vick, I think we better leave before the panther decides he wants dessert."

As they made their way through the cave below the falls everyone was somber, for they imagined they would never see Jared and Jessie again.

As they walked past the first entry way to the cave, lo and behold there stood the panther staring them in the face. Bidzill and Cain backed away from the ferocious creature but Vick stood there waiting for the panther to make the first move. Cain whispered, "Pa, don't you think you should back up a bit?"

Surprisingly, the big cat was trying to communicate with Vick for it kept moving its head, as if, to say come follow me.

"There's something he's trying to tell us," Vick expressed. "I think we should follow him."

Bidzill was concerned with the panther and asked Vick to reconsider.

"If he wanted us we would already be dead," Vick stated.

The men reluctantly followed behind Vick as the panther took them on quite a journey. Finally, they reached the back side of the cave that no one knew existed.

"So, this is how you've been getting in!" Vick said.

For the first time, Bidzill knew there had to be a connection between Vick and the predator.

While the men watched Vick communicate with the panther, Cain tried to explain to Bidzill who appeared to be spellbound watching the exchange.

"I've only heard the story, but Pa says when he and his brother were boys they had an altercation with the panther. From what I understand Pa won the conflict and the panther has always remembered. I reckon he has respect for Pa. That's the only way I can explain," Cain said.

"*No one would ever believe this*," Bidzill thought.

It was exciting to see how well he and the big cat communicated. Acting amazingly calm, they all followed through the dark shadows of the cave behind the panther. The entrance was so well hidden, they would never have found their way into the backside of the cave without the cat leading them.

"Look at this." Bidzill said.

The men followed the panther down a long narrow hall way with very few rays of sun coming through the cracks of the wall.

As they moved along through the cave there were more carvings. Vick stopped to explain the writing and share with the others. One such writing promised that in the last days the descendants of the Original People would prosper and take back their land from those who held them in bondage.

As they continued to follow, Vick stopped at one of the carvings and explained to Bidzill. "This carving pertains to you." It was only a drawing of a stick figure with a line drawn along the top of the head, representing a hat, but something else interesting, the figure wore a necklace with a diamond on it, which shared a close resemblance to the necklace Bidzill had worn for many years.

Vick explained to him that he would become a great teacher to his people, and that through his knowledge of medicine he would share many of the common practices that would safeguard his people from disease.

"Bidzill, this is you, sharing your knowledge with our people."

Hearing that he would be instrumental in teaching to those who needed him, Bidzill became very humbled. Now, he knew his purpose would be to share his knowledge, not only with others but also with his son Rafe whom he knew would follow in his footsteps.

"Come close and look. The carving indicates the treasure is in this room."

"I reckon it's more diamonds." Cain offered.

Vick looked up just as the panther jumped onto a ledge which opened a door to another room. They waited patiently as the rocks moved and two doors opened. The magnitude of what they saw was difficult to comprehend for there were all manner of precious jewels, not only diamonds and rubies but gold, which would make a great difference in helping their people to prosper.

Then men walked around the room examining the riches in disbelief.

"Pa, what are we going to do now?" Cain asked.

Vick who appeared to be in shock gave Cain his regular stock answer.

"I don't know, but we'll know when the time comes."

The men opened chest after chest and examined the contents but there were no moccasins.

Leaving the cave, they saw another room but the Panther kept close guard to prevent them from entering.

"That must be the room where the moccasins are!" Vick said.

"How do you know?" asked Cain.

"Check out the symbol on the door?"

They examined closely, and sure enough there was a carving of moccasins on the door.

"I guess there's no reason to doubt now, is there!" Cain said.

All the time they were walking and examining the contents of the cave Bidzill was in awe of how his life was about to change. He suddenly knew his worldly calling was much more than being a physician.

After making so many twist and turns in the cave, they were sure they needed help finding their way out.

The panther sensing it was time to leave led them through the cave and to their horses.

After seeing so many extraordinary things; the most incredible was when the panther walked toward Vick and became as docile as a house cat.

I'm not believing what I'm seeing, thought Bidzill

It was a lot for anyone to take in but it was certain that the panther had a fondness for Vick that no man would understand.

"If I hadn't seen this with my own eyes, I would not believe any of this," Bidzill said.

When they began to leave, once again the panther jumped upward to another ledge and let out a scream that penetrated throughout the cave. It was wailing as if the panther was sad to say goodbye.

Vick stopped just long enough to lock eyes with the cat and then just as quickly as he appeared he vanished. Only Vick knew that this was the last time he would see the panther.

After leaving the cave entrance, Vick and his party followed the path through the cave, which led them to their horses.

Chapter 36

Return From Panther Holler

So, began the journey back home. They were all yearning to be with their loved ones after facing the reality that Jared and Jessie were most likely dead. Cain had cried all his tears and now he had the task of facing Lucy with the bad news about Jared.

"I don't know how she's going to take the news about our son."

Cain, don't forget who Lucy is. She's the daughter of one of the strongest men I have ever met. If you think about it, she's a lot like Orson.

"I know Pa, but even Orson had his moments. I saw a few of 'em."

After they made it back to Jonesboro, they went by the manor and noticed that no one was home. The two cars were still in the barn just as they had left them. After turning the horses out to pasture Bidzill and Cain chose to ride home together, while Vick followed close behind.

The long drive back to Woodville seemed longer than usual, but they had a prayer on their lips that they would get back in time to receive some good news about Jared and Jessie—there was always that little hope.

When they drove up to the house, Lucy and Elizabeth heard the car and ran out to meet them.

It was apparent by the look on Elizabeth and Lucy's face that something was wrong.

They got out of the car and waited for whatever bad news they were about to hear. They were sure it was about Jared and Jessie.

No sooner than Lucy and Cain embraced, Rafe ran from the house and hugged his father.

"Pa, it's Ma! I brought her to the Porter's house because I thought you'd be here. He was talking so fast that Bidzill had to stop him."

"What's happened, son?"

"It's Ma—she's not gonna make it!"

"What do you mean she's not gonna make it?" he asked.

"One of the bad men burned our house down and me and mama had to jump off the roof. Ma's hurt really bad."

Bidzill removed his hat and walked up the steps to the house. His face was one of despair. Annie Mae met him at the door and took him to see Aggie. He didn't have his doctor's kit, but when he saw her and listened to her labored breathing he did the best he could examining her injuries. He was devastated when he knew that there was nothing he could do to save her. Even if he had his medical kit there would have been nothing that could be done to save her. *It's only a matter of hours*, he thought. He bent down and kissed her forehead.

"Aggie, I'm here now," Bidzill said. "I'll always be with you."

He thought about the first time he saw Aggie aboard the High Stepper. *She was so beautiful, and I knew from that moment that I was in love with her.* Seeing her there so helpless, Bidzill had to excuse himself for a moment. *I can't let them see me cry*, he thought.

He wanted to cry and beg for her forgiveness, but he couldn't. He had mentally shut down with what all he had been through.

She opened her eyes and looked at him, trying desperately to communicate a message that she wanted to see her children.

"Bidzill my love, Jared," she whispered.

He didn't have the heart to tell her that Jared was dead.

"He'll be home soon," he said. He hated that he lied to her, but he wanted to spare her a last moment of hope. Aggie squeezed his hand wondering if she could hold out just a little longer.

Cain, who was distraught with the thought of losing Jared, tried to keep his composure for Lucy. It was a difficult time, but they clung to each other, happy that they made it back home safely.

"Lucy, I'm so sorry that I haven't been here to comfort you."

"Thank God you're home. I didn't know where you were and then Rafe came here with his mother. It was all so overwhelming. You should have told me, so I would have known what was going on."

Cain had no idea if Lucy had guessed the woman she had been caring for was Aggie. *If she does know, she sure is taking it well*, he thought.

Cain didn't have the heart to tell Lucy that the woman they assumed was dead was the woman who had given birth to Jared.

Lucy had yet to guess that Aggie was the mother of Jared, but little things were beginning to gnaw at her that she didn't understand.

There was a lot on her plate for she did not want to give up hope of Jared coming home.

Lucy and Elizabeth were very sad for Bidzill—knowing that his wife only had a few hours to live.

They had been home for a short time when they heard a car approaching the house.

Lucy was sitting with Aggie when she heard the car stop in the drive. Although very weak, she whispered to Lucy that she was waiting to see Jared before she died. This seemed odd to Lucy, especially under the circumstances.

Watching the car door open, Vick recognized his old friend Hop.

Vick was surprised to see him in a car, for he knew Hop always rode his horse. Cain could tell his Pa was glad to see him. They took a moment to say hello and then they shook hands.

"Hop how did we miss you?"

"We just left the manor," Vick said.

"Maybe we were like two ships sailing in the night, and missed each other."

He handed Vick a note, and a package.

"I met a courier just before I turned in here, and he asked if I would deliver this package to you. And this note here was left at the manor and I figured it was for you and Cain."

Vick and Cain looked rather perplexed.

"I had just made it home from dove hunting and this note was left on the kitchen table. It gave me an excuse to get out of town." Hop smiled.

The entire time he was talking Vick figured the note came from Sonny who had Jessie write several notes for whatever reasons he might need them. When Cain saw what looked like scratch, he assumed the person who wrote it was injured. Apparently, when it was written they didn't have a good pencil. "It's hard to read, but I think I can make it out," Cain said.

He read the note out loud, "Pa, we're on our way home. Be there as soon as we can." No one knew what to think. There were mixed opinions and emotions, but Lucy was given hope that the kids were coming home when she heard Cain read it.

Cain opened the package that contained two partly burned accounting books that had the Pecan Plantation seal on them.

"Yes, these are the accounting books that can prove Pecan Plantation was stolen from us, but what does it matter if something has happened to my son," Cain thought.

Bidzill was standing nearby and recognized the two accounting books that Aggie had in her possession when their house went up in flames.

They listened as he tried to explain.

"Cain these are the accounting books that were saved from our house fire. Aggie and I have had them for some time."

Cain was somewhat perplexed.

"I hope you understand, but Aggie still did not know that her siblings were deceased, and she could not chance placing her family in danger. I ask you to please not judge her," Bidzill offered. "You and Lucy can use these books to reclaim Pecan Plantation."

"Thank you, for explaining but we're all family now and what's ours is yours. Understand?" Cain responded.

He heard what he said but nothing mattered except finding his son.

Bidzill hurried back in the house to watch over Aggie, who was still hanging on.

The men were convinced Jared and Jessie were not coming home. It had to be a note Sonny had them write. *What a dirty trick to receive a note like that*, Cain thought.

Besides grieving for the loss of Jared and Jessie, they were also grieving for Aggie who was becoming weaker by the minute. Bidzill imagined she was still hanging on to see Jared and Jessie.

It was late evening when they saw two people in a distance riding up on their horses. As they got closer, Lucy saw Jared and a young woman riding toward them.

"Cain," she shouted. "Is that Jared and Jessie?" Lucy was beside herself seeing her son. She hugged Cain. "I told you they would make it back. Thank God, they're safe!"

She could not contain herself as she ran to meet them. When she got to her son, Jared slipped out of the saddle and picked her up swinging her around.

"Ma, we made it! There were two mountain men who tried to kill us but we managed to escape. We're fine now that we're home."

After the sweet reunion, she acknowledged Jessie and then followed them back to the house, walking beside Jared's horse. Jessie looked like she had been in a fight with a bear, and lost. Her dress appeared to be an assortment of torn and dirty rags, and her face suffered from a lack of sleep.

Bidzill was inside with Aggie as he heard the excitement and bent down to kiss her, but she grabbed his arm and tried to pull him down to hear her. She could barely speak, but he heard her say, "Jared". At that same moment, Bidzill heard Lucy scream, "It's Jared and Jessie, they're home!"

Bidzill knew that Aggie might not make it long enough if he didn't insist that Jared come immediately. *She's been hanging on just to see her son*, he thought.

He didn't wait nor did he think. He just ran and practically pulled Jared off his horse. "Come quick, Aggie's dying, and she wants to see you."

Both Jared and Bidzill ran into the house, leaving Jessie outside with the others. She knew what was happening, and hurried in just in time to see Jared have his last words with his mother. Cain on the other hand, knew that Lucy was about to find out what he lacked courage to tell her.

Jared walked quietly to the bedside where Aggie lay. He bent down and brushed his hand across her forehead.

"Mother, it's so good to see you. Please don't try and talk, just let me look at you," Jared said. He began tearing up knowing that he would never get to know his birth mother the way he had planned.

She managed a smile; for that was the first time she had heard him call her mother. Aggie forced herself to speak but her voice was weak and soft. "I love you, my boy," she said. "Please forgive me." Water welled up in her eyes as she longed to hold him.

Jared was touched so, that tears welled up in his eyes.

"You were very brave, please don't cry," Jared said.

She touched her neck to indicate that she had given him a necklace as a boy.

"Jared knew what she meant. "I'm wearing it now." He pulled the necklace from beneath his shirt collar and showed her. "See, I've worn it since you gave it to me."

Aggie had all her children together and Bidzill could see the love in her eyes. *She's very happy*, he thought. Her lips were very pale, and her long red hair lay around her shoulders as tears trickled from the corner of her eyes. She was beautiful, even near the threshold of death. Her eyes locked with Jessie's for a moment and then she did the sweetest thing. She took Jared and Jessie's hands and placed them together. This was her way of approving of their engagement. Jared was so impressed that he took his eyes off Aggie for a second to look at Jessie. They then heard her sigh and take her last breath. It was difficult for Jared to comprehend, for one minute she was there, and the next she was gone. He did not know how to react to death, for he had never seen anyone close to him die. Rafe, fell near his mother's bed and began sobbing, which upset Jared even more.

Bidzill and Jessie bent down and kissed Aggie on the forehead and then turned their attention to Rafe. Bidzill thought even in death his wife looked like an angel and no matter what, she was in his heart and would remain there the rest of his days. His only comfort came with knowing that they would be together in the afterlife.

Jared turned to Jessie who was standing near. "Oh my God, she's gone. I should have told her I loved her— and I didn't. I didn't have time to tell her I loved her."

Rafe, pulled away from his Pa and grabbed Jared. At first it was awkward and then the two brothers bonded and grieved the loss of their mother. Afterward, Jared became extremely emotional and walked out of the house toward the private sanctuary to be alone. He was crying at the time Lucy approached him who did not understand.

Why did Bidzill make such an effort to have his wife see Jared? It doesn't make sense, she thought. She knew her son had just suffered a terrible ordeal with Sonny, and resented that they exposed him to death when it wasn't necessary.

She walked over to Jared and asked why Rafe's mother wanted to see him.

"Because she's my mother!" he cried out and then walked away.

Lucy was stunned, she could have been knocked over by a feather. She took a moment to think and then everything began to come together and make sense. She wanted to scream for Jared had walked away without any explanation, which deeply hurt her. She placed her hand over her mouth to keep from being heard as she cried. She had never been so hurt in all her life. *This woman is Aggie who gave birth to my son, and she has been living under my roof and never told me who she was. No one has bothered to tell me.* She felt foolish and betrayed by the entire family. *Surely, Elizabeth didn't know. If she did I couldn't bear it!* she thought.

Lucy had to carry on out of respect for Bidzill, but inside she was on fire. *How could they have treated me so badly.* She was extremely disappointed in Cain and for a moment she felt her life as she knew it was over. She tried to hide her anguish, but Cain who sensed Lucy's agony knew it had to do with Aggie. Rather than get into it while Bidzill was there, he decided to wait and sleep on it. He knew that their visitors would be gone by the next morning and they would sort things out.

All that night Lucy kept her distance from Cain and the family until it was time to go to bed. Although he tried to hold her, she did not cooperate. He knew she was brooding about him not telling her about Aggie and thought it best to wait until morning to try and explain things.

It was before daylight when Elizabeth spoke to Bidzill about Aggie. It was extremely difficult since the body had become too stiff to move. He wondered how he would get her home when there really was no home to go to.

Being an early riser, Vick was prepared to offer Bidzill a solution to his problem, and took him aside to discuss it.

"You need to make a decision and consider staying here. We're family now, and this would be a good place for you and Rafe. We have plenty of room and a tact house that is vacant—so think about it and talk to Rafe. It will be the perfect place for you. Besides, this town needs a good doctor and my grandson needs to know his brother. Think about what I've offered and let me know what we can do."

Rafe, who was of the opinion to stay, told his father that he wanted to be close to Jared. Both Elizabeth and Vick wanted them to stay and be part of the family but they didn't know about Lucy.

Up until that time, Bidzill never learned the details of how Aggie and Rafe were threatened after he left them to go find Jessie and Jared.

Heartbroken because of the loss of Aggie, he could hardly function. Rafe pleaded with him. "Pa, can't we stay here where we'll be safe. That bad man may be hiding out someplace and try to find me." Bidzill was vulnerable and had suffered so many losses that he would do anything to keep Rafe safe.

"Okay, we'll give it a try for a couple of months."

After agreeing to stay, Bidzill decided to talk to Elizabeth about his decision, and ask if it were presumptuous of him and Rafe to stay. Of course, Elizabeth thought it was the right thing to do, especially for Rafe.

Vick, who seldom meddled in Lucy and Cain's business, asked Lucy if she would take a walk with him.

After all that transpired, he wasn't about to let what happened with Aggie cause problems with Lucy and Cain, especially with all they had been through.

"I'm glad we have a chance to talk," Vick said.

She nodded "yes" and walked with him over to the sanctuary. There they sat, until Lucy allowed her emotions to get the best of her. She could only keep it bottled up for so long.

"How long have you known? she asked.

"Not long, and neither has Cain," Vick assured.

"Lucy, I know Cain wanted to tell you, but there was never a good time. He was shocked to hear she was alive—we all were. After it sunk in he was afraid to see you hurt. He was going to tell you, but then Bidzill showed up to tell us that Jared and Jessie had been kidnapped. Talk about bad timing, he didn't want to leave you all upset—so he waited until he got home. Sometimes life gets in the way. Not to be harsh, but we have to learn to deal with many disappointments."

Lucy remembered the stories of what Vick went through in prison, but she couldn't shake her feelings of being hurt.

Vick was very tender. "Lucy, you know Cain loves you, don't you?"

"Yes, but he should have told me. What a way to find out! And Aggie never said a word. You know, she could have told me who she was." Lucy countered.

Vick tried to reason with her. "It wasn't Aggie's place to tell you. Had she said something to you, how would that have come across? She was completely out of it with her injury. And, what would you have done if you found out? It wouldn't have been right for her to tell you," Vick stressed. "Cain was devastated, and he knew what this might do to you. You can't imagine what he's been through trying to save Jared and Jessie. He won't tell you, but Sonny stood over him with a gun and would have killed him but by the mercy of God he was spared. You came that close to losing Cain." Vick thought it was best not to go into detail about the panther and the treasure.

"I had no idea," Lucy said. "I don't know what I would have done if something happened to him." Talking with Vick softened her heart toward Cain, but her biggest disappointment was her son who walked past her when he called Aggie "his mother." She would never forget that feeling.

Before Vick walked away, he pulled Lucy close and hugged her.

"I know you have to sort things out, but I hope you can find it in your heart to forgive Cain and Jared. They both need you."

After their conversation, Elizabeth saw Lucy sitting alone and walked over to be with her. She put her arm around her and sat there in silence. When Lucy began to cry, Elizabeth gave her a handkerchief then took her shawl and placed it over Lucy's shoulders. Elizabeth was always there to pick up the pieces.

Finally, Elizabeth explained to Lucy that Vick wanted to move the family back to Arkansas.

"Lucy, when we move, I want you and Cain to move back with us. We're thinking about buying back our old logging company.

I've missed it, and if you'll remember— we made a pretty good team."

Lucy tried to smile, but she thought, nothing ever stays the same.

"I know I've just sprung this on you—but I'm for getting out of Texas and going back to God's country—plus, I miss the manor. So much has happened—and it makes perfect sense," Elizabeth confided.

Lucy listened but she wasn't so sure. They sat there a few minutes before she spoke.

"Elizabeth, it seems like our life has made a full circle and we're about to try it again, and now we have Pecan Plantation.

Elizabeth smiled and chuckled. "Oh no, please—let's not do it again," she belabored. "You know, we have two young men who can run the place for us."

After their conversation, they walked arm and arm back to the house.

~

It was mid-morning of the next day when the family followed the men as they carried Aggie's casket up the hill to a special place dedicated for burial. After Vick and Bidzill performed a short ritual, they watched while the casket was lowered into the ground. Elizabeth, the strong one, offered words of comfort, but before she spoke, the most incredible thing happened. Rafe and Jared noticed Lucy sitting alone and came to join her. They each took a hand and as they sat one on each side of her, she gushed, for the boys were the spitting image of each other. As she studied their features, she felt a soft breeze brush against her face and then a little sparrow perched near Aggie's casket. Lucy imagined that Aggie spoke to her. *"Now you have both my sons— and Jessie."* The magnitude of those words caused her to shiver and for a moment she was overcome with love and compassion for Aggie who had gone through so much trying to save her children.

Jared, who shared the same likeness of his father, whispered into Lucy's ear. "In case you don't know—you're my real mother because you raised me; nothing will ever change that." The special way he expressed himself made her weep. It was an incredible moment with her son.

Elizabeth, who was observing, knew everything would come together—as it should. As always, she was impeccable in her long black dress. With all the attention on Elizabeth they listened as the "strong one" shared her thoughts. She looked rather stately as she held a little black book and spoke softly. After clearing her throat, she began the eulogy.

"My dear family: Today we gather to show our respect to a beloved woman, Aggie Franklin, wife of Bidzill, and mother of two sons, Jared and Rafe and a daughter, Jessie. We have all been blessed to know Aggie, some better than others, but we will never know how much this remarkable woman suffered— for it was hers to bear. We all suffer in different ways, sometimes together and often alone— as I'm sure Aggie did when her heart was heavy. Today we gather here to share A mother's love for her husband and children and to remember Aggie who was taken much too soon."

Elizabeth hesitated as she looked at Lucy who was trying to choke back tears. It was though the last words of Elizabeth's eulogy were meant for her.

Elizabeth continued. "I believe there is another reason we're here—I feel that…. I'm not sure why, but I'm sure in days to come we will know." She was thinking of the life changes Lucy was about to make having not only Jared and Jessie but also Rafe who was the spitting image of Jared as part of her family. Elizabeth was sure that Rafe and Jessie would become a blessing to Lucy as well as the family.

Those words were thought provoking and resonated with Lucy.

After the funeral was over Jared and Rafe were still holding Lucy's hand until Cain approached the boys and whispered to them in true

Cain fashion, "Is it okay if I have my wife back?" The boys smiled and gave Lucy a hug.

"You must be buttering me up for something," she said, trying to control her emotion. Her voice broke and tears began to flow. Her eyes were glistening as Cain took her in his arms and kissed her. It was not a passionate kiss but a sweet kiss that told her everything she needed to know about a husband's love. For a moment, she felt a tinge of shame for her behavior. It was suddenly very clear that through Aggie, Lucy received a special gift— that being Jared, Jessie and Rafe, one that she would cherish in days to come.

She felt such a resolve that when she looked at Jessie and the two boys, she knew that God had granted her the greatest gift of all——A family.

~

As the months and years passed, Vick knew that his time was drawing near. When it was time, he asked Cain and Bidzill to make his final journey back to Panther Holler. Before leaving home, Elizabeth and Vick walked arm in arm out to the barn.

"Lizzie, you take good care of yourself and don't worry about me," he said.

Elizabeth was glad that Cain and Bidzill had agreed to go with Vick since he had reached the ripe old age of 82. Giving him one lingering kiss before he left, she reminisced about when they first met.

"Vick Porter, do you remember the first time we met?"

"That was a long time ago," Lizzie.

"Well, it was not so long ago that I would forget that you threw me off your property."

"Now, why would I throw a pretty little thing like you off my property?" Vick smiled, and then took her in his arms. "I imagine there's a lot of things I need forgiving for, but you'll never have to forgive me for loving you."

He kissed her again, knowing that he may not be returning home.

She had tears in her eyes for deep inside she knew that this would be the last time she would see him.

Watching him ride away was the saddest moment she would ever face.

And so, it was: When Vick rode away that was the last time she saw him. Two weeks later Cain and Bidzill returned home but this time Vick was not with them.

~

For years, Cain would not speak of his father's death until he became ill and was dying. It was on his deathbed that he gave Jared his journal to read to his family.

Thumbing through the pages Jared recognized his father's writing.

Cain tried to move his hand to touch Jared, but he couldn't.

"Pa, you know I will treasure what you have written, but are you sure you want me to share what you wrote?"

Cain's eyes had already glazed over but he was able to shake his head "yes." Elizabeth and Lucy listened intently as well as the rest of the family as Jared shared the journal, for it had always been a mystery of how Vick died.

Jared bent down close to the bed, so his father could hear.

He opened the brown book and began reading the words that were written in blue ink.

"No one knew my Pa like I did and because of that, I am dedicating this last chapter of my life to my father and all those who will come after me.

"Before my father's death, Bidzill, contacted a Navajo Chief who was one of the descendants of the Great Navajo Chief Asta to begin the preparation for the gathering of tribes. They had no idea of the great wealth that was about to be bestowed on them.

"When the day arrived, Pa, Bidzill and I traveled to meet with several Chiefs in a small village outside of Jonesboro, but it was not at all what we expected.

"There was a larger number who attended and every tribe that participated was represented by their Chief and their people. Standing on both sides of a dirt road made especially for the occasion, the Chiefs led the three of us to a large platform that was at least 15 feet high and stood before the crowd. On top of the platform were three very large chairs.

"Momentarily, I thought the chairs were placed there for the Chiefs in attendance, but we soon found that they were placed there for us. After we were physically lifted to the top of the platform another Chief climbed up a ladder and gave us three ceremonial robes to place over our clothing.

"There was something magical about the robes for when we slipped them on, we began seeing many of our people who died along the "trail of tears." Not only did we see the dead but we witnessed the cruelty of the soldiers who forced our people to leave their homes and migrate west of the Mississippi. We were in a dreamlike trance as we saw images of our people who were starved, beaten and exposed to the harshest and most despicable conditions.

"That day we paid homage to all those who had passed on before us. The robes were a blessing and a curse for I have never forgotten the horrible images I saw that day of our people being mistreated.

"As we stood on the platform, we were showered with many tokens as the people formed a single line and walked before us.

The occasion was indescribable as they began to dance in respect to the Great Spirit.

"Before the ceremony ended, five large trucks loaded with an enormous amount of wealth drove in and stopped before the people. At long last their lives were about to change for the better.

After all the years of bondage, they had no idea of the changes they were about to make in their lives. The Great Spirit was approaching the time to lead them on a joyous journey— one which they richly deserved.

"Many fell to their knees in worship, chanting and singing songs of love in their native tongue.

"As we stood there and watched, we could not hold back the tears. Pa climbed down the ladder at the end of the platform and walked among our people. I never saw Pa look healthier; it was though he turned into a young man. As they followed him, there was no doubt that he was the one whom the Great Spirit chose to bless his people.

"The mood was of celebration as they danced to the beat of drums.

"During the ceremony, many of their leaders spoke in their native language and issued instruction for their people to live in peace among all mankind.

"Although it was night, it continued to be bright as day until it was time to leave.

"As the ceremony ended Pa and Bidzill gave a special gift to the Navajo Chief.

"Recognizing Bidzill as a direct descendent of the Navajo, the Chief accepted a map to the cave which bore the primitive writings of their ancient ancestors. Bidzill clarified that in days to come it would prove to be the greatest gift of all, for deep in the writings are ancient cures that will save many lives. He explained his training will help enrich their lives by teaching the people how to care for their sick and afflicted.

"When the day ended, and it was time to leave, many of the Indians wept and rejoiced for the sacrifice that was made for them.

To this day I marvel with what all my Pa achieved. He was not an educated man, but he was much more.

After we left the celebration and Vick began to weaken, he asked Bidzill and I if we would return with him to Panther Holler.

"Pa was weak and sick during the journey and we thought he might not make it. We stopped every few miles, so he could rest and gather some of his strength back.

That night, when it came my turn to see after Pa, I noticed something different about him. There was something uniquely different about his countenance, that intrigued me. He sat upright and talked like he hadn't seen me in years, sharing things about his youth that I had never heard before. As it turned out he began talking about his father and how he had forgiven him for the mistreatment of Sam. "He never mentioned how his father mistreated him—only Sam.

The next morning, when the sun came up, he surprised us being the first one up and impatient to get going. We talked to him about the night before but his only conversation was getting to Panther Holler in time.

"Time for what? I kept asking myself.

"We knew it meant a lot for him to visit the gravesite of Sam one last time but there was something else going on in that head of his."

I'm not sure anyone will believe what I am going to share, but Bidzill and I saw this happen with our own eyes.

Soon after we arrived in Panther Holler Vick began acting strange. He was distracted and somewhat confused, we thought.

Bidzill and I agreed that we should keep an eye on him in case he wandered off and got lost. Observing his behavior, we recognized that he was talking to himself. We couldn't figure out what he was saying, but whatever it was it was very intense as if he was talking to someone personally. Careful not to embarrass him, we let him be. We waited most of the day watching him go about this new routine which we had never seen before. We imagined it was some type of ritual.

Bidzill and I followed him until he stopped just shy of the lake, hiding in a grove of trees—watching. Pa kept speaking to someone as he participated in a ceremony of some kind—and that's when it happened. Out of nowhere—Sam appeared. We were both amazed.

Me more than Bidzill for this was my uncle in the flesh and he was as young as me.

We knew it was Sam for Pa called out his name. There was no denying he was Pa's younger brother for they were the image of each other. Suddenly Pa began a transformation and became young, like Sam.

We had never been part of a revelation before and through our dismay we must have made a noise. Vick and Sam turned and looked at us with the clearest eyes. We had never seen eyes like that before. I would say they were immortal for they were eyes of pure love.

What happened next was a miraculous event—there's no other words to explain. Watching the apparition in disbelief, we witnessed everything that happened. In a matter of seconds the day turned brighter than noonday as a light encircled around them. We watched the transformation continue, which caused Vick and Sam to levitate. Suddenly they were standing in mid-air at least five feet off the ground.

"To this day, I think about what we saw, and I still have difficulty believing it happened.

"After the light engulfed and penetrated throughout their bodies, they became part of the light for only a short time until they reappeared before us. I can only say through that process their bodies became Heavenly. They were so bright they glowed, and we could hardly watch as they began their accent into Heaven.

"Overwhelmed by what we witnessed, Bidzill and I knelt and cried like two children. It touched our hearts so, that we would have gone with them if asked. There was so much love that no earthly person could understand, but we were privileged to experience it for a very short time for our own enlightenment.

"I'll never forget how happy Pa was to see Sam. I think he always knew his brother was in Panther Holler waiting for him to fulfill his destiny."

Cain died shortly after Jared finished reading his journal. It was a peaceful transition as Cain passed through the veil of forgetfulness.

Although Cain never knew Vick growing up, what he learned of his father more than made up for the time he missed.

END

~

There are many legends in the hills of Arkansas were Panthers and Hawks turn into boys bearing the souls of great warriors. Some say in the late evening, when everything is quiet, one can hear the laughter two boys in a place called—Panther Holler.

THE VICK PORTER FAMILY WILL LIVE FOREVER IN THESE THREE BOOKS AND IN MY HEART.